Praise for *Young China Hand*

What is the next generation of China business leaders really thinking? Does it require the experience of an old veteran China watcher to figure out this increasingly important question? Or maybe a newcomer with a sharp eye can better understand the shifting ambitions, mindsets and attitudes of the younger generations of Chinese, particularly the emerging foreign educated elite. If you buy into that increasingly persuasive argument and want a fresh look at new China, then *Young China Hand* is the book you need to read.

-**Tim Clissold**, international best-selling author of *Mr. China*, and *Chinese Rules: Mao's Dog, Deng's Cat and Five Timeless Lessons from the Front Lines in China*

Young China Hand combines a gripping narrative about an epic battle for control between Chinese and foreign partners, with insights into the personalities, powers and policies that shaped China's rise in the aftermath of the 2008 financial crisis. A rare gem among the numerous books about doing business in China, this novel entertains as much as it informs readers.

-**Shao Zili**, Co-Chairman of King & Wood Mallesons China's Management Committee, and former CEO and Chairman of J.P. Morgan China

This is more than just a riveting novel about smart money, fraud, betrayal, and a struggle for redemption. It is also a window into twenty-first-century China, written with clear-eyed realism by two overseas Chinese-Singaporeans with a unique perspective on issues of East-West differences, identity and values.

-**ChinHwee Tan,** co-author of *Asian Financial Statement Analysis: Detecting Financial Irregularities*

Young China Hand brings the reader deep into the opaque and treacherous world of business in China through fast-paced storytelling and vivid descriptions of a changing China. Matt Huang and Grace Hsu have skillfully blurred the lines between fiction and fact, offering a clever blend which will interest both serious China watchers and those less familiar with the rising power of our age.

> \- **Peh Shing Huei**, author of *When The Party Ends*, and former China bureau chief and news editor of The Straits Times

Young China Hand is as much a thriller as it is a case study about China investing, private equity style. This gripping tale exposes the pitfalls of not responding wisely to the evolving demands, vanities and special interests of twenty-first-century Chinese entrepreneurs, financiers and young China Hands. Those who wish to avoid the tragic (and comic)—yet not uncommon—mistakes described in the book would do well to read closely. As a bonus, it also teaches about duck farming!

> \- **Michael Prahl**, Partner at Asia-IO, and Distinguished Fellow, INSEAD Private Equity Centre

The risks and potential of China's economy has become an increasingly important topic in global media and in business literature. What makes *Young China Hand* an outstanding book is its in-depth exploration of the complex environment in which Chinese entrepreneurs, who still form the backbone of the economy, have to operate. The book offers a fascinating character study of a typical Chinese founder, whose new ventures have great potential to provide jobs, invigorate communities, and create wealth for investors, but whose complex psychology and motivations can also pose huge risks for stakeholders—and even the broader financial system.

> \-**Tom Kosnik**, Lecturer and Consulting Professor (Global Marketing and Entrepreneurship) at Stanford University.

YOUNG CHINA HAND

Matt Huang
AND Grace Hsu

ARCHWAY
PUBLISHING

While this novel is inspired by true events and real personal experiences in China, it is a work of fiction. The names, characters, places, companies and events are either products of the author's imagination or are used fictitiously. Any resemblance to actual incidents or businesses or places or persons, living or dead, is purely coincidental.

www.youngchinahand.com

Cover Design and Images courtesy of Sok Hwan Tan,
Xiao Wen Song and Sarah Ng Shu Ting

With the Support of

NATIONAL ARTS COUNCIL
SINGAPORE

Archway Publishing books may be ordered through booksellers or by contacting:

Archway Publishing
1663 Liberty Drive
Bloomington, IN 47403
www.archwaypublishing.com
1 (888) 242-5904

ISBN: 978-1-4808-3161-2 (sc)
ISBN: 978-1-4808-3162-9 (e)

Library of Congress Control Number: 2016907745

Print information available on the last page.

Archway Publishing rev. date: 06/20/2016

Contents

About the Authors

M ATT HUANG IS AN INVESTMENT professional currently residing in China. A Singaporean who graduated from Stanford University with degrees in engineering and management in 2002, Matt has enjoyed a storied investment career spanning the globe, but nothing excites him more than living and working in China. He has been an avid golfer since his move to Beijing in 2008.

Grace Hsu worked as a financial journalist for ten years, five of which were based in Beijing, before becoming a freelance writer in 2014. A Singaporean who graduated with degrees in international relations and business from the University of Pennsylvania and the Wharton School in 2004, Grace currently splits her time between China, Houston, TX and Singapore.

Prologue

I was denounced as a traitor right before we went in to shake hands with the new owner of our embattled China investment project.

Yet it was not my boss's accusations that filled my mind as we stepped into Quanli Private Equity Co.'s opulent Beijing office to meet Mr. Han for the first time. Instead, the only thing I could think about was how weightless Han's fingers seemed. They seemed to float as effortlessly as the cigar ashes they had just flicked away from the rosewood table.

The back of Han's cavernous red leather armchair was turned to us. So all I could see of this Chinese financier, whose identity had eluded me for so long, were his fleshy hands— so bulbous and well-oiled that the skin looked as translucent as a bubble.

Until that smog-clogged evening on December 17, 2010, it seemed as if I would never piece together any substantial information about Han, the co-founder of Quanli. Over the past three months of maneuvering to grab our investment stake in one of China's largest duck-farming companies, he had never once shown his face. Nor did he ever speak to us directly. Instead, he negotiated with us through his army of lawyers, who stonewalled me at every turn when I tried to ferret out clues about Han's age, family background, education, taste in alcohol, preference for spicy Sichuan hotpot or mellow Cantonese broth…or anything of even the slightest interest that I could report back to my own bosses seething away in Singapore.

The more blanks I drew about Han's identity, the more intensely I started to speculate about why the head of a small Shanghai-based fund needed to be so secretive. Perhaps he was a southern Chinese mafia boss dabbling in Wall Street-style debt restructuring to complement his loan shark business, I wondered. Or maybe he represented a corrupt official's mistress, who had the cash and risk appetite to flip distressed assets. Or he could be one of the shadowy princelings whose family ties with top Chinese leaders magically opened doors to plum deals that foreign investors like us could only drool at.

Just two and a half years earlier, I would have dismissed such theories as far-fetched, if they had even occurred to me at all.

At that time, I had just joined All-Stellar Asia Fund L.P., a high-profile private equity outfit based in Singapore, as a junior investment associate. One of the big guns in Asia, All-Stellar had been able to raise an impressive US$880 million from big-name institutional investors at the onset of the 2008 global financial crisis, even as its peers were struggling to even stay afloat. The fund's investment mandate spanned the whole of Asia.

But it was China, with its fast-growing enterprises and its meteoric rise on the global economic stage, which dominated our team's interest and energies. My bosses expected All-Stellar's cash, clout and foreign expertise to be eagerly sought after by Chinese enterprises looking to access international financial markets. So in 2008, they dispatched me to Beijing to gather business intelligence on the ground and to identify the juiciest investment targets among China's nearly ten million private enterprises.

Even though I was the most junior—and at age twenty-eight, the youngest—member of the All-Stellar team, I figured I was up to the task. I could speak, read and write Mandarin. I was born in the multiethnic city-state of Singapore, and graduated from Stanford University. But I could still blend in with the 1.3 billion mainland Chinese people and share their culture through my family roots, which traced back to the southern Chinese province of Fujian. I was also prepared to embed myself in Chinese soil for years, while many of my colleagues balked at the thought of living in a country riddled with food, water, and air pollution scandals.

What's more, I aspired to become more than just a *zhongguotong* 中国通, a term used to describe foreigners as "China experts" to praise their understanding of Chinese language and culture. That label seemed to be losing its currency. Golden-haired *laowai* 老外— Chinese slang for foreigners—speaking impeccable Mandarin were fast becoming a common feature on Chinese TV programs, and dark-skinned rappers spouting ancient Chinese poetry in bars were no longer such a novel crowd-pleaser as they were a decade ago.

Yet it was precisely this growing Chinese proficiency among the laowai that made the real China Hands stand out. Among the millions of foreigners passing through the country every year, these China Hands were the ones who not only stayed long enough to understand the land of "Capitalism with Chinese Characteristics"[1], but had also become specialized enough in their knowledge to interpret its complexity to the rest of the world.

I was gung-ho—or naïve—enough to fancy myself taking on that niche role of demystifying the Middle Kingdom for my western bosses. I was determined not be one of those Asians caricatured as a "banana": yellow-skinned on the outside, white on the inside. If China-savvy could be measured in shades, I would take on the hue of the *Huanghe* 黄河—the Yellow River known as the cradle of Chinese civilization—from which my family name Huang was derived.

And then, China chastened me. Our fund, which seemed such a big deal in western financial hubs like Singapore and New York, was a virtual unknown in China. It was just one amongst the multitude of

---

[1] MIT Professor Ya-sheng Huang used this term in his book "Capitalism with Chinese characteristics: Entrepreneurship and the State." This is a contrast to the term "Socialism with Chinese characteristics" coined over three decades ago by the late paramount leader Deng Xiaoping.

investors crowding into China—sovereign wealth funds, state-owned companies, banks, as well as a host of Chinese companies and high net worth individuals whom I never imagined could command so much wealth. All of them were jostling for increasingly slim pickings in China's state-dominated economy, where the best deals often seemed to be reserved for powerful—and surprisingly young—financiers.

Fortunately, All-Stellar found "a pie falling down from heaven," as the Chinese colloquial saying, *tianshang diaoxianbing* 天上掉馅饼, goes. With the help of a China hand, the fund scored a promising investment deal with Dominant Duck Poultry Farming Co. and became the proud co-owner of thirty-four million birds across six Chinese provinces.

The partnership started off rosily enough as I tried to communicate "the Chinese way," as prescribed by so many business books on the subject. But the tables have a way of being turned at lightning speed in this rapidly evolving country, where split second mask-switching—known as *bianlian* 变脸 (face-changing)—is a famous dramatic art form.

All-Stellar suddenly found itself battling for control over DeeDee and its fifty duck farms. We resorted to solving things the "western way," only to trigger full-blown warfare where I found myself a tormented mediator and messenger. It seemed I could never be Chinese enough for our local allies. Yet, I was becoming too Chinese for my western bosses, who started to question my allegiances.

Still, I tried to console myself that each of those turbulent experiences would bring me a little closer to mastering the art of doing business in China. It was a small comfort I clung to even when Russell Wen, the Principal at All-Stellar, lambasted me as a two-faced traitor after I asked him why he had given me such a shockingly poor performance appraisal.

"You not just sympathized, but even sided with the Chinese. Your refusal to support us in our counter-attack jeopardized the interests of our fund. You also left me at the mercy of Chinese thugs instead of calling in the police," Russell lashed at me, as we rode the elevator up to Quanli's thirtieth-floor offices. We were on our way to sign the papers to complete the sale of our investment stake in Dominant Duck.

"You have the cheek to ask me why we cut your bonus this year by 45 percent this year? You should be glad that I even gave you a bonus, after all the trouble you got us into," Russell ranted on.

I gaped. Just a couple of weeks ago, he had thanked me profusely for "playing a key role" in helping to extricate the fund from its corporate takeover battle across China. So while I did not expect to be rated as an exceptional performer for the year, I had hoped to at least be given a fair appraisal. Yet now, I was being accused of roosting with the enemy.

I opened my mouth, but the only sound that broke the silence was the tinkle of the elevator bell signaling that we had reached the thirtieth floor. Russell stepped out, and delivered his parting shot: "You will be given a final chance to improve your performance for the next three months, failing which you will be fired."

Without waiting for my response, he marched ahead into Quanli's office.

I shuffled after him, eyes glazed. Han's hands floated into view. I willed myself to stand tall in front of this seasoned old master. Even though he had won this time, it wasn't the end of the story for me. If I just persevered in gathering new intelligence about Chinese elements like him, I would slowly, surely redeem myself as a China insider.

And then Han stood up to face us—and my convictions crumbled. I was looking at the young man who would completely redefine for me the meaning of "China Hand".

CHAPTER 1

Easy Grasp

De Xin Ying Shou 得心应手

I T ALL BEGAN FORTUITOUSLY ENOUGH, with the onset of the global financial crisis.

I joined All-Stellar Asia Fund L.P. in August 2007, after a chance coffee meeting with the fund's founder and principal Russell Wen.

It was a sweltering Saturday afternoon in Singapore. I was drenched in sweat as I answered Russell's battery of questions about financial modeling. They were straight-forward enough. But I was still a little unnerved because an impromptu job interview was not what I expected when I popped into a café by the Singapore River to say hi to my friend, a head hunter who had just finished a meeting with Russell.

I was indeed planning to leave my job as a business analyst at a major Singapore government-linked group, where I had helped to execute several billion dollars' worth of investments across the globe over the past four years. And I already had an offer for a third-year analyst position at a major European investment bank. Russell's impressive credentials, however, got me interested.

Born in Hong Kong, then raised and educated in California,

he had worked in Asia since the 1990s as a high-flying investment banker. Russell quickly made a name for himself closing many landmark deals, particularly in real estate. At the height of his career as managing director of the Asian mergers and acquisitions (M&A) division at a US bulge-bracket bank, he left his job and moved to Singapore to set up All-Stellar, an Asia-focused private equity (PE) fund.

"I'm looking for young talent to cover China," said Russell. "There are a lot of Ivy League grads with multiple degrees like you. And most of them have way more experience in PE investing than you do. But they lack the China factor. You mentioned you're proficient in Mandarin?"

I hesitated. It was easy to just rattle off my resume, saying that I spoke the Chinese language at home, studied it in school for twelve years and scored A's in every exam. But those paper qualifications did not prove one could survive, let alone thrive, in China. So I decided to pull out a book I had been reading: *Mr. China: A Memoir* by Tim Clissold.

"I've visited China many times," I said. "But books like this one opened up my eyes to the 'real' China in transition. It also reminds me that being China-savvy is not just about being a Mandarin speaker or knowing a few Chinese business customs. It requires more specialized knowledge about China, as well as traits like grit and adaptability."

Russell nodded. "Tell me about it. Westerners look me and say, 'You've got black hair, black eyes, you were born in Hong Kong, you've worked on China deals for a few years and been there dozens of times, and so you must know China. But I know better. China isn't my cup of tea. Maybe it's my personality. In any case, I know who *doesn't* have the China factor when I see one."

He studied the book cover. "Oh, I think I've seen this before. It became an instant best-seller when it was published a couple of years ago. Is it one of those cautionary tales about the challenges of doing business in emerging China?"

"Well, it's set in the early 1990s. I expect a lot of those challenges still exist today, but to a lesser degree," I replied. "I would like to think China has progressed a lot over the past decade, so problems like corruption, cronyism and the lack of rule of law are not as rife. And the Chinese leadership has made many public comments about the need for Chinese companies to adopt international practices."

Russell's face was expressionless, but his response seemed positive. "If the Chinese companies we do deals with are really easier to work with, and are willing to adopt the western way of doing things, that would please our investors. They're apprehensive but optimistic at the same time about the China market."

The next day, Russell called me into All-Stellar's office for another interview after inspecting my resume.

"Our investment mandate covers the whole of Asia, that's why we are based in a regional hub like Singapore. But I expect you will have to travel a lot to China and even live there, are you prepared to do that?" he asked.

"Yes. I've heard some say that you need to have lived at least five years in China before you can really scratch beneath the surface," I replied.

"Five years…." Russell lifted an eyebrow. "That's good. I want you to know that this fund values loyal employees. We beat up quitters and job-hoppers around here."

Russell was chuckling, but one look at his burly arms was enough to make me take his words seriously. At six foot two inches, he towered above the Asian masses. His athletic frame was still muscular from years of training as a competitive rugby player during his high school and college years. But it was really his gregarious, wisecracking, straight-talking personality that made him stand out everywhere he went. It was clear that he was the life of the party in western circles, and he was gawked at or gaped at by the more reserved Asians in Singapore not used to his boom box style of communication.

"I assure you that perseverance and loyalty are values that I hold highly," I said.

"Well then, Matt, you have a job offer for a junior analyst position at All-Stellar," Russell beamed.

I took it.

That same month, French banking group BNP Paribas admitted to freezing three of its funds, as it had no way of valuing the complex collateralized debt obligations (CDOs) that they held. The subprime debt crisis was gathering momentum. In coming months, a tidal wave of housing evictions and bankruptcies would erupt across the US and other western markets. Global financial markets would seize up; thousands of investment bankers would lose their jobs. As providence would have it, I dodged that bullet by rejecting the European investment bank's offer.

But back then, I had no inkling any of this would happen. CDOs were the least of my fears. My biggest concern was that I did not want to pee into a wine bottle under my desk. That, I heard, was what many associates resorted to doing when insane deadlines gave them no time to dash to the bathroom. Private equity work, I figured, would at least be kinder to the bladder. Russell assured me that the workload at All-Stellar would not be so crazy. As it turned out, I would later find myself peeing into a duck pond in the middle of the night in a remote village in southwestern China, while waiting to be rescued from a horde of angry farmers.

Still, the real draw factor for me to join All-Stellar was the opportunity to work closely with companies serving China's US$4.6 trillion economy. Russell had assigned me to suss out potential Chinese deals. Anything related to China's domestic consumption boom was fair game for us, from lingerie manufacturers to education software start-ups and entrepreneurs customizing natural-fiber cloth diapers for

Chinese families eager to splurge on their "Little Emperors". I relished this chance to get up close and personal with Chinese entrepreneurs, who tended to have vastly different communication styles from the American, European, Middle Eastern, Indian and Southeast Asian businessmen that I had interacted with in my previous job.

The Chinese CEOs I met with were relatively well-travelled and cosmopolitan, but they still had the tendency to talk in a vague, roundabout manner that always left me unsure of what they really meant. I started to have a new-found appreciation for the Chinese saying *heizhongyoubai, baizhongyouhei* 黑中有白, 白中有黑. Translated as "within the black, there is some white; within the white, there is some black," this phrase sums up typical situations in China where people express themselves so vaguely that you can never be certain what they mean, and almost always have to read between the lines to decipher their true intent.

Such ambiguity made it difficult for me to submit any conclusive reports to my bosses who were looking for clear answers about the growth potential of these Chinese firms, but they were still pleased with my overall performance. My year-end review in 2007 turned out to be better than I expected. "Matt is commercial, diligent and highly efficient with his work, which is outstanding," Russell wrote.

As the credit crunch deepened, All-Stellar was enjoying an almost miraculous success in raising funds. While more established PE shops were struggling to raise fresh capital, All-Stellar was in the news for raising US$880 million in less than one year from a string of institutional investors, from western banks to US pension funds, sovereign wealth funds and oil money from the Middle East. These "Limited Partners"—PE lingo for investors in a fund—did not make investment decisions, and their liabilities did not extend beyond their share of ownership in the fund. But there was nothing limited about their clout and influence on a PE fund's operating decisions, as my colleague Randy Cheung explained.

"They set our investment mandates, return targets and deal and sector limits amongst other key issues. More importantly, they pay our salaries with the management fees of up to 2 percent we charged for investing capital on their behalf," he told me on my first day at work. He had joined All-Stellar just three months as an associate before I did, and acted as my mentor.

Randy Cheung, a Hong Kong native, was the brain of our team. He was a financial modeling whiz and had already cut his teeth on an impressive number of big M&A deals by the age of thirty. But what wowed me most was his genuine niceness. He was always smiling and ready to help me, even with my dumbest questions. Even during crunch times when everyone else had lost their heads, he was still mild-tempered—not an easy feat. I liked him a lot.

I also worked closely with Gary Samuelson, who was Russell's former business partner and one of the directors of the fund. A New Yorker with a Buddha-like physique, he had spent most of his twenty-five-year consulting career with multinational companies, but was determined to prove he was no colorless corporate clog in the wheel. Gary was always ready to regale us with stories of his Middle East exploits, braving sand storms and gangsters to complete huge public projects, or coming up with clever ways to win handshake deals with Saudi princes and Dubai sheiks. It was during these adventures that he acquired his enormous beer belly, he claimed. I imagined each of his livers must be the size of a four-pounder Angus beefsteak, since he never once got tipsy even after downing multiple jugs of alcohol in one sitting. That made me wonder how he managed to train up his tolerance in the Islamic states where alcohol consumption was forbidden, at least in public. It was ample proof of his ingenuity, I thought.

Randy, Gary and I were kept busy presenting potential China deals to our investors. They were eager to get more exposure to emerging Asian markets, which they believed could offer significantly higher returns than developed countries at that time. China, in particular, was in the center of their radar.

The big guns—international private equity houses like KKR & Co. and TPG Capital—had already started investing in such companies over the past five years. Now a wave of Asia-focused, US-dollar-denominated funds like ours was rushing into the China market as well.

But deals were snapped up all too quickly. From the grapevine, I learnt that scores of local players, from rich tycoons and government officials to banks and property companies, had been piling into the unregulated industry over the past two years to make a quick buck. Naively, I dismissed this trend as a flash in the pan due to the low barriers of entry in the unregulated market. It would be another few months before I learnt that a good number of these investors weren't just opportunists, but a veritable force to be reckoned with.

Six months flew by, but we were still empty-handed. China deals were much harder to close than I had thought.

All-Stellar's Investment Committee, which was made up of the fund's top brass, as well as representatives from our largest investors, shot down half a dozen proposals. The deals fell short of the strict criteria that the Limited Partners had set, they said, insisting that we should only pick companies where there was a strong alignment of interests between us the shareholders, the founder and management team. They also wanted us to negotiate for significant shareholder rights in the company. If we had a major say in how these unpolished gems were managed, they reasoned, then we would be able to enhance shareholder value, grow the companies faster, and have a better chance at securing juicier returns upon exit.

We searched even harder. But after another dozen proposed deals failed to make it through the initial screening stage, it became clear that we desperately needed a local "rainmaker"—a broker with strong connections to get us to the negotiating table with the right Chinese firms.

Finding the right person to help us land proprietary deals—where the PE investor would be granted exclusive access to negotiate and close the deal before anybody else did—was not easy. Russell wanted someone who was highly influential and localized, yet also fluent in Mandarin, English as well as western corporate finance and international PE best practices. Most Chinese rainmakers with such pedigree were already hired by our biggest competitors, or had struck out on their own.

Finally, in March 2008, Russell called us into his office and popped open a bottle of Moutai, a brand of fiery Chinese liquor which was a must-have staple at banquets for Chinese businessmen and officials.

"We have a rainmaker at last," he announced. "Her name is Susie Wu. She will bring along her protégé Fang Xing to form the new China team."

I was about to cheer, but stopped short in confusion when I saw how grim Russell still looked.

"Our Limited Partners have been calling me every other day to ask when we will be able to close our first China deal. Our competitors have been making a lot more headway than us in China," he said in his usual blunt manner. "If you don't buck up and get some results, you can forget about bonuses this year."

Randy and I squirmed.

"We just need to score one or two big winners, after which it would be plain sailing," Gary said. "That's why getting a China deal soon is so important."

He was right. The siren call of China's frothy equity markets was becoming all the more alluring to investors across the world. With Beijing pulling out all the stops to host a glittering, record-breaking Olympic Games, the Shanghai and Shenzhen equity markets had been roaring with a winners-take-all exuberance. During the heady days of the 2007 stock market boom, PE funds were known to reap 600 percent profits after the Chinese companies they invested in saw their stock prices triple or quadruple after their initial public offerings (IPO). The Chinese stock markets had given up a good chunk of their gains since their peak in late 2007, but many investors still believed that China's long-term growth potential made it an undisputed winner.

Russell was going for gold in China too. "Our target is to get a China deal by the Olympics in August. So we're going to give full support to the Beijing team."

He poured the Moutai into two huge beer glasses. "Drink up," he commanded Randy and I. "And get ready to drink a lot more over the next few months. You two young fellas will be part of All-Stellar's brand-new China team."

Four hours later, we were on board a plane to Beijing to meet Susie.

> *De Xin Ying Shou* 得心应手: **Whatever the heart wants, the hand easily grasps. An idiom describing mastery of a situation or skill.**

CHAPTER 2

The Expert

Hang Jia Li Shou 行家里手

MADAME WU WAS MY FIRST introduction to the rarefied class of young China Hands. And she was nothing like what I expected.

According to Russell, we were lucky to have lured her back to Beijing from her lofty position at a global consumer goods company. She was previously based in Hong Kong, where the multinational company had its regional headquarters, and she managed its relations with the Chinese government. A Beijing native, Susie had become a naturalized British citizen after working for more than two decades overseas, primarily in Europe and Singapore. That made her a typical *haigui* 海归, a term used to describe Chinese people who were born in China, moved overseas, acquired a foreign passport and had now come back to their homeland to tap opportunities in the booming economy.

I had originally pictured a prim and proper Party-Secretary-like matron, who would give us a lecture on how the *weida zhuguo* 伟大祖国 (glorious motherland) has been steadfastly implementing a scientific multi-point plan to restructure and reinvigorate its industries, thereby further improving the environment for domestic and foreign investment. Then one day, I overheard Russell regaling an executive from one of our Limited Partners with juicy descriptions of Susie's champagne-drenched parties at her Isle of Wight home overlooking The Solent Strait, as well as her fancy summer escapades to the Turks and Caicos Islands. That made me think of a hoity-toity, middle-aged socialite whose Chinese roots had disappeared entirely beneath a thick British upper crust.

One look at Susie Wu and I knew I was a buffoon for trying to stuff her into a stereotype. She was supremely friendly, almost irreverent. She was said to be in her early forties, but she looked almost as young as I. Her shoulder-length tresses were dyed with orange-brown streaks that swept back with a dramatic diamond-studded clip said to be favored by nouveau riche Chinese *taitais*, a colloquial term for wealthy married women who do not need to work. Her heavily made-up complexion was a little too taut for comfort, while her eyelash extensions were coming out slightly at the sides, perhaps dislodged by Beijing's gusty spring sandstorms.

She wore a red pair of horn-rimmed glasses through which she examined Randy and I from head to toe with a Mona Lisa smile as we rushed into the Made in China restaurant at Beijing Grand Hyatt Hotel, one of the oldest five-star hotels in the city. It was just a short walk away from the Forbidden City, the imposing abode of Ming and Qing Dynasty emperors over five centuries.

I self-consciously adjusted my tie, wondering if my crumpled suit was a dowdy insult to her ensemble of a hot pink *qipao* 旗袍—a body-hugging traditional Chinese dress—and a snazzy leather jacket. I would later learn that Susie was a patron of up-and-coming Chinese designers such as Ma Ke and Liang Zi, who were making waves on the international stage, and always sought to be one of the first to wear their creations fresh off the catwalk.

"I thought we would get here before her," muttered Randy, glancing at his watch nervously. We were three minutes early for our lunch appointment. We had expected Susie to follow the characteristically late arrival pattern of our various Chinese acquaintances, many of whom seemed to think turning up an hour after the appointment time was punctual enough. Their usual excuse for tardiness was Beijing's notoriously bad traffic. But Susie was not only sitting pretty at a round table by the window, but had sipped half of her jasmine tea. She had also laid out two copies of a report on Dominant Duck, a potential deal she was bringing to the table for All-Stellar. There was an awkward pause as we wondered whether to apologize for making her wait.

Then she chirped, "*Aiyah* why so shy?" with a discernible Singaporean accent, and broke the ice immediately.

"I spent about four years in Singapore during one of my previous jobs as an asset manager," explained Susie, reverting back to her crisp British accent. "So that's where I learnt all those Singlish (Singapore English) phrases like '*aiyah*' and '*lah*'."

In the same breath, she shrilled in pristine Mandarin with the most lyrical Beijing accent I had ever heard: "*Fuwuyuan diancai* 服务员 点菜 (Waiter, take our order now)!"

A waiter hustled over immediately, reciting in well-rehearsed English the restaurant's signature offerings such as Peking Duck and Beggar's Chicken, which were reputed to be among the best in the capital city. These two dishes, said to have originated from the Qing dynasty some 400 years ago, were some of the highlights of the northern Chinese cuisine served by Made in China.

"Let's have two Peking Ducks to celebrate our first All-Stellar China team meeting. May the pair of *yuanyang* 鸳鸯 augur well for our proposed union with Dominant Duck," said Susie gaily.

Randy looked a little confused. But I grinned, pleased that I could recognize Susie's reference to *yuanyang* Mandarin ducks. The Chinese character for *yuan* means "male duck" and *yang* refers to the female bird—which in traditional Chinese culture symbolized lifelong love and fidelity within a marriage. I was very much looking forward to tasting the famous Peking roasted duck, which was a Beijing tourist attraction in itself. Beggar's Chicken, however, was new to me. Susie immediately picked up on this.

"Beggar's Chicken is called *fuguiji* 富贵鸡 or 'rich and noble chicken' but it's really the Cinderella of the poultry world," she explained. "Legend had it that a homeless beggar chanced upon a chicken but was so poor that he didn't have a stove to cook it. So he wrapped it in leaves, slathered it in mud and baked it in the ground. A Qing dynasty emperor passing by was so entranced by the aroma that he stopped to share it with the beggar."

"So that's how Beggar's Chicken won a place on the imperial cuisine roll of honor overnight and became a royal dish," Susie said, adding with an almost impish smile: "Let's order two of those as well—one for us to feast like kings, and another to send to our poor struggling competitor who's begging for cash."

I could not help widening my eyes at this jibe, wondering who it was targeted at. Randy was much quicker on the uptake. "I understand that Mann Brothers is also looking at the Dominant Duck deal?" he asked. "I wonder how long they will be able to last in the game since they are affected by the US subprime debt problems."

I knew that Mann Brothers was the eponymous Wall Street investment bank founded by four siblings in the US. I knew the conglomerate had expanded abroad quite aggressively. But it was the first time I learnt that the bank's private equity arm had already ventured into China, or that Mann Brothers was running into financial problems related to the credit crunch.

Susie flashed her enigmatic smile. "The PE investor has been in talks with Dominant Duck for a few months. Their exclusivity clause is going to expire soon, and we're going to kick them out."

It turned out that Mann Brothers had signed a non-binding term sheet with the company with a six-month exclusivity clause. This meant that the company could only engage in discussions with Mann Brothers during the six-month period, and it was not allowed to entertain other suitors.

The negotiations were falling through, giving us an opening to woo the founder of Dominant Duck. "I heard it from the duck's mouth," Susie quipped. "Chairman Zhou has been a personal friend of mine since 1998. I always made sure I send him a bottle of his favorite *Wuliangye* 五粮液 brand of Chinese liquor every Chinese New Year. It's paid off since he was the one who took the initiative to call me to invest in his company when he heard I had joined All-Stellar."

I wondered if Chairman Zhou was treading on thin legal ice by courting a potential investor while still in negotiations with Mann Brothers. Then a thought crossed my mind: as long as you can get away with it in China, does it even matter? That marked the start of a slippery slope for me. Later on, after being scorned by a local lawyer as an idiot for worrying about breaking a rental contract since it was just a "worthless piece of paper," I would become practically numb to the prevalent legal irregularities and broken contracts in China.

The wine—a 2002 Domaine de Chevalier—arrived, cutting short my internal debate.

Susie proposed a toast to Dominant Duck. "*Shoudaoqinlai* 手到 擒来[2]! May the cooked duck fly from Mann Brothers' mouths and onto our plate!"

I began to see why she had a reputation for being fearsome—a cut-throat hunter gloved with silky western wit. No detail or opportunity escaped her eagle eye. Those traits must have helped her to broker some of the most sensational deals that rocked Asia in the years of frenetic deal activity leading up to the global financial crisis. Her

---

[2] A Chinese idiom which is literally translated as, "to have a bird fly directly into one's open hands". It refers to the easy capture of one's target or adversary.

landmark deals included a hostile takeover of a major national airline, and the acquisition of one of China's biggest meat producers by a state-run group. She had an uncanny ability to match her business contacts with the right investors at the right time. Her track record attracted scores of investment bankers, who often offered her the first pick amongst potential deals.

Susie told us that throughout the decades she worked overseas, she made a point to travel back to her homeland at least once every two months. Her top priority was to forge close relationships with many ambitious Chinese entrepreneurs, many of whom were hungry for capital to expand their businesses.

With the niceties out of the way, Madame Wu proceeded to quiz me, catching me off-guard just as I popped an intricately wrapped Peking Duck wrap into my mouth. The perfect alchemy of flavors— the succulent duck meat steaming in its juices, a film of crispy duck skin roasted until all cloying fat had been melted away, the smooth texture of the steamed flour skin, the cool cucumber strips, the sweet brown sauce concocted with a secret recipe—took my breath away.

"So Matt, judging from your surname Huang, your ancestors were from southern China? Fujian province, perhaps?" she observed. She was right as usual.

"Have you been to China before?" she continued in Mandarin.

This time, I jumped in eagerly, hoping to impress her. "My first trip to Beijing was when I was about ten years old and I went to climb the Great Wall for the first time. My parents are strong advocates of my Chinese education and strongly encouraged me to learn Mandarin since young. They brought me to China a few times to search for my roots, and I've travelled on my own around the country half a dozen times," I rattled off in my Singapore-accented Mandarin.

"I even received a certificate, proving that I had climbed the 'Most Difficult Stretch of the Great Wall'. You know how the saying goes: *Budeng changcheng feihaohan* 不登长城非好汉 (If you have never climbed the Great Wall, you're not a real man)! So whenever I want to impress a blind date, I always bring this certificate along with me."

Usually this joke elicited some mirth from my Singaporean or western friends. But this time I had a tough audience. Susie was not amused. "Being a man nowadays requires buying four walls and a roof. And with housing prices going crazy over the past few years, acquiring a property in a major city like Beijing nowadays is way harder for most young Chinese men than scaling any number of Great Walls," she observed dryly.

I was stumped. Fortunately, Randy saved me by commenting, "Yes it really is crazy how property-obsessed Chinese people are. But it's understandable given the dire lack of other good investment options. The markets for stocks, bonds and even banks' wealth management products are still nascent and state-controlled so it's hard to get any good investment returns."

Susie nodded. "Yes, it's tough for ordinary folks. But if you have a certain type of background, the sky's the limit for making profits, especially in the PE space."

"What kind of background?" Randy asked.

Susie shrugged. "It's pretty obvious what sort of background, isn't it? China's PE industry is dominated by funds set up by PEPs (Politically Exposed Persons)[3]. The interesting thing is that quite a few of them nowadays tend to be relatively young, educated in top universities abroad and well-versed in international practices. Now that you're working here, remember to pay special attention to the young Chinese PE executives, and find out what sort of backgrounds they have."

"By young, you mean those under forty-five?" I clarified. "At least, forty-five years old is the cut-off age for qualification into the prestigious Young Presidents' Organization..."

---

[3] PEP is a term describing a person who holds prominent public office, or someone who is related or associated with this person.

Unexpectedly, Susie broke into a pleased smile. "Yes, I like to think forty-four is still young."

"You both went to the top US schools," she continued. "So you must have had quite a few Chinese classmates, did you make friends with any who were related to princelings?"

This was the first time I had heard of the term princelings, or *taizidang* 太子党. It meant "Crown Prince Faction," and referred to the offspring of China's elite political families. I tried to recall if I even had any significant conversations with mainland Chinese students on campus, but drew blanks. Randy shook his head too. "Most of the Chinese kept to themselves," he said.

"That's a pity that you didn't try harder to interact with them. When I did an executive MBA in the US, I met two young Chinese students who turned out to be some of the best contacts I could ever make in my banking career. Their fathers were…"

Suddenly, Susie's crystals-bedazzled iPhone buzzed with a text message. I smothered a sigh of disappointment as she typed a quick reply, and abandoned the rest of her intriguing sentence.

Madame Wu rose gracefully to go, motioning us to follow. "Chairman Zhou has just confirmed that he will see you both in two hours' time," she said. "I told him you will spend the whole afternoon and evening with him. I hope that's enough time for you to get him to warm up enough to talk a little about the deal. Good luck."

> *Hang Jia Li Shou* 行家里手: **An expert hand in a particular sector.**

CHAPTER 3

Handshake Deal

Wo Shou Cheng Jiao 握手成交

W E ARRIVED TWENTY-TWO MINUTES LATE at the Ten Thousand Joys Teahouse despite setting off almost half an hour early. A car had broken down on East Third Ring Road and occupied the center lane, leaving a hopeless trail of stationary traffic behind it. The jam stoked our anxiety—already stoked by Susie's lack of clear instructions or details about our surprise assignment—even more.

What exactly were we supposed to talk about for the next ten hours? The only clue that Susie gave us before she left was a cryptic tidbit of information: Chairman Zhou had served briefly in the People's Liberation Army (PLA) during his youth. "See if you can get him to warm up to you enough to talk about that. If you can, you will have passed my first test."

Fortunately, Chairman Zhou was even later than we were. So in the fifteen minutes before he emerged from his office building across the street from the teahouse, I was able to order the most expensive items on the menu: aged Pu'er Tea from Xishuang Banna—a hilly tropical haven in southern Yunnan province which is famous for its addictively fragrant tea—as well as braised duck eggs. I also ordered an assortment of local pastries—just to make the table look as full as possible and show Chairman Zhou that we had spared no expense to host him. Chairman Zhou strolled in leisurely, accompanied by his executive director surnamed Meng, who had helped to co-found Dominant Duck.

Chairman Zhou wrung our hands in a hearty handshake, and we exchanged name cards with a profuse amount of head-bowing before sitting down on exquisitely carved rosewood stools. There was a long pause. We all awkwardly watched a *qipao*-clad waitress brewing the dark, fragrant Pu'er tea—a 2003 vintage— in an elaborate ritual. Another waitress hurried over with a steaming hot, damp towel on a porcelain dish for Chairman Zhou to clean his hands.

Finally the man spoke. I expected him to address Randy first, but he took me by surprise by patting me on the back with a fatherly smile: "Your Mandarin is not bad."

I wanted to counter that Randy's strong Hong Kong accent belied his excellent Mandarin, but decided to try the more quiescent approach. "*Guojiang, guojiang* 过奖 过奖," I murmured with a wide smile to deflect this "undeserved praise". Chairman Zhou beamed and raised a toast.

I couldn't help feeling a little smug. "Susie must have been mistaken to think it would take ten hours for us to break the ice. Chairman Zhou and I have obviously hit it off from the start, maybe we will even develop a special bond in no time," I thought, as I calculated how much to bet with Randy that we would be able to persuade Dominant Duck to close a deal with All-Stellar within thirty days.

"Where did you learn your Mandarin?" asked Chairman Zhou.

"My parents are second-generation immigrants from Southern China. My dad was born in Singapore. My mom was born in Chaozhou[4]. We speak mainly Mandarin at home," I replied.

"Yes he has a southern Chinese accent. But his Mandarin is not

---

[4] Chaozhou is a small city in Guangdong province.

bad for a *waiguoren* 外国人 (foreigner)!" Chairman Zhou commented to Mr. Meng, who nodded silently.

He meant it as a compliment, but it jolted me back to reality. Far from being recognized as an insider, I had to get used to being labeled as a *waiguoren* in my grandparents' homeland. From my outward appearance, I could easily pass off as a local Chinese. But I would need more time to work on acquiring a more authentic Mandarin accent to make Chairman Zhou feel more comfortable.

Pleasantries and small talk ensued for the next two hours. We exhausted the topics of Beijing's weather, tea, the upcoming Olympics and the most scenic attractions across China. But we hardly even skimmed the topic of Dominant Duck, apart from some basic information about its operations, which was already available on the company's webpage hosted by China's giant search engine Baidu. Randy and I tried feebly to steer the conversation towards the People's Liberation Army, even resorting to daft off-hand comments such as, "I wonder how the PLA are preparing to ramp up security at the Olympics?" But Chairman Zhou simply gave us a blank look and went back to discussing the magnificence of the Great Wall.

Still, I had plenty of time to study Chairman Zhou's appearance. I had arrived with a mental caricature of a commander wearing an olive green uniform and holding a Little Red Book. But sitting in front of me was a relaxed, decidedly modern man in his mid-fifties, dressed in a tailored gray business suit with a Louis Vuitton black leather man bag tucked under his arm. He was probably around five foot eight inches, lanky with the proud bearing of a self-made man. The only features that gave away his farming background were his tanned, rugged face, and wrinkled hands that still looked crusty in spite of Chairman Zhou's copious use of the wet towel to wipe them— probably the by-product of decades of hardship toiling in the mud to build up his duck empire.

Chairman Zhou was flawlessly cordial, but every time I tried to broach the subject of our proposed investment in Dominant Duck, he clammed up and urged me to drink more tea. I did so with as much gusto as I could, but after the sixteenth cup, I was getting heart palpitations and a strained bladder.

Suppressing a sigh, I reminded myself that an indirect, non-confrontational approach worked best when dealing with Chinese entrepreneurs like Chairman Zhou, who placed great importance on their image, or "face". Giving "face" occupies such a special place in the Chinese psyche. So I knew that simple gestures which exhibited respect for Chairman Zhou's position, such as supporting his elbow, pouring him tea and letting him dominate the conversation, could score points when trying to win his favor. For a newcomer to China, these seemingly insignificant gestures require patient practice. Fortunately, I had the whole afternoon to work on this. So did Randy, who disappeared midway through the conversation and reappeared after twenty minutes with a glum face.

I thought he was having tummy troubles, but he told me later that he had sneaked out to pay the bill. But he ended up having a protracted tussle with Chairman Zhou's secretary, who had been dispatched to do the same thing. The diminutive lady won by—"accidentally," she claimed—shoving him in the stomach, and then stuffing a wad of notes into the cashier's hands.

We piled into Chairman Zhou's fifth-generation Mercedes-Benz Sonderklasse sedan and headed to the dinner venue at Qianmen Avenue south of Tiananmen Square. Cars moved at a snail's pace on the Southeast Third Ring Road, where Chairman Zhou's office was located, all the way to Chang'an Avenue. This road, also known as Everlasting Peace Avenue, is the main artery of Beijing.

Chairman Zhou, noticing us nervously peering at our watches, said matter-of-factly: "The Peruvian President is in town, that's why."

"What does a diplomatic visit have to do with us?" asked Randy.

"They usually close off one of the lanes on Chang'an Avenue to allow the diplomatic motorcade to pass, so we commoners have to squeeze within three lanes."

For most of the trip, Chairman Zhou's chauffeur, who was better dressed than I was, sat stiffly in his pin-striped business suit. His white-gloved hands hardly touched the steering wheel. But whenever Driver Li spotted the slightest opening in the wall of stationary cars in front of us, he would spring into action and rush forward before anyone else cut in. I marveled at his reflexes.

A thirty-minute drive, according to GPS estimates, turned into a ninety-minute ordeal with more small talk about our dinner venue. It was an avant-garde restaurant housed in a *siheyuan* 四合院 (Beijing courtyard) that was tucked in a narrow alleyway known in Beijing as a *hutong*. It was close to Qianmen Avenue, which was famous for its tea parlors and opera houses. Over a century ago, Qianmen was the ending point of two major railroads that transported goods from the western regions to Beijing.

Madame Wu had picked this particular Hunan cuisine restaurant as it was renowned for its excellent *hongshaorou* 红烧肉—cubes of pork belly slow-cooked in Shaoxing rice wine and caramelized with sugar. It was one of Chairman Zhou's favorite comfort foods and the signature dish from Mao Zedong's home province of Hunan.

By now, it was clear to me that we had failed Susie's challenge to get Chairman Zhou to open up to us. But I was still hopeful that once we started chugging Moutai at dinner, Chairman Zhou would loosen up enough to talk real business. It would take me several months to realize that such long-drawn sessions, with seemingly no clear objective or purpose, were the norm in China. Meetings were often exercises in building familiarity and studying the other party's body language and unspoken cues, rather than to work on a specific task.

But on occasion, an opening may suddenly appear, when your business contact lets down his guard or finds some unexpected reason to negotiate more favorably with you. Then your reflexes had to be as quick as Driver Li's to seize the opportunity. And this was what Madam Wu and her disciple demonstrated that evening.

My new China colleague Fang Xing greeted us when we finally arrived at the private dining room in the restaurant. A native of Qinhuangdao, an industrial port city in central Hebei province, he was twenty-six years old and had just tied the knot with his high school sweetheart. They had held their traditional Chinese wedding ceremony just three days ago in their local township. Immediately afterwards, he had hopped onto the first plane back to Beijing to attend tonight's dinner with Chairman Zhou. He was Susie's protégé indeed.

"Lao Zhou[5], judging from the radiance beaming from your face, I presume the afternoon's discussions with my overseas colleagues must have gone extremely well!" Fang Xing boomed, all smiles as he ushered everyone to their seats.

Susie sat regally at the head of the round table, with Chairman Zhou on her right. Fang Xing was about to sit down directly opposite her in the chair designated in Chinese custom for the guest with the lowest status, but was immediately stopped by Mr. Meng, who deferentially gave up his seat next to Susie. After a good five minutes of shoving and loud protestations, Mr. Meng finally allowed Fang Xing to usher him back to his seat. He had a hugely satisfied grin on his face, as if he had been accorded an even greater honor. I watched this whole scene with bemused panic, wondering if I should have jumped in to take that junior seat, since it logically belonged to me.

With calm restored at the table, the toasting began. As Moutai glasses clinked, I studied Fang Xing carefully before my eyes became too glassy from the alcohol. Everything about this young fellow seemed to be brimming. He was chubby with a beer belly a bit oversized for his age, and his cheekbones jutted out faintly beneath

---

[5] In China, people address someone using the word Lao 老 (old) in front of his surname as a form of respect to a close business associate.

his dimpled cheeks whenever he let out a huge bellow of a laugh. His
hair was slicked back with a heavy dollop of styling gel. I looked at
his dandelion-colored left hand, and wondered whether to be more
impressed by the ostentatious turquoise ring on his wedding finger, or
his manicure. It was the first time I had ever seen such shiny, well-kept
nails on a man. He sported a light gray blazer and slick black pants
that night, all by Giorgio Armani. He told us this was his favorite
brand—at least, when he didn't want to look "too flashy".

But what really made Fang Xing's cup run over was his charisma.
It was overpowering. He was dominating yet affable, speaking with an
air of authority on everything from world politics to China's culinary
delights while keeping everyone at ease with light humor. He was
supremely confident yet inclusive, chatting with Chairman Zhou like
best buddies while making sure that Randy and I did not feel felt out.

Before joining All-Stellar, Fang Xing spent three and a half years
job-hopping amongst the major global investment banks. He was
not shy in boasting to us that his biggest strength was in making his
interviewers think he was much more skilled and experienced than
he really was. His maneuvers landed him in a higher new position
each time he switched jobs. By the age of twenty-five, he had already
become a first-year associate—ahead of his peers by at least one year.

Fang Xing and Susie met two years ago while working on an
acquisition of a major commercial real estate portfolio. Susie was
his bank's client. She was so impressed by the young man that she
poached him to be a senior associate at All-Stellar when she joined the
fund. His fresh-off-the-press name cards displayed the rank of "senior
director," which Fang Xing told us candidly was in line with common
practice of inflating job titles in China.

The *hongshaorou* arrived, gleaming cubes of ruddy "brain food,"
as Susie described it. "Mao Zedong would eat two bowls of this every
day to keep him intellectually sharp," she said.

"It's no wonder that Chairman Zhou is so superior in his thinking, since he is a connoisseur of the Great Helmsman's favorite food as well as his sayings," added Fang Xing.

The older man demurred: "I'm just a lowly businessman but I sincerely hope that I have contributed to the modernization of agriculture and a Harmonious Socialist Society under the great red banner of Mao Zedong thought and General Party Secretary Hu Jintao's leadership."

"You can be assured of our whole-hearted support in carrying out your noble mission," said Susie smoothly, as she proposed yet another toast to Chairman Zhou—"an old hand in the duck farm business in China, and an extremely respected Lao Qianbei 老前辈, in the industry." The word Lao Qianbei, or "Forefather," is a term of respect for someone of seniority with impressive credentials and exceptional experience in an industry.

The Forefather returned the compliment, addressing Susie as Wu zong 总 (boss) as a gesture of respect for her seniority. "If this deal goes through, we have a lot to thank Wu zong," he said. "With your support, I'm sure you will present us well in front of your Investment Committee. We have a lot to improve on and to learn from you."

Fang Xing shared Chairman Zhou's story with us, while the protagonist nodded in agreement or interjected with details along the way.

Born in the capital city of Baotou in Inner Mongolia, a northern Chinese province famous for its majestic grasslands, Zhou was a typical northerner—warm-hearted, unrestrained and forthright.

When Mao Zedong's Cultural Revolution to weed out capitalist and traditional elements from society began in 1966, Zhou had just graduated from middle school. Young intellectuals like him were ordered to go the countryside to learn from the peasants, and he was sent to a remote farm in Heilongjiang province to harvest crops and tend to poultry.

In 1979, he was finally sent back to the city, where he enrolled himself in a university and graduated with a college degree in engineering design four years later. The social and political strife of the decade-long revolution had cost him years of his youth, but fueled his determination to change his fortunes. By this time, the country was showing the first signs of economic revival driven by paramount leader Deng Xiaoping's policies to reform and open up China's centrally-controlled market. The reforms intensified after Deng's 1992 Southern Tour, which sounded the clarion call for a rebirth of private sector ownership and entrepreneurship.

Chairman Zhou's first job was as a mechanic repairing vehicles in the PLA, but he also found himself fixing tractors and rudimentary poultry feed equipment for peasants on the collectivized farms. He was "retired" after just six months of work, when the PLA started to downsize.

Inspired by Deng Xiaoping, he decided to move to Beijing to try his hand at setting up a business with Mr. Meng and two other friends. They experimented with various businesses, from trading of agricultural equipment to toy manufacturing, before eventually settling on their least glamorous option—duck farming.

In 1996, the two friends dropped out of the business, so the headstrong Chairman Zhou took control. He persuaded Mr. Meng to stay on as a minority shareholder. That year, he finally opened his first duck farm on the eastern side of Beijing, where one of the capital's major arteries, the East Third Ring Road, now stands. At that time, that road was just a stretch of untouched wilderness.

Business was shockingly good, as orders from tourist-filled roast duck restaurants poured in. Within six months, he set up three other farms along the major river tributaries surrounding the capital city. As China's top leaders scaled back gradually on state intervention in the economy and controls over private entrepreneurship, his duck farm business burgeoned on the back of China's break-neck double-digit economic growth.

With increasing household income and surge of purchasing power, people could afford to splurge on better food on the dining table. Dominant Duck's business in Beijing was flourishing, but Chairman Zhou had set his sights on a nationwide business. In 1998, the company opened its first duck farm outside Beijing in central Henan province, tapping on the business and government relationships of Mr. Meng, who was a Henan native.

By early 2000, the company had hired some 500 staff across China. A year later, revenues crossed RMB100 million (US$12 million). This catapulted it into the ranks of China's top five duck farm enterprises. Then, in March 2007, the company celebrated a new milestone—the opening of its fiftieth farm in Henan province, which brought Chairman Zhou closer to his dream of creating the biggest and most dominant duck farm player in China. The company's English name—Dominant Duck Farming Company Limited—fit snugly into this grand vision.

Still, the name was more of an afterthought, admitted Chairman Zhou. In mid-2007, he had asked a random laowai he met during a business meeting to come up with an English name to make the company look more modern. That was around the time Mann Brothers initiated discussions with him for a potential investment.

That was also the time when he started to harbor dreams of going international. Until then, he had relied on his personal savings, contributions from his family members and recurring cash flows from the business to expand the company within China. The business was a family-run one: many of Chairman Zhou's relatives held key positions, the most senior being the company's chief finance manager—his sister-in-law who had a degree in accounting from a second-rate university in Beijing.

But by 2007, the business had gotten too big to rely on just the family kitty. Chairman Zhou tried to borrow from a mid-sized local bank as well as one of the Big Four state-owned lenders, but was promptly rejected by both. China's banking sector was dominated by government-linked banks which had to contend with political pressure to dish out huge loans at artificially low interest rates to state-owned enterprises (SOEs), while leaving private enterprises—deemed to be more risky—in the cold. So, millions of Chinese dynamic entrepreneurs had to rely on loans from underground banks and loan sharks instead. Chairman Zhou cast around for more options, and realized that some of his fellow entrepreneurs were being wooed by international funds, some of whom were bending over backwards to meet their financing needs.

"One of my friends in the toy manufacturing business insisted he get the investment in hard cash. So, the foreign fund arranged for trucks and trucks of 100-yuan notes to be delivered to his doorstep," Chairman Zhou recounted.

"We can give you more than 100-yuan notes, Lao Qianbei," Susie said. "The previous company you were in talks with could only offer you cash, but they lack the special resources we have."

"What's your dream, Chairman Zhou?" chimed in Fang Xing.

"I want to ai-pee-oo in China," replied the older man gleefully, enunciating the initials "I.P.O.," like a toddler spelling out the letters of the name of his beloved pet for the first time.

Fang Xing snapped his fingers. "Ah, esteemed big boss, that's where you under-value yourself. You're still dreaming too small—All-Stellar has the expertise and network to help a promising company like DeeDee get a prestigious overseas listing like Singapore or Hong Kong or New York!"

Chairman Zhou's eyes widened.

"You will become even more respected among your peers if you cooperate with All-Stellar. Our partnership will raise Chairman Zhou's profile on the global stage," continued Fang Xing glibly.

Chairman Zhou's eyes lit up. "Yes, you are right. I want to build a global company..."

Susie raised her glass to her protégé. I hid my crestfallen face behind the remaining four bottles of Moutai waiting to be consumed by the party. I had spent the whole of the previous night preparing and rehearsing a similar pitch, but it was nowhere as eloquent as Fang Xing's, and definitely would not been delivered with such strategic timing.

"Indeed, you would be a hero for being the first among your comrades from your village and your hometown to respond to President Hu Jintao's call to *zouchuqu* 走出去[6] and win glory for the motherland."

"Glorious, yes it is glorious to get rich," slurred Chairman Zhou, quoting the late paramount leader Deng Xiaoping's famous saying while waving his Moutai glass rather dangerously. "Rich and international…"

Fang Xing gently supported the Lao Qianbei's elbow as he staggered to the waiting car—probably headed for home, I thought— and then turned back to wink at us.

I marveled at how smooth this young Chinese banker was. Randy, after looking over his shoulder to ensure Susie was out of earshot, mused: "Fang Xing and Chairman Zhou must be really close, perhaps they are even related?"

I wasn't sure. Fang Xing had a maturity beyond his years and an uncanny ability to get along with people, even strangers. That made it even harder to ascertain how close he really was to Chairman Zhou—and more importantly, whether he had won the latter's trust.

I was starting to realize that trust is an incredibly difficult thing to win in China. The Cultural Revolution and class struggle of the Maoist era had ripped apart relationships across all classes and social ties. Peasants persecuted landlords; wives denounced husbands; sons beat fathers to death; students tortured teachers; neighbors snooped

---

[6] Walk out of China and go abroad. This refers to top Chinese leaders' call for local enterprises to pursue overseas expansion.

on each other and made false reports. This decimated trust in a broken society.

Once China's markets opened up and socialism receded, the populace plunged headlong into the pursuit of wealth as the only thing they could put their trust and security in. I found strangers tended to be more suspicious of each other, and less willing to offer help, fearful of being exploited or manipulated. Still, money could only go that far in a developing market economy, where contracts were often easily broken with few penalties. The rule of law was not robust enough to ensure legal action against offenders. So cash alone was ineffective to prevent the failure of business relationships.

So the only thing, ironically, that the Chinese could fall back on was trust—putting their faith in people who were close enough to them to rise when they rise and to suffer if they fell.

Therein lay our biggest challenge. For us to win Chairman Zhou's attention was easy, since we had money and could show him that our interests were aligned. For us to win his loyalty was much harder, because he saw no reason for now to pledge his alliance to us. And for me to win his trust, at least for now, was near impossible since he saw me as an outsider. But I was determined to try anyway, and prove to him I could be a useful hand on his side.

At around 11:00p.m., we stumbled back to our hotel rooms. Five hours later, Russell sent an urgent e-mail telling us to attend an eight o'clock meeting at Dominant Duck's headquarters that very morning. Fortunately, Randy and I both slept cradling our blackberries, so we received the summons immediately and rushed to get dressed.

We arrived half an hour early, and a dozen managers were already on hand to greet us. They were all dressed in the same uniform—a charcoal-black coat and red-hued handkerchief in the breast pocket, along with lapel pins of a mascot that looked suspiciously like Donald Duck with a black ponytail. Chairman Zhou was not present, and nobody explained why. But I guessed he must be recovering from last night's heavy drinking.

Mr. Meng, who presided over the meeting, beamed broadly as he waved a paper napkin with some scribbled Mandarin words. "Chairman Zhou and Madame Wu reached an agreement last night to proceed with All-Stellar's proposed investment in Dominant Duck. Our hearts are full of joy as we warmly welcome our new business partners…"

Gesturing to Randy and me, he continued: "Zhang zong and Huang zong, who will discuss with us the details." Randy's Cantonese surname "Cheung" is pronounced as "Zhang" in Mandarin.

We were too stunned to respond. "When was the deal signed?" muttered Randy under his breath. "What happened?"

It turned out that Susie had informed Russell last night that the key terms of All-Stellar's investment had already been verbally signed off. But somehow, that information did not get to us, and we had heard nothing from either Susie or Fang Xing.

This morning, we were supposed to handle the nuts and bolts of conducting due diligence on Dominant Duck—details too trivial for Susie to handle. After all, she had already accomplished a major feat: sealing the deal with Chairman Zhou over a handshake—the most critical milestone of any deal in China, especially in the north—within a week of joining All-Stellar.

Numbly, I went over the next steps with the twelve stone-faced managers sitting across the conference table from us. They diligently scribbled down every word I said into their notebooks, as if I were giving a lecture. Our lawyers would put together a non-binding term sheet[7]. We would discuss a timeline for getting the deal signed, map

---

[7] A term sheet is a bullet-point summary that summarizes the material terms and conditions of the investment. It signals the investor's intention to invest in the company, subject to satisfactory results from due diligence. Term sheets are usually non-binding. Its guides both parties towards a final binding legal agreement, after rounds of negotiations.

out the due diligence we needed to complete, and seek approvals from the Investment Committee.

One manager raised her hand and asked a question after making sure Mr. Meng had nodded his head: "How long will this all take?"

"Typical PE deals can take anywhere between three to six months to close, depending on the complexity of the deal and the due diligence work that is needed to be done," answered Randy. More scribbling.

"Any more questions?"

The managers looked uneasily at the stone-faced Mr. Meng and took their cue to maintain a respectful silence. After a few minutes, I decided it was pointless to wait. "Shall we arrange a schedule for us to visit the duck farms in Beijing as well as other provinces?" I suggested.

Mr. Meng agreed heartily, and we scheduled our first inspection of a duck farm next week. Then we got up to leave, and I made an effort to shake hands cordially with every one of the managers once again. But I could not help feeling how wimpy my handshake was compared to a real China Hand's.

> *Wo Shou Cheng Jiao* 握手成交: **A transaction where a deal is sealed after shaking hands.**

CHAPTER 4

Bare Beginnings

Bai Shou Qi Jia 白手起家

THE FOLLOWING MONDAY NIGHT, RANDY and I were back in Beijing, armed with a long laundry list of eighty-nine questions concerning the company's operations, management and financials. Russell also gave us a one-week deadline to learn everything we possibly could about the business of duck rearing from the different varieties of ducks reared for egg and meat at the company, to how it fared amongst the different competitors in the market.

Russell codenamed the investment project "DeeDee" to keep the company's name under wraps, so potential competitors would not be able to find out that we were actually exploring a deal with Dominant Duck.

"Leave no stone unturned, DeeDee could be our first strategic investment so we have to get it right. And remember, you're not supposed to take anything at face value. Look hard, and look again," said Russell, tapping his "skeptic's left eye" which he claimed had served him well over the years.

We were headed to one of DeeDee's two remaining farms in Beijing. They were located about twenty miles east of the Fifth

Ring Road in the eastern Tongzhou District, near to Chaobaihe, a winding river cutting across Beijing, Tianjin municipality, and Hebei province.

Fang Xing did not come with us, saying he had already visited the farm. Randy and I clambered into the minivan emblazoned with the same Donald Duck-lookalike emblem, where our tour guide—DeeDee's operations manager—was waiting.

Manager Wang Xingsheng was a lanky man in his early thirties. A graduate from an agricultural university in Shenyang, a major industrial city, Wang was clearly knowledgeable about the ducks under his charge. More importantly, he was refreshingly chatty.

"Duck farming is popular and lucrative," he rattled off, not even waiting for us to peel off our winter jackets. "China is the largest producer and consumer of duck meat in the world. Over the past twenty years, the production and consumption of duck meat grew by over 8 percent. Today, China's producers claim to have over seventy percent of the global market share, in terms of duck slaughter count."

I hastily grabbed my notepad, and started scribbling as rapidly as the twelve stone-faced managers had done during last week's meeting. The minivan headed east along Jingtong Expressway, one of the oldest expressways in Beijing, extending from Chang'an Avenue to the east. The key arterial highways in China are named after the cities in which the expressway begins and ends. So in this case, Jingtong means Beijing (*jing* 京) and Tongzhou (*tong* 通). Fortunately, the drive was relatively smooth as we had managed to avoid the morning hour rush by setting off at 5:00a.m.

"I thought that pork is still the most popular meat for the Chinese?" Randy asked. In China, pork is such an important component in the Chinese diet that pork prices are included into the calculation of Chinese inflation figures.

"Correct. In fact, Chairman Zhou originally wanted to start a pork farming business, but the barriers to entry were actually rather high because there were quite a few state-linked suppliers already. Even his attempts to name-drop his PLA connections didn't help," Wang replied.

My eyes lit up when I heard the words PLA. "Did his connections help with duck farming?" I asked.

Wang mulled for a few seconds. "I guess he may have been able to pull strings and get a few prime pieces of land around Beijing for his farm…"

Then he thought better of completing his sentence and hastily changed the topic. "The farm we are going to visit rears just 12,000 ducks at any one time. But despite its small size, it has quite a few loyal customers, like some of the major roast duck chains in Beijing."

The farm was one of the few remaining operations that still existed in the Tongzhou and Miyun municipalities of Beijing, where water was still relatively abundant, added Wang. Beijing's severe lack of water resources had been a major push factor for large-scale companies like DeeDee to find greener, moister pastures in the past two decades. More recently, the property boom caused land prices to skyrocket in the capital city, forcing agriculture-related activities to relocate to the outskirts. In preparation for the 2008 Olympics Games, the Beijing government had also moved out all major duck and chicken farm operations before 2005 as part of the major clean-up of the city.

"So what about DeeDee's farms in other provinces? How big are they?" asked Randy.

"They can produce batches of up to 100,000 ducks. Even so, that's not enough to meet demand," replied Wang and proceeded to rattle off a list of statistics about the annual consumption of duck meat in twelve different Chinese cities. As he talked, he fiddled with his sunhat, handed us bottles of mineral water, typed a quick text on his iPhone, and ogled at a leggy girl waiting at the bus-stop.

Obviously he had conducted this tour for Chairman Zhou's guests countless times.

"The Chinese are becoming more health conscious," he continued. "So poultry meat, including duck, now accounts for over twenty percent of our meat consumption last year. It was only slightly over 10 percent ten years ago. So that's why Chairman Zhou had the foresight to enter into the duck business."

As if his barrage of statistics were not enough, Wang volunteered more: "Ducks typically have a feed conversion of 2.15 to 1. In other words, 2.15 pounds of feed is required to produce one pound of duck meat. I can give you seven additional facts about the type of feed used if you would like?"

I was delighted that Wang had provided me with so many statistics to plug into my financial analyses, but could not help shaking my head at the Chinese's obsession with data dumps. I was starting to appreciate why foreigners in China often complained they were still not getting the relevant answers they needed to their questions, after the Chinese party had spent hours rattling off so many facts and figures that they lost the forest for the trees.

After an hour, we entered Tongzhou. Farmers were driving their horse carts laden with fresh produce to the local wet market, while shepherds led their flocks to graze in the dewy fields. Nearby, rows of billboards touting futuristic-looking shopping malls or skyscrapers stood tall, heralding the onset of industrialization that had transformed many of China's 660 cities into some of the world's most crowded metropolises. The rumbling of cranes and construction equipment across Tongzhou became an incessant background noise, even late into the evening.

We entered a two-lane road that weaved right through a morning market. The minivan inched along gingerly through the crowds bearing their assortment of pumpkins, watermelons, and fresh vegetables for fifteen minutes before we finally reached the farm.

As we drove in through the gate, I saw a bright red banner hung from the top of the three-storey office building with the words written in big white letters:

ENTHUSIASTICALLY WELCOME THE
FOREIGN INVESTMENT TEAM AND
OUR OVERSEAS GUESTS

As we got out of the vehicle, the farm manager by the name of Mr. Lin ran out to greet us. Two young ladies clad in the traditional *qipao* were standing at both sides of the door, bowing profusely while avoiding eye contact with us. We were ushered into the Holding Meeting Room of the farm's Administrative Building Number Two, and seated around an oversized oval Chinese mahogany table with several pots of large Chinese Evergreens in the hollow centre.

I sank into the depths of an oversized black leather chair, and stared at my Chinese name neatly written in Chinese calligraphy on a white signboard placed in front of me.

After a thankfully short fifteen minutes of pleasantries, the farm manager showed us a three-minute corporate video presentation. Chairman Zhou, the protagonist in the clip, was displayed with a serious, determined expression on his face, presiding over an office meeting. Another showed him with a serious, benevolent expression on his face clad in a farm uniform tending to the ducks. Yet another showed him with a serious, patriotic expression on his face shaking hands with some beaming officials at the farm. It was all so very serious.

As the video presentation came to an end, the farm manager applauded enthusiastically, before starting on a power point presentation about DeeDee's history, milestones, operations and grand future. I gave up taking notes, and let myself drown in the numbers.

Finally, it was question-and-answer time. We were relieved that

Chairman Zhou's team was very forthcoming in their responses to our queries. It seemed that they had fielded similar due diligence inspections before. By the end of the two-hour session, I felt satisfied that we had built up a pretty comfortable rapport with the farm manager and his team. And we had checked off roughly half of the questions we had come with—better than I had expected.

Finally, we were off to see the ducks. I had expected the farm to have the stench of poultry manure, but the smell was pleasantly mild. I later found out that Beijing had strict policies governing the construction of duck farms in the city after the Severe Acute Respiratory Syndrome (SARS) that had convulsed the capital city in the early 2000's. Because of environmental concerns, the company had installed a fully enclosed climate-controlled house for the Beijing facilities, even though it was more expensive than the naturally-ventilated shed typically used by most commercial duck farms. The shed was pristine, and we kept tripping over cleaners scrubbing or mopping or polishing something or other.

Prominently displayed on the walls were old photos of a young Chairman Zhou shaking hands with senior officials from the Ministry of Agriculture who had visited the farm in the late 1990's. Farm Manager Lin urged us to stop and admire the pictures. "Let us deeply ponder the significance that DeeDee had received attention from officials at the central government level—the very highest level of officials who report directly to Premier Wen Jiabao, not just any municipal government," he said grandly.

Now I understood why Chairman Zhou chose to maintain small-scale operations and even kept DeeDee's headquarters in Beijing till this day—to be always in close proximity to the political nerve center of the country so that he could always stay abreast with the latest regulatory changes.

I asked for a map of DeeDee's Beijing farm and the surrounding terrain, just to get a visual of the lay of the land. Manager Lin wrinkled an eyebrow and muttered that he did not know where to get one. But Wang, eager to please us, jumped in: "Don't you remember the map that the agriculture ministry officials were referring to when they last visited us a few years ago? It even marked out some of the strategic features of our farm location, including prime access to the water table and the moat of forest and streams surrounding our farm that acted as a natural barrier to keep out the transmission of disease and pests."

I was impressed. "Chairman Zhou was very smart in picking this location for the duck farm then."

Wang nodded. "Indeed, I really must find that map for you, I'm sure we have copies lying around."

Manager Lin hurried off to the administrative building and returned five minutes later, bearing a crumpled black and white map. I smoothed it out carefully and kept it in my folder, as he continued his tour.

"It is said that the former Chinese premier Zhou Enlai called ping-pong diplomacy, Moutai diplomacy and roast duck diplomacy the three great diplomatic manoeuvres of China," Manager Lin said. He pointed to another framed quote, adding: "Here, Chairman Zhou expresses his fervent hope that DeeDee can contribute to the expansion of China's soft power and superior culinary culture globally by promoting the consumption of duck meat overseas."

That seemed like quite a mouthful of gibberish to me, but Manager Lin was so moved— even though he must have read it a million times—that he dabbed his eye with a tissue.

"What this means is that Chairman Zhou aspires to sell DeeDee's ducks in the global market, which is growing at over ten percent a year," Manager Wang explained to us. "Most of the six hundred million birds processed each year in China are consumed domestically. We want to expand overseas as soon as possible."

At twelve noon sharp, it was time for lunch at the staff canteen. While the rest of DeeDee's employees were eating their simple meals of rice and vegetables with stray bits of meat on stainless steel trays, we were ushered into a private room. Here, a sumptuous spread had been prepared specially for Randy and I, as well as the six senior managers at the farm. There was duck meat galore: shredded duck with jellyfish, Hangzhou old duck soup, fried duck tongues with tangerine peels, duck wings with coriander, and Quanzhou ginger duck.

When we had wiped our plates clean and dutifully toasted several rounds of Moutai to everyone in the room, farm manager Lin presented us with a mountain of gifts—air-dried Szechuan-style spicy duck meat, duck necks, duck beaks, duck feet, and two gigantic rubber ducks dressed in charcoal-black coats with the Donald Duck-lookalike company logo emblazoned on their backs. The bounty filled up three passenger seats in our mini-van.

After twenty minutes of handshakes and farewells, we gingerly squeezed into the minivan, taking care not to trigger an avalanche of duck products.

As we headed back to the city, the driver played his favourite CD collection of traditional music played by the *pipa* 琵琶, the four-stringed Chinese lute. Within minutes, we heard a crescendo of snores. Randy was fast asleep.

I grinned at Manager Wang, who took this as a signal to start chatting again. "Huang zong, what a fruitful day—*manzaiergui* 满载而归 (Returning home fully rewarded)!"

He fished out a packet of Double Happiness cigarettes from his left shirt pocket and lit one up for himself. He was about to offer me one, and then thought the better of it. "You don't seem like the type who smokes, just like Fang zong."

"Oh, Fang Xing doesn't smoke?" I asked, intrigued.

"He drinks a lot but only smokes occasionally to keep the Lao Qianbei and his business contacts company. He told me once that he stopped smoking when he went abroad to study because he got fined a few times for smoking in the school compound. Maybe Fang zong is one of those new-age Chinese haigui who has become so westernized that he strictly abides by rules and regulations."

I found Wang's assumption about westerners interesting, but was a little dubious about Fang Xing's reason for quitting smoking. Even after seeing him just once, I could already sense he only followed the rules when it suited his interests.

"How well do you know Fang zong?" I asked.

"Chairman Zhou talks about Fang zong once in a while, and refers to him as *pangzi* 胖子, or the Chubby One. Fang zong must be from some rich and connected family, I guess."

I wanted to probe more about Fang Xing, but decided to try out a more roundabout approach, emulating the Chinese style of cultivating relationships first before extracting information.

"Does your family live around here?" I asked.

Wang laughed. "No we can't afford to, we are too poor to afford to live so close to Beijing—even if this is already the Seventh Ring[8]!"

Born in a village in the outskirts of Shijiazhuang, an industrial city in Hebei province over 180 miles from Beijing, Wang grew up in the middle of the corn fields. He helped his parents to tend the farm from the time his little legs were steady enough to bear the weight of the farm tools and to chase chickens. There were about forty families in his village, and all of them survived on planting and selling corn. His parents made roughly RMB3,500 (US$500) a year. In good years, when harvest was bountiful, they would make an additional 300 yuan to 500 yuan. It was corn grit porridge for breakfast, rice with corn flour boiled into porridge for lunch, and *wowotou* 窝窝头 (Double Nest Head)—a type of steamed corn bread—for dinner. Having meat

---

[8] Beijing's urban planning is organized around massive ring beltways. The first innermost ring road, the Second Ring Road, was built in the 1980s. Since then, the city has grown significantly, with the 188-km Sixth Ring Road becoming fully operational in 2009. There are plans to build a Seventh Ring Road that will exceed the city limits of Beijing.

on the dining table meant either that the family was celebrating some festival of the gods, or it was his birthday.

Every winter, he and his dad went to the nearby forests to cut firewood every day. If they did not come back with enough, the family had to freeze through the night. The brick walls of their hovel were riddled with holes, so when strong winds blew over the flat wintery plains and into their dilapidated home, the long nights were unbearable.

During the summers, Shijiazhuang's temperature soared over 110 degrees Fahrenheit. If he was obedient for the day and finished his school homework on time, his dad would give him twenty *fen* 分, or Chinese cents, to buy a popsicle to cool down. "That was the height of luxury for me," Wang recalled fondly.

One afternoon, his twenty *fen* reward was devoured during a locust plague, which destroyed the fields in a few hours. He recalled putting the coin on a sack of corn just as the sky turned pitch black. Swarms of insects descended upon the area and wiped out every green living thing they could find. "The buzzing sounds became so deafening it felt like the heavens were falling apart," he said. "Before running into our shed, I tried to find my coin but it was gone. I was so upset that I raised my arm in the air and grasped a dozen locusts with each hand at one go. I clenched my fist and crushed all of them."

His parents recounted how Chairman Mao had decided during the Cultural Revolution that of all the pests on earth, sparrows, mosquitoes, flies and rats were particularly detestable. So he mobilized his 650 million comrades in a nationwide movement called the Four Pests campaign to exterminate these four creatures. So with pots, pans, drums, and deadly arrows and slingshots, these creatures were shot down by firing squads. It was good sport for a while, but wreaked ecological havoc, as the harmful pests like locusts multiplied blithely without any sparrows to control their population. Locust populations swarmed the villages frequently and wiped out the very crops and grain supplies that Chairman Mao had sought to protect from pests, leading to the horrific three-year Great Chinese Famine.

His illiterate parents frequently told him this story to remind him that he needed to study as hard as possible to make a new life that would not be ravaged by locusts, or the vagaries of nature. Only education could pull the family out of the vicious poverty cycle, they said. So they scraped together every cent they had to put him through university. At the age of eighteen, he graduated from the only high school from his local township and enrolled in Shenyang Agricultural University.

After graduation, Wang, like many of his classmates, came to Beijing to seek his fortune.

Indeed, young adults from the rural countryside were flocking into urban centers like Beijing and Shanghai in search for better living prospects, lured by the glitz and glamour of cosmopolitan lifestyles there.

Most of the residents of metropolitan Beijing are from other provinces, their identities reflected by a rigid, almost antiquated household registration system which separates the people by their birthplace. With over 1.3 billion people in the country, each province had populations big enough to be countries by themselves. From waitresses and bartenders, to masseuses and truck drivers, these jobs in the city paid double, sometimes triple what they could get if they had stayed behind in their hometowns. In addition, employers usually covered housing and three meals a day, making it a reasonable proposition for most. Some even take up a second job in the evening to make even more money.

Wang had initially searched for a white-collar office job—something his parents thought was a glamorous change from rough peasant work, so they were initially crushed that their only son joined Chairman Zhou as one of the first few employees in his duck farm start-up. "They just couldn't understand why a college graduate would choose to go back to the fields and do backbreaking chores like sweep up duck manure—they thought it was demeaning work and a personal insult to them," he recalled.

"My parents had many brothers and sisters, but for my generation, I'm the only son and my parents' only hope," Wang said, referring to the impact of Deng Xiaoping's one-child policy implemented in the early 1980's. "They spent their last dollar of savings on my college education. So they were relying on me to get a good-paying job to take care of them in their old age."

Wang did not tell them that white-collar jobs in the city were being filled so quickly by a record number of college graduates—rising from 5.6 million in 2008 to a whopping 7.5 million a year by 2015—that real wages for those jobs were shrinking too much to cover the high costs of rental and living in Beijing. And the cushy, high-paying jobs in SOEs were reserved only for those with the right connections and the deep pockets to pay so-called "introductory fees" of as much as RMB100,000 (US$16,000) to land an entry-level position.

Just when he was pondering whether to leave Beijing, he chanced upon a start-up called DeeDee. "Chairman Zhou offered me a starting salary of about 3,000 yuan a month, which was just slightly higher than the secretarial jobs that my college classmates were getting," Manager Wang recalled. "He came from a poor background like me, and yet he had huge dreams of building a duck empire, which was very inspiring for me. I figured that I had a better shot of getting promoted to a senior position than if I were to do a nine-to-five office job in Beijing."

Slaving eighty-hour work weeks and working on all public holidays—even during Chinese New Year when most migrant workers returned to their hometowns for family reunions—paid off after eight years. Wang steadily climbed the ladder and became the youngest middle manager at DeeDee at the age of thirty-two.

"I tell my parents that I could become a millionaire if DeeDee goes for an IPO, but they still can't believe me. Nevertheless, they like to boast to the other villagers that their son is a manager who earns 9,000 yuan a month. That's more than twice the salary of some of my peers in the city who are still stuck in junior positions."

"You have achieved so much, I'm sure your parents must be proud of you, Wang," I said, moved by his story.

Wang shrugged. "People like us, we come from the village. We have to work many times harder than those in the city to make it. But I know that in China today, hard work can only get you that far. Even if I work till I drop from exhaustion, I can still never match up to those special people like Fang zong."

For the first time, I felt Wang had unconsciously spoken from the heart, even though I had no idea what his cryptic reference to Fang Xing meant.

"I'm sure you are not just diligent, but also smart enough to succeed," I reassured him.

"You know, I thought I left the locusts behind in the fields. But now that I've worked for a while in a big city like Beijing, I realize that there are other powerful forces that can wipe out commoners' savings just as easily, like corruption and financial crises. I'm not smart enough to understand all this talk in the news about stock market crashes or asset bubbles, but I still don't have the sense of security that my parents wanted me to have."

The minivan drove up to our hotel. Wang jerked out of his pensive mood, and his bright-eyed, bushy-tailed demeanor returned. He jumped out, piled our duck products into the arms of a startled hotel concierge staff, launched into another round of pleasantries and marketing talk about DeeDee's glorious future, and finally waved goodbye.

Then suddenly, just before the van sped off, he yelled a parting shot to me: "People like Fang Zong may be the big winners in China. But for me, Chairman Zhou is the real hero."

That visit with Manager Wang would be just the first of more than a dozen trips to duck farms Randy and I made across the country. But somehow it was the one that left the deepest impression on me, even though the subsequent interviews with DeeDee employees were just as emotional—even bordering on the melodramatic.

"Chairman Zhou scraped together his savings to bring new technology to our township and introduce modern duck farming methods. We are eternally grateful to him. You will be investing in a company with the most superior farming methods," an employee at one of the farms in Liuzhou county told us with tears rolling down his face.

"Chairman Zhou hired my whole family at his farm. He created so many jobs for people in our village," declared a mother with an infant strapped to her back. She worked at one of the farms in Linyi municipality.

"Chairman Zhou broke his leg once trying to build a dam in the river to ensure that the duck farm would be built in the most environmentally sustainable way. He was too poor to hire a lot of workers, but we all volunteered to help him because we believed in him," said a local village chief in Huangchuan County, where DeeDee's largest breeding ground was located.

The local agricultural authorities also seemed to have synchronized their effusive praise of Chairman Zhou.

"Chairman Zhou has greatly contributed to the local economy and helped create jobs for the people. We greatly welcome a foreign investor like you to our township as it will greatly improve the livelihoods of our people," boomed a potbellied official as he wielded his tenth shot glass of Moutai over a four-hour lunch meeting in Rizhao municipality. "You are going to invest in a great company."

We soon found out that these were standard official statements made at each township we visited, along with the same adulatory spiel about how wise All-Stellar was to choose to invest in DeeDee.

It was only on hindsight a few months later that I realized how skillfully this story of Chairman Zhou as a dirt-poor young rural farmer who rose to become a successful entrepreneur, model citizen and community leader was presented at every single one of our site visits. It was almost as if an invisible hand was orchestrating it. But I was too blindsided then to pick up on this.

Bai Shou Qi Jia 白手起家: **Empty-handed, one builds a house. Describing a person who starts out from scratch with little financial support and uses his two bare hands to build up a successful business.**

CHAPTER 5

Dating

Tian Mi Qian Shou 甜蜜牵手

T HE NEXT THREE MONTHS OF due diligence floated by in a rose-tinted blur of puppy—or should I say, duckling—love.

The elaborate wining and dining at every site visit; the fluffy baby ducks tenderly scooped into our hands by rosy-cheeked farm maids; the cherry blossoms and spring foliage lining our paths as we toured dozens of duck farms across the country; the touching tales of survival and growth by DeeDee employees like Manager Wang and the glowing testimonies about Chairman Zhou's nobility and sacrifice—it all seemed so fetching.

As an aura of hope and ambition swept across China as it readied for the August Olympics, we celebrated a new milestone: All-Stellar officially launched its new Beijing office in a swanky 188-square meter (2,000 square feet) space, which was located within the Central Business District on the east side of the city, close to Chang'an Avenue. The rent for this very respectable address was still less than half the price for the same amount of office space in Manhattan. And renovating it extensively cost us a little north of US$30,000, which was pretty cheap by western standards. We made sure that the office had all the showy luxurious trappings from plush carpets to huge armchairs with gold trimmings that would impress our Chinese partners, as we intended to host client meetings there.

We also hired our lovely secretary, Rebecca Li. Soon after, I convinced Russell to let me spend most of my time in the Beijing office—to cultivate new relationships, obviously. As the world marveled at China's economic rise, we became even more eager to score our first major deal on the mainland. And as DeeDee's managers effusively courted us to "join as one family," I found myself falling into the habit of using the more inclusive Chinese word *zamen* 咱们 (all of us) when speaking with DeeDee managers, rather than *women* 我们 (we) which referred only to All-Stellar.

That was not how due diligence was supposed to be, of course. Our job was to be as skeptical, critical and exacting as possible so that the investigation of the company would be thorough. Randy and I, backed up by a huge team of accountants, lawyers and advisors, had been tasked to drill into DeeDee's state of affairs, size up its real financial position and ferret out any potential tax, operational or technical shenanigans which would raise a red flag for our potential investment.

"Make sure you catch any major negative issues that would be reason for us to abort the deal," Russell instructed us. I was the only one in the office taking the conference call with the Singapore team that day. The opulent décor of our workplace seemed to matter little to Susie and Fang Xing. They never brought their contacts to the office for meetings and rarely even stepped in themselves. Fang Xing would usually dial into our conference calls from outside. He seemed to know DeeDee so well that he was able to articulate and analyse the issues effortlessly, even though—as he told me candidly—he never read the due diligence reports.

It made me wonder again how well he knew Chairman Zhou, whom Randy and I had not seen for the past two months since our dinner meeting at Qianmen. The Lao Qianbei communicated with us only through his senior managers.

The conference call was dragged on as Gary, Russell and Randy debated whether DeeDee may have been exaggerating its output to impress us. Fang Xing had been silent for a long time, but suddenly his voice cut in. "Russell, with all due respect, I think you have to measure privately owned Chinese enterprises like DeeDee with a different yardstick than you would for western enterprises," he said, picking his words carefully.

"What may appear to you to be irregularities, such as revenue numbers that don't seem to tally, may really just be due to the haphazard way first-time entrepreneurs like Chairman Zhou grew their companies," he continued. "He hasn't been exposed to western best practices. What's more, things move so fast in a booming market like China, and he was so busy expanding DeeDee that he may not even have had time to even consider many of the issues you have raised."

"Well, that's why Zhou needs us to step in and kick DeeDee into shape," said Gary dryly. "What we need to know is whether Zhou is willing to learn from us and let us reorganize his company. Any thoughts on this, Matt?"

I did not reply. I was looking up in surprise at Susie, who had just waltzed into the conference room. Rebecca hurried in to hand her a package.

"Hi Russell," she trilled. "I just wanted to update you that Fang Xing and I will be meeting China Stratosphere Investment Group (CSIG) in an hour's time. It's that influential PE fund I was telling you about, Russell, the one run by the former transportation minister's son. They are very interested in agriculture investments, isn't that grand?"

"Oh, they are?" asked Russell, not catching on.

"That's a good sign, Russell," explained Madame Wu. "As I always say, run with the Chinese giants—if a big princeling-led fund like CSIG is interested to invest in farming companies, then it's likely to lift the tide. Valuations of other firms will likely rise as well. So we are on the right track to invest in a poultry enterprise like DeeDee. We need to move quickly to get advantage of this before other big investors start piling in."

There was a short silence as the foreigners on the call digested this piece of information. I, for one, was completely bewildered. I knew about China investors' notorious herd mentality and the volatile swings in companies' valuations this could trigger. But it seemed all too alien to me how betting on whatever the Chinese state-owned giants threw money into would be a sure-win investment strategy.

"Well, you know the China market best, Susie," Russell said at last. "And it's great that you get to talk to such a secretive fund like CSIG. Let us know if they have any, ahem, exclusive information about the new agricultural policy incentives that are rumoured to be launched soon."

"You can trust me to do my job, Russell. It was great chatting with you, as usual," replied Susie breezily. She rose to go, and then suddenly turned back and leaned towards the phone speaker again.

"Oh, and Gary, I've observed that first-generation Chinese entrepreneurs tend to need a lot more latitude in their joint ventures with foreign investors. They don't like too much interference from foreigners. Those who lose too much control of their companies may make you pay."

With that cryptic parting shot, she disappeared again, leaving Gary muttering about what her vague statements really meant. "Can't these Chinese people talk normally and spell out exactly what they mean, instead of dropping all these cliff-hanger statements?" he grumbled.

Over the next few weeks, Randy and I soldiered on with the DeeDee project without much input from either Susie or Fang Xing, who claimed to be hooking up with another potential deal partner after getting a juicy tip-off from CSIG.

After screening multiple versions of due diligence reports drafted by our army of third-party advisors, rewriting our Investment Approval Memorandum and revising our financial model over fifty times, we were exhausted beyond words. But the end was finally in sight: we completed our due diligence in early June and were ready to present DeeDee to our Investment Committee for approval.

Russell put forward the most compelling point to the Investment Committee: the price we proposed to pay for investing in DeeDee would value it at more than 50 percent below the average valuation of similar companies that were already listed publicly. If we could pull off this deal, we would be getting a bargain, since some of DeeDee's peers, which were already listed, were trading at much higher multiples.

"We are confident that we can sell our investment in three to four years' time through an IPO[9]," he told the Committee.

That got our Investment Committee interested. Still, they were concerned about whether All-Stellar would be able to exert enough influence over key decisions in DeeDee.

"The Investment Committee wants to know more about Chairman Zhou and whether his interests are aligned with ours," Russell said in a conference call.

"Susie said the China team has already submitted a write-up on this issue, so let's review it now," he continued. Madame Wu and Fang Xing were out as usual, supposedly chatting up the founder of an instant messaging start-up.

Confused, I looked at Randy. This was the first time I had heard

---

[9] "Buying low, selling high" is the central concept in investing. In private equity, there are generally two methods to exit an investment, either through an IPO and then selling off the shares in the public market; or through a trade sale, which means selling the company to another investor.

the China team had submitted this kind of content to Russell. Randy did not look up, he was already furiously speed-reading through the document that Russell's secretary had just sent him in an e-mail attachment:

"We believe in Chairman Zhou's proven track record. Our confidence in him and in his abilities stem from the more than twenty-five interviews we have had with all the stakeholders at each duck farm we visited. These include the plant managers, customers and suppliers.

Everyone we interviewed praised him for his vision and eagerness to cooperate with us. Chairman Zhou and his team had impressed us with their strategic plans to expand the business in a cost-efficient and highly scalable manner. He fully understands that it is in his best interests as well as the interests of his company to work with us to transform DeeDee's management practices and to operate by international standards. We also believe that his professional management team is stable and has the right mix of industry expertise, local knowledge and strong government relationships.

"What we have seen in Chairman Zhou are the best qualities of a successful Chinese businessman—influential, enterprising, gutsy, relentless, yet at the same time, down-to-earth and hands-on. He is an undisputable leader in his field who has overcome all odds to succeed, and has capitalized on China's phenomenal rise to achieve growth rates that are consistently above industry standards. We believe he can continue to deliver exceptional results in coming years. We are highly convinced this is a sure-win investment and would become a success story for others to emulate."

It was written in Fang Xing's characteristically flowery marketing style, which he claimed he had cultivated during his Harvard Business School days. I had to admit I agreed with all his points. Heck, I could not have written it better myself.

"No more comments or things to add to this?" asked Gary.

Randy and I looked at each other, wondering what to say.

Then Russell spoke again, perhaps assuming that we had all signed off on it and were ready to move on to the next topic: "I think you guys have already established that Chairman Zhou will be a fully cooperative partner, so let's examine the Investment Committee's second concern: they want us to develop stronger protective measures for ourselves, such as vetoes over key decisions[10]. Since Chairman Zhou would remain as a majority shareholder[11] after our investment, we would have less control and influence over company decisions."

"The Investment Committee does have valid reason to be concerned. But we are tying Chairman Zhou down with the profit guarantee that he must deliver for the company over the next two years, so I think our interests are aligned," Randy said.

"Huang zong, what do you think?" Russell asked teasingly, imitating the ingratiating manner in which DeeDee's junior managers addressed me.

"I think we can take comfort that Susie and Fang Xing had already established a pretty robust relationship with Chairman Zhou. In China, that's what matters more than written contracts which are not necessarily enforced enough to protect investors," I said.

Russell seemed pleased with that answer. "I will tell the Committee that we are confident we have key team members on the ground in

---

[10] A veto is a vote that prevents a proposed action from being executed. Having veto rights would give All-Stellar control over Chairman Zhou, because we could overturn his decisions if we thought they did not make sense.

[11] This refers to the shareholder with the biggest stake—and therefore, the biggest voting rights—in the company.

China, who have established a solid relationship with Chairman Zhou and can easily steer the relationship forward. So we have the vital connections to handle disagreements as and when they arise."

Little did we realize that this statement was going to come back to haunt us in the future. But at that time, it seemed only natural to put our faith in Susie's *guanxi* 关系 (relationships) and take All-Stellar's relationship with DeeDee to the next level.

In fact, Russell was already planning his trip to Beijing in August, when we would hopefully have sealed the deal. "And now for the most important thing on the agenda: where's my front-row seat tickets for the Beijing Olympics? You boys had better get cracking on that. It's late May now, so I'm giving you ample time to complete this assignment."

Randy grinned. He had been devising a strategy to bid online for the best seats in the house for hot contests such as the 100-metre men's swimming finals. "We've got that covered, Russell. You will get more than your fill of athletic adrenaline fixes in August."

The mood lightened. After another twenty minutes of discussion, Gary closed the call. "I really like this deal and want it to go through. But just to follow procedure, I need to remind you that it's our fiduciary duty to keep hacking at DeeDee to find its problem areas."

The call closed, and Randy turned to me with a subdued look. "Are you taking up the Fund's offer for us to take up the short-term expatriate assignment in Beijing?"

For me, it was a no-brainer decision. Over the past few weeks, we had already been spending up to two weeks in Beijing at a go—fifteen days was the maximum amount of time I could spend in China without a visa. As we progressed towards late stage due diligence, a deal with Chairman Zhou looked increasingly likely. If we completed this deal, we would be officially in business, our first investment into China and the first for the fund. So it did not make much sense to Russell to have us continue shuttling between Beijing and

Singapore, since our business-class travel was burning a hole in All-Stellar's pocket.

I was enticed by the generous expatriate benefits including tax equalization[12], medical insurance and a free flight home every three months. And it would be a marked lifestyle improvement to be able to stay in a nice bachelor pad instead of checking into a hotel every time I came to Beijing. Rentals had shot up significantly in the months leading up to the Beijing Olympics and there was no sign that prices were receding. After a week of house hunting, I managed to secure a nice cozy one-bedroom apartment in Yonganli, or Perpetual Peace Street, which intersected Chang'an Avenue—or Everlasting Peace Avenue—from the north. Perpetual Peace Street was a stone's throw from Guomao, a prominent financial and business nerve center beside the East Third Ring Road.

"Yes, I've already told Russell I'll move up early next week. But I know you have good reason for not taking up the offer."

Randy preferred the cleaner, more orderly environment of Singapore. His kids were enrolled in schools there and he was concerned that they would not be able to adapt to Beijing's extreme weather and notorious pollution.

"I get the sense that Russell is not too happy with me because I turned it down," he sighed.

I tried to cheer him up. "We've been doing great work so far, and I'm sure Russell's mood will improve once we get this deal across the finishing line. He's just edgy because he is under pressure to establish our first investment by the Olympics."

---

[12] Tax equalization refers to a company's practice of offsetting the differences in tax payable for an employee. This way, he would pay the same amount of tax whether he is working overseas or at home. In China, taxes are progressive and withheld at source. Income at the highest tax bracket is taxed at 45 percent, over twice the tax payable for the highest tax bracket in Singapore. Therefore, tax equalization would be an important consideration for a Singapore-based employee when considering whether to move to China to work.

"It's different for you because you're single and don't have a family to consider. Maybe you could even meet a nice girl here in Beijing."

I grinned, thinking of the opportunities for me to hang out with Rebecca, but tried to hide my excitement. "Well, I see a move to Beijing as a great opportunity to improve my Chinese," I said diplomatically. Secretly, I thought that the stint in Beijing could get me closer to becoming a seasoned China hand and perhaps I could strike my first pot of gold here. And of course, finding the love of my life here would be nice too.

Beijing's balmy spring edged into an intensely hot summer, and Rebecca had started to show off a lot more leg with her new collection of shorts and mini-skirts bought from Alibaba's online marketplace *Taobao* 淘宝. Since I was spending so much time in the Beijing office, I was getting to know her much better.

Born in western Sichuan province, Rebecca moved with her parents back to Beijing, where her paternal grandfather lived, when she was just a baby. Her family liked to think of themselves as *Lao Beijing* 老北京, or old and venerable Beijing residents. There is a deeply embedded sense of exclusivity amongst the native population of Beijing, whose culture was developed through centuries of being the capital of several imperial dynasties, and later as the seat of Red Party power. The *Lao Beijing* are extremely proud of their identity, perhaps even to the point of considering themselves as a class above the rest. While they may appear gruff and rude at times to strangers, and even fellow countrymen from other provinces, their warmth is overpowering once they open up to you. This is why Beijingers have been described as a thermos, cold on the outside, but warm on the inside.

Rebecca's soft features and translucent skin belied the *Lao Beijing* identity she clung on to. She fell into a category of Chinese women known for their elegance, beauty and hot temper—the *Chuanmei* 川妹, or Sichuan girls. The province is famous for two things—its women and spicy cuisine. With just the right humidity and climate, it was the perfect environment for nurturing beautiful women as well as the giant panda—China's national treasure.

Rebecca was brought up in a cloistered environment. When it was time to go to college, her highly protective parents preferred to keep their only child close to them. So she enrolled in Beijing Normal University, majoring in psychology. A young graduate like Rebecca could usually land a job in foreign multinational companies, which needed locals who were proficient in English and willing to accept relatively low salaries. There was a surfeit of fresh college graduates, so a secretarial job at a mid-sized company was almost always filled by someone with at least a bachelor's degree. Even front desk receptionists and waitresses at high-end golf courses in China had to be college grads.

Rebecca and I hit it off from the start. She was a food buff just like me. So whenever I had time to spare from work, she would check out new restaurants with me. Our most memorable meal consisted of rabbit meat cooked in red oil, scorpions barbequed over slow fire, starfish skewers, and stewed duck innards.

These dinner dates were casual and friendly. I would pay for everything when we went out together, since her monthly salary was just RMB4,500 (US$700) a month. I was not sure how she could survive on such a pittance since she was a shopaholic, but consoled myself that her pay was already way above the market norm of around RMB2,000.

Before long, I felt a strong camaraderie with her, even though we were raised in distinctly different environments. Our friendship reassured me I was still inherently Chinese at heart, despite my western education, since I could relate to everything she talked about. Still, our colourful dialogue about Chinese culture and poetry always made me regret not paying enough attention to my Chinese language teacher during my school days. I struggled to match Rebecca, who could rattle off hundreds of idioms and ancient verses.

I wondered how different the experience would have been if we had conversed in English instead. Probably, I would have had the upper hand in directing the conversation towards topics that I could impress her with, like Hollywood blockbusters or stock market tips. Even so, we would have had little to actually talk about, since Rebecca could hardly string a few sentences together despite eight years of rote-learning the English language in school.

One afternoon, Rebecca came up to my desk and waved her hand awkwardly between my face and the computer, "I just checked your calendar, and you're not leaving Beijing the next few days for site visits. Do you have anything planned for the weekend?"

"Yes, I have to revise the investment memorandum again," I said, rubbing my tired eyes from an all-nighter the night before.

"The weather forecast says the weekend weather will be great. Have you been to *Houhai* 后海?" she asked, her face flushed. Was she asking me out on a date? I was hazarding a guess she had never asked a guy out for a date before, judging from her shyness.

"Sure, why not. How about three o'clock on Saturday?" I had been spending too much time in the office—it was time to venture out and explore the capital city of China.

It was a pretty summer afternoon. The heat was manageable with an occasional breeze that ruffled Rebecca's long hair. We walked into Houhai, which literally means "the sea at the back". In fact, Houhai is a man-made lake, with origins dating back to the thirteenth century Beijing, surrounding an ancient water city gate called *yuandadu* 元大都. Some say the lake is actually connected to Zhongnanhai, where China's prominent leaders reside and work.

Famous for its waterfront bars and fancy shops selling traditional Chinese art and craft, Houhai is an ideal spot for tourists and locals alike to laze away an afternoon sipping tea and nibbling local delicacies, before revving up for some spirited nightlife in its famous live music bars. We walked past a roadside stand, where I bought two sticks of *tanghulu* 糖葫芦—a popular Beijing sweet delicacy of honey-glazed hawthorns—and handed one to Rebecca.

While she chattered vivaciously about everything under the sun from the rising price of watermelons to her favorite Hollywood stars, I stared in wonder at the cloudless sky, which had the shimmery blue hue which reminded me of Lake Tahoe. It had been rare to see such a pristine sky over the past few years when Beijing's air quality deteriorated drastically. But now, as China readied for the Olympics, local officials were scrubbing the city clean—from air pollutants to old, ostensibly unsightly buildings and even "Chinglish" words on shop signs. I took a deep breath, immersing myself in Beijing's transformation and in Rebecca's company.

I started to notice something comically seductive about Rebecca's outfit. She was sporting a pink polka-dot patterned miniskirt and bright red stock socks that covered her slim ankles all the way to her knees. The top part of her stockings, usually supposed to be hidden under the skirt, were clearly visible, with part of her thighs exposed. On top of this interesting combination, she wore a pair of bright purple Converse sneakers, mismatched with a gaudy green Gucci handbag.

As I lifted my gaze to the crowds around me, I realized that Rebecca did not stand out too much after all. At a distance, I saw a young girl wearing an orange maternity dress matched with a Hello Kitty bag and seven-inch heels. A few ladies sported an awkward mishmash of leather and silk pieces, with random words like "Armani" and "Hannah Montana" printed on the front of their blouses. If this scene were replayed on Fifth Avenue in Manhattan, I fancied the fashion police would suffer a heart attack.

As we strolled along the lake, I could see several boats in the shape of ducks on the lake. Some were whizzing through the water, steered by elderly couples paddling energetically; other boats were motionless as their young passengers whispered sweet nothings to each other.

"Let's rent one out into the lake," Rebecca exclaimed, and skipped off to get tickets. I blissfully calculated how long it would take to row around the circumference of the lake. One hour. That would give us plenty of time alone together, uninterrupted by unpleasant jostling or spitting from the crowds. My heart skipped a few beats as I pictured a romantic climax on the lake as we drifted into the sunset.

We climbed into the belly of a yellow duck and I started peddling enthusiastically while Rebecca sat pretty. It was much more strenuous than I had imagined keeping the creaky boat on course, and an awkward silence set in as I found myself too breathless to make small talk. Finally, we got to the middle of the lake, and I let the boat drift as Rebecca started to chatter, eager to fill the conversation vacuum. "You know, if you don't tell me, I would never know that you're a foreigner! You are more Chinese than I expected."

I raised an eyebrow, not knowing what to make of this unexpected observation. My own experiences so far interacting with DeeDee's staff had made me painfully aware of the cultural gap between us. Their overly gracious mannerisms only made Randy and I feel all the more distant as we tried to strike up casual chats. Although we looked alike and spoke the same language, I felt that they had already set us apart as outsiders.

Still, I knew that Rebecca was extremely proud to be Chinese, so I thanked her for the compliment.

"Well, I'm a third-generation Chinese immigrant whose family has done reasonably well in Singapore. I'm kind of in the middle—not quite Chinese and not quite foreign," I mused.

"I'm always so impressed by how smart and successful Chinese people are wherever they go around the world," enthused Rebecca. "I've been reading in the People's Daily[13] and on the news portals that they are welcomed as good investors everywhere around the

---

[13] *People's Daily* is a state-owned newspaper and seen as the official mouthpiece of the Communist Party.

world because they are buying assets and properties to help boost the local economies."

I was dubious about her rose-tinted perception that Chinese investors received a purely positive reception overseas, but was not about to spoil the mood with a controversial discussion. So I shifted back to the topic that interested me most: "So do you think I'm more Chinese or more foreign? Chairman Zhou called me a foreigner the other day so I thought it must be pretty obvious from my appearance or way of speaking that I'm different from mainland Chinese."

"Oh come on, you have a handsome Chinese face, yellow skin colour just like me, and speak such fluent Chinese. No one can tell you're a foreigner! " Rebecca answered coquettishly as her fingers worked dexterously to peel some sunflower seeds.

I felt my self-esteem swell with the late afternoon high tide. "So you don't think I'm an outsider?"

"Even though you are not quite like one of us, you do share some of our culture, right?" she replied. "At least, you celebrate the same festive holidays just like us, unlike a lot of the American-born Chinese or British-born Chinese who don't even understand the significance of the Lunar New Year or Tomb-Sweeping Day because they have absorbed so much of the western culture. For you, during the Mid-Autumn Festival, you carry lanterns and eat mooncakes, right? That's a very Chinese thing to do."

That was not quite the comment I was hoping for, but at that moment Rebecca playfully leaned over and popped a peeled sunflower seed into my mouth. Her fingers brushed against my lips. I was in seventh heaven.

Our dinner—pig innards brewed in tapioca paste, salted bean curd and cooked tripe of lamb—was neither romantic nor enticing to my palate. But I loved every bite anyway—the big meal stretched our date out to almost midnight. I started to open up to Rebecca, sharing with her how much more at ease I was with my immigrant Chinese status in Beijing, compared to the identity crisis I had as a Chinese person trying to fit into the Asian-American community during my college years in the US, where my chief existential concern was to avoid being labelled as "fresh off the boat".

Rebecca, who had never stepped out of China, nodded vigorously, although I could tell from her blank expression that she did not quite comprehend what I was saying. Still, she eagerly gave me her take: "Now that you are back in China, you don't have to worry about not being western enough. China is becoming a strong power. We don't need to do things the western way anymore. We can set our own standards and rules for the world."

I chewed on her words for a few seconds, misgivings rising in my throat. I had come to Beijing with high expectations that the Chinese, especially the younger generation, were becoming much more open-minded and would embrace international perspectives and standards. The past few months of dealing with Chairman Zhou and with local officials, who boasted that they had already learnt so much from the West that they were now teaching new foreign investors what to do, had eroded that optimism somewhat. But I figured it was early days yet, and I needed to see a lot more of China before making a judgement.

Finally, I said: "Well, I actually really like a lot of the western ways of doing things, especially the rule of law and you know…err…the more defined, clear-cut way of communication. At least, abiding by the rule of law means people in the West don't blatantly beat red lights and drive against traffic. You know, I almost got knocked down by a speeding car last night when I waited until the traffic light turned green before crossing the street! All the other pedestrians had already run across."

To my surprise, Rebecca giggled. "You're so silly to wait for the green light."

"Anyway, I just wish I could find a good balance and mix of

western and Chinese elements in my identity and in the way I do things in China," I continued.

That suddenly got Miss Li's hackles rising. "Are you not honored to be part of the Great People's Republic of China?" she asked indignantly. "Why do you need to blend in with the West? Did your parents bring you up to betray your Chinese roots?"

Oops, I seemed to have touched a raw nerve somehow. "Of course I'm proud to be Chinese," I hastily exclaimed, jumping to my feet and bowing with a grand flourish to lighten the mood again. Imitating the grandiose speech-making style of the party officials that I had witnessed too many times over the past few months, I bellowed the most exaggerated, sickly sweet oratory I could muster without barfing all over myself. "Family and friends, I would like to take this opportunity tonight to thank my immigrant parents for preserving and passing down the great Han Chinese traditions to me. Mother and Father, without you, I would not be able to share in the rise of our great Motherland and meet such a beautiful Chinese girl like Rebecca Li Xiaohuan who is every man's dream..."

Rebecca seemed to love it. Giggling, she covered my mouth to stop me from talking. "*Youqianghuadiao* 油腔滑调 (Honey tongue)! Silly boy," she scolded gently, and slipped her hand into mine as we strolled into the sticky summer night.

> ***Tian Mi Qian Shou* 甜蜜牵手: Sweetly holding hands.**

CHAPTER 6

Partnership

Zhong Xi Xie Shou 中西携手

I N LATE JULY 2008, FOUR and a half months after we met Chairman Zhou for the first time, we finally received approval from our Investment Committee to invest in DeeDee. There was a catch though: we had to go back to Chairman Zhou to negotiate for better investor rights.

"The Investment Committee remains concerned about the equitability of the deal structure," Russell told the China team glumly during a conference call. "As minority shareholders, we need to make sure that our rights are adequately protected. Under the current terms, we do not have sufficient management control over the business. The Investment Committee still requires All-Stellar to have significant veto rights over key decisions especially on major issues like business expansion, capital expenditure and hiring."

Susie pursed her lips. "I do not think such demands are reasonable for Chinese entrepreneurs who are used to maintaining a lot more personal control over their businesses."

Susie believed that since All-Stellar was still in the initial stages of establishing rapport with Chairman Zhou, we needed to maintain a delicate balance—being assertive in our demands without coming across as being too overbearing."Getting the Investment Committee's approval is an important first step, but we will need a lot more time if we want to get Chairman Zhou's buy-in on these proposed changes," she insisted.

Susie said she would speak to Chairman Zhou on her own in good time. But first, we would test out the company's reaction by breaking the news of the proposed changes to DeeDee's middle managers.

I did not quite understand the logic behind this approach, but Susie had assigned me to speak to them, so I braced myself for a storm. As expected, Manager Wang and his colleagues were livid when I suggested that they work with me to come up with a way to make the proposed changes acceptable to Chairman Zhou.

"We are already under huge pressure from him to close the deal as soon as possible," squeaked Bingbing, a colorless accountant from Hunan province whom I had never seen open her mouth until now. Despite being in her early twenties, she was already in a relatively senior managerial position, and was rumored to be a good friend of Chairman Zhou's niece. "These new demands from your Investment Committee will further delay Chairman Zhou's new projects. These projects desperately needed a fresh capital infusion before they can move forward."

"Since there is so much pressure, wouldn't Chairman Zhou be more willing to compromise so that he can get his hands on the fresh funds faster?" I asked.

"You don't know who you are dealing with," Manager Wang sighed despairingly. "Why do you even ask for our opinion anyway? You know we are not his closest blood relatives, so no matter how capable or loyal we are as his professional managers, we still have very little influence over him."

It had become clear to me that the Lao Qianbei ran his family business with an iron fist. He wielded a meticulously hands-on approach in running the company's daily operations and affairs, having the final word on all business-related decisions and signed every contract. He even personally interviewed every new hire down to the part-time mechanic in his 500-man company. He was the patriarchal figure, revered by all who made up their minds to devote their lives to him. Even his closest aides, the non-relatives at least, were seen to prostrate themselves before him before, during and after each meeting. The employees wavered between fascination and fear of him.

But this attitude made them act in counter-productive ways to keep themselves out of trouble. Assuming that Chairman Zhou would be incensed with the proposed changes, their tactic was to stall for time, and try to find ways to circumvent our agenda. As the days ploughed on, they started to become short-fused with each other, and argue over seemingly irrelevant matters. But they never turned their frustration directly on Randy and I—it was evident that they had been specifically instructed to always remain polite and respectful to us.

Manager Wang, a tea aficionado, invited me out several times. "It's just to *lianluoganqing* 联络感情 (build up our relationship)," he said lightly as we sat down at a table in his favorite tea house one afternoon.

I could not reply. The huge clouds of cigarette smoke he puffed out had rendered me half senseless. Wang did not seem to notice. A hopeless nicotine addict who had picked up the habit "to keep sane" during his early years on DeeDee's farms mending equipment deep into the freezing winter night, he blazed through several packs of cigarettes during our two-hour session.

"It's a very healthy habit, drinking tea," he chattered, as he busied himself with the intricate teapot. "Chairman Zhou does it too."

"How has he been?" I asked, as I pushed open a dust-caked window.

Wang looked at me tentatively. "He is good. He is very appreciative of your hard work and your expertise. We are looking forward to closing the deal as soon as possible so that we can do great things and multiply your investment."

I suppressed a sigh. All this small talk was wearing me down. An hour later, as we parted, Manager Wang finally screwed up the courage and looked at me directly in the eye. "Just expressing my personal opinion—and this is strictly my own personal opinion—I wonder if there are ways to avoid changing the deal? Wasn't it very good already when Chairman Zhou had already closed the verbal agreement with Madame Su-si-er?" He tripped over the pronunciation of Susie's name, and looked even more discomfited.

"If the deal was iron-clad and reasonable in the first place, we wouldn't have to change it, would we?" I retorted. "We are not even sure what exactly the terms were that Chairman Zhou had agreed on with Susie, so we need to have everything clearly spelled out in writing."

"Well, if I were Chairman Zhou, I would say to you that we should just focus on rolling out new projects instead of wasting time refining the terms of the deal…"

I rolled my eyes, wondering why Chairman Zhou kept sending emissaries and dealing with us at arm's length when he could engage with us directly himself. And where on earth were Susie and Fang Xing in the midst of this deadlock?

It took three more weeks of impasse before Chairman Zhou finally decided there was no choice but to meet with us himself, along with Fang Xing. He hosted us to a lunch banquet at the Beijing Kempinski Hotel and for the first two hours, we had another meandering chat about ducks, tea, soap operas and a host of other trivial topics.

Finally, he could not contain himself and addressed Randy and I directly, "So I have just heard from Susie that your Investment Committee wants to revise the contract with us before they can approve this investment?"

"What I don't understand is why it has taken so many months

for you to complete the deal," he continued. "I thought I already worked out the terms with Susie verbally, and also instructed my senior managers to be very polite and support you in your work. So what is there left to do?"

Randy pasted his most disarming smile on his face. "Chairman Zhou, we fully understand your concerns and we are moving as fast as we can, but we need to fulfill our fiduciary duties by completing the required legal, financial and technical due diligence as well as background checks...."

The laundry list did nothing to appease the Lao Qianbei. "I just don't understand why your checks take so long," he burst out. "Three years ago, when I raised RMB50 million (US$7 million) of Chinese money from my friends and family for this business, all it took was a golf game, a drinking session at a Chinese tea house and then a few hours at a night club. Why is it so complicated this time with international investors? And what is all this nonsense about wanting me to give up my rights so we can have a more equitable shareholder structure?"

Chairman Zhou's face was turning beet red. As I tried to offer him some tea to cool down, Fang Xing interjected soothingly: "Lao Zhou, you are an enlightened businessman and that's why so many foreign investors want to work with you. These laowai don't do things as fast as we like, but they can help you to make a lot of money if you are willing to work with them too."

Chairman Zhou calmed down a bit. "The way I see it, international financiers waste too much time, when we could be going full steam ahead to build new projects and earn even more money," he complained.

"Yes, these foreigners do things differently from us, Lao Qianbei. These laowai don't operate on trust and verbal agreements the way we do, but once they finish all the checks and sign the written contract, they usually move much faster," responded Fang Xing. "So as long as *zamen* (all of us) maintain a harmonious relationship, I guarantee you that DeeDee will be able to secure the maximum amount of financing possible to achieve its expansion plans."

"Who the heck is Fang Xing representing now, All-Stellar or DeeDee? Who is he to make such guarantees? And how could he call us 'laowai'?" I grumbled to myself.

Chairman Zhou glanced at Fang Xing, and then cleared his throat. He turned to Randy earnestly: "I'm a simple businessman who rose from a very poor background and fought against the odds to succeed. International investors like these sort of entrepreneurs, right? Shall we provide more information to your investors about my humble origins and more proof of how I will guard this company with my life? Then you don't need to worry about veto rights because I will definitely do what is best for the company, and that will benefit you more than any written contract."

Randy and I smiled weakly, glad that the tension had melted, but still unsure of how to respond to Chairman Zhou's obviously rehearsed speech. So we just chimed in when Fang Xing proposed another round of toasts to "a new cooperative relationship".

Even then, I was still dispirited that we had not made any real headway in resolving the real issues. But at least I had just made an important discovery: Fang Xing had been coaching Chairman Zhou and his managers on how to market themselves to All-Stellar. His strategy had worked, undeniably—we had all been swallowing the Kool-Aid, despite our best efforts to maintain an objective attitude.

Even our Investment Committee had been surprisingly swift in working with us to get the final approval for the deal, perhaps egged on by the heady sense of optimism about China. That exhilaration surrounding China's rise climaxed in August, when Beijing captivated the world with a dazzling Olympics opening ceremony at the intricately designed Bird's Nest stadium. As China scored forty-three world records and 132 Olympic records over two weeks, we edged closer to negotiating a deal but Chairman Zhou still tried to play hard ball by insisting that companies like his were rare gems that deserved much higher valuations and were best run by the founding CEO.

Russell was up for the Olympics. He was in a superb mood as the uncharacteristically blue skies in Beijing lifted everyone's spirits. I suspected he was even turning a little sentimental, humming the Olympics opening ceremony duet "You and Me" performed by Sarah Brightman with a famous local singer Liu Huan:

> *You and me*
> *From one world, Heart to heart*
> *We are one family*
> *For dreams we travel, Thousands of miles*
> *We meet in Beijing*
> *Come together, The joy we share*
> *You and me, From one world*
> *Forever we are one family.*

With the DeeDee deal looking close to the finish line, and we celebrated by splurging a small fortune on buying *huangniu* 黄牛 [14] tickets for one of the most closely-watched races at the Olympics: the 110-metre hurdles opening heat qualifying round on August 18, which featured the icon of Chinese athletics, Liu Xiang.

All eyes were glued on the lanky twenty-five-year-old Chinese athlete. The blaring chants emanating from the 91,000-strong crowd at the colossal Bird's Nest Stadium was almost deafening. "Liu Xiang, *jiayou* 刘翔, 加油 (Go, Liu Xiang)!"

The shotgun blasted. Liu sprung up and sprinted three steps. Then suddenly, his face contorted as he cried out in agony. He clutched his hamstring. His rivals zoomed past him. A deafening silence descended upon the crowd as it dawned on them that Liu Xiang's dream—and that of the entire nation—of a gold medal had crumbled.

---

[14] Literally means yellow cow, a colloquial term for ticket scalpers.

Liu Xiang dejectedly sat down on the tracks surrounded by officials, all alone. He had already earned a fortune from his endorsement contracts with Nike and other leading sports brands and appeared almost everywhere across China on advertisements and billboards. But when the critical moment came, he was not where his sponsors wanted him—on the winners' stand.

Four weeks later, on September 15, news broke on that US investment bank giant Lehman Brothers had filed for bankruptcy protection. The debt-ridden company had leveraged up significantly and amassed huge amounts of US subprime mortgage assets. When the US housing bubble burst, Lehman scrambled for a buyer, but talks fell through. The largest bankruptcy filing in US history triggered pandemonium across the world. But for us, it was a gift.

The financial maelstrom unexpectedly turned out to be the clincher for completing our long-awaited deal with DeeDee. From Manager Wang, I managed to find out that a credit line held by the company had been pulled abruptly in the wake of the subprime loans meltdown. Even before the crisis, the mid-sized Beijing bank had been charging DeeDee a cut-throat interest rate of more than 30 percent above benchmark market rates for the relatively small RMB50 million (US$7 million) credit line, even though Chairman Zhou had been faithfully repaying the monthly installments on time. It did not make sense to me why a Chinese bank would slap such shabby treatment on an SME customer as profitable and credit-worthy as DeeDee. It would have been any Singaporean banker's wet dream—it was growing profits at an annualized rate of over 25 percent and had significant collateral. What's more, it had no prior bad debt and therefore no need to roll over loans, unlike many of the inefficiently-run SOEs.

This was my first introduction to the peculiarities of China's state-dominated banking system, which had spawned unique challenges for entrepreneurs like Chairman Zhou, and in turn affected the way PE players like All-Stellar invested in China. All of China's biggest state banks, such as Industrial and Commercial Bank of China (ICBC) and Bank of China which were two of the largest banks on the planet, are majority owned by the central government. Their key management is carefully selected by the Communist Party. The Chinese banking system is as much a part of the government as it is part of the markets.

These banking giants prioritized SOEs when disbursing loans, since these would be used to fund acquisitions and projects backed by the central or local governments. The lenders offered them sweetheart rates which were often 10 percent to 15 percent below benchmark rates. After all, the likelihood of a default was considered miniscule— it was assumed that an SOE that had problems repaying debt would automatically be bailed out by the government. Loans to SMEs, on the other hand, were deemed as risky, and most state banks preferred to just leave these small customers out in the cold since they were flush with cheap deposits and did not need to compete for loans to reap profits.

Chairman Zhou's solution was to raise some off-balance sheet loans from suppliers and a few companies run by his friends. He also raised funds from some distant cousins, pledging some of his shares in return. Of course, none of these transactions were properly documented in DeeDee's financial accounts.

Then he cast around for foreign PE investors, whom he hoped would not only plow funds into his business expansion, but also help him access international corporate bond markets.

As I would later find out, Chairman Zhou thought he had struck jackpot when DeeDee had caught Mann Brothers' eye. He managed to secure a small credit line from the mid-sized Beijing bank by boasting to their managers during a raucous karaoke session that a big Wall Street player was about to become DeeDee's major shareholder. It was only when the subprime crisis erupted—and its repercussions ripped up DeeDee's credit line in Beijing—that Chairman Zhou realized how precarious his situation was if he did not close the deal with All-Stellar as soon as possible.

All of a sudden, Chairman Zhou became extremely friendly and flexible. The deadlock was broken. Negotiations which had dragged on for almost two months were suddenly completed within just three hours, and that same evening, as Chairman Zhou agreed to include the veto rights which we insisted into the contract. Once the papers were signed, he exuberantly invited us out for a grand celebration of our union, seven months after our first blind date.

The first stop was the elegant Beijing roast duck restaurant called Duck de Chine. We emptied at least four bottles of 46-degree *baijiu* 白酒—an extremely potent distilled Chinese spirit. Half drunk, we were then chauffeured to the post-dinner activities at Beijing's majestic Number Eight KTV and Nightclub, notorious for hosting business entertainment orgies.

As we drove up, I vaguely made out the words "Number Eight Bathhouse" on the neon sign on the top of the building. The bright lights were shrouded by the polluted air, adding a sense of mystery to that place. I followed the pack into the castle-like nightclub, where we were greeted by eight girls dressed up in the traditional Chinese *qipao*. They bowed with military precision, smiles tilted up at the exact same angle to reveal rows of perfect white teeth.

We entered Room 308. It was one of the classiest KTV rooms I had ever seen, with two seventy-inch LG flat screen televisions and black cow leather sofas. There was also a private bathroom with gold-plated door handles and taps. I felt like I was hallucinating as we were escorted to our seats like kings ushered onto their thrones.

Shortly, we heard a scurry of high-heeled feet along the corridor. "Line up, girls get ready to greet your handsome guests. Put on your friendliest smiles. Stay in order," yelled the club manager, commonly known as "Mama-san". There was a hushed silence in the room as gusts of assorted perfume fragrances assaulted our senses, heralding the entry of "Beijing's Top Beauties". Every one of the girls was at least five feet seven inches tall. It was quite a stunning sight—I could not find any girl in the cohort who did not boast Barbie Doll body proportions.

The girls began their routine greetings: "Gentlemen, good evening. Welcome to Number Eight KTV and Nightclub. We hope you will have an extremely satisfying time with us." They then bowed in unison and started to introduce themselves. "Good evening, my name is Xiaofen, and I come from Hunan." Good evening, I'm Xiaozhen, from Chongqing." "Good evening, handsome brothers. My name is Xiaolu, from Chengdu." In Chinese culture, where hierarchy is paramount and age is directly correlated to the respect one deserves, introducing oneself with *xiao* 小 (little), before one's surname is a way of showing reverence to someone who is older or holds a higher social status.

I ended up with a girl by the name of Xiaoling from the eastern coastal Chinese province of Jiangsu. She had a demure, fresh-faced look that mesmerized me, and stood out from the rest even though she wore minimal makeup. She sat down beside me, her eyes trying to avoid direct contact. Her gentleness touched my heart.

"So what are we drinking now? *Baijiu*, or *yangjiu* or beer?" Fang Xing asked, addressing his question to Chairman Zhou. Yangjiu was a colloquial term for "western alcohol". We eventually settled on a combination of beer and brandy, although even a novice drinker like me knew it was a bad idea to mix different types of alcohol in one sitting. Deciding the intoxicating poison of choice for the night was usually reserved for the host footing the bill. Sometimes, the host would ask the guest for their preference as a show of respect. Somehow that night, the roles were reversed—Fang Xing acted like he was playing host.

In my drowsy state, I just went with the flow. Before long, the waitresses, communicating through internal walkie-talkies, had moved a dozen cartons of beer into the room. Manager Wang's girl was busy smothering him with kisses, while Randy's girl was whispering sweet nothings into his ears.

"Cheers to Chairman Zhou and wishing your business to prosper to the end of the age!" Fang Xing shouted over the KTV music, with a bottle of beer in one hand, and the other hand caressing his girl. The *baijiu* over dinner seemed to have minimal effect on Fang Xing. While we raised our beer bottles up together to celebrate the start of our fledging relationship, I noticed Fang Xing's turquoise wedding ring was missing.

The night went on with singing and playing dice games. Xiaoling was eagerly feeding me cherry tomatoes, and accompanied me to drink the brandy mixed with sweetened green tea. I asked for hot water to wash down the alcohol. She knew I was not feeling too well and decided to give me a shoulder massage. Stroking me with her soft hands, she laid her head in the hollow of my shoulders. Before long, we started kissing.

The night went by like a whirlwind. Before long, the clock ticked midnight. "*Maidan* 买单 (Get me the bill)!" Chairman Zhou hollered at the Mama-san.

He fished out a big wad of bright red notes from his pocket and counted five pieces for each of our girls. This was their salary for three hours of drinking and kissing—every girl looked forward to that moment. Five hundred yuan meant a lot to them, as most have left their villages and townships to strike it rich at large cities like Beijing and Shanghai. In one night, these girls could easily earn half their monthly household income sitting with these rich gentlemen, even more if the guy wanted to pay for extra services.

"Thank you *Dage* 大哥 (big brother), please come again," Xiaoling whispered softly into my ears as I gave her up reluctantly. In China, people can be complete strangers, yet address each other as older brothers or younger sisters to convey an almost eerie sense of intimacy.

"Give me a *fapiao* 发票[15], and include all the girls' tips into it,"

---

[15] The word *fapiao* means a receipt. Usually machine printed, but sometimes handwritten, a *fapiao* serves as proof of expenditure. Vendors pay tax to the local authorities when they issue *fapiaos* to customers. With an official *fapiao*,

bellowed Chairman Zhou to the Mama-san. The bill came up to around RMB15,000 (US$2,400). Each of the waitresses and the bar boys also got 100 yuan each. Not exactly big money for us, but clearly a livelihood for the girls working in this sector.

On November 8, the lawyers signed off on the lengthy completion checklist of conditions which Chairman Zhou had to meet before we would inject the funds into DeeDee. We wired US$ 77 million over—an amount considered very substantial for a foreign investment in a Chinese agriculture company—and officially became owners of a 30 percent stake in DeeDee Duck. Not surprisingly, All-Stellar's maiden investment in China made waves in the local investment circles, and a few Chinese PE fund managers started to reach out to us for networking dinners.

Our timing was fantastic: the very next day on November 9, Chinese premier Wen Jiabao made international headlines by unveiling a massive RMB4 trillion (US$586 billion) stimulus plan aimed at stabilizing the Chinese economy, which was suffering a rapid downturn in exports from its western counterparts. Before long, analysts and media were hailing the dragon economy as the brightest growth spot in the world.

Our investment prospects could not have been better. The Investment Committee was gratified. But somehow, I felt a strange sense of unease. The euphoria of chasing the goose had worn off a little. Now that we had her in hand, I could not help wondering if she was indeed as golden as we thought she would be.

> ***Zhong Xi Xie Shou*** 中西携手:
> **Partnership between East and West.**
> ***Zhong*** 中 **refers to China,** ***Xi*** 西 **refers to**
> **the West.** 携手 **means "joining hands".**

Chairman Zhou could expense the bill that night as a legitimate tax-deductible entertainment expense.

CHAPTER 7

Obstacles

Die Jiao Ban Shou 跌脚绊手

T HE BITTER WIND CHILL AND dry air forced blood to drip from my nose as we walked into our long-awaited inaugural board meeting with the DeeDee management. The newly-formed DeeDee Board of Directors consisted of Chairman Zhou, Mr. Meng, Susie and Randy.

It was already December 2008—more than a month since we injected our funds into the company. We were finally holding this important board meeting, which had been delayed repeatedly by DeeDee's management. They had claimed they were so busy sorting out business issues that it was nearly impossible to nail down a date for the meeting.

As I fumbled for tissues to stop the nose bleed, Fang Xing made a grand entrance, vigorously shaking the hands of the two directors from the Chinese side while reeling off compliments to the Lao Qianbei about how good and high-spirited he looked that day.

In reality, Chairman Zhou looked like a thunder cloud. He was livid that we had not delivered our investment funds the very next day after signing the final contract in end September, and instead had waited another month before wiring in the US$77 million. "Where is your boss?" he snapped at me. "I am very angry that because of your significant delay in sending us the money for investment last month, our new projects could not start up in time. You'd better explain what the heck is going on."

Russell, who was coming separately from his hotel, was stuck in traffic. Susie was away on yet another business trip—Russell was her proxy for the inaugural board meeting. This meant that until Russell arrived, it was left to Randy, Fang Xing and me to deal with Chairman Zhou's wrath.

Glaring at us, he continued: "Your investment money came in one month late. In future, we must minimize such delays; otherwise it will incur huge losses for you and for us because we need to move very quickly in our expansion. We want to make it worth your while to invest in us."

By now, I was already well-rehearsed in All-Stellar's standard reply on this issue: "There are strict governance processes we had to adhere to as an international fund, and many conditions that DeeDee had to satisfy first, before we could wire the money over. But I assure you, Chairman Zhou, that we will make up for lost time."

I resisted the temptation to add: "If your employees would only cooperate with us in completing the conditions we listed, we would have moved much faster as well."

The past month had been grueling for us as we prepared for this board meeting, as we encountered new stumbling blocks at every turn.

The first was the resistance from the company's rank and file. During the due diligence period, only the close aides of Chairman Zhou as well as DeeDee's senior management based in Beijing had interacted with us. When news about our investment finally spread to the rest of the company, the local operations and finance directors across the various provinces were flabbergasted by our requests for detailed monthly financial and operational figures. They were even more stumped by our deadline: all data had to be submitted within two weeks, so that we could rush out documents for the board meeting.

After much resistance, they turned in just four pages of gibberish that I could not decipher. It would take another three months, and a lot of detailed instructions before they finally provided the numbers in a decent format.

The DeeDee employees were even more mystified when we explained to them our top priority for the board meeting: to institutionalize the company's business processes. This would include issuing monthly reports to gauge the business performance, none of which existed before we came on board.

"What is a monthly report? We just tell Chairman Zhou whatever he wants to know, whenever he summons us in," said Mr. Meng. That sounded ridiculous to me. How could Chairman Zhou run the operations in such a haphazard fashion? It would take me a few more weeks before I could see the man in action, and understand what Mr. Meng really meant.

We also under-estimated how long it would take to just churn out documents for the meeting, which had to be in both Mandarin and English, since Russell could not comprehend Mandarin. Translation was an onerous job which Fang Xing, who was arguably more bilingual than me, managed to avoid since he managed to convince Russell that he had to devote all his waking hours to bring in a new lucrative deal. So it was left to me—along with Google Translate and a host of other online tools I tried to harness to speed up the laborious process.

Finally, Russell strode in.

This time, Chairman Zhou got straight to his point. "My goal is to *ai-pee-oo* by the end of next year in an overseas market like Hong Kong or Singapore," he declared to the rapt audience of board directors and senior managers. "Our revenues for this year crossed 700 million yuan, and our net profits are about 210 million yuan. My goal is for DeeDee to double those numbers by 2010."

The All-Stellar team gaped. A growth target of about 40 percent a year was extremely aggressive by industry standards. I shuddered to think of what methods Chairman Zhou would use to achieve this goal, while keeping profit margins at 30 percent.

Chairman Zhou went on to emphasize that nothing was more important to him than expanding the company as quickly as possible, so it would look good for an IPO in an overseas Asian market. He was maddeningly stubborn about achieving his objectives in the shortest possible timeframe. We knew, of course, that this was going to take longer than he expected. International equity market investors would not be dazzled simply by the company's size. They would scrutinize every single detail of the company, from its financials to its business processes, and the quality of the management team.

I thought Russell would explain all this to Chairman Zhou, but he seemed to have wised up to the fact that the Chinese management had become almost allergic to the very mention of "fiduciary duty". Mr. Meng had gone berserk last week when I told him it was our duty to do things the proper way. "The proper way of doing things is just an excuse for wasting time and losing money-making opportunities," he had retorted.

Russell simply said, "I think we need to be realistic that preparing for an overseas IPO could take longer—perhaps one year or more."

The older man started to turn crimson at this statement, but Russell cut him short: "I hope you understand, Chairman Zhou, that our interests are clearly aligned. A faster listing means that we can sell off our stake earlier and get a higher rate of return from our investment. So you can be assured that we want the best for DeeDee, and we are not trying to make things more difficult for you when we ask for changes to be made to the company. It is critical that we have a constructive first meeting today to lay a good foundation for the IPO."

Chairman Zhou nodded grudgingly as I translated this statement. For the first time, the meeting went according to plan. Within four hours, we had agreed on key business objectives. Russell convinced the DeeDee team to moderate the original ambitious revenue target from 42 percent to around 30 percent a year, with a view on hitting 1.2 billion yuan by 2010. We had also mapped out our strategies for growth and acquisitions over the coming five years.

Eager not to lose this momentum, Randy and I worked feverishly through the night to churn out meeting minutes. We delivered the thick document to DeeDee the very next day, blissfully anticipating a smooth work flow now that all our objectives and plans had been neatly written out.

Needless to say, we were soon disappointed.

A week later, we had a showdown with DeeDee's senior management over why we needed to do any strategic planning at all. In our minutes, we had taken great pains to stress the importance of international best practices such as writing a business plan, which would spell out concrete steps to achieve our growth targets.

But when we arrived for a scheduled meeting with DeeDee's senior management to discuss how to write the plan, we were told that Chairman Zhou had already left for Henan province. "He is in discussions with local government officials to build a brand new slaughtering facility in Henan province," said Manager Wang.

"What facility? Is it in our Proposed Usage of Funds table[16] which both parties had signed off on?" stammered Randy. "We need to do a strategic mapping of potential new production locations so we can optimize the use of our limited financial resources. We have told you before that we feel there was already some overlap in the facilities DeeDee had previously built in Henan. So we recommended that DeeDee locate new farms elsewhere in provinces where it has not expanded to yet…"

"Respected Sir, Chairman Zhou told me to pass on this message

---

[16] This stipulates the projects that Chairman Zhou could invest in and the respective amounts, based on our detailed analyses of the funding needs of each project.

that time is of essence. You have already caused a lot of delays, so it is even more important now to use the fastest methods to achieve our IPO goal," said Ming Ming, a junior finance manager, meekly.

"But we need to think of the long-term costs and benefits of doing things in this manner without any big picture planning," protested Randy. "Building the Henan facility might be faster and yield quicker results than trying to set up a facility in a new market. But these sorts of shortcuts will only hurt the company later. What DeeDee needs are the analytic problem-solving skills that All-Stellar can offer."

Mr. Meng, who had been sitting passively throughout the conversation, let out a derisive snort. "Results-based management, operational excellence, balanced scorecards, bullshit. I really must wonder whether this bombastic management lingo that you keep using is just invented by foreigners to make them look superior. I don't see how they can solve the real problems we face on the ground in China."

"Well, you haven't even tried it yet, how would you know?" I protested. "Meng zong, you do know that the US$ 77 million we invested in DeeDee is just enough to fund the equity portion of the proposed new facilities. We would have to get bank loans soon to top up. We need to make sure we strictly adhere to the use of funds both parties agreed on earlier."

The curt reply was: "You are free to write the business plan yourselves and submit it to the board for approval at the next board meeting."

We trooped back to the office dejectedly and tried to explain our latest conflict to Russell.

"Are these idiots trying to shut us out?" he fumed.

"Ambitious Chinese companies inspire to become international players. Yet, at the same time, they are not willing or able to adopt the proven management strategies that had become the norm for top western companies. That's the problem we face with Chairman Zhou and his team..." Randy began.

"Yes, yes, I know all that," snapped Russell. "But Susie had assured me that Chairman Zhou is so eager to associate with foreign investors that he would bend over backwards to suit us. What I want to know is whether she's correct, or whether you have discovered anything different which suggests this Lao Zhou is too set in his old ways of doing things, and only wants All-Stellar to window-dress his business."

"I think Chairman Zhou is reasonable and willing to work with All-Stellar. But he is acting very defensively right now, because he is worried we will try to exert too much control over his company. We need to win his trust first..." I said tentatively.

"Yeah yeah, win trust. All the books say it's the first rule of investing in China, right? Problem is, we don't have the luxury of time or patience to wine and dine him for another six months before he finally decides to open up his heart to us and do things our way," growled Russell. "What I want to know is: how do we get them to trust us in the shortest amount of time? Find that out for me, Matt."

I was stumped. Fortunately, another incoming call for Russell cut short our conversation, and I was left to ponder his questions. I was too green to know what to do. The only person I could think of who might offer a real solution was Susie. I just needed to find her first.

> *Die Jiao Ban Shou* 跌脚绊手: **To be obstructed by one's feet and hands, to meet with obstacles.**

CHAPTER 8

Encumbered

Ai Shou Ai Jiao 碍手碍脚

"You must be desperate to come all the way here just to talk to me," Susie said, as I rushed up to meet her at the arrival gates of Beijing International Airport.

I had not seen Madame Wu for almost three weeks. She had been on back-to-back business trips, and she conveyed all instructions for the China team through curt emails or through Fang Xing. Only Rebecca was allowed to call Susie directly, and she kept the poor girl manically busy with her endless special requirements for flight bookings, airport transfers, accommodation and ground transport. Susie had unique preferences for which particular airline to fly on, which hotel to stay in, what kind of pillows and what brand of tea she wanted in her hotel room, and insisted that perfection down to the very last detail.

I heard from Rebecca that Susie would touch down at 9:40p.m. on Friday, and decided that I would have to intercept her there if I were to get a proper meeting with her. I knew she would not have much time to entertain me, but even a few minutes of discussion was better than nothing. Since she was the brain behind the deal as well as Chairman Zhou's personal friend, she would have the best solution to the thorny situation at DeeDee. And I needed to hear it from her directly, not through Fang Xing.

Thankfully, she did not seem upset to see me as she emerged from baggage claim, perhaps because I rushed up to offer to carry her bags. "So what brings you here? Looking for some tips? I have ten yuan here…" she asked in amusement.

"Yes, Ma'am, I really need your valuable guidance on how to smooth out our relationship with Chairman Zhou," I said meekly.

"Why is this question so urgent that you need an answer right now?"

I decided to pour out the whole story of the disastrous board meeting, our clashes with Chairman Zhou as well as his staff, and Russell's daunting questions. I finished talking just as we reached her black Audi A6. The chauffeur opened the door for her. I wondered if she would invite me into the car or just zoom off. She seemed to be pondering the same question. Finally, she took pity on me and motioned me into the car.

"Fang Xing already gave me the update last week, so I'm aware of the issues we are facing," Susie said coolly. "I've been testing you guys to see how you handle this."

"Yeah right, thanks a lot," I thought. Out loud, I cut to the chase: "With all respect, Madam Wu, can you give me some pointers on what ways we can use to convince Chairman Zhou more quickly to accept the new changes we recommended to DeeDee? What should we do to make the Chinese staff at DeeDee more willing to cooperate with us?"

"So you're asking me how to change Chinese people's behavior overnight?" Susie asked in amusement. "Are you even Chinese?"

I took a deep breath, willing myself to stay calm. "Yes, I know very well that there is no magic formula to winning Chairman Zhou's trust overnight. In fact, it seems like patience is the only answer I can come up with so far. Maybe we need to trust them first, before they can trust us..."

Susie seemed pleased with this answer. "A lot of westerners who come to China may see the kind of relationship-building process required in Chinese business dealings as a huge waste of time. But that is just the way this society is wired."

I nodded. "I'm just starting to appreciate how some changes in China could happen overnight, yet other proposals could lie dormant and simmer over months, or even years."

"It may seem that the Chinese drag their feet because of distrust, customs and reels of bureaucracy. But you'll also be surprised just how fast the Chinese move when they put their mind to it," said Susie, gesturing to the construction sites littered along the highway as we sped towards her bungalow in the elite Shunyi district about fifteen minutes away from the airport.

"It's always this rhythm: wait to rush; rush to act, and then wait again. Just look at the physical transformation of China. It can be dormant for a long time and then move incredibly fast when policy winds turn. Whole stretches of expressways can be up and running in a mere two months. Entire townships can be constructed in less than a year. I just heard about a property entrepreneur who completed a high-rise building in Hunan province within just ninety days, after waiting years for approvals. These are just metaphors of how business opportunities in China move."

I wondered if shoddy construction and the risk of collapse from over-acceleration were part of the metaphor. Out loud, I said, "I overheard Chairman Zhou telling his managers once that it's all about capturing opportunities at lightning speed in China."

Susie nodded. "When Chairman Zhou makes deals with local partners, he has to strike while the iron is hot before those guys change their minds or terms overnight. When he goes ahead and signs new projects, it's because he reasons that he can't wait a week or a month for us to debate the decision and check our strategic plans and then give him written approval. The deal with the local partner would have been long gone by then."

I could not stifle a sigh. "But Russell does not understand this, nor would he condone Chairman Zhou's actions even if he understood."

Susie shrugged. "Well, then Russell has to work on his own trust issues first."

My heart sank. The quickest solution was to put my boss in a freaking therapy session?

"It's inevitable—the teething pains when the foreign investor and Chinese partner first get together and try to thresh out their differences. At least, if it's just teething pains, the two sides will grow up and get used to each other. But often, they just knock each other's teeth out and end the relationship badly. I used to be in the thick of all this, but now I prefer to take a step back and wait for the dust to settle."

I did not know what to make of this. But I knew time was running out, so I asked Susie point-blank, "Madame Wu, is there anything I can do about the situation?"

Susie laughed heartily. "You are a dogged one. Not giving up— that's a good start. Well, for one, you can learn to be more Chinese in the way you think and behave."

I suppressed a sigh. "I've been brought up in a traditional Chinese way and learn about the Confucius classics, so my thinking should already be quite similar to my *balinghou* 八零后 (the generation born after 1980) peers in China."

Susie smiled, but her response was gritty. "You're still an outsider, and you haven't personally experienced the after-effects of the Mao regime and Cultural Revolution. I don't know many outsiders who can really catch on to the Chinese way of thinking, no matter how much they know about the country."

"Argh, what is the deal with this 'outsider mentality'? China has fifty-six ethnic groups, and yet these people still can't be a little more inclusive?" I fumed to myself.

"Well, I think I'll be able to learn quickly since I'll be spending a lot of time in China, and maybe even live here," I told Susie as confidently as I could.

"Living here does help. At least you could learn to speak like the locals and gain acceptance more easily," Susie conceded. "Based on my own experience, it seems much easier for Chinese elites to succeed in the rules-based western system, compared to foreigners like you trying to win in a complex system like China's."

"Are your lenses already too dyed by your western education and upbringing for you to see things through the mainland Chinese's eyes?" she challenged me. "Even if you were able to understand their perspective, you may lack the ability to do things the way they do—which is what really matters."

I couldn't catch Susie's drift, and asked meekly: "Do what sort of things...?"

Susie shrugged. "You'll see for yourself. Chinese people never say things directly, so you have to learn to read between the lines."

"Since you have been out of the country for over twenty years, how do you keep in touch with the Chinese way of thinking and doing things?" I pressed.

She smiled coolly. "I may have been in Europe, Southeast Asia and the US, but I always made sure I spent most of my free time with wealthy new immigrants from China. In fact, there are so many of China's richest families and top officials who have secretly taken up citizenship abroad nowadays that I have to be selective in whom I want to network with."

She leaned over and added in a lower voice: "They speak more freely abroad than they would back in China."

I paused momentarily, wondering if I should start seeking out wealthy mainland Chinese immigrants in Singapore to network with.

As it turned out, Chinese movie stars like Jacky Chan, Jet Li and Gong Li all had properties and the equivalent of green cards from the tiny island-state. But the ones I was really interested in were Chinese officials and tycoons—and trying to track them down was much more difficult since they were careful to lie low.

Just then, Susie's car stopped outside a pair of iron-wrought gates. She waved me away. "There's a cab waiting right here to send you home. It was nice talking to you. Goodnight."

———◦◦◦◦———

Two days passed after my random and unsatisfactory conversation with Susie, which threw up more questions than answers. I was starting to despair, when Chairman Zhou made an unexpected announcement: he had come up with "the perfect solution" to make us happy.

"I've hired an American white guy as my *dongmi* 董秘 (Board Secretary). He can speak English and is familiar with your western ways. So he will be able to improve our communication and trust by leaps and bounds, and upgrade our cooperative relationship to the highest level," he declared triumphantly.

The Board Secretary held a divine role at a Chinese company. He was the company's chief meeting organizer and communications specialist. He was responsible for relaying instructions from top management and ensuring that the people below executed on them. An experienced board secretary also helped the Chairman organize work at each functional department, such as finance, human resources, and operations, and often acted as the company's chief spokesperson.

We were elated at the prospect of working with an American executive who would wield real power and influence in DeeDee's operations. That would hopefully make it so much easier for us to implement our asset management strategies.

And then, Chairman Zhou trotted out Mark Hensworth.

An energetic twenty-eight-year-old lad from Missouri, he had qualifications that were not exactly what we expected: he had no real prior working experience except for a stint at Wall Street English, a popular private English language school sprouting up at almost every street corner across China. Mark had taught there for about six months.

He candidly admitted it was his slight resemblance to Brad Pitt, rather than his teaching skills, that turned him into the school's star attraction for hordes of young Chinese eager to learn English from anyone who looked like the cast of the sitcom Friends. "My Asian American friends, who are better at English grammar than me, never got hired as teachers because they didn't have the look the students were looking for," he told me later.

Mark had arrived in Beijing three years ago to study Mandarin at Beijing Foreign Language University, and could now manage simple business Mandarin. After tiring of the hum-drum Wall Street English classes, he dropped his resume randomly across a number of online career portals such as 51job.com, applying for a range of jobs from marketing to business development. Somehow, he caught Chairman Zhou's eye.

"Look at him, doesn't he look so...so...westernized?" beamed Chairman Zhou, pointing enthusiastically at Mark's blond hair and baby blue eyes. "Don't you think that now, with foreign investors and an American board secretary, DeeDee is boldly transforming into a truly international company?"

I tried in vain to stifle a giggle and a sigh. It was only too clear that Mark would be a mere figurehead and a glorified mailman to deliver Chairman Zhou's instructions to us, while the founder remained firmly in control.

Fang Xing, in contrast, kept a perfectly straight face. He heartily shook Mark's hand, and said solemnly, "Indeed, Mr. Hensworth is a rare gem. He has the honor of becoming Chairman Zhou's first foreign employee, and very likely, the youngest foreign board secretary in the history of Chinese companies. This is a historic moment."

Mark's job—at least for the next few months—was to answer any questions that the All-Stellar team had and to try to keep us out of Chairman Zhou's hair. I met Mark every Thursday to touch base, and our formal office meetings quickly evolved into culinary expeditions as we tried out new Beijing eateries while chatting about work.

At the start, things did seem to get easier, since we had a dedicated concierge helping us to arrange meetings, chase for DeeDee's monthly reports, and present our proposed business plan amendments to Chairman Zhou. Even these tasks were already a challenge for Mark, since the DeeDee staff were naturally suspicious of him and did not accede to his requests for information readily. Still, he seemed to be enjoying every moment of working at DeeDee.

"Why did you decide to work in a Chinese SME?" I asked him one evening, as we rode the elevator down from DeeDee's office.

"Working here makes perfect sense really," he replied. "I'm a simple guy, and my goal right now is simply to improve my Mandarin proficiency. What better way to do so than immerse myself into a completely Chinese environment like DeeDee where no one speaks a word of English?"

"Well, I guess you could hook up with a Chinese girl. A lot of laowai I know do that to practice their Mandarin and they get a lot of side benefits too," I offered.

"Nah," drawled Mark. "I've got a sweetheart waiting for me back in Missouri. She doesn't get what the heck I'm doing here in China. But she knows I really like linguistics and Chinese history—even though it doesn't earn much money—and she's got my back. It's hard to find someone like her, who is very understanding and who doesn't care much for materialism."

I smiled, thinking of the several casual dates I had had with

Chinese girls who asked me point-blank during introductions how much I earned, and whether I could buy them a "greeting present" such as a pair of earrings or a bag. I turned to a different subject. "When will we receive the January consolidated numbers?"

"You know, these Chinese people…" Mark began cursing, before discreetly lowering his voice, realizing that he should not have assumed the Chinese around him could not understand English. "I'm still trying to get the numbers from the Changsha and Hengyang subsidiaries, and the numbers from Hunan and Shandong provinces don't tally. I'm trying to figure out why," he whispered. Changsha and Hengyang are two major municipalities in the central province of Hunan.

"You mean Hunan's numbers are too big to be true? Yes, I don't understand why your initial report stated that Hunan's revenues are bigger than the earnings reported by the other provinces like Shandong, Henan and Guangxi, when the Hunan operations are smaller in size," I sighed.

"I think it's just a mix-up in the way they report the numbers, maybe there was an extra zero or two somewhere," Mark said as reassuringly as he could. "I'll figure it out soon."

"You know the report is over two weeks late, and Russell is already breathing down my neck. What's more, Chairman Zhou still needs time to sign off on the reports…" I continued.

As we walked out of the building, Mark suddenly stopped dead in his footsteps.

"Damnit!" he screeched.

"What happened?" I asked in alarm.

"I forgot to punch the card before leaving the office," Mark spluttered, dashing back to the elevator. I grinned in sympathy. Mark had complained many times about this archaic practice of signing in and out of the office, which was still prevalent in many Chinese companies. Employees who did not register their attendance, arrived late or left early were fined. Some also had their salaries docked. A few Chinese companies I knew even implemented fingerprint technology to rule out possible fraudulent behavior of people signing in and out on another's behalf.

When he came back down a few minutes later, I had already hailed down a cab and we set off for Mark's favorite barbeque Sichuan fish restaurant on *Guijie* 簋街, a famous food street with red lanterns, traditional courtyards and hundreds of restaurants serving stewed rabbit heads and spicy pepper-encrusted scorpions. The foreigners call it "Ghost Street," a technically incorrect translation because the character *gui* 簋—a word so complicated even the ordinary Chinese had trouble writing it—is pronounced the same way as the character "ghost" in Mandarin but actually means "a large food vessel".

"How has the first two months been working at Chairman Zhou?" I inquired, as we dug into the three-pound barbequed eel drenched in a pool of recycled cooking oil and chili peppers together with my favorite assortment of seaweed, mushrooms, dried beancurd skin and lotus roots.

"Hell of a ride," Mark grinned.

I stared at him, not comprehending.

"My Mandarin has improved tremendously. I can now read an entire feasibility study in less than two hours," he said smugly.

"That's awesome…but uh, I was referring to the state of affairs at DeeDee. So what has Chairman Zhou been busy with nowadays?"

Mark put down his bowl of rice, and hastily chugged a bottle of icy cold, sour plum juice. He might have accidentally chewed on a spicy pepper and was trying to extinguish the fire in his mouth.

"Just the usual…Chairman Zhou is still very concerned about how to raise additional financing from the banks," he said.

"Yes," I said glumly. "He says if DeeDee is going to achieve the revenue and profit growth targets we set this year to prepare for the IPO, he will need at least RMB580 million (US$88 million) to expand the capacity of the existing farms and acquire bigger farms from competitors. But we are a PE fund, we can't go raising a corporate debt in our own name and use the proceeds for DeeDee, it's simply unacceptable."

"Well, Zhou harangues me every day about how to make you guys step in to procure a big bank loan on behalf of DeeDee," pressed Mark.

Chairman Zhou had made clear just how bitterly disappointed he was that DeeDee's association with a top-notch international fund like All-Stellar had not reaped the benefits he wanted. He had been led by Susie to believe All-Stellar would help him to access international debt markets quickly and painlessly.

With the launch of Premier Wen Jiabao's stimulus plan that reportedly flooded the markets with some RMB10 trillion (US$1.5 trillion) of credit right after All-Stellar came on board, it seemed like all his financing troubles would vanish.

But as it turned out, the bulk of the stimulus was pumped into— who else?—the SOEs, leaving only crumbs for private businesses. Chairman Zhou's team set up meetings after meetings with the state banks, but discussions were slow and laborious as the credit officers resisted lending to smaller businesses which were more difficult to price for risk and rushed off ever so often to approve ostensibly safer projects for SOE customers.

We were unable to help Chairman Zhou with any of his unorthodox requests: we refused to bribe; we lacked the contacts to pull strings with the state banks or any of the unofficial channels; it was impossible for us to take out any loans on behalf of DeeDee from foreign banks; and we could not lend DeeDee money from our own fund.

I explained all this for the fifth time to Mark, who nodded with a vacant look on his face. Undeterred, I pressed him again: "So besides loans, what else is Chairman Zhou up to?"

Mark brushed off my question with an innocent look on his face. "He seems to be meeting with a lot of folks from Yunnan province, but I haven't been in the loop," he said lightly. "Oh by the way, have you been to any tourist attractions outside Beijing recently? Want to go check some out?"

I wondered if Mark had also started to adopt the typical DeeDee Chinese management's style of evasive small talk. As I watched him work dexterously with his chopsticks at the remains of the eel on the coal-fired metal plate, I felt that he had become localized more quickly than I had over the past few months.

I was still curious why Mark, who was the first in his extended family to learn Mandarin and venture out of the US, picked the road less trodden by joining a Chinese SME. I asked him about his unconventional choice.

"Unconventional?" he repeated, surprised. "I'm just one of the millions of foreigners who come every year to China to study and work because this is supposed to be a hot market. And all these American CEOs are taking Mandarin lessons and making annual pilgrimages to Beijing and Shanghai to pry open the China market. I just read an article about Mark Zuckerberg[17] studying Mandarin the other day. He's about my age, did you know?"

"That's true, I replied. "But most foreigners would still pick a more comfortable way of getting China exposure on their resumes— attend Mandarin classes, do summer school here, attend a big university in China, get an internship, or maybe try to work for a large foreign firm in Beijing. You could arguably get just as much

---

[17] Mark Zuckerberg, the founder of Facebook, has spent several years learning Mandarin since 2010. As of the publication of this book, he has joined the Tsinghua University School of Economics and Management Advisory Board, and even hosted a dialogue with Tsinghua University students entirely in what Chinese media reported as "undeniably impressive" Mandarin. Facebook is banned in China, but Mr. Zuckerberg has met with several top officials, including President Xi during the latter's diplomatic visit to the US in September 2015.

language immersion—not to mention more pay and less grief—as you would in DeeDee."

Working for a militant, control freak boss like Chairman Zhou—who was only willing to pay Mark a pittance of RMB20,000 (US$3,000) a month and piled him with often unreasonable work demands—was not every foreigner's cup of Chinese tea. It certainly was not mine.

Mark grinned. "Well, I guess I'm kind of a linguistic perfectionist. I want to be really deep inside the system to understand the Mandarin language.

"You know, I loved reading the writings of young Americans who had grown up in China like Pearl Buck or the American diplomats like John Paton Davies and John Service. I always felt that they grew up eating and drinking the Mandarin language with their local playmates. They internalized the Chinese world view much better than other authors who wrote about China from the outside looking in."

I was intrigued. "Those American diplomats…they're the Foreign Service officers who gathered intelligence in the 1930s in China, and then got persecuted back home in the 1950s when the Chinese Communist Party took over the country?"

"Yeah. Unlikely heroes, but I always felt somewhat inspired by their perseverance to find out the real situation on the ground about the Chinese Commies, and to tell it like it is to those paranoid politicians back home—even if that meant their patriotism would be questioned for advocating cooperation with the Reds."

"They're the original China Hands," I agreed. "Did you come to China to become a *zhongguotong* too?"

"Isn't that what you fancy becoming, Huang zong? I wouldn't want to compete with you for the title," Mark teased. Then, turning serious, he chewed on the question for a while. "I did aspire to be a sinologist initially, and I find it really fascinating to get up close and personal with the Chinese. It's fun to mingle with the younger Chinese crowd. They are so cosmopolitan nowadays and some even know more about American pop culture and brands than I do. But what's most interesting to me are enigmatic characters like Chairman Zhou. He's caught between the times—socialism and free-market liberalisation."

I grinned. "Yes, the Lao Qianbei cracks me up with his curious mix of Maoisms and capitalist ambitions."

Mark continued, "But now I sometimes wonder if I might start disliking myself if I became so *ruxiangsuisu* 入乡随俗 (localized). I'm not sure the values and thinking of many young Chinese in big cities—people like Fang zong for example—is something that I want to get sucked into. I suspect that the process of becoming a *zhongguotong* involves getting into the minds of the Chinese and also doing what they do…which could mean getting one's hands dirty…."

Then suddenly, he stopped short and said anxiously, "I'm not claiming that western morals or culture are superior, or that Chinese young people are immoral, ok? I've been chewed up so many times for saying politically incorrect stuff, so I get a little antsy airing my views in China now."

I smiled broadly to show that I did not take offense to anything he said, while stifling a groan as the Chinese spices swirled insanely within my stomach. Just then, my phone beeped with a message sent via *Weibo*, a popular Chinese microblogging website which is akin to a hybrid of Twitter and Facebook. One of my Chinese friends had just forwarded a poem that had been posted online. "Even though I don't know who the author is, but I felt like he/she was a soulmate because the poem really spoke to my heart as an 'outsider' and a non-native in Beijing," he commented.

> *Beijing*
> *An imperial capital which foreigners find mysterious yet starkly real*
> *An imperial capital which non-Beijingers detest yet look forward to*

An imperial capital where Beijingers feel helpless yet remain proud of
An imperial capital where poor people don't dare to come and rich wives don't wish to leave
An imperial capital where false sentiments permeate so you can never be lonely
Have you decided to come here? Or have you decided to leave?

As I elbowed my way through the subway crowds to get home, I mulled over the motivations and circumstances that had led me to the heart of the most populous country on earth. Even though my forefathers came from China, I was increasingly aware of just how different my Chinese peers operated, compared to what I was used to at home. Their thinking, as Susie and Mark had observed, was also because rules and values here were often malleable.

Now that I had come to Beijing, what would it take for me to succeed in an environment where the most incredible dreams can come true—but often at a formidable cost? Was I to adapt by changing my personality and shifting my principles, or could I still remain true to myself?

After making no progress in extracting further information about Chairman Zhou out of Mark, I decided that the best way to make my life less miserable was to get close to Chairman Zhou myself.

So I summoned the courage one day to march into his office and ask if I could join him for a site visit to the duck farm in the municipal county of Liuzhou. This was located in the southwestern province of Guangxi, which boasted a rich history spanning 2,100 years. It was home to one of the three regional headquarters of DeeDee.

I knew that Chairman Zhou travelled extensively across the country to visit his duck farms every month, and had found out about his December schedule after slipping his secretary an imported

Johnny Walker Blue Label whisky for her husband and a bottle of Midnight Poison, Dior's latest perfume, for her.

I was not particularly excited about visiting the local farms since it always involved heavy drinking—not to mention nauseating duck poop manure—which made it hard for me to keep a clear head or even maintain coherent conversations. But I figured it was the only way to really get to know Chairman Zhou, and to start trusting him myself.

He was scrutinizing a pile of engineering design drawings as I knocked on the door, and I heard him bark at a nervous young manager: "How do you expect me to sign off on this when the design drawings for the incubator facility are missing? How many times must I tell you to not submit something to me that is incomplete?"

He only noticed me standing at the door when the trembling manager tiptoed out, and was so surprised he almost fell out of his chair. "Who…why…" he stuttered, as he tried to regain his composure. "How are you, Mr. Huang?" he finally said in an awkwardly formal tone.

"Please do just call me *Xiaohuang* (Little Huang). Sorry to interrupt but I was wondering if I may come in for a few minutes? I just wanted to bring you a special organic *Tieguanyin* tea that was freshly picked from the Yunnan highlands. I had bought it for you when I went to Lijiang last week."

Chairman Zhou looked taken aback, and then he melted when he saw the tea, which I knew was his favorite type. His calloused face broke into a broad smile: "You are too kind, thanks very much, Xiaohuang. So what brings you here today?"

I took a deep breath and blurted out my request. That made Chairman Zhou even more flabbergasted.

"Liuzhou? What…er…that is very far for you to travel you know," he stuttered.

I could see Bingbing, the young accountant who was next in line to enter the office, hiding her mirth at seeing her usually imperious boss so discomfited. Another three giggling staff stood in line behind her, each holding piles of paper and files.

Not knowing what to say to me, Chairman Zhou searched for a distraction and spotted Bingbing. "Come in. What do you want?" he demanded.

She hurried in, holding out a gigantic printout detailing every employee's basic pay and performance salary amounts for the month. She needed Chairman Zhou's signature before she could process payments, which were already overdue by almost a week.

"I remember Lin Fang was late for work twice this month. Why does the spreadsheet only say once? And he was late for over thirty minutes. This means he gets no basic salary for that day!" he snapped.

He immediately called the next person in. "Have you worked out the new budget for the office stationery? I heard that we are still buying pens from that store which charges ten cents more than the price available online. What is going on?"

Then he picked up an old Nokia phone, thumbed out a text and turned to me with an apologetic expression. "Xiaohuang, that is very kind of you to suggest spending your precious time with me on the trip, but I just recalled that I have an important meeting in Beijing next week, and will not be able to travel. Shall we arrange to go to Liuzhou some other time?"

I knew that was my cue to disappear. "Of course, I wouldn't want to inconvenience you, Chairman Zhou. Thank you very much for your time."

I left the office despondently. If only he would apply the same military precision and urgency to responding to our team's proposals for transforming DeeDee, as he did to managing the company's microscopic affairs! "I'd have to go back to work on my relationship with Mark instead for now," I sighed.

Back and forth, back and forth, two steps forward one step

back—that seemed to be the rhythm of doing business and building relationships in China.

Five greasy dinners—ranging from more Sichuan food to applewood-roasted BBQ ribs at a Texas roadhouse—later, Mark opened up a little.

It was another ghastly cold night. We strolled casually up the street towards the junction at the Second Ring Road where a gigantic food vessel monument stood, overlooking the entire Ghost Street. It was almost ten o'clock at night but it seemed people were just streaming in for dinner. Empty beer bottles stood precariously on the edges of tables, with any remaining available table space cluttered with remnants of empty crab, baby lobster and conch shells. Billows of smoke wafted up gently in waves from the makeshift *kaochuan* 烤串 (skewer) stalls at street corners, emitting a flavorful, burnt smell. The skewers, which can range from meat slices to chicken wings, gizzards and even goat testicles, are barbequed over slow fire and sprinkled with chilli powder, cumin and a slew of other spices.

"Three yuan for one mutton skewer! Ten yuan for four!" bellowed the street hawker. Prices of the mutton skewers had gone up again. I remembered it was only two yuan last year.

We bought a bunch of twenty skewers each and sat on squat stools by the roadside chewing and counting the number of top luxury cars passing by. After just seven minutes, we had spotted one lime-green Maserati, three Rolls Royces and one creamy white Ferrari, at which point Mark suddenly decided to offer me a little tidbit that convulsed me so much that I almost jabbed the wooden skewer into my throat.

"This morning, Chairman Zhou was entertaining some officials from Kunming. I think we may be buying over a portfolio of duck farms over there soon," he said nonchalantly. Kunming is the capital of Yunnan province located in the far southwest of China.

"What?" I stuttered, horrified. "Kunming? I thought we already agreed with him to stop looking for new projects until we settle the bank financing package for the existing duck farms!"

"Chairman Zhou believes the duck farms in Yunnan are more profitable as they have a lower cost base for feed. He has asked me to raise this up to you guys at the next board meeting for approval," Mark replied.

I stared at him, momentarily lost for words.

We had been trying to implement a two-step approval process for new projects, where all potential new investment opportunities must first be subjected to an initial screening stage, before being signed off by both parties. Only then could they be explored and developed further. This concept was entirely new to DeeDee's management, since Chairman Zhou alone had made the calls on investments in the past. From what Mark just told me, it was obvious he was defiantly blocking us from making the change.

We had also advised Chairman Zhou that DeeDee's main focus for now should be to secure the bank financing for the existing projects as soon as possible. But Chairman Zhou was furious that we were undermining his top priority of expanding the business. He was fanatical about achieving growth at all costs, even if it risked bankrupting DeeDee. So he had insisted the board give a blanket approval to all new projects.

Our relationship with Chairman Zhou was becoming increasingly tense. I was starting to think it was impossible for a stubborn Lao Qianbei, with his tentacles in every aspect of the business, to accept the way international investors like us insisted the business ought to be run. Even trying to convince him of the merits of setting up a proper delegation of responsibilities, so that he did not have to sign off on every single company purchase down to office pens, was like asking him to drink poison. After all, that would mean diluting his stronghold over the company.

But there had to be a way to bring him around. Fang Xing was still the best card we had to play. I just needed to get him involved first.

> *Ai Shou Ai Jiao* 碍手碍脚: **To block another's hands and feet; prevent the other party from proceeding.**

CHAPTER 9

Free Spenders

Da Shou Da Jiao 大手大脚

WE CRUISED DOWN CHANG'AN AVENUE in Fang Xing's swanky crimson Aston Martin V8 Vantage S Roadster. He had the hood down, even though it was so cold that the heavy morning dew had formed frozen beads on the flanks of the magnificent beast.

Shortly after All-Stellar signed the deal with Chairman Zhou, Fang Xing had placed his order for this 4,300 cc red beast, which was to be imported directly from Warwickshire. But he had to wait four months—the dealership blamed exceptionally high demand for the delay. In fact, nouveau riche Chinese's insatiable appetite for luxury goods meant that waiting lists for high-end cars could take up to half a year.

Fang Xing finally picked up his new toy two days ago, and wasted no time showing it off. "You're my little baby's first guest passenger!" Fang Xing exclaimed, before rattling off the properties of the six-speed sports shift, semi automatic gearbox. I had never felt more flattered in my life. I must be doing something right to make Fang Xing like me this much.

It was only later that I realized he told almost every acquaintance that came on board the exact same thing. And I eventually found out that I was not really his first guest passenger. His wife, whom I was going to meet shortly, was not either.

Fang Xing had both hands on the leather steering wheel, and one foot ready on the accelerator, waiting to speed off when the light turned green. Finally, it was time to go—he barely made it three feet before we were stopped again by snarling traffic. For the first time, I was actually very pleased that the jam made the journey so much longer. This gave me a rare opportunity to chat with Fang Xing and get to know him better. He had surprised Randy and I by inviting us to his apartment for "a casual housewarming party," and even offered me a lift from the office.

I noticed Fang Xing's unique turquoise wedding ring back on his finger, but knew better than to comment on its re-appearance. Instead, I picked another item to comment on. "What an exquisite pair of cuff links you have on today. They are in the shape of golf balls!"

"Yeah, they are limited edition. I got them at Oriental Plaza last week," he said nonchalantly, although I could detect a gleam of pride in his eye.

"They're from Mont Blanc right?" I said.

After spending almost nine months living in Beijing, I had become an expert in identifying luxury good brands. It was a skill that I never expected to acquire, since I had always been quite a brand-blind slop in Singapore, and could not have told Chanel apart from Gucci, let alone spot a Maserati through the smog on a Beijing street.

My education in luxury items came from becoming a pack mule for Rebecca and other Chinese friends over the past few months. They enthusiastically checked my overseas travel schedule and bombarded me with requests to buy duty-free goods. On my return flights to Beijing from Singapore, my carry-on luggage would be bursting to the seams with L'Occitane Immortelle precious serums, Louis Vuitton handbags and Mont Blanc jewellery. These precious commodities,

I estimated, would cost them several months of salary. I struggled to comprehend how my young Chinese friends could afford these expensive products. But to them, this was still a great deal. The higher taxes in China on overseas luxury goods meant huge price differentials for similar products, so buying from duty free shops overseas meant significant savings.

As the demand for high-end luxury goods thrived, international luxury firms flocked to China as their traditional, more mature markets suffered a severe slowdown. The world's most well-known luxury brands opened up store after store as the Chinese rushed to buy the latest spring collection of Louis Vuitton handbags and Hermes accessories, even though these stuff were priced much higher than overseas with the luxury tax slapped on.

Mike Yeo, a Singaporean friend who has been in this industry for over a decade, had recently switched jobs and was poached to join the Cartier sales team based in Shanghai. He told me finding a sales job in the luxury sector in China was very easy and his career was so good here that he was prepared to stay in Shanghai indefinitely. "Even with an economic slowdown, there are still enough rich people to keep business going. They are hooked on branded items. The only thing that could make this party stop would be the end of corruption. Even then, old habits die hard in China. So I think I won't be going home to Singapore anytime soon," Mike said blithely.

But what really woke me up to the wonders of China's luxury boom was observing people like Fang Xing and my new business contacts like thirty-two-year-old Chinese billionaire hedge fund manager Donald Wang. His Mandarin name was Wang Pai 王湃, which sounded like the Chinese phrase for "trump card". As for his English handle, he may have inadvertently named himself after Donald Trump, after consulting a fortune teller who told him that he should immediately take on an English name "Donald" to multiply his fortune.

According to this Chinese Trump, if you wanted to make it into the highest echelons of society, you needed to prove that you could afford such luxury non-essentials. "These cars mark my status in society and help me win business from clients. It is a necessary part of my work," Donald told me earnestly as he opened his garage: a Rolls Royce, a Ferrari, a Porsche, two Audi's and three Mercedes SUVs.

Donald and his wife began each day with the mind-boggling task of deciding which key to draw out from the safe to drive to work. But even all those swanky cars had become mere pittances—his goal now was to own his own private jet or yacht to prove that he was really in the ultra-rich league. "Once you make your first hundred million bucks, your obsession is how to make your first billion," he said.

Fang Xing, I figured, also shared this mindset. From what I gathered so far, he was already well on the way to making his first billion. And he certainly had the trappings to prove it. But I was still unprepared for just how magnificent his possessions were.

We arrived at his apartment at Swan Palace, one of the upscale neighborhoods along the Fourth Ring Road. It was a 366-square-meter (almost 4,000 square feet) south-facing penthouse on the twenty-sixth floor of the building, with a sensational city view. In China, people are obsessed with the direction their apartment windows face. South-facing apartments are the priciest because it is most favored amongst the local Chinese as you get the most sunlight no matter which season throughout the year.

Fang Xing had hired an interior designer hailing from New York City, and told us that he had spent an additional RMB1.5 million (US$230,000) to refurbish the house. It was reminiscent of a chic downtown Tribeca penthouse. I loved the modern open design and the high floor-to-ceiling windows. The Brazilian rosewood furniture and Dali marble floors were fused together in an immaculate match of East-West elements.

Around the apartment were several other Chinese paintings,

calligraphy, and sculptures from famous contemporary Chinese artists such as Yue Minjun and Zhang Xiaogang, names which I had never heard of before until Fang Xing rattled them off, as he gave us a grand tour of his house. I did not know that Fang Xing was such an art connoisseur.

As I walked around ogling at Fang Xing's collection, my eyes fell upon an exquisite clay statue sitting at the foot of the staircase. It was of a young girl fighting a big fat bear. "This sculpture should be worth at least 1.5 million yuan now," Fang Xing told me. I gasped. The value of the artwork was equivalent to the cost of renovating the entire penthouse!

"How about this one? What is it? A bubble?" I asked, pointing to an abstract art drawing of a bloated object suspended in mid-air. Fang Xing shrugged. "No idea. Maybe it's a dandelion, since I like them. That was a gift from a friend in one of the state banks who took up modern art painting as a hobby. I just hang it up in a corner to give him face."

I wondered enviously how Fang Xing could have amassed so much money at such an early age to afford such a gigantic penthouse and his private art collection. I guessed he must have several projects running simultaneously on the side, but I was not exactly sure. Maybe he came from a rich family? Maybe he had deployed his huge risk appetite shrewdly, and was now reaping the profits thanks to surging asset prices? Gazing at the opulence around me, I wondered when I would finally decide to commit my hard-earned cash to buy a property in China.

A butler served us a 1996 Carruades de Lafite in a set of Zalto crystal stemware, and we all started to relax, as the sumptuous smell of grilled wagyu beef prepared by Fang Xing's personal chef wafted from the kitchen.

Sitting beside Fang Xing was his wife Yuan Ting. A slender, soft-spoken girl from the same township as Fang Xing, Yuan Ting's fair complexion contrasted with the black Burberry lace dress she wore. Her wavy hair was tied up in a sleek ponytail that reached down to her narrow shoulders. She looked radiant and sporty, with a tinge of light makeup on her face. As she sat down quietly beside her husband, her eager eyes rolled swiftly, as if wanting to join in our conversation. Her husband boasted to me how smart she was—Yuan Ting graduated with a first class honours from Singapore Management University, while he had only managed a second upper.

"Did you enjoy your time in Singapore?" I asked Yuan Ting, as she contoured her lips with a Bobbi Brown party rose semimatte lipstick.

"I love your country very much. I would love to go back there to live one day. It's such a good place to bring up children!" replied Yuan Ting, fondly patting her slightly bulging tummy. She looked at her husband, who gave a nod of approval.

"Fang Xing tells me a lot about you. You moved to Singapore at an early age?" Yuan Ting continued.

"No, no. I'm a true blue Singaporean. I was born there and grew up there," I replied.

Yuan Ting was about to ask another question, but Fang Xing cut in, "Hey Matt, do you play golf? Let's have a round sometime."

"Sure, but I'm not very good…"I started.

"Oh that's okay. I suck at it too. I just can't hit straight. But it's a good game to play anyway," he replied. "You should consider buying a golf membership in Beijing. Prices are skyrocketing nowadays! One of my friends just bought a golf membership at CITEE Golf Club[18], and guess what, he actually got his driver to drive a carload of

---

[18] This was a luxurious high-end golf course in Shunyi, a sprawling district cluttered with lavish mansions in the outskirts of Beijing. CITEE Golf Club was leveled in early 2013 after just a few years of operations. Its influential owner signed a design-build-operate-manage contract with Nicklaus Group of Companies (owned by legendary US golfer Jack Nicklaus) to build the Bear Club's first Nicklaus-branded

hundred-yuan notes into the clubhouse to pay for the membership!"
he continued.

I smiled. This reminded me of the news I read lately about the
villager who walked into a local car dealership with one-yuan notes
and fifty-fen coins to buy a car for his fiancée. The entire staff at
the dealership had to work overtime to count the money so that this
poor villager could drive the birthday gift home to his fiancée before
midnight.

A loud beep sounded from the kitchen. "The banana walnut cake
is ready!" Yuan Ting exclaimed.

As we finished dinner, we moved to the living room. Yuan Ting
was busy brewing coffee with the new Nespresso coffee maker Fang
Xing had bought her for her birthday. The coffee went very well with
the Yuan Ting's homemade cake. I saw a book *Du Lala Shengzhiji* 杜
拉拉升职记 lying on the coffee table.

"Do you want to borrow it? It's an excellent read," Yuan Ting
offered.

The story of Du Lala had taken China by storm. It was a fictitious
story about a young white-collar graduate by the name of Du Lala,
who decided one day she would no longer be buried in an obscure,
low-level position. She then developed a series of tactics to climb up
the corporate ladder in the fastest possible way. The story struck a
chord with many young job seekers. Du Lala quickly became their
role model, and an enduring icon of personal freedom and aspiration.
A movie based on the book had been released, followed by a thirty-
two-episode TV drama serial. Even a play was made. I borrowed the
book from Yuan Ting, even though I reckoned I only had enough
spare time from work to finish watching the movie.

The Chinese young adult like Du Lala grew up amid a seismic
shift in the country's value systems. Unlike their parents who suffered

---

golf club outside the US. The new Nicklaus Club Beijing opened in March 2014
amidst great fanfare.

through periods of upheaval such as the Great Leap Forward and the Cultural Revolution, the younger generations of Chinese have largely enjoyed a rapid improvement in their standard of living within a stable environment. Many of those born after 1978, when the late paramount leader Deng Xiaoping launched watershed reforms to open China's market, even take upward mobility for granted. From the decollectivization of agriculture to allowing foreign investors and local entrepreneurs to start businesses, Deng's policies fundamentally changed the Chinese economy. More importantly, it changed the mindsets of its young people. Getting rich was not just glorious. For many, it might well be the raison d'etre of their existence.

This obsession with getting richer faster seemed to be reflected in the incredible frequency at which people job-hopped. It wasn't just a case of waitresses or blue-collar workers changing jobs to get a 500 yuan raise in monthly salary. Highly-paid professionals like Fang Xing saw job-hopping as "the fastest way to get up the corporate ladder". Before joining All-Stellar, he had averaged just slightly over one year at each of his three previous jobs, he told us proudly. "I was able to negotiate a promotion and a bigger pay raise every time I moved."

"Doesn't it look bad on your resume if you move too frequently?" Randy asked in astonishment.

"There is no shame in doing whatever it takes to improve one's lot, right? Everyone works for himself. Local employers operate by that principle too. That's why stupid workers risk getting exploited and even go without pay. It's their job to keep their best employees happy, so that they will stay on." reasoned Fang Xing.

Of course, one could argue that Fang Xing had advantages that not many of his Chinese peers could match up to. An only child born into an upper middle-class Chinese family with important connections, he was endowed with the self-confidence of one who was very rarely rejected, or forced to deal with failure. Bilingual and well-connected, he was plugged into both the western mindset as well as China's big trends. So I fully believed his boast that he could set new rules of employer-employee engagement and command a higher premium for his services.

As I left Fang Xing's apartment that evening, I could not help wincing at how far I lagged him. As Fang Xing flaunted his possessions to me that evening, he was indirectly giving me a slap on my face. He had made it and I had not. It was a wake-up call for me. How was I going to catch up with Fang Xing? I was already in China and had no excuse for not making it big here.

<hr />

After seeing Fang Xing's penthouse, I started to get interested in the property craze around me.

The credit boom had leaked into the stock, commodity and property markets. Assets were starting to bubble effervescently. Every day, I could see advertisements for new property sales splattered across English and Chinese newspapers, and bumped into property agents in their smart pinstripes at every crossroad junction. Property developers were in for a ride of a lifetime, with new units snapped up at soft openings within minutes. The crowds at property showrooms were carefully controlled, each visitor given a queue number and date to return for the soft opening without any guarantee that there would be any units left. Visiting new property showrooms became common lunchtime activities for my Chinese friends. Some of them even made their property purchases over a phone call without ever once stepping foot into the showroom, egged on by enthusiastic housing agents.

"Let me tell you, 23,000 yuan (US$3,500) per square meter is a steal in Beijing's CBD. Just watch, it will rise to 35,000 yuan (US$5,500) by the middle of next year," Mr. Dai, the real estate agent who had helped me to rent my apartment, prophesized. He turned out to be dead accurate as prices skyrocketed far beyond the means of most middle-income families. It would climb further to reach almost RMB70,000 (US$11,000) per square meter by 2014, a jump of over 300 percent in just five years.

Chinese people seem to have a peculiarly intense love affair with property that bordered on a compulsive obsession. In other countries, owning a property means also owning the land it sits on. But in China, the land is owned by the government, which leases it to the property owner for a maximum of seventy years. After that time is up, theoretically, the property would be worthless. The poorly-built buildings probably would not last that long anyway. Yet, somehow, the craving to own a property is an essential part of Chinese culture.

Many of my friends, including Rebecca, actually confessed they felt incredibly insecure living in a rented place. The dream of property ownership extends all the way down to the lowest rungs of society. Lower-income Chinese like my house help, Cai *Ayi* (Aunt), worked seven days a week to keep up with the mortgage payments on a tiny one-bedroom apartment in her rural hometown in the eastern Chinese province of Anhui. Property prices there had become so inflated that it would take Cai Ayi another forty years to pay off the mortgage with her meager monthly earnings of several thousand yuan.

The property bubble was fuelled further by China's gigantic stimulus plan, with banks starting to lend aggressively to businesses which they believed were credit-worthy. The large SOEs became the biggest beneficiaries. However, amid dwindling external demand, expansion plans for most companies had stalled alongside deteriorating growth prospects. Since these firms had easy access to cheap credit, they amassed loans and poured the debt monies into the property market. Some even became lenders themselves, through special purpose financing vehicles, to less fortunate borrowers such as loan-hungry private enterprises which were given the cold shoulder by state banks. Almost every company in industries ranging from agriculture to consumer products reportedly dabbled into property investments, resulting in increasingly dangerous asset price bubbles.

Meanwhile, Chinese consumers started to exhibit their financial prowess abroad, snapping up property overseas in markets like the US, Canada and Australia, armed with their stronger currency. My friend, who was a real estate agent in Singapore, told me gleefully about his mainland Chinese customers, who hauled in suitcases of cash to snap up entire floors of private apartments in the Garden City.

What fascinated me most about this whole phenomenon was the way the ultra-wealthy in China tried to distinguish their property buying sprees from that of the masses. In an economy awash with loose credit, borrowing money was looked down upon in wealthy Chinese circles. As Fang Xing told me, "The rich bosses I hang around with think that using credit to buy houses—or any kind of big-ticket item for that matter—is only for the poor who cannot afford a high-end lifestyle."

His own apartment, of course, was paid with cash. And he was already planning to get a new bungalow in the elite Shunyi district with his next annual bonus. As for the remaining loose change, he was contemplating an exclusive golf membership at CITEE. I wondered if I would be able to afford an apartment when my annual bonus letter arrived in March. I could hardly wait.

> *Da Shou Da Jiao* 大手大脚: **Literally translated as "big hands and big feet," this idiom describes a person who spends lavishly and freely.**

CHAPTER 10

Departures

Ren Shou Liu Shi 人手流失

FEBRUARY ROLLED AROUND, AND WE were getting very close to holding DeeDee's second board meeting. But we were nowhere closer to convincing Chairman Zhou to adopt our new ideas to improve DeeDee's business processes, than we were after the first board meeting.

Fang Xing had started appearing more frequently in the office over the past four months. Susie, however, had faded out of the picture almost completely. She rarely even held her usual weekly teleconferences with the China team, but I did not dare to comment on this to anyone back in headquarters. With Randy focusing more on other projects as he spent more time in Singapore, I was glad to have Fang Xing's company. We grew a little closer over lengthy lunches with business contacts. One day, I decided to broach the topic that had been causing me sleepless nights.

"Fang Xing, what should we do with Chairman Zhou? He does not seem very interested to talk to us. I'm getting worried that our business plan would never get moving at this rate," I asked him, as we stumbled back to the office after yet another alcohol-laden lunch meeting with DeeDee's senior management.

During the lunch, I had almost worked myself up into a fit trying to convince Chairman Zhou to delegate less important decisions to middle management so we could all work more efficiently. But my efforts fell on deaf ears. I had used as obtuse and tactful an approach as I could possibly muster, but I was starting to wonder if that only made me look weak.

Fang Xing had been of no help at all in persuading Chairman Zhou. Instead of backing me up, he merely dropped an occasional joke to lighten the mood. By now, I knew better than to try to involve him in efforts to implement procedures that could potentially dilute the Lao Qianbei's control.

Fang Xing patted me on the back patronizingly. "You are worrying too much," he said, taking a leisurely sip of his Starbucks macchiato. I looked him enviously. He never needed the double shot expressos that I survived on to get through the all-nighters spent preparing for each weekly meeting with DeeDee.

"You foreigners worry too much," he continued. "In China, things work differently and it has been this way for thousands of years—don't expect to change things in just five months. And don't try too hard to push Lao Zhou to change or do things your way. You can influence him but don't do it in front of his employees. Chinese entrepreneurs don't like to be bossed around. They like to be in control."

I pondered this for a minute: did Fang Xing mean that if we gave Chairman Zhou sufficient autonomy, we would come out fine? How could it be that simple?

There was clearly so much that we needed to do to improve DeeDee's business processes, before it could achieve its ambitious growth targets and make its IPO dream feasible. Yet Chairman Zhou was sidelining and delaying much-needed reforms, while pursuing growth at any cost. But how much longer could it sustain these crazy double-digit growth rates? If this continued, wouldn't the company inevitably fall off the cliff?

Fang Xing rolled his eyes at my worries. "Even if DeeDee burns up all its cash, it can still sustain its growth through off-balance sheet borrowings until it raises IPO funds, right? As long as it can find a way to keep the ball rolling, it's not going to crash. Right now, the most important thing is to give the external world the confidence that the company is enjoying spectacular growth, then it can get all the new projects and loans it needs."

I wanted to pursue this further but Fang Xing walked off, texting a reply to a new message with cheeky smile on his face.

I sunk back into my ruminations about how quickly the cracks were surfacing in my once-pristine image of DeeDee—and of China as well. The country was reeling from reports that over 300,000 infants had been sickened by milk formula tainted by the deadly chemical Melamine, which had been added to increase the powder's protein content. A massive public outcry had erupted over the unscrupulous behavior of Chinese milk producers, further fuelled by revelations that the scandal had actually been discovered before the Beijing Olympics, but had been deliberately concealed so as not to overshadow the games. The World Health Organization labeled the incident as "a large scale intentional activity to deceive consumers for simple, basic, short-term profits."

I realized shortly after that the melamine scandal was not an isolated incident. Report after report about China's tainted products rolled out. There were fake eggs made of chemicals, fake mineral water that was actually bottled tap water, fake organic vegetables, fake luxury goods—the list went on.

Around me, friends were sharing their personal stories. One incident left a deep impression on my mind: my friend Wen Wen, a twenty-four-year-old sales manager at a Chinese high-end cosmetic products firm, resigned from her job in Beijing after falling out with her boss over his underhand tactics to cut costs. The company had built its reputation and credibility on the promise to customers that it would only use genuine organic ingredients. But as the customer base grew and profits rolled in, her manager had gotten greedy and ordered the company's production line to mix cheaper sub-standard products into the final product. When she protested that this was unethical, he had told her pointedly: "Be street-smart. Everyone does it. For most Chinese businesses and officials, the first pot of gold is never clean. And the rest of the pots probably aren't either."

For the idealistic and pampered Wen Wen, a single child who took great pride in her father's position as a low-level Communist Party official in western Sichuan province, and often boasted about her rich family's lofty business principles, this statement was like a tight slap to her face.

I was not as naïve as Wen Wen to believe China's corporate profits were generally pristine. But her account did challenge my previous optimistic view that Chinese businesses were fast adopting international best practices and were more inclined than before to do things above board. I started to look more warily at everything around me, from China's economic data to the ridiculously expensive baijiu I had bought for Chairman Zhou as a Chinese New Year gift, and even Rebecca's new Prada handbag. I wondered if these, too, were fake and adulterated.

Rebecca's dressing had become increasingly fancy over the past few months. She looked especially fetching when we met for dinner on February 9, 2009—the last day of the fifteen-day Lunar New Year festive period—in Solana, an upscale shopping mall in northeastern Beijing. Dressed in a white fur jacket and a fiery red Max Mara dress that was perfectly color-coordinated with her shiny Prada bag, she looked vastly different from the sweet young thing who had held my hand at Houhai last fall.

"Perhaps she is dressing up more to impress me," I thought to myself, rather pleased. "But I do hope she is not over-spending since her salary is so meager."

I bought her a pair of exquisite freshwater pearl earrings at Solana after dinner, and basked in her delight at the unexpected gift as we took a cab to her apartment.

"So why did you decide to stay in Beijing for Chinese New Year instead of going home to celebrate with your family?" asked Rebecca.

"Well, I have a lot of work to do here. And I also figured that spending the New Year here would be very different from what I experience back home. For the first time in my life, I bought firecrackers and set them off in the streets," I replied.

The abundance of pyrotechnics sold on many street corners turned Beijing into something of a warzone. One could be strolling serenely on the sidewalk and suddenly trip over frozen spit and charred firework ribbons, or find oneself stung by exploding fireworks set off just a few feet away by crazy revelers.

"I have an idea—let's light some firecrackers tonight when we get to your apartment?" I exclaimed excitedly.

I expected Rebecca to smile. Instead she turned to a new topic as if she never heard my suggestion. "How was the ride in Fang Xing's new Aston Martin?"

A little taken aback by her abrupt question, I stammered: "It was great! I've never sat in such a cool car before."

"Yeah, isn't the crimson exterior dashing? Fits Fang Xing's status perfectly," Rebecca beamed.

"Yes, indeed. And the exquisite cow leather seats and that sporty steering wheel. *Yifenqian yifenhuo* 一分钱一分货 (You get what you pay for). He invited you to sit in it too?" I asked.

Rebecca giggled. "Not only did I just sit on the passenger seat, Fang Xing actually let me race with it one full round along the Third Ring Road yesterday night. It took me only thirty-five minutes. It was eleven o'clock at night and with fewer cars on the road, I could really test the acceleration."

I stared at her incredulously. I could not visualize Rebecca behind the wheel of any vehicle swerving in and out of traffic in Beijing, let alone in a 4,300cc red Aston Martin owned by Fang Xing. And as if this was not enough, she added, "I chose the red color for him."

"Lucky you," I murmured, not knowing what exactly to make out of her latest comments. I wondered if she was the real first passenger in Fang Xing's car.

I peered curiously out of the cab window at the Third Ring Road, which was horribly jammed up. Traffic had come to a complete standstill; drivers and passengers leapt out of their cars to gape an unexpected spectacle. The Television Cultural Center, adjacent to the headquarters of China Central Television (CCTV), was engulfed in an inferno. We stared up in horror at the massive blaze, which had already consumed much of the forty-four-storey building. The wedge-shaped structure, whose radical design by Dutch architect Rem Koolhaas had earned it nicknames such as "Termite's Nest," cost an estimated US$730 million to build, and was scheduled to be completed in May 2009.

"Probably some fireworks were misfired into the building?" I speculated.

I was right—horribly so.

It turned out that CCTV officials had authorized a display of almost 700 highly explosive pyrotechnic devices on the construction site, ignoring three straight police warnings not to set off the fireworks. A brand new Beijing architectural icon went up in smoke, and it took no less than 600 firefighters to quell over five hours. One firefighter died, and seven other people were injured. The news was sidelined by state media.

We sat in silence for almost an hour. The cab had moved slightly over half a mile. Finally, we gave up and took the subway instead. I insisted on sending Rebecca home first. She lived in a *minzhai* 民宅, one of the public housing development projects scattered within the older districts of Beijing. While most of her single peers chose to live with their parents to avoid the extra burden of rental costs, she decided to be different and move out immediately after college. She shared an apartment with a housemate who worked at a local children's hospital nearby.

I knew she was hooked on American sitcoms, such as CBS' Big Bang Theory, NBC's Friends, and FOX's New Girl. For Rebecca, these shows glamorized the uninhibited freedoms enjoyed by young adults who lived on their own with their best friends and romantic partners, away from the prying eyes of helicopter parents. The condition of her place, however, was a far cry from the comfy apartments in big cosmopolitan cities like New York City featured in the sitcoms.

Many of these *minzhai* had no elevators. We climbed up the stairs to Rebecca's apartment on the sixth floor in pitch darkness, guided by the torch lights on our phones. Normally, the lights in the corridors and stairwells could be activated by sound sensors. But on that particular night, no amount of stamping or clapping triggered any lights. We stumbled to the door and Rebecca rummaged through her bag for her door keys. In the moonlight, I could barely make out the vague silhouettes of an old bicycle, carton boxes and rat poison canisters scattered along the corridor. There could not be a starker contrast between this place and Fang Xing's imposing mansion. I waved goodbye to Rebecca and stumbled my way out.

In the darkness, I felt the disappointment sink in. The fireworks I had hoped for in my relationship with Rebecca in the New Year had indeed happened. But far from being a romantic catalyst, it had filled me with even more foreboding about how quickly and unexpectedly things could blow up.

⊰─◆─⊱

Beijing roared back to life after its Lunar New Year hibernation. Shops re-opened, millions of migrant workers swarmed back, the smog returned, and we resumed our hectic work routine.

I was assigned to travel to a remote small county called Huangchuan, which was part of Xinyang, the southernmost city in Henan province. DeeDee was opening its third Henan farm there. Chairman Zhou wanted a representative from our fund, specifically a foreigner, to attend the opening ceremony and make a speech. This would impress local officials—hopefully enough to convince them to sell DeeDee farmland at prices much cheaper than the official published rates. The local officials tended to be more willing to offer incentives to businesses that brought in not only new jobs, but also glamorous foreign investors, since this was said to be a key item determining their promotion prospects.

Randy was supposed to fly from Singapore to represent our fund. But at the last minute, Susie sent me instead. I was mystified by this decision: Randy's distinctive Hong Kong accent and his sophisticated air would have made him the ideal person to make the speech. One could immediately tell he was not from mainland China, whereas I was sometimes mistaken for a southern Chinese—not always a flattering category even in modern China. In any case, Randy was the most senior after Susie in the China team, so he should have been sent to represent All-Stellar instead of me.

But here I was, in the middle of a duck farm, cutting countless yards of red ribbons with a beaming municipal governor. We were surrounded by a throng of enthusiastic local media, who dutifully reported our two speeches word for word the next day without any editorializing.

"We thank the government of Xinyang City for providing our company a platform to grow our business," I started off with my much improved Mandarin, adding the occasional local slang to show how localized, or *ruxiangsuisu* 入乡随俗—which literally means to enter a village and follow its customs—I had become.

"The local cooperatives in Huangchuan county are our highly valued partners. We will remain faithful in supporting the livelihoods of the local people," I declared, to roaring applause.

Next, I visited a local agriculture co-operative in the nearby city of Nanyang. It was part of my routine job of building relations with local officials wherever I went in China. I spent an entire morning in the office of a village elder, smiling until my cheeks ached at a presentation about an agriculture co-op that his son was in charge of. Again, I was surrounded by local party cadres, who kept staring at me to check if I shared their brimming pride in Nanyang's agricultural innovations. The truth was, I could hardly understand most of the presentation, since the officials were speaking in a local dialect which I had difficulty following.

The only thing that held my attention was a king-sized bed in a corner of the room. I knew it is common practice for the Chinese to take an afternoon nap. But it was still a novelty to see for myself how comfy a low-level county official's bed could be, decked out with four duck-feather-stuffed pillows, silk bedspreads and even a stuffed bear that the village elder claimed were his granddaughter's.

A village elder noticed me stealing longing glances at it, and smiled: "Don't you have a bed in your own office? I heard that some Europeans take naps too, but the Singaporeans and Americans don't do this. What a pity—this is a very good Chinese practice that should be adopted in all the top economies, it helps improve productivity."

I smiled weakly, not sure how to answer. Fortunately, the alcohol arrived. An hour later, I felt my inebriated body being carried onto a van and transported to a restaurant for more drinking, followed by a visit to a local market, a park and a labyrinth of aged buildings that my hosts introduced as the Ancient Government Office of Nanyang—a top tourist spot. Somehow I made it onto a plane. I finally woke up fully from my stupor at 11:00p.m. to find myself dragged by two air stewardesses down the aisle of an empty plane at the Beijing Airport.

A week later, Randy called me to explain why I had been dispatched to Henan instead of him.

"I've resigned, Matt," he said simply. "I'm moving my family back to Hong Kong."

"What...? Did something happen in Singapore...?" I was too shocked to complete my sentence.

Just a few weeks ago, Randy was still in excellent spirits as we enjoyed a Kobe steak together at Fang Xing's new apartment and made no mention of any desire to leave. Then again, Randy was always Mr. Sunshine, calm and composed with a perpetual smile imprinted on his face. I could never really tell what he was really feeling. Only someone with a discerning eye could detect any trace of frustration in him. It was only after working with him for a year that I had finally picked up on his angst about the lack of progress DeeDee was in getting bank financing.

"Everything is fine, Matt. I just miss the wonton noodle stall near my childhood home in Hong Kong too much," Randy laughed.

"Is it about Susie? Or is Russell giving you grief over DeeDee? This all seems so sudden," I pressed.

"Nah, I just got a decent job offer in Hong Kong, that's all. Suits me better—more financial modelling and less alcohol," he replied lightly.

"That's true, you are such a number-crunching genius that it would be a waste not to use that talent fully in your job," I agreed, careful to avoid any mention about how much he performed at drinking sessions when negotiating with Chinese partners. It was his biggest sore point that after three shots, he could not even add ten plus ten.

I never found out the real reason for Randy's abrupt departure, but I suspected Susie was a key factor in his decision. She had made clear that she thought Randy was not up to the job and aggressively pushed for Russell to promote her own guy, Fang Xing. With her territorial mindset of pre-emptively defending her territory against a new foreign employee, she never really gave Randy a chance to prove that he was neither a mole sent by Russell, nor a threat to her own position.

I had avoided her criticism so far since I was still very junior. I was also willing to take the plunge to move to China, and to build up rapport with Chairman Zhou's local team members such as Manager Wang and Mark. That seemed to convince Susie that I was still useful to her.

Spring finally arrived at last—I had survived an entire winter season in China. Green shoots appeared, and the early blooms produced wisps of pollen that made my eyes water. With the change of seasons came a new emergency.

In March, a day after the annual bonus was announced, Susie suddenly dropped a bombshell: she was resigning. She had barely spent a year with us.

She announced that she was leaving to move back to the UK for personal reasons. But we all knew the real push factor was the very public row she had with Russell over his refusal to sign off on one of her expense claims. She had insisted that the claim of over US$10,000 was a legitimate expense because she had hosted eight distant relatives of a top Chinese leader to a private dinner party. This meeting, she claimed, could potentially give All-Stellar access to exclusive deals and pave the way for it to collaborate closely with state-linked funds.

Russell did not buy this explanation. "Where are those exclusive deals to show for all your outrageous expense claims?" he had demanded. "And in any case, our fund has a duty to our Limited Partners to steer clear of any actions that could be construed as bribery or shady dealings with a PEP."

Some Chinese bankers in our business circles could hardly believe how stupid we were. In their eyes, Susie's business relationships were so valuable that Russell should have done everything to retain her. In fact, US$10,000 seemed quite a bargain to meet with such an illustrious family—if Susie's claim were true. The gold coins hidden in Mid-autumn Festival mooncake gift boxes for big clients were already worth much more than that, they reasoned.

But some of my western banking contacts insisted that Russell was right to fight with Susie, who had not provided any concrete proof that she had indeed held a real princeling party. More importantly, condoning such a practice could potentially get All-Stellar and its American investors in trouble with the US regulators.

⸺⸱⸱⸺

With Susie's departure, Russell came up to Beijing more often than before, often bringing his trusted aide, Gary, along. Most of their trips were never more than two days, which included twelve hours of flying time. This did not give them much time with us on the ground, but that was not the biggest of our concerns.

All-Stellar's relationship with Chairman Zhou was getting increasingly rocky. Russell and Gary had replaced Susie and Randy on DeeDee's company board of directors. Unfortunately, neither of the men spoke a word of Mandarin. So they passed all messages to Chairman Zhou through either Fang Xing or me.

This greatly displeased the Lao Qianbei, who felt that he did not get the respect he deserved. Based on the unspoken rules of hierarchy and business etiquette, he felt that only someone of Susie's rank or higher was qualified to talk to him about changing the way he ran his company. In the past, Susie had been able to pick up the phone and ring Chairman Zhou directly to discuss issues whenever they cropped up.

But now, even important issues like hiring a suitable Chief Financial Officer (CFO) were left to me, the most junior member of the China team, to negotiate with Chairman Zhou. Russell believed that DeeDee desperately needed to install a CFO to get the company's finances in shape for the IPO. The ideal candidate would speak English, understand international accounting standards, and have many years of experience dealing with international auditors. More importantly, we needed a CFO who was not simply a yes-man—a problem prevalent in many Chinese companies where one single major shareholder unilaterally made all the decisions. Since hiring international talent was All-Stellar's area of expertise, Russell went ahead to approach headhunters, who conducted a detailed market search and introduced several candidates to us.

I was dispatched to present the options to Chairman Zhou. No sooner had I outlined our recommendation for a compensation package—RMB1 million (US$160,000) in base salary with cash bonus and share options—than the Lao Qianbei threw a fit. "That's way too much! I won't pay more than a quarter of a million! How dare you decide for me who my CFO is and how much to pay him?" he yelled.

I reported this to Fang Xing. He smiled smugly. "I knew it. Let's just wait and see. The winds move so fast in China."

Before long, Gary even took the initiative to come on his own every week to bond with the DeeDee team over rowdy drinking sessions. He held his drink well with our Chinese counterparts, but his confrontational personality was starting to get on their nerves. Most of the older DeeDee managers did not understand Gary's English, but his hostile non-verbal cues sent a clear message to them that this western investor was disgusted by the way they were running DeeDee.

Banging the boardroom table one day, Gary interrogated Bingbing. "It's already end of May. Why is the revenue for the first five months less than 40 percent of the budget[19] for the first half? Give me a satisfactory explanation," he demanded.

The diminutive accountant raised her glasses up a notch, and stuttered, "Mr. Samuelson, we copied the number straight out of the company's accounting system. You can be assured that our

---

[19] Companies develop detailed financial budgets at the beginning of the year to guide the company to achieve planned sales, costs, assets and liabilities and cash flows for the year. As budget inputs have to come from all subsidiaries, related companies and departments, preparing, adjusting and finalizing the budget is one of the most painful processes the company's finance team has to undertake each year.

accounting system is extremely scientific and reliable. If you give me some time, I will thoroughly investigate and find out how the number was derived."

Gary laughed incredulously. "So you don't know? Does anyone here in this whole freaking company even know the real financial state it's in?"

Bingbing dissolved into a puddle of tears. Her colleagues muttered curses under their breath.

"I would cry too at the sad state of affairs in this company," Gary huffed. "If I weren't genuinely concerned about reforming this company, do you think I'd be sitting here trying to get to the bottom of this crazy mess?"

I hastily jumped in to translate: "Mr. Samuelson says he would also shed tears because he sees this company like his own first born son. He feels deep joy when the company is doing well and feels deep pain when it faces any problems. He says he is willing to join hands with all of you here to eradicate problems and bring DeeDee to new heights. Please understand and pardon his manner of speaking which is more suited to western boardrooms, where direct and strong feedback is given."

Bingbing sniffed. "Huang zong, can you please translate more truthfully next time? Some of us understand English, you know."

⬤◆⬤

Four days later, Gary e-mailed me. "We need to talk to DeeDee again. Let's discuss what I can do to improve the situation at Chairman Zhou's. I will be up in Beijing next Monday."

At first, I was gratified that Gary seemed so eager to discuss ways to mend relations with DeeDee's staff. My elation lasted all of twenty minutes, when Gary's secretary in Singapore clued me in on the real reason why he was making another trip to Beijing so soon.

"You blocked out six hours in Gary's schedule for meeting DeeDee?" Annie called me to complain.

"Is that too little?" I asked, alarmed. "Would Gary like me to arrange dinner with the DeeDee team too? Nine hours to resolve twelve outstanding issues is ambitious I know, but…"

"Are you crazy? Two hours is more than enough for Gary *lah*," she retorted.

"Why would Gary want to fly all the way to Beijing for such a short meeting?" I stuttered.

"Oh Matt, don't you get it? After this flight, he will make it to the Solitare PPS Club."

My jaw dropped. To become a member of this exclusive club, a traveler had to accrue a cumulative S$250,000 (US$180,000) in spending on Singapore Airlines Suites, First or Business Class travel within five consecutive years. Gary had the DeeDee project to thank for his accelerated ascent into this stratospheric V.V.I.P. club.

Monday afternoon's meeting with DeeDee accountants passed quickly. Gary asked a few curt questions and then cut short the meeting, saying he had another important appointment. We sped off in a shiny Audi A8 that Gary had booked for the evening.

"You know I sit on the board of one of the biggest energy conglomerates in Hong Kong. They are so organized and on the ball," Gary began, after handing the chauffeur a slip of paper with an address that made the latter raise his eyebrows slightly. "Their CFO, an American I hired onto the team after our investment, makes sure that his finance manager and Chinese accountants always give me the monthly reports on time. I can never find a single grammatical or calculation error in them!"

I knew he was indirectly criticizing me for failing in my job as an asset manager. But I knew better than to try to explain to him why my own reports were always late because I had so many numerical discrepancies to fix.

For example, the count of ducks at each farm was almost always wrong, and the monthly sales numbers did not tally either. Sometimes, it was due to sloppy calculations by the local farm managers. More often, it was because we had difficulties reconciling our excel spreadsheets and reports, since the Chinese count numbers by *wan* 万, or ten thousands ('0,000), unlike the western system of counting by the thousands ('000). For 50,000 tons of duck feed, a careless Chinese accountant would input the number "5" into the spreadsheet, and then I'd have to waste time later changing it to "50" after detecting the error. After a while, I resigned myself to the fact that old habits die hard for my Chinese counterparts, and got used to being the only one who cared enough to correct every single discrepancy.

However, Gary, who had barely clocked thirty days in China until this week, blew up every time I tried to bring up the topic. "Why can't they just switch to thousands? It's just simple math, isn't it? Aren't they supposed to always get the top scores in Math?"

I kept quiet, while Gary continued ranting. "You know, we should really fire that stupid accountant of Chairman Zhou's. I don't care what connections she has with his relatives. Incompetence should not be tolerated in any organization."

Just then, we pulled up in front of a courtyard emblazoned with the red bright letters "Maggie's". It looked like any ordinary bar that foreigners liked to frequent—until we walked inside.

It turned out to be one of the most infamous bars in town, touted as *the* place in Beijing for foreigners to enjoy a sailor's den experience— washing down their wanderlust with strong ale and picking up girls for a one-night stand. A captain's bell hung above the bar. Gary strutted up to it, reeling a little from having downed three shots of vodka in as many minutes. He rang it thrice. To my amazement, this resulted in a standing ovation from all four corners of the pub—Gary was going to buy drinks for the entire house!

As if on cue, scantily dressed girls with frosty pink lipsticks sauntered into the room. Most of these girls were not of Chinese descent. "Go ahead and choose a girl you like. But come back with a solution to resolve the issues at DeeDee by the end of the night." Gary ordered me, as he boldly scanned a leggy Russian blonde, and a curvaceous Mongolian maiden up and down. He waved me away, and I knew that signaled the end of the "important evening work meeting" that he had told Russell and Chairman Zhou he would be having tonight.

I conveyed Gary's credit card to the bartender, and discovered that this was hardly the first time that he had treated the house. Big spenders like Gary helped buffer Maggie's against unexpected dry spells, like the few months leading up to the Beijing Olympics when it was forced to close. During that period, the Chinese authorities reportedly clamped down on activities that might affect the city's image.

Three hours later, it was time for me to send a drunken Gary back to his hotel. The Russian chick went along in the chauffeured car. He had spent over RMB12,000 (US$1,900) that night.

Very early the following morning, I was woken up by a call from Chairman Zhou: "The behavior of your small boss Gary over the past few weeks has been unacceptable. People like him are not welcome in my boardroom. Please convey my message to your big boss Russell not to send Gary to meet with us anymore."

"Chairman Zhou, Gary may have his own style of communicating which may appear unfriendly, but he is really trying to help. Gary is a very sincere man," I began. I immediately regretted my choice of words as soon as they came out of my mouth.

Chairman Zhou dropped all pretense of being civil. "Sincere? More like disrespectful! Offensive! Shameful!" he yelled. "He thinks he is so smart that he can solve all our problems and he interrogates my staff as if they are criminals. He knows nothing about China or about us. He is only making the matters worse! I'm banning him from all future meetings. And if this bald fatty ever steps into DeeDee's premises again, I myself will boycott all the board meetings."

I soon found out that Chairman Zhou did not just throw Gary out. He was ready to alienate the rest of the All-Stellar team as well. A week later, I met with Mark Hensworth, who had thankfully warmed up enough to become my regular drinking buddy. He told me about an intense meeting that had taken place on the same night that Gary had been rocking the captain's bell and the Russian blonde at Maggie's.

Mark recounted how Chairman Zhou had summoned a dozen employees, including Manager Wang and himself, back to work at nine o'clock at night. Zhou had decided to charge ahead with buying more duck farm assets in southern China, with or without All-Stellar's approval.

"Wang, call Yan tomorrow. Tell him we are ready to sign the agreement to acquire his duck farm operations in Yunnan," the Lao Qianbei had instructed. "We will pay him thirty percent upfront within two weeks. The rest will come through bank loans. Tell him we are already in discussions with the local banks to close the funding gap."

After firing off more orders to the other employees, he turned to Mark: "Call Manager Li and tell him to fly to Kunming on the earliest possible flight tomorrow to sign the agreement. He has our *gongzhang* 公章[20] for the Guangxi province subsidiary. You know who I am referring to, right? Li Yuechao?"

Mark shook his head. There were just too many Li's and Yuechao's in the company for him to keep track of. He was also confused why

---

[20] The gongzhang is a red company chop issued by the local Administration of Industry of Commerce in China, a licensing and regulatory body akin to the state revenue agency in the US. It is like the company's thumbprint or seal, and is needed in almost every aspect of business operations, from opening bank accounts to contract signing. It is so essential in Chinese business that it is not uncommon for a company's chairman to carry it physically with him at all times.

he was being roped in to handle such errands when his role was to manage communications with external parties like All-Stellar.

"Our Guangxi General Manager. Make sure you do not call the wrong Li Yuechao, the assistant finance manager at Rizhao muncipality in Shandong province. Do you understand?" continued Chairman Zhou, spewing globs of saliva over Mark's hand and notepad as he worked himself up into a fit.

"From now on, Mark, you don't need to communicate with anyone from All-Stellar, except Xiaohuang. But you can only talk to him when I give you permission. After this Yunnan deal is done, you can tell him that we cannot afford to waste any more of our precious time at their board sessions. We will not be writing any long meeting minutes or generating useless reports. We need to *ai-pee-oo* fast. We will teach them how to do things *our* way."

> *Ren Shou Liu Shi* 人手流失: **Literally translated as the "loss of people's hands," refers to staff departures.**

CHAPTER 11

Horse Cloud

Gao Shou Ru Yun 高手如云

AFTER LEARNING ABOUT CHAIRMAN ZHOU'S outburst, Russell finally decided it was time to switch tactics. He sent me to play golf with the Lao Qianbei.

Originally, he wanted both Fang Xing and I to work on improving the relationship with Chairman Zhou, but thought the better of it after the former—who had just been promoted to director of the China office—complained about how much work he already had to do. Fang Xing had managed to impress Russell with his uncanny ability to bring a constant stream of new deals to the table. At every conference call, he would drop names of illustrious Chinese businessmen that he had just secured meetings with, and rattle off new investment ideas. These included a convertible bond investment into a major third-party logistics player in Shenzhen which was supporting the millions of small businesses selling stuff through Taobao every day; a Series C funding round in a three-dimensional printing start-up in Guangzhou; and a joint venture with a major Hunan-based pharmaceutical conglomerate.

But as the weeks passed, we discovered that his proposals

invariably came to nought. Still, Fang Xing always had entirely valid and reasonable reasons: the intervention of a state-owned monopoly to block foreign investments, or new policies that made the business environment too volatile for us to risk entering a particular sector immediately. Once, Fang Xing was straightforward in his answer: "We can't invest in this plantation deal because a powerful official told us not to, it's his territory." And that ended the conversation. Despite our best efforts to probe into the identity of the official, Fang Xing was absolutely tight-lipped.

Russell was not sure what to make of a subordinate like Fang Xing, who was always very respectful but who made clear he would not be controlled or ordered around. With Susie gone, Russell was careful not to do anything to trigger her protégé's departure as well, since we needed a new China rainmaker. I had yet to build a deep contact base across China, so the task of tackling the tumultuous relationship with Chairman Zhou naturally became my main responsibility.

As it turned out, Chairman Zhou was also increasingly keen to talk to me. He saw me as an important chess piece. He knew that our Singapore team trusted me more than Fang Xing, so I was the better conduit to convey his messages to Russell and press for decisions. Since neither Chairman Zhou nor Russell could pick up the phone to call each other due to language differences, I became their go-between.

We started meeting regularly at Chairman Zhou's local members-only golf club. His game was as unpredictable and volatile as Beijing's air quality. On good days, Chairman Zhou could shoot what Tiger Woods carded on a bad day, which was not bad for an amateur golfer.

The first three trips, on the surface, seemed like an utter waste of time. We only spoke when Chairman Zhou felt like it, which was once or twice every hour, and only about the most trivial topics. I felt a bit like a caddy instead of a companion golfer since I was always obsequiously rushing to help him find his ball in the bushes, or compliment him profusely on his strokes. But he seemed to enjoy my company as he practiced his strokes, perhaps because he did not have to worry about "losing face" in front of a junior acquaintance like me.

As time passed, we established an unspoken rapport. I found myself more and more at ease, and was able to play my normal game without having to let him win every time. We even started to bet on who would win each game, with the loser buying a round of cheap beer.

For the first time, I was so thankful I had heeded advice from my bosses in my previous company to take up golf as a business skill. At that time, in my early twenties, I did not think much of hitting a small white ball over 200 acres of landscaped grass, preferring the rough and tumble of a soccer match or basketball game. But now that I was in China, golf took on a whole new meaning. It paved the way for closing secret deals, it provided a gel to mend strained business relationships, and—as I would later learn in a dramatic manner—it could also offer a platform to kill deals off.

My Chinese golf buddies told me that this was *the* sport for the highest echelons of society in China. While golf had a relatively short history in emerging China with the first golf course opening in 1984 in Guangdong province, the heart of Deng's experiment with Chinese capitalism, it held special meaning in the eyes of the Chinese. It was a trendy and healthier way to discuss business outside the usual venues such as the smoke-clogged KTV lounge or a restaurant where heavy drinking was invariably expected. Mega deals were often struck on the golf course, sometimes on the 19th hole. This is a slang term for a pub or bar where golfers hang out for a drink after golf. In China, the 19th hole would also take on a human form, referring to the karaoke hostesses that golfers would bring home after a post-game KTV session.

Many Chinese golf aficionados loved to discuss about how observing a person play golf could accurately reveal his disposition and temperament. Such characteristics would manifest themselves in business dealings. For example, if a person cheats at golf, one should think twice about partnering with him in business. How the person manages his game and his etiquette on the golf course tells you a lot about him.

My golfing experiences in Asia and the Americas turned out to be a useful tool to engage Chairman Zhou's interest, since he aspired to play on the world's most prestigious greens one day after he retired. I regaled him with descriptions of the various golf courses that I had played at during my years as a business analyst with the Singapore conglomerate. His favorite was an exclusive golf course in Santos, Sao Paulo. Owned by a rich Japanese family, it was set in a pristine Atlantic forest with a unique mix of tropical and subtropical broadleaf forests, grasslands and savannas. "That day, there were just seven players, including our party teeing off," I boasted. Chairman Zhou's eyes had widened with something almost akin to envy as he surveyed the rowdy groups of Chinese golfers around us. I heard him muttering "Santos, Santos" under his breath.

⎯⎯◆◆⎯⎯

We walked up quietly together onto the first tee box and got ready. As I splattered sunscreen on my face and arms, I saw Chairman Zhou fiddle with the old driver he had pulled out from his well-used gold and white golf bag. Despite his ambition to play at high-end golf estates, he could not override his thrifty habits, and stuck to using the same set of clubs he had bought eight years ago when he picked up the sport.

His shot had landed slightly behind mine, about ten yards away. I respectfully waited as he gestured to his favorite buxom caddie to hand him a seven-iron. His practice swing was great, but he eventually duffed his shot. I felt a surge of confidence as I swung my nine-iron nicely to set up a birdie.

We finished our game, and he fished out two crisp 100-yuan notes to tip our caddies, who squealed with delight and thanked him profusely. Then he turned to me, eager for yet another well-worn story. "Tell me about that Royal Colombo Golf Club in Sri Lanka again?" he asked.

"It's the second oldest Royal Golf Club outside the United Kingdom," I started off, knowing that this factoid was always something of special fascination to him. I described the course, and the Guv'nors Bar at the clubhouse, with its regal décor including the names of past captains and Presidents carved on its archival wall. "I only scored 108, thirty-six shots over par, that day and decided to have an English mojito to console myself. I took an extra ten minutes to sip it because it was so delicious. If I did not have that drink at the bar, I could have been killed," I said melodramatically.

"When I got back to my car, the driver was panicking and told me that a bus bomb just went off about ten miles away from where we were on the main road. Many passersby died on the spot and there were severe casualties. It dawned on me that if we had started to drive ten minutes earlier, we could easily have been at the epicentre of the bombings."

For some strange reason, Chairman Zhou enjoyed listening to that story over and over again. He liked close shaves and skirting the edge of the cliff, and once commented that if he were not so consumed with expanding his duck empire, he might have taken up sky-diving as a hobby. He definitely had a huge risk appetite in his investments.

Once, he had invested RMB10 million (US$1.5 million) of his savings in a jade excavation site that his friend said had just been discovered in Mutianyu—one of several sites for tourists to climb the Great Wall—in the 1990s without even bothering to see the site first. "My wife was very furious because that money was supposed to be for our son's college education, and to purchase a house for his wedding gift," he recalled. "My son was just one year old at that time. I thought, what the heck, big risks means big money. If we make a killing, we will have enough money to secure a place at the best university overseas for our son, right?"

It turned out that the jade was real. But corruption and pilfering whittled away Chairman Zhou's share of the profits, so he just made a meager 5 percent return at the end. "At least I didn't lose money," he said cheerfully.

Several weeks later, as we ended our golf session, Chairman Zhou lamented, "Your bosses sitting in Singapore really don't understand China. Do they even understand our industry or try to help us solve our problems? All they know is to organize board meetings, ask us for useless monthly reports, and criticize the way I run my business."

I decided we had reached a comfort level where I could be frank with him. "Chairman Zhou, all these board meetings are designed to help you run your business better and make rational decisions. This is the best way we can help you to solve your problems. We also feel misunderstood and disappointed when you ignore our advice. For example, you really shouldn't have just signed the contract to buy the Yunnan duck farms without our approval. When Russell heard the news, he was upset and scolded me for a long time. That made my life very difficult."

"Ah, *xiaohuozi* 小伙子, you don't know, that was a rare opportunity. *Lao Yan* was selling his Yunnan farms dirt-cheap. He had some financial troubles, so we acquired the farms at an unbelievable price," Chairman Zhou explained, addressing me with a slightly derogatory term that meant "young fellow". This label was typically used by older people to address youngsters who did not know any better.

"But if an asset is not in the company's best long-term interests, even getting a super good price may not be the best decision," I protested. "We have expertise that may benefit you greatly. Wouldn't it be better to involve us in your decision-making process so that we can help you make the best investments?"

Chairman Zhou shrugged. "Please manage your bosses for me," he said, patting my shoulder.

I was heartened that he did not flare up at me. Even though we still did not see eye to eye on many matters, I sensed that he was starting to understand my point of view, even if he had too much pride to heed any advice from a young lad in his early thirties.

Part of the reason why he resisted listening to me or to any "outsider" was psychological—the cut-throat business environment had conditioned him to trust only in his own judgment and nobody else's. As he shared with me once, he always assumed people, even his own relatives, were out to cheat him, while bigger companies were always bent on grabbing his share of the pie.

It wasn't just him. A senior European diplomat once told me that he had lived in China long enough to learn the golden rule: doubt everyone and everything. And many of my Chinese friends claimed that suspicion and skepticism was increasingly a social norm in China. A key reason, it seemed, was that China lacked a rule of law. Many small businesses and individuals found out the hard way that the legal system was still relatively undeveloped and not sophisticated enough to protect personal interests. This was unlike the systems in the West, where individuals with grievances could take on even the largest corporations through lawsuits and generally count on a fair hearing.

For Chairman Zhou, building an inner circle of employees whom he could absolutely trust in the company was often more important than hiring the best talent. Typical of many Chinese family-run businesses, DeeDee was filled with Chairman Zhou's close relatives and time-tested friends. They ensured that Chairman Zhou's authority was unchallenged in virtually every situation. Employees with no ties to the founder generally did not get the most senior positions in the company. The majority of the extended Zhou family's wealth was also tied up in the duck farm business.

But even among his loyal supporters, Chairman Zhou was still intensely selective about who he trusted. Only people who had made enough sacrifices for him were allowed into his inner ring and his strategic planning meetings. Mark, the board secretary, and other senior executives were often left out of meetings, so information across the company was often disjointed. In fact, it seemed Chairman Zhou deliberately created the information dissymmetry to keep a complete version of the facts obscured from anyone who had no need to know.

Finally, after over a dozen golf sessions with him, he invited me to his office one Wednesday afternoon. My eyes had lit up at the significance of this—Susie used to have secret regular meetings with him on Wednesday afternoons as well. It looked like Chairman Zhou now trusted me enough to have me take her place, since he did not invite Fang Xing.

Exactly at three o'clock, I walked into his office with a little swagger in my gait. The room was scantily furnished, with some faded wall cabinets which looked like they were culled from one of the second-hand flea markets in Beijing. A gaudily decorated purple gift box sitting on his table immediately caught my eye.

"Who is that for? For your *xiaosan* 小三 (mistress)?" I asked teasingly, pointing at the box.

In Singapore or in the West, it would have been a huge faux pas to mention a touchy topic like mistresses so directly to a business contact.

But in China, mistresses had become so in vogue that they were openly boasted about by nouveau riche entrepreneurs and officials, who were trying to outdo each other in wealth trappings. Here, mistresses are named after numbers. The words *xiaosan* means "Little Three" in Mandarin, third in position after the lawful wife who is second in the household. The husband, the head, is number one. A second mistress is called *xiaosi* 小四 (Little Four), and so on. It is quite socially acceptable for very rich older men to find mistresses a few decades younger than themselves. Once, a drunken county official confided to me that he had felt inadequate after he attended a "no-wives-only-mistresses" gathering with his rich friends, and realized that his high school-age chick was not as classy or elegant as the other well-educated Little Threes in the room. He had asked if I could introduce some "sophisticated foreign women" whom he could bring as a date to the next gathering to "recover his face".

As for Chairman Zhou, while he was probably too thrifty to splurge on Little Fours or Little Fives, I could tell that he was not lacking in flings with buxom young things. But he probably exercised the same amount of caution and wariness about picking a Little Three as he did with his inner ring of employees, so I had yet to hear him mention that special someone.

Today, he seemed a little antsy when I asked him about the gift box. I could see his pulse quicken a little as he took a deliberately slow sip from his tea flask, but he replied nonchalantly: "Just a pair of Hello Kitty crystal earrings for my son's girlfriend. He is quite serious about her, so he is bringing her to dinner at home for the first time to meet the parents. He said she likes this brand of jewelry."

"Meet the parents? That is a big thing in China!" I said lightly. A question crossed my mind: with his net worth and social status, he could surely afford something even more expensive for a potential daughter-in-law?

"I grew up so poor that I only ate meat once a year, during the family reunion dinner on the eve of Chinese New Year," mused Chairman Zhou, talking more to himself than to me. "So I still can't bear to waste any money on expensive food, not to mention impractical frills like crystal earrings. If it were a gold ring, it can at least be a store of value for rainy days. But this...useless plaything, I cannot understand why young people nowadays cannot be more practical in what they like."

I smiled. Chairman Zhou was indeed thrifty to the extreme. When he did not have any business entertainment at night, he would always head home for a simple home-cooked meal. Our meals together were always in hole-in-the-wall eateries that served cheap but excellent local delights. Even his gifts to clients and suppliers during key traditional Chinese festivals such as Mid-Autumn Festival were modest, in contrast to the extravagantly-decorated mooncake boxes sold by five-star hotels that were all the rage among businesses at that time. While China's deeply-ingrained gifting etiquette meant that Chairman Zhou could not ignore the custom, he insisted on ordering his mooncakes from cheaper local pastry shops and wrapping them himself with gold paper.

"All the mooncakes in Beijing are made in the same few factories in the outskirts of Beijing," he declared. "They just slap on a beautiful box and wrapper, and charge you ten times more. I'm not wasting money on this rubbish."

A steady rapping on the door interrupted our conversation. The door swung open and Manager Wang hurried into the room.

"Ah you're here at last! Did you see the fax that came in last night from *Lao Li*, the feed supplier from Linyi city in Shandong province? He is raising prices by 10 percent starting next month!" Chairman Zhou cursed, letting out a string of expletives.

Manager Wang started to talk about rising inflation, but was drowned out.

"He has the audacity to raise prices without even giving me a call in advance! Must be that smart-ass son of his who is taking over the business from his father," roared Chairman Zhou, slamming down his tea flask. "Get *Lao Cai* from the Fine Feed Suppliers Group on the line later. I think they have a Linyi sales team. We haven't given them much business since last year. Get a quotation from them for delivery next week."

Manager Wang disappeared immediately.

Chairman Zhou turned to me. "Xiaohuang, since I like you, I

will tell a piece of good news: I have already made a handshake deal to acquire some new duck farms in Guangxi province. We will need to sign the paper contract once the Yunnan deal is complete and we have found enough cash to fund it."

He smiled broadly, but I turned pale. He had once again flouted our investment agreements, which stipulated that DeeDee must get All-Stellar's approval before it could sign on new projects.

"I need you to tell your bosses to come up with ideas about how to secure some new loans for DeeDee so that we can fund our new acquisitions. I'm sure they will agree that this is the best way they can help us to achieve our IPO dream."

I took a deep breath and started to speak as fast as I could before he cut me off: "Chairman Zhou, I am sure that you have heard our point of view many times at our board meetings. We do not want the company to commit to any new projects at this stage, since this would put severe stress on its balance sheet and cash flow. If DeeDee were to apply for a listing in such a state, its IPO valuation and investor interest will surely be impacted…"

"But I have already said many times at board meetings that we need to get a lot of new, important projects to impress investors and make our *ai-pee-oo* big. Your bosses will get me the money and loans to make these projects happen. This is easy for All-Stellar to do because the Chinese government's stimulus plan will make it easier for private companies to get loans," he growled.

I raised my eyebrows as high as I could go to signal to Chairman Zhou that we both knew this was fiction: Russell and Gary had spoken at length about how the stimulus money flooding into the Chinese banking system was largely benefitting the state-owned enterprises, while small businesses were still largely left in the cold.

"Chairman Zhou, Russell has said that we will explore law-abiding and above-board ways to get loans for DeeDee. But we must also be prepared that if DeeDee were not able to get the new bank loans, it would be operating on negative working capital[21] in three months' time," I said.

Scowling, Chairman Zhou picked up the phone and called a customer to discuss raising prices. After the second heated phone call, he motioned for me to leave.

I left dejected. When I started working with DeeDee, I had grand ambitions of using the new asset management system All-Stellar had prescribed to transform the company into an international powerhouse, and enhance shareholder value. Six months later, it all looked like a sham. Now, it was a struggle to get Chairman Zhou to even attend the regular board meetings.

At Russell's meetings with All-Stellar's investors, the latter would grill him on how he planned to mitigate the problems with DeeDee. He had no good answers, so he would turn around and lash at me for not managing the relationship with Chairman Zhou better.

It was then that I truly began to appreciate the importance of guanxi as the basis of business deals in China. It was conventional wisdom that investment agreements and legal contracts in China are invariably worthless pieces of paper, unless they are backed by a solid business relationship. But now I finally understood why Susie liked to say that the defining characteristic of a China PE hand was the ability to leverage multiple power relationships to fix problems that neither the law nor money could really solve.

I found myself wishing I knew more people who had influence over Chairman Zhou, so that I could use those relationships to subtly shift his thinking and bring him around to our point of view. But I knew no such person. The only person I could recall the Lao Qianbei openly expressing deep admiration for—besides Mao Zedong and top

---

[21] Negative working capital means liabilities the company needs to pay within one year exceed the current assets to be monetized over the same period. This is detrimental to a company's health because it would not be able to continue running for much longer unless it gets more capital.

Communist Party leaders—was Ma Yun 马云, who founded Chinese e-commerce giant Alibaba in 1999.

Until then, I only knew Ma Yun, whose name can be literally translated as "Horse Cloud," as the man whom Rebecca credited for elevating her to Cloud Nine every day, when she browsed Taobao, China's answer to Amazon.

The first time I saw her on an online shopping conquest, she was so excited that I thought she had just struck jackpot. It turned out that she had just grabbed the last five polka dot dresses of varying shades that was being sold at half price, just forty yuan each. I watched her negotiate for ten additional freebies from the online seller, typing furiously in a heated debate replete with exclamation marks and emoticons. Finally, the seller caved in after she threatened to post a horrible post-purchase rating. Rebecca triumphantly completed the purchase through Alipay, Alibaba's online payments service within mere seconds. "On to the next purchase: orange-scented, four-ply toilet paper with gold trim for my mom," she declared exuberantly.

One of the crown jewels of Alibaba, Taobao was China's dominant e-commerce marketplace. It was cluttered with virtually every type of product you could find on the planet, from live fish to smart phones and exotic toilet paper. Alibaba has eight other lines of businesses ranging from online payments to an e-commerce platform for small businesses and cloud computing.

As I researched more about Jack Ma, as he is better known to the English-speaking world, I started to appreciate why Chairman Zhou was so attracted to this larger-than-life business leader.

Ma Yun was already famous for building one of the most successful business empires in China, tapping the immense power of the internet to help enterprises and individuals buy and sell goods.

A few years later, when Alibaba launched the world's biggest IPO ever in history, every detail of Ma's colourful personality as well as his journey from an English teacher to a billionaire entrepreneur would be widely reported by international media. In September 2014, Alibaba would make history by raising over US$20 billion on the New York Stock Exchange. It would surge 38 percent on its IPO debut and net underwriters of the sale a windfall of over US$300 million. Among the winners in its IPO were reportedly scions of top Chinese party leaders who had invested in the company prior to its listing. Reflecting Ma's strong official connections, he would later be seen accompanying top party leaders such as the current President Xi Jinping on state visits to South Korea and the US.

But way back then, in 2009, Chairman Zhou had no way of knowing that Alibaba and Ma Yun would become such a global sensation. All he knew was that Ma Yun was being praised in local media for having the qualities of a Chinese entrepreneur that he himself was trying to cultivate—an iron constitution, a "never-say-die" attitude, ingenuity and ambition. All these traits, he felt, formed the core of the new Chinese entrepreneurial spirit that has spawned so many billionaires and built up China's prosperity in the process.

I decided to use Ma Yun to help me engage Chairman Zhou at our next weekly meeting.

"I was reading one of Ma Yun's interviews with the media, and I'm very inspired," I began. "He constantly emphasized *jianchi* 坚持 (perseverance), and said this trait was one of the vital keys to his success."

The Lao Qianbei beamed. "You know Ma Yun too? He is indeed a *gaoshou* 高手—a high hand, an expert hand—to be able to build such a great company against great odds, and to be so successful in managing international investors like Yahoo."

I was surprised to hear this, as I had the impression that Alibaba's partnership with Yahoo was hardly the stuff of a *yuan yang* duck fairytale. It initially did seem like a perfect match in 2005, when Yahoo executives including Taiwan-born co-founder Jerry Yang praised the "cultural alignment" they felt with Alibaba and Ma, who spoke fluent English and was comfortable dealing with foreigners. Yet clashes soon arose after Yahoo became Alibaba's largest strategic shareholder in 2005. Ma reportedly realized that he may have sold the 40 percent stake in Alibaba too cheaply and had relinquished too much control. It was his first major lesson working with international investors. In 2010, Yahoo and Alibaba could not come to agreement on a share buyback plan. A year later, the relationship frayed further when Ma spun off Alipay and took it under his own control. Ma claimed to have good reason for this, but critics lashed out at him for blatantly deviating from principles of full disclosure.

To my surprise, I found out that Chairman Zhou had followed the entire saga since 2005 closely, saying that he gleaned a few lessons from watching the way Ma dealt with foreigners. In particular, he heartily approved of the way Ma had regained control of all the underlying companies that Alibaba operated in China, including Taobao.

"For a China business to grow well in the first decade or two, I believe it is very important for the founder to be squarely in control. If any problems crop up, the founder should be the chief strategist and mastermind," Chairman Zhou lectured me.

"Only the Chinese would know how to run China businesses best, and now that our country is prosperous and strong, we do not need to learn as much from the West as we did in the past. We may still need their money, but we do not have to take orders from them," he continued, as my heart sank deeper and deeper into misery.

"Ma Yun said he aspired to build a company that will survive 102 years, spanning three centuries. I share the same vision for DeeDee. With the IPO, I'm confident that I can fulfill it," he concluded smugly, with a special emphasis on the pronoun "I" in his sentences.

I had no idea how to respond, let alone persuade Chairman Zhou of the benefits of letting All-Stellar prescribe a new way for running the business. It looked like Fang Xing was right – trying to make

Chairman Zhou relinquish too much control would actually be counter-productive.

All-Stellar would need to find other ways to convince Chairman Zhou to do what we wanted, while thinking that it was actually his own idea. Since I could not pull any strings, I would need to win the Lao Qianbei's trust in order to influence him. Time was ticking, I had to move quickly if we were to avoid a catastrophic collapse of our investment.

> ***Gao Shou Ru Yun*** 高手如云: **Expert hands as numerous as the clouds. In this chapter, this phrase is a pun on Jack Ma's Chinese name, referring to an expert hand like Horse Cloud.**

CHAPTER 12

Smart Money

Yan Ming Shou Kuai 眼明手快

As I tried to get closer to Chairman Zhou, Fang Xing started to become more distant from the All-Stellar team.

I hardly saw him during official working hours, though we managed to meet up for drinks occasionally. Unless Russell and Gary flew up to Beijing, Fang Xing saw no need to turn up in the office at all. Since he was now more senior in rank, I had no reason to question his absence. Most of our meetings with Chairman Zhou's team and the Singapore headquarters were now held over conference calls, so Fang Xing would instruct Rebecca to circulate a dial-in beforehand each morning. Only Rebecca was kept aware of Fang Xing's whereabouts. However, she would sometimes look clueless or shake her head when I asked where he was.

Many mornings, Russell and Gary would call our Beijing office to spot check on us to make sure we were diligently at work and not lazing at a foot massage parlor somewhere. Fang Xing could usually be reached on his mobile, but there was always a constant buzz of activity at the other end of the phone line. In the background, there were sometimes faint murmurs. At other times, I could hear machinery humming in the background. On one occasion, a young girl was cajoling him to come over to sit with her.

Fang Xing was street-smart, and a natural at Chinese private equity deal-making. He was a networking fiend, who could name-drop his way into any inner circle if he didn't have the direct connections to get invited. He also had the knack for making people feel that they were the smartest people in the room for following what he had advised them to do. So he was always on the phone with eager Chinese entrepreneurs lapping up his investment tips and funding ideas. The way he could jazz everything up and make seemingly impossible deals become alive and attractive to buyers and sellers always filled me with a mixture of awe and alarm. To top it off, he had an uncanny ability to make small talk and broker big deals, even when he was under the heavy influence of alcohol.

Making a deal work meant pounding the pavement, and constantly looking for new relationships. I was struck by his resourcefulness and energy—he thrived on just five hours of sleep a day. He used to say if one shook the fruit tree hard enough, fruits will fall off and the harvest would be plentiful. Of course, it had better be a fruit tree in the first place. If Fang Xing found himself in a rubber tree plantation, he would quickly leave it and find a more rewarding apple orchard elsewhere.

From his perspective, whether the deal was good or bad depended on whose side you took—so he never took sides. Closing the deal was far more important for him. If there was no deal sealed, there was no money on the table to be made.

And for Fang Xing, time was of the essence. So he focused on very concrete goals: always zoom in on deals that were most likely to close. He did not waste time on deals with uncertain prospects, and certainly did not spend time on business plans or analytical spreadsheets like most western investment professionals did. "For people who like to contemplate, ponder and formulate strategies,

China may not be the place for you," he told me once, after I claimed I needed to study China's investing landscape a lot more first before I could put my own money into deals.

Despite being so sure of himself, he still seemed to have an irrepressible urge to show off to me. Perhaps we were of a similar age and had somewhat similar backgrounds, so he felt the need to put me in my place on his turf. During a particularly heavy drinking session one night, he was unusually chatty and shared a little more of the story behind his meteoric rise. That opened up a whole new dimension of his personality.

Fang Xing knew even before he graduated with a business master's degree in the US that he would return to China to earn his first million. His home country was where he had "the biggest edge," he said.

"Before the financial crisis, a lot of my Chinese classmates were still dreaming the American dream and wanted to stay in the US. There was a growing minority returning back to China because they had to take over the family business. But I was different from all of them—I had the luxury of choice and I knew the smart choice was to go back to China once I got some US job experience on my resume," he recalled.

"Because it's one of the fastest-growing economies in the world, so it's easier to make money here?" I hazarded a guess.

He looked at me as if I were dumb-witted. "Oh c'mon, that's the Kool-Aid we feed to the foreigners. China is one of the hardest markets to navigate and make money, really. The environment and policies here are in constant flux. And there is a maze of state-linked interests to factor in. All that can shift goalposts overnight so you need to always be vigilant to make sure you are still shooting for the right targets and that your investments don't go sour right under your nose."

I sighed. "Yes, I'm starting to see how unpredictable things can get in China. It seems so much harder to understand this system compared to the western system."

"Ah ha, you got it. That's why, if you know the system from the inside, and you have some western pedigree—which is important, but frankly overrated in China—then you can easily get ahead of other 99 percent of investors blindly putting their money in here. There are so many money-making opportunities to exploit if you know how to handle risks the Chinese way."

Learning all this did not come easy, even for him, Fang Xing admitted. "I had family connections, but that's not enough. I needed a master to teach me how to really do things on the ground. And my lucky break came when I met Susie."

After he had won Susie's trust, he was tasked to follow up on the smaller deals that Madame Wu had no time to attend to. Later, he piggybacked on her name to build up his own connections with influential people. At age twenty-four, he made his first million as a broker and dealmaker through so-called "finder's fees". The going rate for such fees was up to five percent of the funds raised. Since these projects were large, often costing millions of dollars, the finder's fees could be pretty substantial. In all these projects, money changed hands in two ways: payment of cold hard cash up front, or bank transfers to distant relatives' bank accounts. Such methods were more likely to evade scrutiny and taxes. Fang Xing's goal was to become such a trusted broker that he would also become a third-party conduit for the funds.

Fang Xing's next big break came when he became well-connected and successful enough to gain access to an obscure but powerful brokers' network where everyone called each other *tiegemen* 铁哥们, literally translated as Iron Brothers and referring to buddies who were as close—or even closer than—blood brothers. Only friends who had absolutely no secrets amongst them could be called *tiegemen*. There were only men in this particular club. Susie was said to be part of an even more influential network of male and female members, including a few princelings. But it was so secretive and fluid that it did not even have a formal name.

"Because of such solid relationships, brokering deals became much easier and the cut got bigger," boasted Fang Xing, drinking with uncharacteristic abandon. I was starting to wonder if he had quarreled with his wife, or something had gone wrong for him to let down his guard like that.

"Now, deals like DeeDee just provide me with small change," he added.

The wheels in my brain spun furiously. Was that how Fang Xing got his pocket change to buy his new Aston Martin? Did he get a cut from helping Chairman Zhou raise money from All-Stellar? I was sure that he was not getting anything from our fund, so his "small change" must have come from the Chinese side?

"With China's IPO market set to become one of the biggest in the world in the next few years, there's so much money to make," he drawled. "I just had lunch with one of the investment bankers at Merrill today. We may have a new deal!"

"Fang Xing, you are really a shrewd deal-maker," I said, a little begrudgingly.

He seemed very pleased by my comment. "Come with me tomorrow when I meet them. They're from the US, so it will be easier for you to talk to them too."

The next day at 8:30a.m., we met with the chairman of AEXI Capital. The fund had been an active investor in the global food and beverage sector since the 1990s. It made its first foray into China in late 2005, picking up a 30 percent stake in Chili Sisters, the fledging hotpot chain serving pricey hotpot meals. The deal had seemed like a gamble at that time since the brand was relatively unknown, but it turned out to be a brilliant move. Chili Sisters tapped into the huge consumption boom among the increasingly affluent Chinese middle-class and enjoyed a five-fold growth in revenues over the past three years.

"These guys are now looking to raise additional capital for the hot pot business from new investors because Chili Sisters want to expand their chain across another fifteen provinces," Fang Xing claimed, as we headed to the Ritz Carlton hotel in the latest addition to his sports car collection—a canary yellow Ferrari. "I'm also persuading them to sell us part of their existing stake in Chili Sisters so that we can hopefully build up a sizeable stake in the company."

"Why would they want to part with some of their shares when Chili Sisters is doing so well and might head for a listing soon?" I asked dubiously.

"I sold it to them on the grounds that the valuations of companies in China's F&B sector have hit historic highs, so they should take advantage of this to take some profits. And I said, you never know if China's policies on listings might change, for all you know, it might become more difficult for smaller companies to list, so it's better to hedge your bets rather than wait to cash out everything at an IPO."

"And…why would we be keen to take over their stake if the prices are at a historic high and listing policies might change?" I asked, unable to keep up with his reasoning.

Fang Xing rolled his eyes. "Because I'm confident we can play the game better than they can. Right now, the IPO market is going crazy. We just need to have the right connections and enough flexibility to get out of the investment at the right time," he said.

I would recall Fang Xing's throw-away comments later on, when we were mulling the limited options to exit from our DeeDee investment. As it turned out, China's IPO market soared to become the world's largest for new share sales in 2010 with a record US$71 billion raised and then froze up for 14 months when the Chinese securities regulator slapped a moratorium on new IPOs to tighten supervision. Even after Fang Xing's repeated observations about how quickly and unexpectedly things moved in China, it still blew my mind how completely unpredictable the Chinese stock market was, and how impulsive the state's reactions to its gyrations could be.

We sat down to a light breakfast of egg whites, toast, and roasted vegetables with Mr. Eaton Steinberg, a seasoned venture capitalist so thoughtful in his observations about China's trends that I wondered if Fang Xing was simply being too cocky to think he could beat AEXI Capital at the game.

He had already met several potential new investors earlier in the week, and ours was the last meeting before his flight back to San Francisco at noon. But his enthusiasm about China's potential was still undiluted, even after giving the same presentation for the sixth time: "We got the big trends right: strong growth in Chinese consumers' disposable income, the policy shifts to support a more consumption-driven economy, the evolving lifestyle choices of younger Chinese who are more willing to splurge on dining experiences and not just on the food. And we figured these trends were powerful enough to support the growth of an upscale chain like Chili Sisters, even through periods of slower economic growth."

"But we were still taken by surprise at how robust demand continued to be even when the global financial crisis set in," he continued. The downturn might have roiled the Chinese stock markets in 2008, but it did little to dampen Chili Sisters' sales. Perhaps it was the huge stimulus boost, which leaked into the local financial markets and also into local officials' pockets, he hinted. All this in turn boosted a lot of business entertainment dining which helped boost the chain's sales.

"We realized that we had hit a jackpot with the high-end brand positioning of Chili Sisters—Chinese consumers are incredibly 'face-conscious' and brand-conscious, so they are always splurging on premium items when they dine here to show off to their business partners or friends. Each month, we import over a ton of wild

Alaskan cod and Ecuador tiger prawns through the centralized procurement unit, which then distributes it to each store based on the budgeted demand. Imported seafood is always the best sellers since it's a health fad now."

I nodded. "The herd mentality is very strong among Chinese—be it the latest food fad or investing in stocks or buying big brands."

"Yes. But at the same time, the Chinese consumer is also a lot more flexible and willing to experiment than we expected—a population that was almost exclusively a tea drinking culture for centuries can get hooked on coffee within just a few years, for example. And now, viola, China is Starbucks' top consumer market."

Fang Xing chimed in: "Starbucks is making such a killing here, and supplies 70 percent of the café market. And it's no surprise given China's sheer size. It's just mind-boggling how much consumption capability it already has—it's the world's largest consumer of pork, rice, apples, beer, oil…you name it."

"Indeed, and this sheer size is why we still see such a vast potential for Chili Sisters," said Mr. Steinberg. "Now, I like to get straight to the point, so shall we discuss valuations and what kind of investment you would like to make?"

Within less than half an hour, we had agreed in principle to submit a non-binding letter of intent to invest in Chili Sisters. A letter of intent was usually the first step towards more serious discussions. The meeting was short and succinct—a refreshing change from the protracted Chinese meetings with objectives that seemed vague and subject to change.

Before we parted, I tentatively asked Mr. Steinberg about AEXI Capital's experience working with Mr. Yan, a fifty-three-year-old entrepreneur from Sichuan province who had founded Chili Sisters. "How much autonomy do you give to your local partner to run the business?"

"That's an interesting question…" Mr. Steinberg pursed his lips pensively, as if mulling how candid he should be with a potential business partner.

"Well, we've experimented with different approaches, but it looks like giving Mr. Yan more leeway to run the show may be the best way to go for us."

Fang Xing beamed. Turning his gaze on me, he said, "See, this is just what I told you earlier—Chinese entrepreneurs don't like to be controlled too much."

Mr. Steinberg nodded. "I know we started off—like a lot of foreign investors do—wanting to inject international best practices into the Chinese company and trying to influence the way things are run. But chances are, you will meet so much resistance from the Chinese entrepreneur that you will wear your relationship out, and wear yourself out too."

"So is there still a place for foreign investors to share their expertise and improve operational and management practices?" I asked, still not quite convinced.

"I can't speak for everyone. But in our case, once we did our due diligence and figured out that Mr. Yan was a relatively reliable partner—at the very least, he is not a crook and seemed serious about building up a long-term business—we eventually left him to control most of the business while we supported him and provided feedback from the side lines," said Mr. Steinberg. "And as time went by, as we built up more trust, Mr. Yan also returned the favor in giving us more latitude to influence operations. It was a slow and arduous process though. Be prepared to be very patient."

After the meeting, we rushed to the west side of town to have lunch with some bankers who were assisting Chairman Zhou develop a financing package for the duck farms. Most of the big global and state-owned banks had their headquarters along Financial Street, a wide boulevard lined with offices and classy five-star hotels a few miles west of Tiananmen Square.

I dreaded these lunches because they were long and tedious. To make things worse, heavy alcohol was usually served, incapacitating me for the rest of the afternoon. After over a year in China, my ability to hold alcohol was still pitifully pathetic. Compared to the local Chinese, especially the ones that came from the North, I was a novice drinker who would get tipsy over two glasses of red wine.

By the time we finished, it was already three o'clock in the afternoon. The five of us—two bankers, Fang Xing, Chairman Zhou and myself—had downed four bottles of red wine and a dozen bottles of beer. As I stumbled back into the office, I was filled with wild ambitions: perhaps I could emulate Fang Xing and broker some deals of my own too? I had just received an unexpected call from Donovan Loy, a friend I knew a long way back and an ex-colleague of mine from Singapore who offered me a "chance of a lifetime to make a killing".

Donovan was one of the top revenue-earners in my previous company. Every year, it was rumored that he was always ranked among the top three performers in the company. He also had great interpersonal skills and got along very well with the senior guys. I was quite surprised to find out he had left the company shortly after me.

He was his usual cheery self when he called me out of the blue. "Good morning. Happy new year to you! I heard you're in China now. Making big bucks, eh?"

"Oh hi, Donovan, I heard you've left the company. I thought you were doing very well! What are you up to nowadays?" I replied.

"I'm doing some consultancy work and deals, and guess what? I am working on several projects in China now. It is such a big playground here with so many money-making opportunities—we must ride the wave. Plus, it's much better to be your own boss. A lot more autonomy," Donovan continued.

I nodded my head in agreement, "Yah, that's so true. How I wish I could be like you. I'm overworked and underpaid here! So how can I be of help?"

"I have an interesting business opportunity in China that I'd like to see whether you want to be involved in," Donovan said.

"Like what?" I probed.

"I am in Zhengzhou, the capital city of Henan province, now. I am working on this very profitable hospital construction project. Would you like to invest some money in this venture?" Donovan asked. He did not provide more details, but suggested we meet up soon. We agreed to meet on my next business trip to Henan.

In May 2009, I took a ninety-minute bus ride to Zhengzhou from Deng Feng, a municipal city about forty miles away. Best known as the birthplace of Chinese Kungfu, Deng Feng's Shaolin Temple attracts throngs of people from all around the world every year eager to learn martial arts. As the Chinese saying goes: *tianxia gongfu chushaolin* 天下功夫出少林 (All martial arts under heaven arise out of Shaolin). Countless movies were made along the Shaolin theme, the most recent of which was the martial arts comedy "Shaolin Soccer" by famous Hong Kong actor and producer Stephen Chow.

Earlier in the week, I was in Deng Feng to interview potential candidates for finance manager at DeeDee's Henan subsidiary. The previous finance manager had lasted only six months at her job. She cited personal reasons for her sudden departure. But it was widely known that she could not get along with the Head of Finance in Beijing, who was Chairman Zhou's sister-in-law.

After completing the interviews and finalizing the offer for the chosen candidate, I called up Donovan. He had just been hired as a consultant to help John Tan, a seasoned Taiwanese-Singaporean businessman, raise money for his new project—a high-rise commercial complex housing a mall and a large number of high-end medical suites, which would be located in the core of Zhengzhou's Central Business District. The medical suites would be leased out to specialist doctors engaged in independent practice. I knew little about the healthcare industry, though it was clearly a great sector to invest in, since the Chinese population was rapidly ageing. I recalled reading somewhere that this sector was still not open to foreign investment.

Donovan told me that he had great confidence in the project because John, the lead investor in this project, had very close relationships with key officials in the Zhengzhou medical federation. These people even held some shares in John's company through a proxy, and were helping him to pull strings to garner support for his new project.

The project company was raising its final round of financing of about RMB30 million (US$4.5 million), and had already secured the majority of this amount. Donovan told me that he had already invested over RMB500,000 (US$75,000).

"The number one lesson to learn about investing successfully in China: always find a reliable local partner who has skin in the game. That way, they will be incentivized to work for the same objectives as you. John has worked closely with these Chinese guys in the past, and assured me that they are reliable," said Donovan. "You can't go wrong with this project."

⸺◆⸺

It was an arid afternoon. I stood under the scorching sun waiting for the car that was supposed to pick me up to the construction site for the new commercial building. Glancing briefly at my watch, the metallic hour and minute hands glinted fiercely, reflecting the intense afternoon sun. It was two o'clock, and there was still no sign of Donovan. I whipped out my cell phone and reread the text I received from him the night before. "Meet at 1:30p.m. at the west side road of Zhengzhou Central Railway Station." He was already half an hour late.

Then suddenly, I saw a black Audi A6 driving towards me, screeching to a halt within a few inches of my foot. I looked at the number plate—it matched what was in Donovan's text message. The middle-aged driver heaved himself out of the car, and rushed to open the door for me. "Mr. Huang, I am extremely sorry to be late," he said, without looking very apologetic.

I was surprised to see that he was alone.

"Where is Donovan?" I demanded, a little impatiently.

The driver looked a little bewildered.

"Who is Duo-nuo-wan?" he asked.

He continued, "Our boss Mr. Tan is waiting for you at the construction site."

"Mr. Tan? Is that John, the Taiwanese investor?" I asked.

"Yes, I think some of the foreigners call him John, but we call him Chen zong," the driver replied, nudging me into the car.

I wanted to ask more questions, but he had whipped out his cell phone with his right hand and started chattering away in a heavy local dialect that I could not comprehend. His left hand skillfully maneuvered the steering wheel, weaving the car through a labyrinth of haphazardly-parked cars. He continued to talk for the next forty minutes, as the car swerved and jerked through heavy traffic all the way into the city center.

Zhengzhou was a typical second-tier Chinese city, boasting a rapidly growing urban population and a steroid-driven building spree. On virtually every street, I saw construction of every kind of structure—stately government offices, skyscrapers, malls, and what seemed like far too many condominiums—taking place. I looked around for the middle-class residents that all these buildings would cater to, but my view was obstructed by a pack of peddlers hawking laminated maps of China, mobile phone car chargers, and live turtles to cars as soon as they stopped at a red light. A feeble old man hobbled over as well, waving a rusty can and forcing a smile as he asked for loose change. We passed a disused basketball court by the side of the road, where a bunch of elderly folk were doing stretching exercises in one corner.

"Are there many young professionals in the city?" I asked the driver, when he finally put down his phone.

"The brightest young people, or the more well-to-do ones, all go to the first-tier cities which used to be seen as the most glamorous," he replied in heavily-accented Mandarin. "The older folks like me, we stay here to take care of the grandkids."

"Your own children are living in a bigger city?" I asked, glad that the driver seemed so chatty.

"My son went to Beijing after he graduated, because he thinks the pay is higher there. His wife joined him there too, not long after she gave birth," he said. "But now that there are some fashionable malls and high-end entertainment facilities being built here in Zhengzhou, my son says that he doesn't mind moving back in the future, after he has earned enough money."

I wanted to ask more questions, but the driver started to puff on a cigarette, while turning at almost every road junction. I was getting giddy. Where was he driving me to? This was the first time I visited Zhengzhou, so I could not find my bearings.

Then, suddenly, the car abruptly stopped in front of a construction site. Two men approached. I recognized one of them as Donovan. He still looked the same after all these years, jovial, bespectacled and slightly nerdy. The other guy, who was probably in his late forties, must be John. He sported a Givenchy biker jacket and a pair of matching Armani sunglasses. The large, platinum-plated buttons on his sleeves glinted in the afternoon sun.

John took off his sunglasses, revealing a big black mole next to his right eye. We exchanged a brief handshake. "So, this is the piece of land owned by my Chinese partner. Once constructed, it will be the tallest building in the Zhengzhou Central Business District," he began, without wasting any time on pleasantries.

"Based on the current project time-line, the building will be operational in two years' time," added Donovan.

I had visited countless construction sites like these before, during my previous few years working as a business analyst. I scrutinized the site, marveling at the size of the land parcel. It was definitely big enough to house two skyscrapers. In the middle of the site sat two idle Liebherr construction cranes and a Caterpillar bulldozer. I did not see any workers, and was surprised at the lack of activity. John detected my concern at once.

"Construction is about to start. Where you're standing right now is where the temporary construction office will be built. In one month's time, it will house the entire project team," he explained.

It was already dusk. I looked up into the cloudless, orange-streaked sky, and pictured a beautiful tall skyscraper. Crowds of sharply-dressed professionals were leaving their offices for the day. "*Chi f-huan quba* 吃饭去吧![22] I have booked a nice seafood restaurant. We can talk during dinner," John said.

It was a very pleasant evening. Even though this was the first time I met John, there was an unspoken camaraderie among Singaporean countrymen. John ordered a sumptuous spread of hairy crabs, abalone and sea cucumbers, topped off with bird's nest in rock sugar for dessert. The decadent feast was casual without the heavy drinking that accompanied typical Chinese business dinners. We could also speak freely in our own Singlish accent. In Chinese style business dinners, it was always overly elaborate; overflowing with alcohol and the host invariably had a hidden agenda. One had to remain sober enough to ask intelligent questions, and pick up on the host's veiled requests or business propositions. At this dinner, I felt an unusual sense of calm. I was in familiar territory and could let down my defenses.

John told me about his background. He was born and grew up in Taiwan. When he was in his early teens, he followed his parents to Singapore. He freely admitted that he never excelled in his studies

---

[22] In Taiwanese Mandarin, f- becomes hu-. The Taiwanese accent is the subject of constant entertainment for the Chinese people.

and scraped through technical school with a diploma in business administration—the only subject that truly interested him. When he graduated in the early 1990s, the job market was bleak and he found himself doing odd jobs to earn his livelihood, from selling insurance to waiting on tables. He tried to start several businesses, but barely broke even. A year later, he joined a mid-sized Taiwanese firm that imported machinery parts from China. The firm sent him to China six months later to deal with its local partners.

"It was through this random assignment that I first came to China and discovered that I like doing business here," he recalled. "I'm comfortable with working with locals and building guanxi with them. At the same time, I can do things in an organized way like a Singaporean, so the foreigners like me too."

He left the Taiwanese firm after a year to do his own construction projects with local partners, and has stayed ever since.

Donovan did not talk much during the entire time. But as dinner drew to an end, he urged me to consider this investment seriously.

"We will send you the business plan tonight. Take a look," he said. "It includes a full set of financial projections. The numbers look good."

"What is just as important for you to consider is that we have very solid Chinese partners backing us," John added. "They want to make sure that we succeed."

We shook hands, and I left for the station, just in time to catch the last bus back to Deng Feng.

The next morning, I received an e-mail from a lady by the name of Ms. Bai, who signed off as John's secretary. "Good morning. As instructed by John last night, please find attached the business plan, financial model and photocopies of the land title and other legal documents for your perusal." It was very professionally crafted, a refreshing change from Rebecca's shaky English. The only part that did not look so slick was the e-mail address: 2003819508@qq.com.

The business plan was impeccable even by western standards. Spanning over thirty pages, the PowerPoint document summarized the business opportunities, identified the key market trends, and explained why the medical suites industry was on the precipice of explosive growth in China. It also had every element that I expected to see in a professional business plan, from a SWOT (Strengths, Weaknesses, Opportunities and Threats) analysis, to a detailed Gantt chart showing the construction schedule for the next twenty-four months. The sources and uses of funding were meticulously spelled out, right down to the last cent. I could not spot a single grammatical or spelling error. The financial model was obviously created by experienced investment bankers: it was extremely thorough with fifteen worksheets, and a balance sheet that was refreshingly balanced.

I was very impressed that a company in a second-tier city like Zhengzhou could produce such a pristine piece of work. John and his Chinese partner must be doing something right. In Beijing, we could not even put together a proper business plan with DeeDee after so many months.

Shortly after, my phone rang. It was Donovan. He was checking in to see whether I had received the business plan from John.

"There is no better time than this to invest in real estate, the boom is just starting. You're going to regret it if you delay any longer," enthused Donovan.

I tried to keep myself in due diligence mode, and to avoid getting too caught up in my friend's excitement. The deal was indeed very enticing, but there were some parts of the business plan that seemed to have overly optimistic projections.

"It looks like John Tan's Chinese partners acquired the land at a price way below the official market rates. How did they pull that off?" I asked.

"Connections and grease obviously. You know how things work in China. What other things are you worried about?"

"How are they going to get all the proper licenses within such a short timeframe laid out in the business plan?" I asked. "From what I know, setting up a Chinese medical facility can require up to seventy different official stamps of approval from different levels that could take months and years. It sounds like John's partners will be doing a lot of greasing to speed things up?"

I heard a guffaw on the other side of the line. "Nihenjiche 你很 机车 (You're so motorbike)!" exclaimed Donovan. The word *Jiche* (机车), or motorbike, means "you're really annoying" or "you're a pain in the ass". It is a euphemism for the word *jibai* (雞掰) which is a slang word for vagina. Donovan's response immediately conjured up the image of John Tan and his biker jacket in my mind. He had obviously passed on Taiwanese slang to my Singaporean friend after hanging out together so much.

"Relax, relax, brother. You are getting worked up for nothing," reassured Donovan. "In a developing country like China where there is still a lot of bureaucratic red tape, the only way to get things done fast is to follow the local practices. But they are very experienced and shrewd so they won't do anything that draws attention or gets them into real trouble.

"These Chinese, they may appear unscrupulous in their business dealings at times—at least by international standards—but they know how to stay on the right side of the local laws," he added.

As Donovan spoke, I recalled Mr. Steinberg's comment during our breakfast meeting that local Chinese partners tended to operate their businesses in "ways that may make American businessmen squirm". "Even the most scrupulous businessmen may find themselves in very gray legal areas, if they want to get things done here without having to wait ten years," he said.

I decided to call another Singaporean friend, Ching, who had worked in China for over fifteen years and was now the China head of a multinational automotive company. I wanted to pick his brain about some of the issues in China investing that had bugged me for the past few months, before deciding on my next course of action.

He sighed deeply when I asked him about how gray things could get in China. Was it inevitable that one had to engage in some of the more questionable practices such as bribery, creating off-balance sheet vehicles to fund projects and hiring the offspring of top Chinese officials in order to get deals done? I asked him. This was an issue that I had pondered about deeply as our All-Stellar team scouted for new deals and found ourselves at a disadvantage because of our exacting due diligence process.

"Sometimes it's easier not to find out exactly how gray things can get, or you would never get anything done," Ching confided.

"But you also don't want to get caught with your pants down—and not know it— if the Chinese securities regulator or other authorities start to probe into your joint venture," I pressed.

"Yes, exactly, that's why we make sure that our own operations are perfectly above board," he responded. "We sometimes still have to close one eye—by letting local partners run most of the show, and do things their way without getting you involved. And if you're worried that you might get screwed if you cede too much control—well, I've learnt that if you make sure your interests are aligned with the Chinese side's, they are less likely to sell you out. Chances are, you'll be fine in the long run."

I chewed over these conversations for a while. I still had some lingering concerns about how realistic John Tan's targets were and whether the deal was inherently a risky one. But what clinched the decision for me was the assurance that John had good references from Donovan, who was a fellow countryman. True, John had become so deeply immersed in China's business culture and practices that I could have sworn he looked like a local, but I figured that this trait was actually an asset. He could be trusted to keep my investment safe since he knew his way around China. "Another plus factor: he's a co-investor who has skin in the game and money on the line," I reasoned.

Donovan suggested that I co-invest RMB200,000 (US$30,000) in the form of a short-term loan for a period of six months at a monthly interest of 5 percent. This came to an annualized 60 percent return, beating any investment product I could find in the market.

At my insistence, Donovan promised to send me a loan contract, but not before offering me another commentary. "You know as well as I do that contracts are just mere pieces of paper in China. What you should base your confidence on is not this contract but the fact that we are good at what we do here, and we have a relationship of trust."

"Yes I know this, but I still want a contract signed—I'm still used to the Singaporean way of doing things properly," I replied.

"Ok sure, take a look at the contract. If you're comfortable with the terms, you can sign it, mail it back to me, and wire the money to the designated bank account."

A day later, the deal was done. I felt a flush of exhilaration as I daydreamed about the interest appearing in my bank account in a few months. In a few years, I might finally be able to buy my own swanky apartment in Swan Palace...for Rebecca perhaps.

> *Yan Ming Shou Kuai* 眼明手快: **Sharp vision and quick hands. To act quickly and astutely.**

CHAPTER 13

Reignition

Miao Shou Hui Chun 妙手回春

WITH FANG XING CONSTANTLY ON the road scouting for new deals, it gave me a lot more time alone with Rebecca in the office. After the night I sent her home and witnessed her living conditions, I found myself constantly dreaming about dating Rebecca in a more serious relationship. It was probably not a great idea to let my imagination run wild given that she was actually my subordinate, and All-Stellar strictly prohibited employees from dating in the office. Nevertheless, I felt this irrepressible urge to provide for her and give her a better life.

Lunch or coffee breaks were great opportunities for me to get closer to Rebecca. We would chat about interesting facets of Chinese society, such as her parents' obsession with setting her up on blind dates referred by their relatives, friends and even strangers. They were among the crowds of elderly Beijingers who routinely gathered in Zhongshan Park near the Forbidden City to exchange photographs and biographies of their children in the search of the "right partner" for their precious offspring. Many also came with a list of criteria:

compatible academic qualifications, to stable job, good income, house
ownership and even a compatible zodiac sign.

While the culture of arranged marriages is a thing of the past
especially in China's booming cities, many Chinese parents continue
to play an active role in their children's search for love. This gross
interference, Rebecca complained, stemmed from the prevalence of
single-child families in Chinese society, which made parents paranoid
about making sure their only offspring married well. Rebecca had
been forced to go on many a blind date to placate her mother's
hysterical anxiety attacks.

Rebecca's latest ordeal was a date with a twenty-seven-year-old
engineer, who barely even looked at her the entire time while their
mothers chattered nervously non-stop. The guy had just completed
graduate studies in the US and had been described by Rebecca's
parents as a "very eligible bachelor from a well-to-do family". In fact,
he was a distant relative, the son of Rebecca's mum's third aunt's
nephew.

"He was so weird and rude, and did not even register my existence.
He kept thumbing away on his iPhone during the entire dinner!"
Rebecca complained.

"Ha…" I smiled at her foolishly, fumbling with the cell phone
I had in my hand and pushed it quickly under the pile of working
papers on my table.

"I would never touch a guy like this with a ten-meter pole!"
Rebecca lamented, imitating the "ten-foot pole" English expression
that I often used. "The successful guys like Fang Xing are all taken.
What should I do?"

"That guy is blind not to appreciate what a great girl you are. You
have so many suitors; you can afford to be a lot pickier…" I began.

"Haha, yes, Rebecca is so picky, so are you! Maybe both of you
should just date each other!" Fang Xing interjected jovially. Rebecca
and I had been so engrossed in our conversation about mate selection,

that we did not even realize that Fang Xing had stepped into the office. Rebecca coiled up in her seat, smiling sheepishly. I saw a triumphant grin on Fang Xing's face, seemingly satisfied with himself that he had finally succeeded in catching us red-handed flirting with each other.

"Hi Fang Xing, haven't seen you for a while! Did you come into office to gossip about who got promoted in our fund?" I asked.

"You've been made a director, right?" he responded. "I came in to claim my dinner treat from you! I'll pick the place. Let's go to Nobu."

I nodded a little dismally. After two years on the job, I had finally attained my long overdue promotion, and was finally on the same level as Fang Xing in terms of rank. That meant—in theory—I did not have to be bossed around anymore.

But in reality, the promotion was nothing much to cheer about. Fang Xing still lorded over me because he had a much better handle on the China private equity business than I did. What was worse, I had only received a title promotion without any salary increase. At the same time, I was given much more responsibility: as a director, my head was now on the chopping board if our investment in DeeDee flopped.

On top of this, I was told that I would soon be "localized" and would no longer be eligible for tax equalization, a benefit expatriates to China enjoyed. So I would have to start paying China taxes of up to 45 percent, deducted upfront from my salary each month. I suddenly found myself contributing a substantial portion of my income to Beijing's Chaoyang District Tax Bureau.

I knew of many foreigners who painstakingly planned their travel schedule so that they would spend no more than 183 days in China to avoid paying China taxes. It probably made a lot of sense from a tax perspective. However, I always wondered how these foreigners could really claim they were immersed in China, if they were so busy jetting in and out?

As I sat glumly nursing my Japanese sake in celebrity chef Nobu
Matsuhisa's restaurant, Fang Xing snapped his fingers at me and
mentioned a well-known name. "I heard that this guy's grandson,
who is in his mid-twenties, is interested to take Susie's job. Did Russell
mention anything like that to you?"

I was startled. "What? No, I thought Russell has always tried to
steer clear of PEP hires. You know how sensitive some of our Limited
Partners are to such things because of US regulations."

Fang Xing snorted derisively. "PEPs and Chinese PE often go hand
in hand, that's what Susie always says. Russell should be flattered that
he even wants to have a stint in All-Stellar for the experience, instead
of setting up his own fund right away. It's an opportunity of a million
lifetimes to hire someone this blue-blooded."

I fumbled for a response. I knew the thorny issue of Russell's stand
on PEPs always got Fang Xing worked up. When Fang Xing first
joined All-Stellar, he had proposed a co-investment deal in a cash-
starved Chinese online provider of matchmaking services, alongside
a PE fund set up by a retired official's son-in-law. Fang Xing had been
extremely proud of this potential deal, which he claimed he invested
a lot of time and "relationship capital" to secure. But Russell had
refused to submit this proposal to the Investment Committee, saying
that the allocation of US$10 million was too small.

Two years on, the PE fund had magically turned the struggling
company around and recently sold its stake to a major conglomerate—
for a tenfold profit. When he heard this news, Fang Xing had stormed
into the office to vent his frustration to me, cursing Russell and
smashing a thousand-dollar porcelain vase in the process. Luckily,
Rebecca mustered all her Taobao-trawling powers to buy a replacement
vase which looked exactly the same, and cost just thirty bucks.

Recalling that episode, I furtively moved the sake bottle away
from Fang Xing, and said soothingly, "Well, I heard from a reliable
source—Russell's secretary—that he has been interviewing a few

Chinese candidates. The interesting thing is, they all seem to be pretty young. Under forty-five."

Fang Xing sniffed scornfully. "There are plenty of young PE professionals in China, just as the industry itself is relatively young. That doesn't mean anything. Did you at least find out if any of them has a famous family name? Your intelligence is pretty lousy, eh?"

I changed the topic. "Who knows, after that spat with Susie just before her departure, Russell may have done a lot more thinking about the issue of PEPs."

"Whoever Russell picks, I hope it's someone tough who can revive our China operations quickly and keep Fang Xing in his place," I added to myself.

In late May 2009, I went home for a much-needed break. But after just two days of gorging on Singaporean culinary delights like char kway teow and fried carrot cake, I got a call from Russell. He was so excited that his sentences tumbled out almost too quickly for me to make out the words.

"I know you are on leave, but can you make a trip to the office tomorrow afternoon? I have good news and bad news, which do you want to hear first?"

I took a deep breath. In the past, questions like these would have stumped me because I hated surprises—even good ones. But after spending one year in fast-paced China, where changes were part of the norm, I had grown accustomed to the unexpected. In fact, surprises— from government policy shifts to Chairman Zhou's crazy maneuvers to expand the company behind our back—were so common that I would get a queasy feeling in my stomach whenever things remained calm for more than a few days.

"Let me guess," I said lightly. "The good news is that you want me to cut short my leave and go back to Beijing early. So what's the bad news?"

Russell's laughter boomed over the line. "Glad to hear you're taking it so well. This is the dedication that we like to see, especially for new Directors like you! Yes, you need to go back to Beijing tomorrow, and we're coming with you. We've finally found a replacement for Susie."

I was stunned. I did not expect an appointment so quickly.

"The guy's name is Alan Dong and he's got great qualifications," continued Russell. "Let's hope he is bad news for Chairman Zhou—we really need him to take that stubborn old farmer in hand and make him do things our way."

The next day, with my luggage in tow, I met Alan, a forty-year-old haigui. Born and raised in Shanghai, he spent the greater part of his education and career in the US. He had done stints at banks such as Citibank and Morgan Stanley, where Russell had also spent a few years. He had sharpened his command of English to the extent where he could converse with us in a polished American accent just like any Wall Street banker.

I was hoping to find out more about Alan's background, particularly if he had any influential connections. But I did not learn much during our brief meeting before we headed to the airport. During the cab ride, Alan explained to me why he decided to return to China.

"All the activity and money are in Asia now. So All-Stellar made the right move to focus on the region, especially on China," he said. Russell and Gary beamed.

The four of us settled into our Singapore Airlines business class seats. Russell fell asleep. Gary inhaled cocktails. Alan opened his laptop and started attacking the speaking notes that Russell had instructed him to prepare for the first meeting with Chairman Zhou. On his lap was the eighty-four-page investment memorandum we prepared the year before, when we tabled the deal to the Investment Committee. He kept flipping the document back and forth with a furrowed brow, which made me a little worried. I would have loved to catch up on sleep, but did not dare to do so in front of my new boss.

So I made a big show of tidying up my own notes, before discreetly looking out of the window once the lights were dimmed.

I usually loved sitting by the window of planes. I enjoyed gazing out into the clear blue sky and the ocean of white clouds beneath and clearing my thoughts. For a few hours, I could safely switch off my Blackberry and phone without having to explain why I did not reply to emails in time. How I treasured these moments of solitude at 38,000 feet.

But this time, of course, there was no peace and calm for me. I flitted from speculation about what Alan would be like as a boss, to fantasies about striking it rich.

The plane had just completed its cruise above the South China Sea, entering China airspace through Guangdong province. The most populous province in the world's most populous nation, Guangdong is home to the world's biggest production center for everything from shoes to bras and iPhones. The impact of Deng's economic reform policies in the 1980s were the most evident in Guangdong, beginning with the formation of special economic zones in Shenzhen, Zhuhai and Shantou, and then transforming entire fishing villages into prosperous cities. Billion-dollar businesses like internet giant Tencent Holdings and the largest Chinese property developer Vanke were built here; stock market millionaires were minted daily; dozens of major market and currency reform initiatives were launched, offering hope to China watchers that President Hu Jintao was serious about opening up the vast market to foreign investment.

But as nightfall descended on the Middle Kingdom, all I could see was bottomless blackness with the odd patches of light below. As the plane headed northeast towards Beijing, we cruised over enormous Chinese townships, some with populations larger than whole countries. Having grown up in a tiny nation like Singapore, I was still blown away by China's staggering proportions even after living here for almost a year. Navigating China was a daunting experience as it overturned all my previous assumptions of size and overwhelmed me with its contradictions. It was a vast land but suffered a scarcity of clean water and fertile arable land. Here, huge urban populations squeezed into congested, haphazardly built cities; huge swathes of new residential properties lay uninhabited—"ghost towns" like those in Inner Mongolia's Erdos city were the big story in international news—while university graduates in Beijing crammed like ants into dank basements and slums because they could not afford costly urban housing. China's immense possibilities were only matched by the seemingly impossible scale of its problems.

I recalled my first trip to Beijing with Randy on that fateful winter morning in 2008. I had told myself that coming to China to work was the beginning of an exciting journey that could lead to riches and glory. I believed that as long as I persevered, I would succeed. If I spent enough time immersing myself in Chinese society, I would become like one of the seasoned China hands. If the white Westerners could succeed in China and publish their stories, I could do just as well—or better—especially since I had no barrier of language and skin color.

But one year later, I was struggling with self-doubt. Had I really become more China-savvy? I had polished my Mandarin considerably, but that seemed like an insignificant qualification now. Spending most of my time here was also not enough to help me get ahead. It seemed that even older China hands, who called this land their second home, may struggle to decipher the fast-changing China code, as an increasingly confident Beijing sought to shape rules for the world.

Meanwhile, my conversations with Fang Xing and other young Chinese like Manager Wang opened my eyes to the intricacies of guanxi in China business. There was guanxi, and there was Guanxi with a Government link. As China's economy expanded amid the global financial crisis, it seemed to have become dominated even more by vested interests and state-linked vehicles. In increasingly important but still immature industries like private equity, knowing the who's who behind the deals was as important as it was to have the know-how in executing deals.

I could not wait to see how Alan Dong, with his blend of East-West skills, would pull all this off.

———◆———

We paraded Alan at DeeDee the next day. "He will be of great value to your company, Chairman Zhou," Russell beamed. "And you'll be glad to hear this—he has extensive experience raising money in the US for big companies, so he can definitely help solve DeeDee's financial problems."

Chairman Zhou's eyes lit up after I translated this, but he still kept a stern, unsmiling face. He did not like outsiders—let alone laowai—highlighting the fact that DeeDee had any kind of financial problems in front of his employees. It made him lose face, he would complain to me afterwards. And Alan's western credentials did not impress him much—"I've never heard of most of those western names anyway. How big are those Flower Flag or Big Monster banks?"

I stifled a giggle. The Flower Flag Bank, or Huaqi 花旗, that Chairman Zhou had referred to was actually Citibank, while the Big Monster Bank, Damo 大摩, was actually Morgan Stanley. The word mo 摩 actually means engine, but Chairman Zhou mistook it for another word with the same sound mo 魔, which means monster or devil.

Alan stood up, and began in his mother tongue: "Chairman Zhou, as investors, we remain completely and wholeheartedly committed to you and your company. My role here is to allow both parties to reengage with each other to bring our amicable relationship back on track. Today marks a new chapter in our bonding. Let us forget all the past issues and misunderstandings. As the saying *tongzhougongji* 同舟共济 (We are in the same boat together) goes, our relationship should be centered on mutual trust and commitment. We should seek to achieve common goals, and face external parties with a unified front."

"Cool!" I thought. "Alan has that same familiar officious style of making lengthy speeches that do not promise anything concrete, but mean a lot to the Chinese."

By now, I had heard the phrase *tongzhougongji* more than a hundred times, used by officials of all ranks, from Premier Wen Jiabao's comments on US-China ties down to the county officials in Liuzhou who loved to study the Chinese leadership's pet phrases. And here was Alan, using the same phrase to remind Chairman Zhou that he was in the "same boat" as All-Stellar, and it did not do either party any good to remain fractious with each other. I nodded vigorously in agreement, and looked over enthusiastically to see if Alan had already defused the blistering tensions with DeeDee staff. They still looked uncertain about how to respond. Chairman Zhou remained stone-faced.

So Alan brought out his trump card a week later: a trip to the Chinese KTV lounge to reignite the sparks in All-Stellar's relationship with Chairman Zhou.

He had already gotten approval from Russell, who had left Beijing the same day he arrived, to splurge on this assignment. So he picked the crème de la crème: the infamous Tianshang Renjian 天上人间, which means Paradise on Earth. It was such a well-known karaoke joint among foreign men that the place had the most appropriate English nickname "Passion Club". After an elaborate dinner, Alan discreetly told Chairman Zhou the place he had picked for "evening entertainment". Finally, the Lao Qianbei let a slight smile slip.

Passion Club was notorious as an orgy house for the rich and powerful. It was strategically located in the center of downtown Beijing in the five-star Sheraton Hotel on East Third Ring Road – within close proximity of many big Chinese companies' headquarters.

KTV rooms here had to be reserved at least a day in advance, as they sold like hot cakes despite being overpriced. Fang Xing told me that this was a place "that made people embarrassed to enter even if they had ten thousand yuan in their wallets". The *zongtong taofang* 总统套房 (presidential suite) which we had chosen for Chairman Zhou cost RMB8,888 (US$1,400) per night. The number eight sounds like the word "prosperous" in Chinese and is a lucky number.

Such an exclusive suite conferred a high social status on the guests. More importantly, the hefty price tag meant we treated Chairman Zhou as a VVIP, and gave him mianzi 面子, or face. It showed that he was important enough for us to spend big money to maintain this relationship. Apart from that, the room did not look much different from the room we had at Number Eight KTV and Bathhouse, just slightly bigger.

But what set this place apart from the normal KTV joints with escort services were its high-end hostesses, most of whom were college graduates. Some were even postgraduates from famous art colleges like Beijing Film Academy, where Dan Dan—Chairman Zhou's girl for the night—claimed she was currently studying.

We were spoilt for choice. After a few rounds of selection, Fang Xing picked a girl dressed in a diamond-studded evening gown who was from Sichuan province, while Manager Wang picked another from Gansu province. They looked like photocopy images of each other and I thought they were twin sisters, until I realized that many hostesses underwent plastic surgery. Alan preferred tall ladies with strong features and picked a girl from Liaoning province who was studying at Beijing College of Music. My girl Ran Ran was from eastern Jiangsu province.

Chairman Zhou and Alan exchanged pleasantries. A few shots later, the Lao Qianbei and Dan Dan stood up, picked up the microphones, and started performing a classic love song from the 1990's. They sang beautifully together and received uproarious applause.

Chairman Zhou slumped down beside me, as Dan Dan hurried

to pick up his wine glass from the other end of the table. "Chairman Zhou, you are such an incredible pair! Your girl is so pretty. You have great taste for women," I yelled into Chairman Zhou's ear while raising my glass to the couple. As a form of respect for Chairman Zhou, I had to raise a toast to his girl as well.

Chairman Zhou was already a little high from the alcohol. His girl gently took the empty wine glass away to refill with more vodka. It was a practice among many Chinese businessmen, for whom dining etiquette using specific glasses for different types of alcohol was a completely foreign—and largely irrelevant—concept.

Chairman Zhou stumbled over to me and looked me in the eye. I thought he was going to crack a joke, but he pointed his index finger at me and roared: "Remember, these girls are just after your money. Don't get a wife that is too pretty. They will run away eventually! Beauty comes with a price." I looked away a little embarrassed, feeling like a son chided by his crusty father.

That evening, I managed to practice some of the new tricks I picked up from the Internet about how to keep sober at long entertainment sessions in China. One particularly useful technique was to keep a half-empty glass of water on hand. Instead of drinking from it, you slowly spit out the colorless alcohol into the glass when no one was noticing, and then immediately get the waitress to replace the glass. Then there was the "wet towel" technique: slowly defuse the alcohol from your mouth into a hot towel that you are pretending to wipe your face with.

Of course, there was the ultimate "abstinence" technique: tell the people at the table you were abstaining due to health reasons or that you were allergic to alcohol. But that obviously would not work when drinking with people you already knew. I spied Alan, who was under the most pressure to drink copiously since he was the host, fumbling with his wet towel and wondered if he was deploying the same techniques.

In another corner sat Manager Wang, playing dice games with his girl. He seemed to be losing every single one. He had been a bundle of nerves all evening. As he downed glasses of beer as a penalty for losing the dice games, I could see him occasionally clutching his fist and burping hard, as if trying to drown the butterflies in his stomach with the alcohol.

In the end, it was not how expensive or luxurious the presidential suite was, nor how decadent the night went that made it truly unforgettable. The climax for me came at the end of the night when the girls bade us goodbye.

Alan, who was red-faced and barely able to walk, shook Chairman Zhou's hand vigorously and said, "See you tomorrow, Lao Qianbei." I hid a smile as the older man stiffened.

Then suddenly, a gleaming BMW Z4 zoomed into the driveway. In the driver's seat sat Fang Xing's girl. She was almost unrecognizable, sporting a demure, girl-next-door look. She wore a sophisticated, yet toned-down Fendi outfit that was obviously calculated to give her the appearance of a *fuerdai* 富二代, a second-generation wealthy heir. I watched in disbelief as she motioned to Fang Xing to hop in.

Fang Xing had been strangely quiet that evening, although I did briefly recall hearing him grunting as he grinded feverishly against his girl in a corner of the room just before we called for the bill. He hopped into the car and the pair sped off into the night.

By now, I was used to seeing Fang Xing take off with hot chicks. What stupefied me was just how much this girl had managed to save from working just two years at Passion Club. She could now afford a luxury car that most of her peers in the city— let alone her childhood buddies in her village hometown – did not even dare to dream about. Passion Club was fulfilling the dreams of young girls who had the college qualifications to land white-collar jobs, but who would rather embrace the quickest methods to elevate their status.

"There is a kind of dignity and honor in being able to acquire the next Ferrari, Fendi or Ferragamo, that you cannot get from just being a simple professional," Rebecca told me philosophically when I related the episode to her later.

"But isn't that *chongyangmeiwai* 崇洋媚外? Worshipping the West and chasing after foreign things is a practice you disapprove of, right?"

"When a Chinese working girl relies on her own effort and can buy western brands that 99 percent of westerners cannot afford, that can be glorious too," replied Rebecca calmly. I gave up trying to reason with her.

The next morning, we arrived at DeeDee's headquarters bright and early before 9a.m.. All the Heads of Department were present at this meeting. The mood was solemn. It was as if all the ecstasy and euphoria of the previous night had vanished at the break of dawn. The sole agenda that morning was how to resolve the deadlock with the banks. The company was in desperate need of additional bank capital to build new duck farms. Manager Wang was due to make his weekly report on his discussions with the local banks. He had been ordered by Chairman Zhou to travel across the country to talk to the local banks in the various provinces and had made some progress with a state-linked lender. As the whole room stared at him, his voice cracked with nervousness. "Last Friday, the assistant general manager of the operations department of the corporate loan division at the Liuzhou City Branch tells me that our loan application is still at the preliminary credit approval stage," Manager Wang began.

"I brought him to the KTV to probe further and even gave him a carton of Double Happiness cigarettes. He then revealed to me privately that our application is stuck in a backlog, and we are number 234 on the list," he said. Everyone in the room gasped at the words "number 234".

"We need to reach out to someone more important than an assistant general manager within the bank. Someone more senior who can make decisions and can expedite the process," Alan barked.

After a minute of silence, Manager Wang whispered, "Chairman Zhou….?"

The Lao Qianbei was furiously typing away at his phone. He looked up momentarily. "What about China Merchants Bank? Or Bank of Communications? Or ICBC? How about the local Guangxi rural cooperative banks? Have you tried all of them?"

Unable to suppress his frustration, Manager Wang groaned. "Of course we did, otherwise how could we face you today? Li Yuechao, our Guangxi General Manager, and I have tried every contact we have. We hope to give you an update next week."

Two hours passed with not much progress, and finally, Chairman Zhou called an end to the meeting. Alan hurried over to talk to him privately, so I excused myself and wandered into Manager Wang's room.

He snapped at me the minute I entered. "Where is this new boss of yours from, this Alan? How can he criticize me like that in front of Chairman Zhou earlier? Does he even know any senior bank officials himself? If his skin is so thick, then why doesn't he try calling all the bankers himself, the way that I did?"

"I'm still trying to figure him out, honestly. I heard his *laojia* 老家 (hometown) is in Shanghai so I'm hoping that he has some powerful banking contacts there. He has great credentials, that's for sure."

Manager Wang ignored me and kept seething. "What are we going to do about the bank loans?" he moaned at the wall. On it hung a scroll with the words *fuyousihai* 富有四海 (prosperity across the four seas) written in bold calligraphy. I smiled at Chinese people's penchant for covering their doors and walls with auspicious four-word idioms in the hope of attracting fortune.

"Ah heavens, will it be more difficult for the stars across the four seas to be aligned, than for the banks to lend to us?" Wang lamented.

I decided to change the subject. "Your birthday is coming up, how are you planning to celebrate?"

Wang shrugged. "More work and alcohol, I guess," he said wearily. "When I was young, my parents would bring me during my birthday month to spend three days burning incense and praying for health and prosperity at *Wutaishan* 五台山 (Five Peaks Mountain). But I don't have time to go anymore."

Five Peaks Mountain was the most famous of the four legendary religious peaks in China. The region of Wutaishan encompassed a total area of almost 230 square miles and was located in the northern province of Shanxi.

"Since we have the IPO coming up, maybe I should make another trip during Chinese New Year to pray," he mused.

"Why Wutaishan of all places? If you stayed in Beijing, for example, you could visit many famous shrines, like the Lama Temple?" I asked.

"Because Wutaishan is most 'spirited'." Wang said. He meant that the gods were most active in Wutaishan, and would be most likely to hear his prayers and grant his wishes.

"During my trip a few years ago, I even brought back a rock from Wutaishan to contribute to the *fengshui* 风水 of Chairman Zhou's water structure," he added, pointing to the pond at the entrance. "His wife and relatives were so pleased that they gave me eight packets of cigarettes." Fengshui, the Chinese geomantic in which spatial arrangements are designed to harmonize spiritual forces and direct flow of energy, was a Zhou family obsession.

I strolled over to the elaborate artificial water landscape directly facing the entrance to the office. I had often seen such fanciful exhibits in the offices of Chinese companies. But it was the first time, after countless visits to DeeDee's headquarters, that I scrutinized this pond.

I looked in disbelief at the constant stream of water flowing through the gold-plated water fountain, wondering how the thrifty Lao Qianbei, who scolded employees for leaving lights on in the conference room even for ten minutes, could have brought himself to install this extravagant structure. I counted the fish in the pond carefully: eight goldfish and a lone black-colored goldfish. As their bright heads bobbed in the water, I contemplated the number nine, representing prosperity and longevity.

————————◆◆◆————————

The day's conversations about fortune reminded me about my own investment in John's business. Two months had passed and I had not heard any news since I wired the money over. Construction must have started by now, I thought. They must be busy securing government approvals and dealing with the contractors on the ground. I decided to reach out to Donovan to get an update as I had a work trip to Zhengzhou on Friday. I would stay the weekend there and check out the sights in Zhengzhou.

My Chinese friends did not have many good things to say about this city—it was notorious for its rogue traders and swindlers, they warned. But from my online research, I knew it also had many beautiful tourist attractions worth visiting, and its people were said to be welcoming and industrious. I told Donovan to book me in the same local business hotel that he stayed in, since he knew the hotel manager and could get me a special rate of only RMB188 (US$29) per night.

I had expected the same five-star treatment that I had received from my previous visit. So I was in for a rude shock when I checked into the hotel room, which looked like a dormitory from the 1980s, with a rusted, boxy television; a rickety bed made of plywood; a mottled mattress; and a red thermos flask filled with tepid water. Instead of the sumptuous dinner of hairy crabs, abalone, sea cucumbers, and bird's nest like the one John had treated me to during our first meeting, we had a simple meal at a cheap local Cantonese restaurant opposite the hotel. John said that his Chinese partner, who was supposed to come meet me, had "an emergency to attend to" and could not join us.

Over sticky rice and steamed prawn dumplings, John updated me on the project while Donovan interjected occasionally with some details. John said the final papers were already being processed by the relevant authorities and construction was going to start anytime now.

After the unsatisfying dinner, John brought me to a foot massage at the basement of the building. Most local hotels in second-tier and third-tier cities I visited had seedy foot massage and spa parlors at Basement One. This one was no different. The elevator door opened directly into the foyer with outlandish furnishings and mismatching neon lights. It looked as if they were trying very hard to recreate a high-class ambience but failed miserably because they could only afford substandard materials. We were ushered to three gigantic brown leather armchairs that could recline at the press of a button. From the long menu of services, I picked the Chinese medicinal foot massage, which was touted to improve blood circulation and help my body detoxify.

Three masseuses shuffled in, lugging huge wooden basins with scalding water with a strong herbal aroma. My masseuse was a teenager from a rural village in Jiangxi province, who scrubbed my feet using sandalwood-scented lotion with the rigor of a farm girl used to scrapping mud off just about everything. She wore a red miniskirt with swirling dragon patterns on it, which could have been quite seductive—if not for her sleeveless translucent blouse, which showed off her unshaved armpits in all their raven glory.

Donovan chatted with me while John busied himself flirting with his masseuse. The latter had filed for a divorce with his wife of seven years just a few days after moving to China, Donovan told me quietly. Their son now lived with his ex-wife in Singapore, to whom he paid alimony every month.

"After his failed marriage, John became a pituizu 劈腿族[23].

---

[23] Pituizu literally means a "split" in athletics, but nowadays used to describe a lifestyle in China where one maintains multiple love partners concurrently.

This huahuagongzi 花花公子 (playboy) now has a gorgeous, live-in girlfriend from Sichuan province who is fifteen years younger than him. He also has several other girlfriends on the side!" Donovan added.

"John must be enjoying his freewheeling lifestyle in China," I commented.

After the seventy-minute massage which was only RMB68 (US$10) each, we called it a night and went upstairs. I was still hungry, so I ordered some room service. While I was in the shower, the doorbell rang. Thinking it was my room service order, I quickly rinsed off the shampoo, wrapped myself up in a towel and opened the door.

My jaw dropped. Standing at the door was a sweet-faced girl, dressed in a pink dress that barely covered her smooth thighs. Her perfume, which had already invaded the entire corridor, made my head spin. "Hey *shuaige* 帅哥 (Handsome Brother), do you want some service?" she shrilled. She sauntered into the room without waiting for me to answer. Here I was, wrapped only in a towel, but this girl – who was probably no older than 18 years old – did not even bat an eyelid.

"For full service, 650 yuan or a hundred US dollars. Partial service also available," she recited calmly. She gestured to a wide selection of birth control devices on the countertop beside the bathroom sink, and then looked back at me expectantly. The condoms were labeled in English: "UNCOMPLIMENTARY," or "not free".

By this time, I was breathing heavily as she ran her fingers through her silky long hair. But somehow, I struggled to lay my hands on such a young girl. She looked so much like the teenage daughter of one of my Beijing friends.

Finally, after what seemed like eternity, I muttered, "Sorry, Miss". I gestured for her to leave. She was so surprised that she froze, and I had to half-push, half-shoo her out, shutting the door firmly behind her. I stared blankly at the emergency escape instructions on the back of the door. Absolute silence ensued. No entreaties of "*shuaige,* let's talk". No sound of departing footsteps. After a few minutes, a huge, colorful pamphlet was shoved under the door. A telephone number was printed at the bottom, along with a jumbled sentence: "University students, models, second-rated and third-rated movie stars, European blondes, Russians, Japanese, Koreans, for premium massage service."

It was filled with photographs of school girls, nurses and air stewardesses. There was even a young blonde in Communist party garb that was unbuttoned and cut up in so many strategic places that I wondered if even Mao Zedong, who was described in several foreign books and biographies to have quite a lascivious appetite for young virgins, might have found it a little too *zhongkouwei* 重口味 ("heavy taste," or racy).

I cancelled my room service order and went to bed hungry.

Miao Shou Hui Chun 妙手回春:
Magical hands purported to effect a miraculous cure and bring the dying back to life.

CHAPTER 14

Jubilation

E Shou Cheng Qing 额手称庆

OVER THE NEXT THREE WEEKS, my new boss and I made a daily pilgrimage to Chairman Zhou's office. I could tell Alan was trying his utmost to woo him, and initially he seemed to win the old man's favour when he set up a "special financing task force" to negotiate bank loans for DeeDee.

However, it soon became obvious that Alan, having just returned to China from overseas, did not have the right relationships on the ground to get any real discussion going with the tight-fisted state-owned banks.

DeeDee was seeking an additional RMB580 million (US$88 million) of bank financing to fund new expansion and acquisitions. Alan tried to name-drop by touting All-Stellar's well-known institutional investors and managed to secure a few meetings with bankers. But the managers who were available to see us were not senior enough in the banks' convoluted hierarchy, while those that did wield influence were not serious about meeting up and often stood us up.

After a deputy senior manager—whom Alan and I had spent

two months wooing and who had seemed very forthcoming during the lavish banquets we treated him to—did not show up for our scheduled meeting, Chairman Zhou lost his patience. He told Alan point-blank to stop turning up at his office every day since he was "wasting too much of his time".

"I think Alan is really messed up. He tries to act like he is very Chinese, but honestly, he is neither from the East nor from the West," Chairman Zhou complained to me during one golf session, which he insisted Alan did not attend.

I kept quiet and focused on messing up my shot so that the Lao Qianbei would win the game. I knew he was in a foul mood because DeeDee had drained almost all its capital, as the new acquisitions sucked up more money than expected. He had to resort to borrowing again from underground lenders at unfavorable rates. But he was still hoping for a loan from a major bank which would lend credibility to DeeDee and boost its chances of getting additional bank financing down the road.

"Alan might have a fancy western resume, and he may have been born and raised in China, but he still doesn't understand how companies operate in China because he doesn't care enough," continued Chairman Zhou as we walked back to the club house.

I was taken aback. "Alan doesn't care…?"

"That Gary, he is a pig head but at least he gets genuinely worked up about finding ways to solve our problems. But that Alan, his *xinsi* 心思, his heart and mind are truly not on his job or on us. He goes through the motions but he doesn't exert himself enough. And he doesn't spend enough time broadening his guanxi. What are these young people up to nowadays?" he ranted on bitterly.

I was struggling for a reply when our attention was distracted by a stream of bubbles blown right into our faces by two kids. I was a little annoyed that they seemed to have aimed straight for my eyes, but Chairman Zhou patted them good-humoredly and said, "Little friends, what are you playing with?" It was obvious he was very fond of kids.

"I have these Unbreakable Bubbles! They are very sticky and don't pop!" giggled one little boy, as he opened a new bottle of viscous solution. He carefully blew a huge bubble that floated for a surprisingly long time before finally landing on Chairman Zhou's hand. It settled for two seconds before deflating. "Amazing, the bubble is so sticky!" exclaimed the Lao Qianbei. "I should get some of this stuff for my staff's kids on Taobao."

I beamed, relieved that he had forgotten about Alan.

On August 31, 2009, after we had held over fifty meetings with senior bank officials and brought them on over a dozen site visits to DeeDee's duck farms, the company finally secured the debt financing. It received a ten-year loan of RMB520 million from a state-owned bank, which covered about 90 percent of DeeDee's financing needs.

It turned out that Chairman Zhou had enlisted the help of a friend whose technology company had a powerful shareholder—a relative of a central government minister. That friend put in a call to the general manager of a state-owned bank branch in Beijing, obliquely mentioning his powerful shareholder, and grandly portraying Chairman Zhou as an influential businessman backed by a top-notch foreign investment fund. The bank manager was impressed enough to include DeeDee in the bank's lending quota for the month—for an undisclosed introductory fee. Chairman Zhou also refused to tell me the interest rate. Getting a loan from a SOE bank would open so many new doors for DeeDee that any expense was worth it, he insisted.

We heaved a sigh of relief when the loan was finally disbursed. Now we could stop worrying about bankruptcy, and could finally move on with expansion plans. Earnings from the new Yunnan operations were finally starting to trickle in, and it looked like we would meet our 30 percent revenue growth target for the year after all.

The mood at the company was triumphant. After the friction and acrimony of the past few months, the relationship between All-Stellar's senior management and DeeDee's staff finally made a turn for the better. In fact, everyone suddenly became so chummy that it felt as though we had all popped ecstasy pills and forgotten our past troubles.

A giddy Chairman Zhou surprised everyone in the office by distributing a few hundred bottles of Unbreakable Bubbles, and even demonstrated its use. In a sudden fit of excitement, Alan grabbed a bottle and joined him, dragging me along. Before long, the usually meek DeeDee staff were all giggling and playing with bubbles as we celebrated the upcoming IPO.

Barely a month later, amid comatose stock markets, we started our preparatory work for the company's international IPO like warriors heading back to the battlefield. This was a big step forward to achieving Chairman Zhou's ultimate China dream of running an overseas-listed firm.

Several investment banks came to pitch for the lead underwriter[24] role. Lawyers, independent directors and other third-party intermediaries were appointed. The company's auditor, Bean and Counters (B&C), one of the world's largest auditing firms, commenced work to prepare the company's historical three-year audited financials for the IPO prospectus[25].

DeeDee's urgent need to hire a qualified CFO, a thorny issue that had lay dormant for almost a year due to the impasse with

---

[24] A lead underwriter is typically an investment bank whose primary directive is to organize an initial public offering. The lead underwriter usually forms a syndicate together with other investment banks to create the initial sales for the company's shares to be sold to institutional and retail clients.

[25] The prospectus is a legal document issued by the company which is offering its shares up for sale. It contains vital information about the company, including its history, financial statements, use of proceeds, business and growth strategy, management team, legal opinions, and key risk factors.

Chairman Zhou, was suddenly resolved. At the advice of the underwriters, Chairman Zhou immediately embraced the concept of hiring qualified professionals wholeheartedly. With his blessings, we hired Steven Chen, a twenty-five-year veteran experienced in helping Chinese companies list, to lead DeeDee through the IPO process.

I could not believe our luck. Just two months ago, we were still trying to resuscitate an almost moribund company. Yet now, we were back on our feet and readying to make a killing on our investment. The tide had turned in our favor and now fortune was smiling on us.

———————◆◆◆———————

While Alan and I were working doggedly with the banks on the IPO preparation, Fang Xing was busy courting TingCher, a Chinese brake supplier which was looking for additional capital to expand operations internationally. TingCher touted McLaren and Ferrari as its top clients. With the Formula One SingTel Singapore Grand Prix coming up in a few weeks, the TingCher factory in Shenzhen was a flurry of activity as its production teams and engineers geared up for the race.

Fang Xing, in his weekly update call with the Singapore team, heaped praises on Tingcher's organizational processes and its well-run corporate machinery. He also regaled us with a story of how Ms. Cindy Chow, TingCher's business development manager and a former car model, had spent two hours late at night showing him around the TingCher campus, explaining to him the entire manufacturing process in minute detail.

Fang Xing, with his sales flair, easily convinced Russell and Gary to allow him to pursue this deal further. After we finished the conference call, Fang Xing shared with me an even more interesting tidbit of information: he had casually mentioned to Ms. Chow at the end of his tour that he had yet to watch a Formula One race live. Ms.

Chow, who appeared to have been smitten by Fang Xing's charms, offered him two tickets to the Singapore Grand Prix's Paddock Club. She explained that a major client had invited her bosses to Singapore, but one of them could not go and thus there were two spare tickets.

"It's even better than building relationships on the golf course!" Fang Xing added glibly. "I've already told Russell I'm going to Singapore to network the TingCher management and hopefully seal the deal."

"How many tickets do you have?" I asked, secretly hoping that perhaps I could escape from the laborious drafting sessions for the weekend and make a quick trip home to Singapore.

"Two tickets. I'm bringing my wife. She needs a break after giving birth. She hasn't been sleeping much since the baby was born," Fang Xing responded.

Glumly, I turned my eyes back to page 169 of the draft prospectus I was reviewing.

"So, why is it that Fang Xing gets all the fun and I'm stuck with the tedious and boring proofreading work?" I complained to Rebecca as we knocked off for the day. "After all, we're the same rank now. Do you know he's going to Singapore with his wife at the end of the month to watch the Formula One? I think the Backstreet Boys, Beyoncé and Chinese stars like Jacky Cheung and A Mei will be performing at concerts during the race," I said.

"Wow! Jacky Cheung is my favorite Hong Kong singer!" Rebecca gushed. Then she paused, deep in thought. "Well, goodnight, you'd better go home and get some rest," she finally said, waving me away.

The days lurched by in humdrum tedium. Scanning the headlines in the Singapore news, I could almost feel the frenzy building up to the September 28 Formula One race, even as I sat thousands of miles away in a stuffy lawyer's office drafting IPO documents.

It was a dreary Friday evening, and I was looking forward to rushing back to the office in time to catch Rebecca before she left work for the day. As I mentally rehearsed my casual invitation to her to join me for drinks in a new trendy bar, I suddenly saw my blackberry light up with an e-mail from Rebecca to Alan, copied to me:

> *Dear Dong zong,*
>
> *Sorry I have some urgent matters to attend to, and cannot come in on Monday. I will apply one day urgent leave.*
>
> *Faithfully,*
> *Li Xiaohuan*

When I saw Rebecca's e-mail, I wondered what emergency had cropped up as she had not mentioned anything to me when we met in the office that morning. I attempted to call her, but she did not answer, so I left her a message expressing my concern.

The weekend passed in a melancholic daze as I worked dispiritedly to clear yet another pile of legal documents. Rebecca had turned off her cell phone and did not reply to any of my emails or text messages. I was starting to get worried about her. Finally, on Monday evening, I searched online for Rebecca's microblog, where I knew she loved to post photos of her food, shopping and daily activities.

A freshly-uploaded picture appeared on the screen—showing a beaming Rebecca surrounded by the giddy sights and sounds of the Formula One race in all its glory. I gasped, then cursed, and repeatedly hit the Refresh button on my browser as I waited for new photos to appear. My glazed eyes could hardly take in the scenes as they unfolded…the Formula One Paddock Club, the plush interior of a private jet, an enormous bed in the presidential suite of Singapore's famous Raffles Hotel.

Desperately searching for more clues, I chanced upon an old microblog post that read "Go to my blog for further commentary". I did not know Rebecca had a blog!

I searched high and low online, using every desktop research technique I had picked up during my past seven years of preparing corporate analysis reports and PowerPoint slides. Finally, two hours later, I finally found it: "Carefree-Becca's Blog" on sina.com.cn. I zeroed on a newly-posted story, littered with exclamation points and over-the-top Chinglish expressions, about a young working girl named Becca, and her boyfriend Fred Zhao:

September 25, 2009

At 5:30p.m. on Friday, Fred burst into the office, ran towards Becca's desk and instructed, "Go home now, pack your bags, we're going to Singapore! I'll pick you up at ten o'clock tonight. Remember to tell your big boss you will not be in on Monday!"

Becca shrieked and jumped up, eyes shining. "You're so *man*!" She could hardly believe her luck. Fred must be hopelessly in love with her to bring her to see The Formula One SingTel Singapore Grand Prix—the first night race and the first street circuit in Asia.

"Have you got your visa from the Singapore embassy approved?" Fred shouted as he rushed towards the elevator, bag in hand.

"Yes I did, boss!" Becca replied. "What about you?"

Fred rolled his eyes. "Didn't you know I got a US green card a few months ago when I made that huge real estate investment? I don't need to apply for visas anymore."

At 10:00p.m. sharp, a black unmarked car with tinted windows pulled up at Becca's apartment block. It was not Fred's Aston Martin. The car door swung open, and a burly man jumped out, grabbed her bags and said, "Let's go, Ms. Li. Mr. Zhao will meet us at the airport."

In a daze, Becca climbed into the car. Almost an hour later, they turned into an unmarked road. Where were they going? Becca wondered. She had never been to this part of Beijing before. Before long, the car arrived at a huge metal gate, almost the size of the doors to the Forbidden City. The sleepy guard at the gate snapped to attention and opened it.

Becca gasped. Floodlights filled the entire compound. In the middle of the compound was a sleek, silver-colored Dassault Falcon 7x. The compound was bustling with activity as the plane was being loaded and fueled. As she gazed around, she noticed someone walking towards her. It was Fred!

"Becca! Welcome! We'll be ready to take off in a moment. Let's get on board." Fred took her arm and steered her up the flight of red carpet stairs towards the cabin.

"Pinch me! I feel so *haiii* (high)!" Becca squealed, as she entered the cabin. It was set up like a luxurious six-star hotel suite. In the center of the cabin was a four-poster bed covered with freshly plucked rose petals. A table for two was set up with the finest silverware. On either side of the table was a plush armchair with seatbelts—the only hint that they were on board a plane. She whipped out her iPhone and started snapping pictures of the cabin.

As a lavish supper was served, Fred kissed her and exclaimed, "Baby, I can't believe we're actually doing this! The story you concocted for me to convince my wife to let me go alone for the Formula One actually worked! She finally relented this afternoon and allowed me to go off for the weekend while she stays at home to look after the baby. I was so afraid she would insist on coming, since I did invite her to come with me several weeks ago. Baby, you're a genius! Let me offer a toast to you…and to us!"

Becca raised her glass and smiled. She could now have Fred all to herself for the next few days. How much fun that would be!

"Off to bed! It's just a six-hour flight so we won't have much time to enjoy this gigantic bed!" Fred said, as he scooped Becca up in his arms.

September 26, 2009

The plane landed at Singapore's Seletar Airport. A black Volvo S80 whisked them off to Raffles Hotel, a colonial-style hotel named after Sir Stamford Raffles, the founder of modern Singapore. After freshening up, Fred brought Becca shopping for a suitable outfit to wear to the Formula One Paddock Club. "There is no way you can appear at the Paddock Club in these ugly Converse sneakers," he told her in no uncertain terms. "The Paddock Club is *the* place to be during the F1, and my business partners will be there. You need to look high-class so you can 'put radiance on my face'!"

September 27, 2009

"How do I look?" Becca strutted up and down the Raffles Hotel presidential suite in her brand new Jimmy Choo shoes. She wore a sleek gown which Fred told her had been designed by none other than the darling of Singapore fashion, Francis Cheong.

"Gorgeous, simply stunning!" was all Fred could say, his eyes glued to her hourglass figure.

An entourage of black Volvos at the Raffles Hotel conveyed Fred and Becca, as well as a host of other guests, to the Paddock Club. The lead car suddenly stopped as a team of policemen hurried to remove the street barriers. A moment later, the entourage was racing around the actual circuit! "A special treat for you, Mr. and Mrs. Zhao," the driver quipped.

Soon after, the entourage pulled up to the Paddock Club.

As Becca stepped out of the car, she felt as if she had entered a completely different world. The glitz and lights dazzled her. A waitress in a white mini dress and knee-high black boots handed her an ice-cold wet towel, followed by a glass of Dom Perignon rose champagne. It was the best champagne she had ever tasted, and clearly others agreed—Prince Charles and the late Princess Diana had chosen it for their wedding!

She looked around for Fred. There he was some feet away with his arms draped over the shoulders of two curvy waitresses, who were trying to drink his champagne at the same time.

Becca felt jealousy well up and sting her throat. She decided to walk around on her own to cool down. As she surveyed the guests around her, Becca's eyes grew larger and larger as she recognized international celebrities and politicians. Surely that was Justin Bieber…and "Little Li" Leonardo DiCaprio…and…was that her beloved idol Jacky Cheung?

"Ah, there you are! I was looking for you! Shall we get some food?" Fred slid up beside Becca. They headed up to the Nobu Suite where world renowned chef Nobu Matsuhisa and his team were whipping up mouth-watering treats. Fred and Becca methodologically worked their way through the masterpieces, with Becca taking a photo of each plate before tucking in.

After dinner, it was time for the Pit Walk. This was a rare chance to get up close to the cars, the crew, and perhaps even the drivers. Fred was distracted by the Russian models posing with the cars. Becca did not care this time, she was too busy drooling over a snapshot of her idol Lewis Hamilton, who had appeared briefly in the McLaren-Mercedes garage.

Fred and Becca then headed back to the Nobu Suite, as it had one of the best locations in the circuit to view the race.

They stood by the window and watched as the race flagged off just shortly after 8:00p.m. After twenty-six laps, an accident involving Adrian Sutil and Nick Heidfeld, and several pit stops, Becca started to get bored.

Nearly two hours after the race started, the drivers were down to their final laps. As Hamilton completed his final lap to take the checkered flag in a little over one hour and forty-five minutes, Becca shrieked in delight, "It must have been the kiss I blew him earlier that helped him to win the race!" Fred looked none too pleased but kept smiling as he chatted with two Singaporeans in business suits.

It was time to return to the hotel. Becca gave Fred a kiss, thanking him for the whirlwind trip to Singapore. Fred winked, popped open a bottle of bubbly champagne, and said, "Who says the evening has ended?"

Accompanying this breathless tale was a slew of photos of the Formula One race and other Singapore sights, but images of the two protagonists were conspicuously missing. I mulled over the diary entries deep into the night, imagining Rebecca and Fang Xing together.

On Tuesday morning, Rebecca was back in office on time. The only hint of her weekend escapade was the two cups of double-shot expresso she had already drunk.

After reading a glowing report submitted by Fang Xing about the progress he had made in his "highly advanced negotiations with TingCher senior executives" in Singapore over the weekend, I strolled over to Rebecca. "So did you resolve the urgent matter? I was very worried about you," I asked casually.

She did not look directly at me as she mumbled a response. "Yes, it's fine now."

I decided to confront her. "I've seen the pictures you posted on

Weibo! Who did you run off to Singapore with? You know I'm from Singapore, so if you were going there for a holiday, you could have asked me to help you with the itinerary."

This time, she looked at me straight in the eye. "I went with Fang Xing," she replied matter-of-factly. "And I turned off my phone the entire time I was in Singapore."

"Fang Xing?" I asked, feigning ignorance. "Why?"

"What do you mean *why*? Don't you already know that Fang Xing is the man of my dreams? My mother even hopes he may divorce his wife to marry me and bring me to the US to have our baby one day," she said nonchalantly. Her words hit me like a ton of bricks.

Suddenly, it all made sense to me. It was as if a light switch had been turned on. Some time ago, Fang Xing would quiz me each time after I went out with Rebecca, asking me how the dates went. Now I finally knew why he was so interested. He was trying to figure out if I could become a third party in their relationship.

I had always wondered whether the initial sparks that flew wildly on the duckie boat at Houhai during our first date could have culminated in a romantic relationship. I never found out until Fang Xing told me the answer—Rebecca never would marry a foreigner like me because she could not get a real sense of security and belonging from such a relationship.

While she liked the idea of migrating to a developed country like the US or Singapore to give her kids a foreign passport, she also held a complex bond with her motherland. She wanted her husband to work in China and to help her maintain strong ties with family and friends there. A foreigner, she felt, could not be depended on because he would inevitably tire of his China career and return to his homeland, never to return.

What's more, I didn't meet her mother's criteria: I had no house under my name. Neither did I own a car. I did not have enough zeros in my bank account. I had insufficient proof of financial capability. In

China, *luohun* 裸婚 (naked marriages)—a slang for getting married without first buying a property or a car—was still frowned upon by many parents.

Still, what really blew me away was the realization that Rebecca would rather have a fling with a married Chinese man than settle down with me. What was it about Fang Xing that made this social butterfly so attractive in the eyes of women? I had previously assumed that since he was a married man and a father, Rebecca would not seriously consider hooking up with him since he could offer her neither emotional security nor a real future. So what did that say about her values that she chose to be a *xiaosan* anyway? Was Fang Xing's ability to achieve incredible riches at a young age such an irresistible X-factor in China that even Rebecca's mother approved of him? Why was Fang Xing's foreign citizenship actually a plus factor for him in attracting girls like Rebecca, but a liability for me—a descendant of Chinese immigrants?

The revelation in Rebecca's blog that Fang Xing had acquired a US green card did not surprise me at all. He almost always brought up the topic of investment immigration when chatting with contacts in our private equity and business circles. What usually followed were heated debates about relative merits of different jurisdictions from the US to Europe, Singapore and Australia. The details they shared proved just how seriously many rich Chinese were considering migration. Many, in fact, had already taken action to get their green cards.

Later on, surveys showing that a growing proportion of Chinese multimillionaires—almost 60 percent by 2011—were considering immigration would spark surprise and controversy among the Chinese masses. But for some of my PE colleagues, who had spotted this trend much earlier, such news only reinforced their private joke that many of the juiciest deals in China still go to foreigners—that is, China-born elite haigui with foreign passports.

Dejectedly, I told myself to let go not just of Rebecca, but also the naive notion that I was qualified to be a young China hand.

Gone were the days where young Chinese women were caricatured for marrying foreign men just for the sake of getting their money and a green card to get out of the country. Equally obsolete was the cynical joke that old China hands tended to be a bunch of foreign teachers, business consultants or middlemen with a general knowledge of the Middle Kingdom and a specific interest in dating local beauties. As China prospered to become the world's second largest economy, affluent Chinese were acquiring their foreign identities with cold hard cash. Meanwhile, foreigners like me were finding it harder to prove our worth in China. Was there anything that would set me apart from the increasingly formidable haigui?

> *E Shou Cheng Qing* 额手称庆: **To put one's hands to the brow in rejoicing, exulting at one's fortune.**

CHAPTER 15

Alone

Dan Shen Zhi Shou 单身只手

I T WAS A BITTERLY COLD morning in early March 2010. I squirmed in my heavy wool coat, trying to readjust to the city's choking smog. I had just returned from Dandong, a coastal city in Liaoning province just west of the border to North Korea, where I had spent the weekend teaching English to young adults at a local coffee house. The air there was so refreshingly pristine that I felt almost suffocated the minute I reached Beijing.

No one really knew the source of the pollution. But the prime suspects were the heavy industries from nearby Hebei province and the nearly five million cars on Beijing's roads that consumed what some claimed was substandard gasoline. China had just become the number one automobile market in the world back in January this year.

To keep the pollution in check, the Beijing government decided to implement policy measures where cars with number plates ending with certain digits were not allowed to travel on the roads on specific days. On top of this, car owner wannabes had to participate in a lottery for new license plates which took place every month. However, the odds of success were slimmer as time passed, as unsuccessful applications got rolled over to the next month. This was bad news for me, since I was planning to buy a car—the first item on my checklist to make me into a more eligible bachelor in China. Worse yet, all these draconian measures seemed to do little to improve the air quality.

I pondered all this as I stared out of the office window waiting anxiously for Russell's e-mail letter informing me of my annual bonus payment. If it were substantial, I would finally be able to afford a down-payment on my first apartment.

On top of that, I might also potentially be entitled to a carry bonus worth a mid-range Aston Martin if DeeDee successfully listed in April—just one month's time. All-Stellar's investment bankers had told us that the fund's shares would be worth at least three times of its initial investment. Based on this valuation, if we successfully sold our shares in the market, I could be in for a windfall since I had played a significant role in this deal.

I looked around me. For the first time in many months, Alan, Fang Xing, Rebecca and I were all in the office together at the same time.

I strolled into Fang Xing's room, where he was listlessly surfing the internet for information about wealthy Chinese's investments in European vineyards. "Is that a new deal you're proposing to Russell, or is that what you're planning to buy with your bonus?" I asked jokingly.

He grinned. "How did you guess? With a penthouse, exotic art, an Aston Martin, and a Patek Phillippe watch, the things I'm still missing are a private jet and a vineyard. I think I'll spend my bonus on cultivating my own Bourdeax first, it's always been a dream of mine since I was a teenager."

I was crestfallen. Here I was envisioning my first set of wheels, while Fang Xing—as usual—was miles ahead of me, planning his first vineyard.

"Wow, you have big dreams," I muttered.

"Of course, you have to dream big to get far in a big place like China, right? You know Ma Yun used to joke with his friend, 'If I'm not a millionaire by thirty-five, please kill me'? Just look where he is now. One of the richest men in China," replied Fang Xing.

I nodded silently. But this time, I did not feel the usual twinge of envy that surged whenever Fang Xing showed off his riches. Perhaps I was starting to get a little jaded by the frenetic pursuit of material possessions around me. I was also starting to understand the sacrifices one had to make to strike it big in China. To get ahead, I was now more than willing to risk my health—breathing in hazardous air in Beijing was just the beginning—and to blunt my conscience doing things I would have been uncomfortable with in Singapore. And I sensed that there were many more risks I would have to take, and more shenanigans to deal with, if I wanted to get my hands on the China prizes Fang Xing had already acquired.

Fang Xing broke my reverie. "So what have you been up to these three months? I've been on the road so much that I haven't had time to catch up with you."

I shrugged. "Nothing much, working like crazy on the IPO, that's all. I did follow Manager Wang to Wutaishan in January. I needed some fresh air and scenery to clear my head."

"So how was the trip?"

Staring at the wall of gray particles suspended right outside the office window, my mind flashed back to the sunlight-drenched, jade-green landscapes that we had passed as Wang steered his Beijing Jeep Cherokee southwest down the Beijing-Kunming Highway that cold January morning.

When we reached Wutaishan National Park, I had been overwhelmed by awe. The mountains jutted their jagged peaks into the fluffy white clouds, while incense-filled mist clutched at their ankles. Multicolored flags waved in the breeze, representing the five elements: blue for sky; white for air; red for fire; green for water and yellow for earth.

Wang led the way to the Five Grandfathers' Temple, the favorite shrine for those praying for fortune or romance. "The famous abbot here once said to me that each person should not be greedy. Three wishes. Nothing more, nothing less," Wang said.

We walked gingerly down the silvery cobblestoned path, which seemed to rumble with the monotonous chants of monks within. At the entrance of the temple, Wang pulled out two crisp red 100-yuan notes from his pocket and handed it over to a monk, in exchange for two fat bundles of joss sticks. He shoved me a bundle. "Pray to the Buddha inside, and your wish will definitely come true!" he urged me. I nodded and smiled to show my respect for his beliefs, but did not join him inside.

He knelt down in front of the giant Buddha statue, closed his eyes, and clasped both hands in front of his chest. His three prayer requests were already written on his forehead: a successful IPO in early 2010; lots of money to cash out from his company options; a future filled with material abundance, prosperity and two children.

I rushed over to help a severely hunched elderly lady over the temple sill, and decided to give her the joss sticks Wang had bought. Smiling in gratitude, she clutched the bundle as she struggled to kneel down in front of the Buddha statue. Wang was two pillows away, eyes still closed, chanting an incomprehensible prayer. I stepped back to watch them again, contemplating a quote posted on search engine Baidu's questions and answers page (http://zhidao.baidu.com) which I had recently read while researching Wutaishan:

> *Today, as I reminisced at the moments I stood on Wutaishan praying for things to come, I laughed at my innocence and childishness of yesteryears. The smiles on my face revealed not the first fruits of joy and sweetness when I prayed at Wutaishan for the first time, but a painful revelation at the extent of my unanswered prayers with a tinge of bitterness. One sincere heart, one true desire, engulfed by the vicissitudes of reality, leaving deep scars down to the core of my heart.*

It was written by an anonymous Chinese netizen. I hoped that Wang, who had become a good friend to me by now, would never be scarred by the kind of disappointment expressed by the author. But there was still an uneasy foreboding I could not fathom; a sense of dread that had swelled ever since I realized Alan was not quite the China hand I had expected.

I did not share all of this with Fang Xing, however, knowing that he did not care for anything mystical or religious. I simply answered: "It was a great tourist experience and the temples are interesting—if you care for that sort of thing."

I went on to describe all the different temples on Wutaishan: If you wanted love or needed money, Five Grandfathers' Temple was the top recommendation. For success in your career or good grades for your children, Buddha Peak would be your best bet. If you craved wisdom, or if you had difficulty conceiving a child, pray to a statue inside the Special Idol Temple.

"If you went to the wrong temple, would your prayer be ignored?" asked Fang Xing flippantly.

I shrugged. "You should ask the millions of people who flock to Wutaishan every year. It's an age-old tradition for them."

Fang Xing shook his head incredulously. "Why do these people even need to go so far to pray?" he said scornfully. "Superstition is such a waste of time, just go out and get what you want."

"Sounds like you are an atheist or an agnostic, since you don't believe in such stuff?" I asked.

He looked me blankly. Those terms were meaningless to him. "It's just a matter a time before old customs and beliefs must give way to the new. All I know is: if one does not embrace the future, time will pass you by. Before long, you realize you're left behind. So we have to grab every opportunity to enrich ourselves and get ahead."

His comment sparked a revelation for me. Fang Xing represented a generation of young Chinese who have been brought up to believe only in themselves. He was his own greatest supporter and fan. Self-achievement ranked higher than religion or faith, and he worshipped at his own altar.

Just then, Rebecca let out an excited squeak. "The letters are in..."
We rushed to our laptops.

Russell had given me an excellent appraisal, commending me for my "hard work, acumen, and ability to connect with key stakeholders on the ground". His only criticism was that I had not brought in any new China deals. That made me reflect rather regretfully on the proposal Fang Xing and I had submitted to buy a minority stake in Chili Sisters, the spicy hotpot chain. Fang Xing had left it to me to present the investment rationale, and I had explained to Russell that AEXI Capital was a reliable partner.

"We would not go wrong co-investing along a relatively seasoned foreign investor who had a proven track record in buying and exiting investments in China and who had already built a strong relationship with the Chinese company," I had argued.

But as it turned out, AEXI Capital decided against teaming up with us. They had found an influential Chinese investor who offered a much better price than what Russell had finally signed off on after discussing my proposal.

I was disappointed, but Fang Xing had consoled me at that time by explaining there was no way All-Stellar could have competed to get the deal. "That Chinese investor is a serial entrepreneur who can get any kind of bank loan he wants, and can provide useful local government contacts to help Chili Sisters break into new markets," he had said. "We can't match that sort of value proposition."

Even though the deal had not materialized, I was still given a six-month bonus, in line with my expectations.

From the looks on Fang Xing and Alan's faces, they too seemed reasonably satisfied with their bonuses. I overheard Alan calling his personal banker in the US to tweak his personal portfolio allocations, while Fang Xing was already heading out for celebratory drinks with Rebecca.

I sat there alone in the dim office, wondering why I was not more ecstatic that my longed-for new car and apartment were finally about to become a reality.

Was it because I, as an honorable Beijing taxpayer, would have to contribute almost half of my bonus to the tax bureau first? But even that deduction did not sting as much anymore. Chairman Zhou had earlier offered me a fresh new perspective to look at it: "Paying taxes was a whole lot better than having no bonus at all."

Perhaps it was that nagging feeling of floating in the calm before a storm, which no amount of self-belief or Wutaishan chants could quell.

A week passed. We had almost completed the preparation work for the IPO. All we needed now was for DeeDee's auditor to issue the final audited report, and then the financial figures in the IPO prospectus could be finalized. Chairman Zhou and the management team would begin their global management road show[26] shortly after.

At 10:50p.m., I got an unexpected call from Fang Xing. "I have just tendered my resignation. I just received another offer from another PE outfit. You should leave with me. This place pays peanuts!"

I was speechless. It was all too bizarre. Why was Fang Xing leaving so abruptly? He had been with us for less than two years. It was mystifying that Fang Xing would leave when there was low-lying fruit to pluck with the IPO taking place in a month's time.

"Fang Xing, this is your deal. You brought it to the table with

[26] The management roadshow is a critical part of the IPO process, where the company's management, together with their underwriters, travel around the world to give presentations to analysts, fund managers, and potential institutional investors to secure orders for the company's shares.

Susie. The company is going to list in a month. If you stick around, it will mean a big fat carry check! Why are you rushing to leave when you're about to make so much money?" I asked in bewilderment.

After a brief moment of silence, Fang Xing replied jokingly, "The offer is irresistible. Anyway, if I leave, wouldn't you get a bigger portion of the carry? It's time for me to move on to a new opportunity."

He refused to tell me anything about the new PE outfit he was joining. I reckoned Fang Xing's new employer must have dangled such a huge sign-on bonus that it would far outstrip even the largesse he would receive from DeeDee's IPO.

The next morning, I found myself alone once again with Rebecca in the office. She was sitting at her desk aimlessly. I figured she had already finished her Taobao shopping for the week. Fang Xing's desk had been cleared overnight, apart from a few paper files he left behind and a self-help book entitled "Awaken the Giant Within".

"Why do you think Fang Xing decided to leave?" I asked Rebecca.

"Better pay, better benefits? I'm not surprised at all. Or maybe he found a new sweetheart and decided to abandon us?" she replied chokingly.

I sat down at the edge of Fang Xing's empty desk, trying to make sense of his abrupt departure. I sensed there was more than meets the eye, but I tried again to convince myself Fang Xing's resignation was just a minor hiccup and that I would be better off holding a longer-term view by sitting through the investment.

His parting shot floated through my brain again: "You should leave with me. This place pays peanuts!"

Was he really suggesting that his new firm would offer me an even higher-paying job too, or was it merely an off-hand comment he didn't mean?

Should I leave anyway? I was the only one left from the original China team. With Susie, Randy, Fang Xing gone and Alan—who had only been on board for a few months—also showing signs of wanting to leave after DeeDee listed, I could well be completely alone in a year's time. I was unnerved at that thought.

But I decided to stick on and see the deal through out of loyalty to Russell, who had put quite a lot of confidence in me so far.

Some part of me was also gleeful at the thought of taking over Fang Xing's share of the carry bonus. Together with the outstanding interest on my loan to John Tan's hospital project, I would be able to afford a nicer apartment in downtown Beijing.

> *Dan Shen Zhi Shou* 单身只手: **A lonely hand, describing someone who is all alone and without help.**

CHAPTER 16

Scrambling

Shou Mang Jiao Luan 手忙脚乱

ANOTHER WEEK WHIZZED BY. PHONES were ringing off the hook with calls from our lawyers and IPO sponsors as we raced to finish our preparations. I accompanied the research analysts who were preparing initial coverage[27] on site visits to DeeDee's duck farms around China.

Then, six days after Fang Xing's departure, the unthinkable happened. DeeDee's new CFO, Steven Chen, called Alan in panic.

"Our auditor has resigned!"

I was in the office when Alan received this news, and heard a strangled screech come from his room. "What do you mean? You're saying our audit firm B&C actually resigned? How can they resign? When did they resign? How can they possibly resign at the eleventh hour, right before the IPO?"

Alan listened to a frantic yelling on the other end of the line

---

[27] Research analysts from the investment bank's research team will often "initiate coverage" on a new stock listing if there is sufficient buying interest. After commencing coverage, the analyst will usually publish a report on the stock, followed by periodic updates.

for almost five minutes. Finally, he slammed down the phone and staggered out of the office.

I did not know what had actually happened, but whatever I could glean so far had already made me fear the worst. The resignation of B&C meant that DeeDee would no longer be able to get its set of historical financial statements signed off by an external audit firm before the IPO—a requirement that was as fundamental as submitting SAT scores or a set of recommendation letters in order to apply for college. Investors, as well as the public, rely on external auditors to provide an unbiased and independent view on a company's financial health, and to assess whether its financial statements are in line with accounting standards. DeeDee's IPO was doomed if it did not have the audit reports.

I found Alan huddled in the bathroom and we started to list out the questions that Russell was bound to demand answers to immediately. The abrupt turn of events threw up questions that Alan and I had no way of answering quickly. What did B&C find out that led to their decision to quit? Why was there no prior notice? Instances of auditors resigning so close to the IPO were extremely rare.

At almost midnight, with no clear answers in hand, Alan and I finally broke the news to the All-Stellar team in Singapore. Russell was predictably livid, and unleashed a torrent of curses even more colorful than those yelled by Beijing cab drivers stuck in traffic.

"How could this ever happen? What the hell is going on?" he howled, after calm had finally been restored in our emergency conference call.

"In the weeks leading up to their resignation, the auditor had raised certain outstanding questions about the financial position and performance of the company," Alan began tentatively. I could see his knees literally knocking together.

"Yeah, we heard about that. B&C had requested that Chairman Zhou's team provide the additional documentation to support their audit work," snapped Gary impatiently. "That's no big deal—most audit firms raise questions during the normal course of audit. As long as the company's finance team responds promptly to their requests, there's nothing to be worried about. What's the problem?"

"Yes, having audit issues is normal and do not necessarily spell trouble," responded Alan. "But in our case, the auditor raised the issues at a very advanced stage. In fact, as late as last Thursday, the B&C senior audit partner met up with Steven and the IPO underwriters to discuss the auditor's concerns and possible solutions."

"Fang Xing had attended this meeting to represent All-Stellar, but he did not report any significant concerns when he returned to the office," I added.

"So did they come up with any solutions at the Thursday meeting? Why didn't you alert us of this meeting?" growled Russell.

Alan was silent for a few moments. It was clear from his expression that he was regretting not attending the meeting himself and sending Fang Xing—who, at that time, had not yet tendered his resignation—instead. He decided to dodge the question. "The audit firm discussed some possible solutions with us, and we thought they were satisfied with our answers," he said.

"But this afternoon, with no warning, they fucked us. They issued a statement to the stock exchange stating that they will relinquish the role of company auditor with immediate effect. They will retract all their statements and filings submitted to the stock exchange.[28]"

Russell was too flabbergasted to speak. Gary started hyperventilating. I silently pulled out the letter that the auditor addressed to the shareholders of the company. At Alan's bidding, I read it aloud: "We have noted several inconsistencies in documentation in our audit for the three years ending December 31, 2009 for Dominant

---

[28] Prior to listing, a company's auditors and lawyers, together with the IPO underwriters, have to sign off on the official IPO prospectus before it is printed and distributed.

Duck Poultry Farming Co. and can no longer act as the company's auditors. We hereby resign as auditors and reporting accountants with immediate effect."

Dead silence. We all pondered the implications of this statement. It was like the final nail in the coffin, killing off Chairman Zhou's IPO dream and our goal of making a 300 percent return on our investment.

A full three minutes later, Russell finally spoke. "And where the hell is that China man?"

"We haven't been able to reach Chairman Zhou on his cell phone, nor his office line today," I replied despairingly. "When we asked the company management where he is, their coordinated response was that he is away on *jiankang liaoyang* 健康疗养 (medical holiday)."

I did not add that I had just seen Chairman Zhou looking relaxed and in high spirits during our meeting just one week ago. He told me he had just gone to his favorite tailor to make new suits so he would look spiffy for the road show.

"What kind of shit is a 'medical holiday'? Is it typical for Chinese CEOs to run away on long breaks when crises pop up?" Russell bellowed. Alan wisely did not answer.

Then, Gary finally stopped gulping air long enough to scream: "Go find that idiot now before I strangle all of you!"

So I rang up Mark Hensworth.

"Chairman Zhou has been extremely stressed out ever since the company commenced IPO preparations. He has worked non-stop for the past six months and the doctors have advised that he needs some rest. When he recovers, he will be sure to reach out to you," Mark recited mechanically. Even his staunch refusals to discuss anything remotely related to the Lao Qianbei sounded very well-rehearsed.

"Wait, Mark, can you at least tell me if Chairman Zhou is still alive?" I asked desperately.

The line went dead.

With the auditor's abrupt resignation, the investment banks had to resign as sponsors to the listing. DeeDee was forced to withdraw its listing application. We were back to square one. Our backbreaking work over the past six months came to naught in a matter of hours.

The next day, Alan and I went to DeeDee's headquarters. It was buzzing with activity. Everything looked like business as usual. The only thing that looked amiss was that Chairman Zhou's office door was firmly shut and there was no long line of nervous managers waiting outside to see him.

We urgently needed to speak to someone at the company who had the authority to make decisions during Chairman Zhou's absence so that we could figure out the next course of action together. But no one dared to even say hello to us without getting his approval first.

"It seems that we are stuck until Chairman Zhou decides to reappear," Alan reported glumly back to Russell.

"If you can't get those fucked-up ducks to talk to you, then at least drill the fucking bean counters! Tell them we will sue if they don't explain properly why they bailed out on us!" Russell screamed. A pretty reasonable recommendation, it would seem. The only hitch was that B&C was only willing to entertain a meeting with us if the majority shareholder—that is, Chairman Zhou—was present.

Our Limited Partners blasted us about the auditor's resignation. But apart from telling them the embarrassing truth that we were unable to locate Chairman Zhou, there was nothing much more we could say. Alan and I raced through many all-nighters to prepare a detailed memo for them on the history of this investment and chronology of events leading to the auditor's resignation. In it, we tried to come up with a proposed plan to mitigate the damage. However, without real facts to back up our case and without any first-hand accounts of what had actually happened, we could only make educated guesses about why the auditor had resigned. We were utterly exhausted from trying to make sense of this impossible situation.

It was during this period of upheaval at DeeDee that China experienced one of its fiercest droughts and dust storms in recent years, paralyzing large swathes of China's western and southern provinces. Perhaps the heavens were giving us signs of more ominous times to come.

Certainly, for myself, there was worse news to stomach when I tried to contact John Tan to get an update on my loan to his company. The repayment was overdue by three months, but I had not heard a word from him. That was not all. On top of the RMB200,000 (US$30,000) I had co-invested in the hospital project, I had actually lent Donovan an additional RMB100,000 (US$15,000) last September, as he said he "needed money to tide over this difficult period." He told me he had paid some esoteric consultant a big sum of money to pull some relationships in the government to expedite the license approval process. He promised he would return me RMB150,000 (US$23,000) one month later, equivalent to a glitzy annualized return of 600 percent. It did not take me long to take up the offer. I did not even sign a contract with him.

"Please do not worry about the money that I owe you. If you can be a little more patient with me, I shall be happy to more than make up the money you have put in the project." This was the last time I heard from Donovan, when he had e-mailed me in late January. Since then, he had been unreachable on both his Singapore and China cell phones.

The only small consolation was that I was still always able to reach John. Every time I called, he gave me hope that there was some new solution that he was working on to repay me my money. This time, he said that the company was expecting a new deal after Chinese New Year and was in advanced discussions with a US business group who was going to repay the loan and buy up the Chinese partner's shares at the same time. But with Russell breathing down my neck and the crisis at DeeDee consuming all my waking hours, I never managed to go back to the construction site, nor was I able to meet the Chinese partner.

I was still reeling from the shock of my own investment fiasco when Chairman Zhou finally reappeared from his "medical holiday" almost two weeks later. He sent me a text saying he was ready to meet. Alan immediately shot out an e-mail to the All-Stellar team in Singapore with the subject header: "CHAIRMAN ZHOU HAS FINALLY COME OUT OF HIDING."

Russell dashed onto the next flight to Beijing. The next morning, we walked into DeeDee's office, where all the senior managers were dressed in the same charcoal black suits, lending a funeral mood to the meeting.

We expected to see a visibly refreshed Chairman Zhou after his long break, but were greeted instead by his fatigue-battered face and bulging eye bags. "I do not agree with the judgment and conclusion of the auditor," he started forcefully, slamming the table for emphasis. "The auditor wanted us to reduce the previous year's net profit number by ten million yuan. We found this absurd and did not agree."

He motioned to Steven to flash a power point presentation on a TV screen. Steven spent over an hour laboriously explaining why DeeDee was still qualified for an IPO, since its sales were really much higher than what the auditor had estimated.

We all sat in silence listening attentively but I could tell Russell's despair was deepening by the minute. It was obvious to us that any attempt to explain what had gone wrong with the auditor's assessment was futile by this time. We had already delayed too long in providing a satisfactory response to our Limited Partners, and the negative press around our pulled IPO had sealed our fate—it would be impossible to return to any stock exchange to list in the foreseeable future.

At the end of the presentation, Chairman Zhou tried to put on his best gung-ho face: "So that's why we need to keep fighting and pressing on in our revolutionary fervor to bring our IPO to fruition."

Russell was too weary to shoot snarky comments about the Red capitalists. "Chairman Zhou, shall we arrange a meeting with B&C as soon as possible, now that you have reappeared? It's been almost one month since they resigned, and we need to speak to them directly."

But the long-awaited meeting only served to thicken the plot further: the Hong Kong-based senior audit partner who had led the auditing process did not even attend the meeting. A senior manager, Mr. Ling, was sent to meet us on his behalf. It turned out that audit partner had already left B&C last week.

Mr. Ling was a bony and angular man in his mid-thirties from the northern coastal city of Tianjin. His grey-streaked hair was parted to the side, exposing his heavily receding hairline. He looked so thin that I fancied he could have been blown over by the blast of Russell's wrathful demands that B&C explain its "senseless resignation".

"B&C is a big audit firm. We audit state-owned companies and privately-owned enterprises with the same level of vigor and professionalism," Mr. Ling began.

"Your senior audit partner, who has just resigned, wanted us to reduce our previous year's net profit number by ten million yuan at the very last minute. He did not give us any chance to state our case properly. This is completely absurd and unjustified," Steven retorted.

Mr. Ling adjusted his glasses a few times, carefully avoiding Steven's glare. "In performing the audit work for the past few months, we noticed several irregularities in the company's financial statements. We sent people to Liuzhou in Guangxi province, as well as to Huangchuan in Henan province to verify the facts with the local government officials. They are telling a different story from what you have described to us."

Russell, Alan and I sat bolt upright in alarm. This was the first time we had heard about these issues. Somehow, none of this had surfaced during our due diligence checks. Chairman Zhou's stoic face betrayed no emotion at all.

Mr. Ling proceeded to read a prepared script out mechanically:

"We found out Dominant Duck had an outstanding land title dispute with the Huangchuan local authorities. The management team tells us it has been resolved but our investigations on the ground suggest otherwise.

The audit team also went down to Guangxi province to conduct an audit of Dominant Duck's farms in Liuzhou. We found out that the land bureau of the provincial government in Nanning did not recognize Dominant Duck as the owner of the land on which its farms had been built.

In addition, we have reason to believe some sales contracts are falsified. In light of this, the revenue that Dominant Duck reported to us has been artificially inflated.

Dominant Duck's management told us to overlook such accounting irregularities. This is unacceptable."

Steven once again leapt up to protest. "What bullshit! DeeDee is without doubt the rightful owner of the land in Liuzhou! It was granted the rights to the land by the Liuzhou agricultural authorities and also got approvals from the environmental bureau to build the duck farm! B&C were the ones who fucked up by going to the wrong government department for information!"

"B&C went to the land bureau in Nanning. As you should know, Nanning is the capital city of Guangxi. It holds much more authority than the Liuzhou bureau. The officials there said they had no records of Dominant Duck's contracts," Mr. Ling replied coldly.

"What idiots!" hissed Steven. "Come on, you know full well the quality of communication between local government departments, and the kind of record-keeping they do. Guangxi province is so huge. It's really not that surprising that the Guangxi officials know nothing about DeeDee's contracts in Liuzhou!"

"B&C does not comment on the way local governments operate," stated Mr. Ling, turning more robot-like by the minute.

"Well, what about the land title dispute? Surely you will agree with us that DeeDee was simply following legitimate local practices in a small county like Huangchuan? That was the only way to guarantee our business interests there!" protested Steven.

"You had claimed that DeeDee (Huangchuan) Company Limited owned the agricultural land that its farm was located on. But when B&C went to check with the local land authority, the officials told us DeeDee's land license had not been renewed for two years," recited Mr. Ling, reading again from his prepared script. "The staff's living quarters were illegally built on agricultural land. You should have applied for a property development license to build the hostels. Please explain why you insist that you are following legitimate business practices."

Steven was turning blue in the face. "We've explained this situation to your colleagues so many times and you still don't get it?"

The robot looked blankly at us.

Chairman Zhou spoke up. "Mr. Ling, I personally went down to Huangchuan to sign a ten-year working arrangement with the local agricultural cooperative. They helped us to acquire the land through their connections and promised to support our future manpower requirements for the duck farm, on condition that I pay for the construction of the co-op staff's living quarters on the agricultural land."

"Where is the official contract for this deal? Where are the written approvals from the land authority officials?" asked the robot.

"Some of the local land authority officials were present at the dinner when I made the deal with the co-op chief," replied Chairman Zhou. "They fully approved of DeeDee's commitment to help improve the livelihoods of the co-op members by providing jobs and living quarters for them."

"So where is the written proof of their approval…"

Steven totally lost it. "Mr. Ling, are you really stupid or faking stupid? You know as well as we do that these small counties do not issue written contracts for everything. You are obviously just trying to nitpick at small technicalities because you have no solid case for why B&C resigned so abruptly! Why don't you get that audit partner who resigned last week to come back and explain the real reason why he fucked us up?"

"B&C maintains that we have a solid case, especially on the issue of the sales contracts," recited Mr. Ling dully.

"Those damned sales contracts again. We admit that we had not been able to produce the originals," sighed Steven wearily. "One of our local operations managers – who left the company a year ago and went to Africa to work – had filed them away somewhere but we haven't been able to locate them. But we were able to reproduce the exact same copies of the contracts from our customers, and also had them officially stamped. Isn't that enough for you?"

Mr. Ling was unmoved. "Based on our investigations and our understanding of the issues, we decided not to recognize the revenues from the falsified sales contracts and from the Liuzhou operations. We also chose not to recognize part of the revenues generated by the Huangchuan operations. We continue to stand by these decisions," he stated.

By now, Steven was too choked up with frustration to respond. Chairman Zhou, whose silent rage made him look much more menacing than when he was yelling death threats at his staff for wasting electricity, spoke for him. "DeeDee has always played by the local rules and did not deviate from what was deemed as normal business practices in China," he barked. "Either you international auditors are so dumb that you do not understand how business is done in China, or your senior auditor was viciously trying to block our IPO. Now you are left clutching at empty reasons to justify what was obviously a wrong decision for B&C to resign as auditor."

Russell, who was already drenched in sweat from hearing all these revelations about DeeDee for the first time, squirmed in his seat. Chairman Zhou was throwing some pretty damning accusations at B&C.

Still, I could not help wondering: if the audit partner had been a local Chinese firm, would DeeDee have passed the audit? Probably yes. But even so, that might not have helped it to successfully list on one of Asia's top stock exchanges. Investors wanted no less than an all-clear from a top international auditor on DeeDee's accounts, after being spooked by a recent spate of fraud scandals at a handful of Chinese firms listed in Asian markets like Singapore and Hong Kong.

The next two hours dragged on as each side repeated their stand ad nauseam. What bothered me most was that the accounting issues that B&C had highlighted did not sound overly controversial. Maybe they could even have been solved if both sides stopped being so hell bent on pinning the entire blame on the other side. But Mr. Ling repeatedly made clear that he was merely a messenger and had not been directly involved in auditing DeeDee's accounts. So he refused to be drawn into a constructive discussion of how to resolve the issues.

Finally, we ended the meeting, defeated and lost.

Russell had no choice but to go back to the Investment Committee with the bad news that B&C refused to retract their allegations that DeeDee's accounts had major irregularities.

"Our sincere and heartfelt opinion is that the auditor had meted out a sentence too harsh for a company that was simply trying to raise capital for expansion. We believe that DeeDee did not deliberately falsify the accounts," he wrote in an e-mail to the Investment Committee. I was not in the loop to read the replies, but I imagined they must have been scathing.

It finally crystallized for me just how conveniently Fang Xing had timed his departure. Did he know about B&C's resignation ahead of time? If not, why would he resign just weeks before the company he had introduced to All-Stellar was about to enter into the honorable league of overseas-listed Chinese firms?

I suddenly recalled Rebecca complaining that Fang Xing's cell phone had been engaged for a very long time after he returned from the final meeting with B&C, and she could not reach him. Was he already plotting the fastest way to get out of our sinking ship?

> *Shou Mang Jiao Luan* 手忙脚乱:
> **Hands and legs in a flurry, to act with confusion.**

CHAPTER 17

Pandemonium

Cuo Shou Dun Zu 搓手顿足

I T WAS A STIFLINGLY HOT day in late May 2010—about two years since All-Stellar first invested in the company, and over two months since the auditor resigned.

The conference room in DeeDee's Beijing headquarters was crammed with sweating people, mostly from All-Stellar. All of our top brass was there, as well as a bunch of associates and even two interns who had been flown to Beijing from Singapore for the sole reason that they could speak Mandarin. Russell wanted everyone who could possibly communicate with the Chinese side to be there for the meeting. This was the most "face" we had ever given to Chairman Zhou. The problem was, we were not even sure he would turn up for the meeting.

He had not been seen for the past three weeks, having disappeared on his second "medical holiday" without any warning. Not surprisingly, this made our entire team freak out. We were clearly losing our handle on Chairman Zhou, and DeeDee's situation was increasingly dire. Cash flow pressures were mounting, and two dozen employees had resigned. Finding a replacement auditor was also an impossible task—even if there were no material misstatements in the financial statements, which auditor would dare to pick up the broken pieces and assume responsibility for a set of numbers that another auditor had expressly refused to sign off on?

After twenty days, I finally managed to reach Chairman Zhou on the phone and persuade him to come into the office. By this time, Russell had come around to the realization that the Lao Qianbei was really the only person who could help us salvage our investment. So he was anxious to mend broken bridges and win him back to our side, and instructed Alan to sweet-talk Chairman Zhou as much as possible.

Forty minutes dragged by. To pass the time, I scanned the news on my cell phone. One headline read: "Passion Club Among Four Top Nightclubs Ordered to Close Down." Beijing police had launched surprise spot checks at several high-end entertainment venues in May 2010, shutting down four of them and arresting 557 escort girls.

The Passion Club was where Alan had earlier brought Chairman Zhou for a raucous night of merrymaking, in the hopes of reigniting the spark in All-Stellar's relationship with DeeDee, I recalled. Now the club, once thought to be immune to corruption crackdowns thanks to its powerful clientele of elite businessmen, officials and military officers, had fallen under the axe of a political campaign which famous state TV anchor-man Bai Yansong described as "challenging the privileged class, and cleansing the social environment". Some local media even portrayed its shut-down as a "magnitude-ten earthquake" which had "meaning of epic proportions". Others speculated that it was somehow linked to the massive triad-busting activities in Chongqing, which had been led by the western municipality's then-party chief Bo Xilai.

Another news item that gripped my attention was a scandal involving Chinese textile maker Hontex International Holdings. It had listed in Hong Kong in December 2009, but was now under scrutiny for disclosing false or misleading information in its IPO prospectus. On March 29, 2010, the Hong Kong securities regulator had gone to court to freeze Hontex's assets in the city, stating in a press release that the company was alleged to have materially overstated its financial position in its prospectus.

Hontex was just one of a growing number of Chinese companies listed in Hong Kong, Singapore and the United States that had become embroiled in accounting scandals over the past two years. In Singapore, at least six Chinese firms listed on the stock exchange had been exposed since 2008 for irregularities such as questionable cash transactions and inflated sales. In the US, investors in listed Chinese firms were losing billions of dollars as allegations of fraud ravaged stock prices[29]. I had followed all these developments with interest, and wondered if DeeDee would have been hit by the wave of negative investor sentiment about Chinese IPOs, even if it had managed to list during this sensitive period.

Suddenly, the door swung open. The Lao Qianbei marched into the room with his managers in tow, and glared defiantly at the crowd of foreigners around the table.

All of us in the All-Stellar team leapt to our feet. We launched into a long round of effusive greetings and introductions. A beaming Alan shook the Lao Qianbei's hand for what seemed like eternity as he cooed, "Chairman Zhou, there are no issues too difficult for both parties to resolve together in an amicable manner. It would be best if

---

[29] Fraud schemes involving small-cap Chinese firms listed on the major US exchanges may have cost investors at least US$34 billion over the past five years, according to a study conducted by financial web publication TheStreet.com., which published its findings in an article headlined "SEC Probes China Stock Fraud Network" on December 21, 2010. The study calculated the market capitalization losses for 150 stocks that appeared to have been used to bring Chinese companies to US exchanges. These 150 stocks included those directly implicated in fraud allegations, as well as those damaged by association with such issues.

you can work together with us instead of going off on official breaks without telling us first."

I could sense a little stuttering in his voice. Russell was smiling as civilly as he could through clenched teeth.

"Why do I need to inform you all?" Chairman Zhou snorted derisively. "I had good reason to go away. I was out speaking to potential buyers to buy up your stake in DeeDee."

That was yet another bombshell to shatter any remnant of trust we had in Chairman Zhou. So he had been maneuvering behind our backs to get All-Stellar out of his company? After his return from his first "medical holiday," he had agreed to our request that both parties maintain constant and frank communication on all issues, and resolve all problems together. Now Chairman Zhou was blatantly violating the investment agreement by going out unilaterally to market our stake to potential buyers.

"What the..." stuttered Russell. "Why were you speaking to potential investors on our behalf?"

"I am sure it is in everybody's interests that we find a new investor to replace you," Chairman Zhou replied coolly. "Your team seems too busy to do it, and I have much better guanxi than any of you, so I thought I'd give you a helping hand."

Russell was stumped for a minute. It was true that All-Stellar now needed to consider the option of exiting from DeeDee much earlier than planned. But how were we going to sell out at a reasonable valuation when the company had no audited financial statements? We were loath to sell out in a distressed sale, where shares of a company are sold in an urgent manner and often at a loss. For us, approaching potential buyers at this stage would be suicidal, but Chairman Zhou could not care less. He had just gone ahead and unilaterally put our stake up for sale.

"Please explain why you deemed it your responsibility to help us find a new investor," challenged Russell, trying to remain calm.

The Lao Qianbei shrugged off the question. "We will try to get a price that allows you to still make a tidy profit out of investing in us."

Alan tried protesting, persuading, reasoning and cajoling in turn for another half an hour, but Chairman Zhou simply sat with his arms folded, stoically silent. Finally, he cut Alan off in mid-sentence with a parting shot: "Please focus on your other investment projects instead."

That was a low blow. Chairman Zhou knew well that we had no other investments in the pipeline apart from DeeDee, as Alan did not have the right contacts on the ground to win new deals so far. Even when Fang Xing was around, he always had convincing reasons why he brought so many deals to the table but none of them came to fruition.

I studied Chairman Zhou's clammed-up face before he stalked off. He was always a man of few words, and this dialogue was already more than he usually deigned to engage with us in over the past few tumultuous months. Given that I had gotten to know about him much better over the past few months, I got his message immediately: "Hands off from now on, you damn foreigners!"

Recalling his bubbling enthusiasm not too long ago about bringing international investors on board to help him expand DeeDee, I sighed at how quickly the winds had changed once again.

We went back to our office dejectedly, and started yet another brainstorming session. Preventing Chairman Zhou from taking any more drastic actions now became the top priority for us.

"We need to take control of the situation. We cannot let Chairman Zhou play us like this anymore, it's disgraceful," Gary fumed. He had been uncharacteristically mouse-like during the meeting earlier with Chairman Zhou, but now he was back to his usual loud, livid self. "I smell a rat somewhere: no matter how poorly managed the resignation was, the auditor must have found out something about the company we did not know about. I do not trust this China man a bit."

After a brief moment of silence, Gary exclaimed, "Fraud! There must be fraud in the company!"

Gary's remarks sent a chill down our spines. If Fang Xing were around, I was certain he would have fought back at this accusation and taken Chairman Zhou's side. As for myself, I was not sure how to respond. Perhaps I was just too dazed and confused, or had no guts to defend Chairman Zhou, even though I instinctively felt that he was not the kind of entrepreneur who would have deliberately committed such financial shenanigans.

For the rest of the week, the accusations about fraud continued. Alan's head was on the chopping board.

"I'm disgusted at your incompetence in handling this matter, Alan. How could you not have known there was something fishy with DeeDee's accounts? You must find a solution fast," Russell raged at Alan during one conference call.

I could not help but felt sorry for Alan. He had not even been present when the deal was forged, and had spent less than a year as the head of a decimated China team. Yet, he had to deal with the fallout when the deal imploded, as well as the brunt of the criticism for not fixing it fast enough.

Was Alan really incompetent? I did not think so. He was just lacking in experience to effectively manage a very local Beijing entrepreneur hardened in his own ways, and accustomed to local tactics of doing business. Chairman Zhou was a *ditoushe* 地头蛇, or a "local snake," someone who knew the business environment so well and insisted on absolute control. But the problem was, Alan and Russell both had no idea how complex Chairman Zhou really was. They thought the Lao Qianbei was a country bumpkin entrepreneur with primitive knowledge of international accounting and business.

"How could you not know that the auditor resignation was coming? You are hired to be on the ground to manage the process. It is your responsibility to know what goes on at the company," Russell continued. "Do you speak to the CFO and the girls working in the finance team often enough?"

Finance is usually the most prized function within a privately held Chinese company. Its ledgers and bank balances were held in strictest confidence by the Chairman, the CFO and possibly one or two other trusted aides, usually family members. It is common for Chinese companies to transfer huge sums of money between affiliated companies through a web of shareholder loans, off-balance sheet cash injections and withdrawals, as well as agreements between "related parties".[30] These intertwined dealings are either left undocumented, or governed by simple contracts usually not more than a few pages in length.

Company founders like Chairman Zhou liked it this way. It was actually a form of "corporate governance with Chinese characteristics," as he even tried to reason with me once. It ensured that outsiders— greedy capitalists, disloyal workers and the like—had no chance to sabotage the company or cook the books. "I'm the most honest one because I founded this company and I would not do anything to hurt DeeDee's future for generations to come. But I don't trust other people—they are only motivated by greed and short-term gain."

Try convincing foreign auditors of this. Most of them would hate this arrangement, because they needed transparency to make informed judgments about the company's state of affairs. To them, Chairman Zhou was out to make DeeDee's financial reports convoluted, inconsistent, or worse still, misleading.

I wondered if there had been some real miscommunication between B&C and DeeDee's finance team—who were never briefed by Chairman Zhou on the complete picture of the company's affairs—on some accounting issues. The auditor might have decided

---

[30] These are techniques used by many Chinese private companies to make it difficult to trace certain financial transactions and movements of cash.

it was easier to resign, than to struggle to figure out DeeDee's messy financial affairs.

Even if B&C had accepted Steven's explanation for the discrepancies, it might still have balked at Chairman Zhou's style of corporate governance—or lack thereof. So might minority shareholders, who were often not the real winners in Asian listed companies. Many of the region's publicly traded firms were effectively controlled by the founders or their family, a significant number of whom had become very rich overnight. But this had failed to trickle down to minority shareholders, as ChinHwee Tan and Thomas R. Robinson had pointed out in their book *Asian Financial Statement Analysis*. Asian stock markets such as China's had grossly underperformed, even as GDP rates soared[31]. The lack of corporate governance was partly to blame, and B&C had probably become more sensitive to this problem amid a public outcry over accounting scandals involving Chinese companies that were listed overseas.

Of course, I could never figure out if my theories about why B&C resigned held water. There were just too many stakeholders, each of them holding bits and pieces of the puzzle. Few were willing to tell me the real side of their story. Still, as time passed, I grew increasingly convinced that the crux of the issue was neither fraud nor a blatant disregard for rules, but differences in cultural perceptions about what was legit and acceptable for a company to do.

I never got to share any of these views with Russell, however. He was too busy mauling us. "You were supposed to gather intelligence for us about DeeDee, and build up rapport with Zhou to get him on our side. You play golf with him every week right? Yet you didn't even have a clue how to find him when he is on medical holiday. Were you

---

[31] Tan, ChinHwee; and Thomas R. Robinson. 2014. *Asian Financial Statement Analysis: Detecting Financial Irregularities*. Hoboken, NJ: John Wiley & Sons, Inc. The book listed China as an example. Despite China's strong economic growth that saw its GDP more than double over the past decade, the domestic Shanghai Composite index virtually stayed at the same level since 2001.

so busy drinking and merry-making that you missed all the warning signs about DeeDee's financial irregularities?" he yelled.

Alan and I could say little to defend ourselves against these tongue-lashings. So we feverishly devised ways to stop Chairman Zhou from further mischief—or God forbid, more medical holidays.

I called the Lao Qianbei every single day, and showered his secretary with gifts to persuade her to keep me updated on his whereabouts. Alan wanted to put bugs in Chairman Zhou's car and office to eavesdrop on his conversations. But he chickened out of doing it himself, and did not make much headway outsourcing the job. Whether any of these actions actually proved that the China team still had some real value to offer to headquarters was unclear. But it did not matter. All we cared about was that we did not lose whatever tiny remnant of faith our Singapore bosses had left in us.

It was only later that I realized that Russell and Gary no longer even expected us to come up with any solutions. They had already sidelined the China team.

> *Cuo Shou Dun Zu* 搓手顿足: **Anxious hands and clumsy feet, describing someone who is frantic and frustrated.**

CHAPTER 18

Control

Chang Ying Zai Shou 长缨在手

B Y EARLY JUNE, A TEAM of over twenty restructuring specialists and lawyers had been assembled for a volcanic showdown with Chairman Zhou. All of them claimed to have China experience averaging twelve years. At their advice, the Singapore headquarters devised a plan to take over management control of DeeDee. Since they had such formidable China credentials, they did not need to consult the China team or get feedback from the ground.

After three weeks, Alan and I were finally summoned to Singapore for a strategy meeting to execute the new foolproof plan.

"We note that Chairman Zhou had breached several clauses in the investment agreements," Gary began. "For example, they had failed to furnish us with the required audited financial statements every quarter."

I winced. This sounded more like nitpicking on legality. How could a company whose auditor had just resigned fulfill the requirements of this clause?

"Under the legal contract, any breach gives the investors the right to exercise their remedies, but this is only done as a last resort," pronounced Tom, a newly-hired American lawyer, exuding supreme confidence as he stretched out his lanky legs.

"As part of any PE investment, the founder's shares in his own company are usually pledged to the investor to protect our rights in case the founder breaches his side of the bargain. In private equity speak, exercising remedies means we could legally take over Chairman Zhou's shares in the case of a breach," Tom explained very slowly for our benefit, as if teaching a group of interns.

What our bosses liked about this approach was that it appeared to instantly catapult us from weakness and passivity to a moral and legal high ground. Chairman Zhou had blatantly disobeyed the instructions in the legal agreements. Now he deserved to have his company taken away from him.

Like many Chinese entrepreneurs, Chairman Zhou held the shares of his onshore company, DeeDee, through offshore holding company structures. So the easiest way for All-Stellar to wrest control of DeeDee was to target his offshore shares.

Once we had taken over the company's shares and operations, we could exercise full control over the future of the business and our own fate, the advisors reasoned. We could easily replace Chairman Zhou's team with new and more competent management who had run duck farm businesses before and who would finally obey our instructions to follow international best practices. With attractive remuneration, we could get the new management to listen to our demands and run the company the way we wanted. Perhaps the current employees would benefit from a fresh management style and be more motivated to perform?

Still, I was worried that if we really went down this "winner takes it all, loser loses it all" route, the situation might spiral out of control and there would be no turning back—as the Chinese phrase *yifabukeshoushi*—发不可收拾 aptly describes. We risked getting into an all-out war with Chairman Zhou, who would fight to the death to save the company he had painstakingly built up over two decades. It was his baby, the first fruit of his blood, sweat and tears. To topple such an incumbent on his home turf was not going to be easy.

I glanced at Alan, who was sitting there passively. I wondered if he had the same barrage of questions I had: even if we really succeeded in the takeover, would we be able to reform the company successfully? What about the various business and regulatory relationships Chairman Zhou built up at each province? How long would it take for us to cultivate the same depth and breadth of guanxi that he had? Had we thought long and hard about the consequences of our actions, or we were simply out for vengeance? Could there be some middle ground we could strike?

Finally, I decided to speak out, even if my China boss remained silent. "Russell, I wonder if we can come up with a less confrontational solution. Declaring war must be the last resort, would you agree? I fear that we might be maneuvering the relationship with Chairman Zhou to a dead end…"

"We have had enough of Chairman Zhou's nonsense. He broke our contract and our trust, so we need to teach him a lesson he'll never forget!" Russell snapped, cutting me short.

I shut up. Who was I, with a mere two years of PE experience, to question the veterans of the profession? Russell and Gary, with their years of international experience, must have calculated the odds of success, weighed the risks and decided this was the best way out.

I knew my job from now on was not to challenge or improve the takeover plan, but simply to provide information whenever my bosses asked for it. As the only surviving member of the original China deal team, I had the most knowledge of the company and the deal. So my role would be reduced purely to a messenger reporting the situation on the ground in China.

I wondered how people like Susie and Fang Xing would have defused the situation. Would they have spoken up as I had, or kept on the sidelines like Alan did? Or perhaps they never stuck around long enough in any role to manage such crises?

The only clue I had to how a local Chinese might react to the takeover plan was Rebecca's look of disbelief when I explained the strategy to her, followed by an expression of utter detachment. She had an "I'm thankful I'm just the secretary" look on her face. Something in her dispassionate attitude disturbed me.

"So what do you really think?" I pressed her.

She shrugged. "Why do you guys need to make it so complicated? I think you guys should still proactively reach out to Chairman Zhou and try to settle amicably. Chinese people will make you regret it if you ambush them like this."

But we were already locked into the takeover battle plan. What the Singapore team and their advisors could not figure out was how to execute it.

Our first problem was getting hold of Chairman Zhou's precious *gongzhang*, or seal. I knew Chairman Zhou locked it in the metal safe in the finance office, with a passcode known only to a select few. We would need the company *gongzhang* in order to freeze DeeDee's bank accounts, change out the existing bank account signatories, and effect the necessary change of shareholding at the local registry of companies.

Then we realized that we would also need to get hold of the *yingyezhizhao* 营业执照 (business registration certificate, equivalent to the business license in most countries). Each Chinese company is issued one original and two certified copies, one of which is typically displayed on a prominent wall in the office. I knew Chairman Zhou hung only a photocopy on the wall, not the real copy.

Two divergent camps emerged among the army of advisors we had hired on how to snatch these two critical items.

"We should raid the offices at night to seize the safe with the company chop, as well as all the company files and computer databases.

If we attack at night, we will encounter the least resistance. We just need to hire a professional team to break open the front door," argued representatives from the more offensive camp.

This met with vehement opposition from the more conservative camp. "This stealth plan is absurd. We are DeeDee's rightful owners— we have the authority to act openly. Why do we need to engage in such covert behavior?" they retorted.

But when it came to how we were going to implement either approach and who would do it, neither camp could offer a concrete plan on the logistics and practical details.

The discussions went back and forth for days on end. Sometimes, Russell and Gary would fly up to Beijing to meet with local lawyers. At other times, Alan and I were summoned back to Singapore for internal strategy sessions and Investment Committee meetings. I felt like a primary witness standing in court, grilled by lawyers who reeled off questions like a machine gun on automatic firing mode:

> "*What is the amount of registered capital in the Beijing company?*"
> "*How many employees have resigned since the IPO flopped?*"
> "*How much did Chairman Zhou miss in terms of the profit guarantee he promised last year?*"
> "*Is the legal representative of the Henan subsidiary a close blood relative of Zhou?*"
> "*Are the operations at the duck farms really suspended and for how long? Are the ducks still alive?*"

It was only then that I realized just how little anyone in All-Stellar knew about the DeeDee deal apart from me. Even Russell and Gary, despite having flown up to Beijing so many times, seemed to be clueless about many of the details about DeeDee's operations—let alone the intricacies and idiosyncrasies of how businesses are run in

China. It was also clear to me by now that none of the experienced China experts who were advising us had ever lived in the country before, nor had they interacted in any significant way with Chinese entrepreneurs.

On one occasion, I endured an excruciating interrogation session in Singapore from 8:00a.m. to 4:05p.m. Russell wanted me to return to Beijing that very evening to gather more information for the advisors, so I rushed like a madman to catch my 4:50p.m. flight. I reached the Singapore Changi Airport eighteen minutes before the scheduled flight departure time. The friendly Singapore Airlines ground staff, who by now recognized me as the guy who was perpetually late for his flights, shoved me off on a buggy to the departure gate. I reached the gates a mere two seconds before they closed, and heaved a sigh of relief.

Once I reached Beijing, however, my frustrations surged again. There was no smog that day, so we landed on time—and then spent the next hour sitting on the tarmac. Two Chinese passengers sitting next to me started speculating about which international political figure or business hotshot or high-ranking official was about to arrive in or depart from Beijing. That must be the reason why the lesser mortals like us had to stew for so long while our commercial airplanes waited for the traffic jam to clear, they reasoned. I was intrigued by this theory, but soon got worked up thinking about all the inexplicable flight delays—lasting as long as eleven hours—I had endured over the past few weeks as Beijing's worsening air traffic hit the headlines.

Could it be possible that every single one of my flights coincided with smog, bad weather or the arrival or departure of a big shot? Had Beijing's new Terminal Three airport, which had opened before the Olympics and had been mocked as a white elephant for its over-capacity, suddenly become overcrowded? Was the internet chatter about increased military surveillance in the region that disrupted Beijing's civilian airspace not so nonsensical after all? I found myself struggling with questions whose answers were indeed available, but were too complicated to find out—a state that seemed to sum up my roller-coaster China experience so far.

Finally, heaven sent me an unexpected reprieve. After seven grueling trips to Singapore, I fell so ill that the doctor had me hospitalized immediately. Thankfully, All-Stellar had put me on a medical insurance package that covered my expenses for a one-week stay in a one-bedroom suite in the private Beijing United Family Hospital. There, the soothing background music, elegant Chinese paintings on the walls and fresh bedside flowers provided me the most pampering I had gotten in months.

It was a world of difference from the local public community hospitals my local friends went to when they fell ill. I had visited these public institutions in the past, and found that trying to get treatment in there was akin to rushing for the train at Beijing Central railway station along with tens of thousands of migrant workers returning home for the Chinese New Year festive holidays. From the time the hospital doors opened at eight o'clock in the morning, long lines snaked out onto the sidewalks as patients waited to purchase queue numbers to see a doctor. This is known as *guahao* 挂号, or getting a queue number. It was the first step before one could see any physician. The *guahao* for the popular doctors ran out in minutes. Once they were sold out for the day, you had to come back the next day and try again.

The best public hospitals, known as Class 3A or *sanjia* 三甲 hospitals, suffered a perpetual shortage of beds. Medical costs were heavily subsidized by the state, so there were always many times more patients than the number of beds the hospitals had available. But this dire overcrowding did not daunt local Chinese like my friend Lucy, who was hospitalized at the incredibly popular Chaoyang Hospital. She spent four days lying on a makeshift bed parked along a dusty wall in a corridor leading to the main hospital ward. But she was all smiles when I visited her. "At least I managed to get a bed that several hundred—maybe even thousands—people would have loved to sleep on. And I saved fifty yuan (US$8) for a corridor bed, compared to a regular one," she told me gleefully. I marveled at her delight.

My dedicated house nurse, Chen Qing, reminded me of Lucy because of her sunny disposition. She would bounce into my room to deliver meals and medicine, chattering away vivaciously in an attempt to cheer me up as I glumly checked my blackberry every few minutes for updates from the Singapore headquarters.

On my first day, the conversation naturally started with our family backgrounds.

"So where are you from originally? You said you are from Singapore. So were you born there, or are you a haigui like many of the other patients here?" she asked. I could tell she found me interesting because she could not really tell whether I was a foreigner or not: I toggled between Singaporean and Beijing-accented Mandarin, spoke English with a peculiar lilt, blended in quite well with the local Chinese, and yet seemed most comfortable with the foreign doctors in the hospital.

By now, I was used to this question, which my local acquaintances invariably asked when they met me for the first time. Usually, my first reaction was to simply reply that my ancestral home was in Fujian province's Quanzhou city, to avoid being labeled as an outsider. When my late paternal grandparents left the Fujian coast to chase their dreams of a better life in Nanyang—or Southern Sea, referring to Southeast Asia at large—in the 1930's, Quanzhou was still a sleepy fishing village. Today's Quanzhou, a respectable, large-scale city by Chinese standards, had flourished into a metropolis teeming with skyscrapers and shopping malls, as well as a population the size of New York City.

Chen Qing seemed very impressed. "Wow, your hometown has really done well. My township is still a backwater today, hasn't changed much over the past few decades. That's why I had to leave it to earn money in a bigger town when I was sixteen years old."

She recounted how she left home for the nearest industrial city of Handan in the northern Hebei province as a teenager to work as a waitress. She needed to support her younger brother through junior high school. Although she had qualified for a top-tier university, her parents could not afford to send her there as they were saving up their money for their precious son.

Chen Qing took all this in her stride, recalling how lucky she was to get a scholarship to study at a small nursing vocational institute. After graduation, she managed to land a job at Beijing United, where her salary of RMB3,500 per month (US$550) was a little higher than that of her local peers. Half of that sum was sent home to help defray the family's expenses. That left little for her to spend on food and transport, let alone the occasional indulgence such as a dress from the wholesale clothes market in western Beijing.

"But even though I hardly have any savings, I'm glad I don't have as much stress as you do," she chirped.

I slowly opened up a little about my work troubles, finding Chen Qing's sympathetic ear a much better panacea to my grinding migraine and stress-induced nausea than any amount of bed rest.

By the third day, Chen Qing felt familiar enough with me to call me *"qin," or "my dear"*. *"Qin,* you shouldn't be working when you are sick!" she chided me gently.

"My bosses and I are taking over the company in the next few weeks. You wouldn't understand..." I began.

"What do you mean 'taking over'?" she scratched her head, confused. "Aren't you guys a business partner with this Chinese company? I thought partners work to solve problems together?" she asked.

I beamed at her comments. Finally, someone was paying attention to me.

On the fourth day of my medical break, Russell called me. "How are you? Are you feeling better? We are making some progress but need you back."

I inhaled deeply, trying to draw out every particle of courage. Then, with Chen Qing smiling encouragingly at me, I blurted out the speech I had rehearsed with her so many times over the past two days: "Russell, I really want to make sure we succeed in our first investment. You have put me in Beijing, and I want to make it worth your while. I am sure Chairman Zhou will fight back but not sure how. I still think it is too risky to engage in combat activity in other people's home turf…"

Before I could explain my rationale, a derisive snort on the other side of the line cut me short.

"If you had real concerns, you should have raised it long ago," sneered Russell. "Our team made the decision to go ahead. Are you trying to chicken out now? I expect you to be professional in your job."

The next day, I scanned the headlines listlessly as I waited for Russell's call. A string of natural catastrophes was ravaging the country, from coal mine disasters to devastating rainstorms in Southern China that resulted in massive flooding and the evacuation of nearly 750,000 people.

The phone rang. Russell sounded triumphant. "We have now successfully taken over full legal custody of the company and are ready to execute on the takeover. We have assembled the best international and local lawyers in China who are backing our action against Chairman Zhou. The momentum needs to be maintained."

"Yes sir," I said.

"We have finally devised a foolproof strategy, and need you back to help with the execution. When are you discharged?"

"I'll make it tomorrow," I said falteringly. "I will head to the lawyer's office once I get out of hospital."

"Ok here's the deal. During the time you were away, we took control of all the existing offshore shares of Chairman Zhou's company. The company is now 100 percent controlled by us. It will take him a few days before he finds out," Russell said.

"We will do an office raid next week and install the new management team," he continued. "We are afraid that Chairman Zhou will be in the office that day and thwart our takeover action, so we want you to invite him out for golf with us. On the golf course, we will make him resign from DeeDee. Our lawyer will hand him a board resolution that we will make him sign to make his resignation official."

I struggled to process the mad plot that Russell had laid out.

"Err…I haven't spoken to Chairman Zhou for a month. You want me to invite him out of the blue to play golf, and then ask him to resign from his own company?" I stammered. "What if he doesn't want to play golf with us, or he suspects something when I call him all of a sudden?"

"Yes, you are the one who must invite him out, because you are our only channel of communication with Chairman Zhou now," replied Russell. "You'd better make sure he doesn't smell a rat. If any of our plans are leaked out, we would have to abort the entire mission and you will be held solely responsible. Now go pick the golf course and make sure Zhou gets there on time."

"There are over seventy golf courses in Beijing…"

"Great, we are spoilt for choice then," snapped Russell. "Pick one that is far enough from central Beijing so that he will not be able to react and rush back to his office in time to stop us. This is our only chance to grab power from Chairman Zhou.

"Oh, and I forgot to update you earlier: we've already hired a new CEO and an Operations Director to succeed Chairman Zhou and his Head of Operations. DeeDee's CFO resigned last week, so our restructuring specialist will assign a temporary senior manager to manage the finance function until we find a replacement."

He hung up.

I started shaking. Russell was making me betray the Lao Qianbei, whose trust I had painstakingly built over the past three years. Yet, if I opposed Russell's instructions, I would be unprofessional and fail to perform my fiduciary duties as a manager of the fund. In fact, opposing my boss' direct orders would be the last thing to do if I still wanted to keep my job.

An hour later, Chen Qing found me under the bed, my body contorted into such a tight knot that I was unable to get out on my own. "How did you even get yourself into this position?" she exclaimed, as she dragged me out.

> ***Chang Ying Zai Shou*** 长缨在手: **Holding a long cord of firepower in one's hands, meaning to control the situation.**

CHAPTER 19

Off Guard

Cuo Shou Bu Ji 措手不及

S TILL COUGHING AND WHEEZING, I staggered back to work the next day and pondered how to invite Chairman Zhou to golf.

Three hours later, with my head still spinning from the medication, I finally decided to send a text instead of call. I knew he would be quick to notice how strange it was that if I sounded so ill and yet wanted to play golf with him.

"Chairman Zhou, is everything well? We haven't spoken for a while. Russell is in town tomorrow and would like to invite you to golf next week. Perhaps it's better to meet in person to chat about business issues?" I wrote.

Within a few minutes, my phone beeped. It was Chairman Zhou.

"OK. Which course and what time?"

"Diequan Golf Course, next Monday, say at 12:30p.m.?" I replied. This was three days away—on July 5, 2010, the day for our planned takeover. In fact, Gary had insisted on July 4, Independence Day, for some bizarre reason. He had been crestfallen when a quick check of the calendar revealed that July 4 fell on a Sunday. We eventually settled for one day later, a Monday, which technically was still July 4 in the US. I got Rebecca to call the club to confirm they were open as most golf courses closed on Monday for routine maintenance, and it turned out they were open for booking in the afternoon.

I knew the exclusivity and glamour of this location would pique Chairman Zhou's interest. Better known as Beijing Cascades Country Golf Club to foreigners, Diequan was a new championship course designed by Arnold Palmer, one of America's most enduring golfing legends. The greatest players in US men's professional golf history, the likes of Palmer, Jack Nicklaus and Gary Player, had spotted the huge growth potential of the sport across Asia, and were actively involved in designing, building and operating golf courses in China.

Over just a decade, some six hundred golf courses had mushroomed across the country, compared to about 15,500 in the US. But the US figure included 11,500 public courses—a concept that did not exist in China since the public does not play golf. Only the rich do. Taking this into account, the number of private golf courses in China was actually about 15 percent of the 4,000 private courses in the US. Property developers, who were betting on the sport becoming more popular among Chinese officials and the mass affluent, started to flood my phone with texts like these:

> *"New thirty-six-hole championship golf course nestled in the pristine forests of Penglai, a city in Shandong province with fantastic views of the Bohai Rim coastline. Founding membership starting from RMB88,000. Only for people with keen eye for prestige. Interested, please call 1358 977 3865"*

Chairman Zhou and I had spent hours during previous golf games discussing the risks and merits of investing in new golf courses like the Penglai project.

But even the daring Lao Qianbei was daunted by the massive gray area that these developments were mired in. Many of the golf courses, as well as the bungalows and apartments that surrounded them, were not entirely legal. They were built by developers who leveraged power relationships, as well as lucrative side deals signed with local government offices, to exploit regulatory loopholes. Golf courses in China were regulated by multiple ministries, including the National Development and Reform Commission, Ministry of Land and Resources, the Ministry of Construction, the State Administration of Environmental Protection, the General Administration of Sport and the State Tourism Administration, just to name a few.

"I heard from my friend who is a golf course developer that out of the seventy-plus courses in Beijing, only about three or four are completely legitimate and have the proper licenses," Chairman Zhou told me. I remained dubious about his claim until much later, when I read Dan Washburn's book *The Forbidden Game: Golf and the Chinese Dream*. It described the widespread lack of regulatory approvals among the hundreds of golf courses that had sprung up in China over the past decade. Perhaps only a dozen courses in China could claim to have a business license that specifically mentioned the word "golf"[32], Mr. Washburn had written.

The industry flourished vibrantly and haphazardly. Golf courses sprouted up like wildfire, deterred only by environmentalists in China who protested that golf courses polluted the underground drinking water while gobbling countless acres of farmland as well as precious water resources. The public had a valid cause for concern—the water shortage had already become so severe in China's northern regions that a mega infrastructure project, the "South-to-North Water Diversion Project," was being built to move over 45 billion cubic meters, equivalent to eighteen million Olympic size swimming pools, from southern China to the north.

Despite all these factors, Alan was a die-hard believer in the

---

[32] Washburn, Dan. 2014. *The Forbidden Game: Golf and the Chinese Dream*. London: Oneworld Publications Ltd.

potential of China's golf courses. He had already splurged most of his bonus on buying memberships in few upcoming prestigious projects in Beijing. He often urged me to jump in as well, claiming I could get returns of up to 600 percent by selling the golf memberships to rich Chinese after the courses had been built and opened. I wondered why he did not spend more time actually on the greens playing golf with Chairman Zhou or other businessmen to cultivate deals for All-Stellar.

Just then, a text broke my brooding. Chairman Zhou had replied. "OK."

Relatively simple and pain-free. I felt a smidgen of smugness: nobody in All-Stellar apart from me could have gotten this done within just ten minutes. Seeing the way golf helped my relationship with Chairman Zhou blossom—just as it now served as a tool to destroy it—also erased all doubts about how a little white ball and a set of expensive metal staffs could help my China career.

The elation lasted for barely a minute. Anxiety overtook me again as I joined in the All-Stellar team's feverish preparations for the takeover. My main task was to train up Mr. Xie Youyi, who was going to be DeeDee's new CEO after All-Stellar's planned takeover of the company. Russell felt that Mr. Xie, whose Mandarin name could be translated literally as "thank you friendship," would obey All-Stellar's orders and not sympathize with Chairman Zhou, since he was the senior manager of DeeDee's bitter arch rival Lingma Poultry Farming Company. He poached Mr. Xie by offering him an irresistible package—a salary way above market rates, along with company options. I spent fifteen hours with him to get him up to speed with everything I knew about DeeDee, all the while struggling with a growing burden of guilt. While I knew that my loyalty was to All-Stellar and to Russell, I could not help feeling that I was backstabbing Zhou, whom I had grown to respect and even view as a friend.

I firmly told myself that All-Stellar had the legal rights to carry out its plan, and the situation would be better for everyone—including Chairman Zhou—once we had executed our takeover and turned DeeDee around.

Even so, I started to get terrible nightmares. Chairman Zhou would chase me down the fairway with his seven-iron, shouting," Why did you abet the landlord class to snatch away what rightfully belongs to the peasants? This is my blood and sweat and life, I will kill you for your treachery..." I ran for my own life, tripping and scrambling and tripping again until my sweat-drenched body finally jerked awake.

Before I knew it, Monday morning had arrived. I was an emotional wreck as I called Russell to tell him I would not turn up at the golf course. I had already done what was instructed of me so the mission to serve Chairman Zhou the papers could proceed without me, I said.

The truth was that I really did not have the guts to meet Chairman Zhou face to face. I could handle the fear of Russell firing me, but I did not want to be there in person when Chairman Zhou was fired from his own company.

Russell was out of his mind with fury at my decision to absent myself. But after his threats to cut my bonus fell on deaf ears, he commanded me to follow Gary's SWAT team to DeeDee's offices and provide Mr. Xie with any additional support he needed when dealing with the staff.

Chairman Zhou must have sensed something was amiss and sent me a longer than usual text, which read, "You're coming for the game later this afternoon, right? If you're not coming, let's just call it off. I don't want to see Russell nor want to play golf with him. What's more, it's really hazy out there, I don't want to play golf in this kind of environment."

In a blind panic, I typed "yes"—the single word that proved crucial in the final moments before the takeover.

Staring tearfully at my phone, I realized how low I had sunk. I knew that Chairman Zhou was a man of his words and would not stand me up. I also knew my text would soon demolish every particle of respect and trust he had for me. Underhand tactics were not uncommon in China, but barefaced lies to a friend—like the one I had just told to Chairman Zhou—would be deemed a personal attack and a declaration of war. My choice to not join Russell on the golf course, which I had earlier hoped was a slightly redemptive move, would not make me less of an enemy.

It was a long, excruciating wait until the 12:30p.m. tee-off time. My blackberry was beeping every few minutes with emails from the advisors. The team assigned to take over Chairman Zhou's office were readying for the green light from mission control.

12:20p.m.

Russell shoots out an emergency e-mail, addressed to me and copying everyone: "Zhou has not showed up! I want you to call him to find out where he is. Tell him we are ready to tee off when he arrives. If all it takes for him to come is for you to show up at the course, you should hurry over now!"

12:25p.m.

My phone beeps. It is a text from Chairman Zhou: "Arrived. Where are you?"

12:28p.m.

I scramble to find my blackberry and shoot out an e-mail: "He has just arrived at the golf course."

12:29p.m.

Gary emails an update: "We are all on standby at the lobby of DeeDee's offices. Waiting for instructions to proceed, Russell."

12:40p.m., Diequan Golf Course

Russell strides up to Chairman Zhou and says, "Lao Zhou, good to see you. I would like to introduce Philip Poteri, our lawyer. We hereby remove you from your position as Board Chairman of Dominant Duck."

12:55p.m., Dominant Duck's Beijing headquarters

A team consisting of Gary, the four lawyers, six security guards, as well as DeeDee's new interim CEO and CFO burst into the DeeDee office. I follow meekly behind, trying to keep as much distance as I can from them without getting yelled at.

The entire office is still dark—on Chairman Zhou's orders, all the lights were turned off during lunch break from twelve noon to one o'clock every day, a rule that saved the company a few thousand yuan each month.

The employees troop back from the cafeteria. Many exclaim in surprise when they see all the office lights in full blaze. Our SWAT team immediately herds them to the big conference room. There, big tabloid-size bilingual notices had been pasted on all four walls, notifying the fifty startled staff that Chairman Zhou had resigned as Board Chairman. Printouts drafted by our restructuring specialists are distributed to each employee, describing the management changes at the company and reassuring them that their jobs would be protected.

1:05p.m., Master Administrative Conference Room One, Dominant Duck's Beijing headquarters

"We would like to inform you that with effect from noon today, the senior management team at Dominant Duck has stepped down from their positions," Mr. Xie, the newly appointed CEO, announces over a loudspeaker.

"We have just met with Mr. Zhou, the previous Chairman of your company, who has informed us he will be leaving the company for personal reasons. We will work closely with all of you to ensure that the business will soar to greater heights," Mr. Xie concluded.

The staff eye him warily.

1:20p.m.

The meeting ends. The staff leave the conference room looking even more confused than when Mr. Xie announced the takeover. There are still too many questions left unanswered.

Suddenly, a shrill cry rings from the far end of the office, where the finance and accounting cubicles are located. "The company safes and our computers are gone!" Bingbing shrieks. "And the accounting files too!"

At the ground floor lobby, the six security guards finish loading the safes, computers and file cabinets into the metal truck, and drive off.

> *Cuo Shou Bu Ji* 措手不及: **Hands caught unprepared, describing someone who is taken by surprise and caught off-guard.**

CHAPTER 20

Power

Yi Shou Zhe Tian 一手遮天

ALL-STELLAR'S VICTORY PROVED ALL TOO fleeting.

Just one day after our surprise takeover of DeeDee, we found ourselves under siege.

At around 10:30a.m., I was about to enter our office building when a rickety old yellow school bus screeched to a halt in the driveway. About forty middle-aged men waddled off the bus, still greedily sucking on their two-yuan-a-pack Five Cows cigarettes. From their tired faces and dust-caked overalls, they looked like they had just spent ten days straight laboring at a construction site without taking a shower.

They unloaded five large boxes and took out a bunch of bright red banners. Then the leader of the pack, like a tour guide leading a throng of gawking local tourists through Tiananmen Square, waved a red flag, signaling to the workers to follow him into the building.

They laid out the banners carefully in the center of the spacious lobby, each piece of cloth lined up against another on the marble floors with military precision.

"*Huanwo xuehanqian* 还我血汗钱 (Return our blood-earned salary)!" one demanded.

"*Zhongguo wansui* 中国万岁 (Long live, China)!" another proclaimed.

All-Stellar Asia Fund L.P.'s Mandarin name and office address were prominently featured on all the banners.

The workers then marched back to the bus, and unloaded crate after crate of Harbin Beer, blocking the entire entrance to the building. They leisurely fished out the bottles and lined them in neat rows behind the banners, all the while chattering in an indecipherable Chinese dialect.

Curious passersby gathered to watch, as the leader whipped out packs of poker cards and distributed them to the workers, who were already eagerly seated on the floor or on top of the empty crates. They launched into a rowdy game of dalaoer 大老二 (Big Old Two), a popular poker card game played in China. Wads of one-yuan notes, gambling chips and globs of beer-tinged spit were soon scattered all over the polished floor.

The building's management had alerted Rebecca, and she rushed down to join me. We surveyed the mayhem in growing alarm, but did not dare to approach the revelers without our bosses' instructions. So after I had informed the Singapore headquarters about this latest bizarre development, we hid in the crowd waiting to see what would happen next.

As I watched, images of John Tan and his shiny biker jacket suddenly flashed through my mind.

Panic surging through my veins, I recalled the empty construction site, and forced myself to confront the very real possibility that it was all an elaborate set-up. Had my own investment disappeared into a black hole? Had my judgment been so clouded by John's show of professionalism and western management techniques that I had blindly put my trust in a conman?

I had little recourse to recover my money: a police report was useless; trying to sue him for fraud in court would be a protracted struggle; chasing him down would require copious time and resources that I could ill afford now, with All-Stellar's investment in DeeDee on the rocks. "And it's not like I could retaliate by sending protestors to John's office to demand my money back," I sighed to myself.

By now, it was almost noon. The demonstrators had set up the stage just in time for their target audience—the lunchtime crowd. More than a hundred curious onlookers had gathered. Some snapped photos of the raucous scene and gleefully posted them on their microblogs.

The workers, emboldened by the growing number of spectators, stopped gambling and started to shout slogans about the glorious justice of the Chinese Communist Party. The office building management did not dare to stop them from chanting, but they hastily circled some yellow barrier tape around the performers to make sure things did not spiral out of control. "The workers may exercise freedom of expression, but must be confined to linger and voice their views within this designated area," a roly-poly manager nervously told the leader.

I could not help marveling at how quickly the tables were turned. It had taken us almost a month to devise a strategy to overthrow the incumbent leadership in DeeDee. But twenty-four hours were all Chairman Zhou needed to recover his footing, regroup his troops, and devise this outrageous demonstration to wrestle control of his company back from us. Enraged by the trap he had been lured into at the golf course, Chairman Zhou had launched a blistering offensive to make us regret starting this war.

———◆———

For the next three weeks, the rioters would appear without fail at All-Stellar's doorstep. Every morning, the workers showed up religiously at a quarter past eleven with their alcohol, poker cards and banners, and they would leave at 4:00p.m. sharp. The staged revolt was starting to look increasingly like a carnival.

At that time, we had no way of knowing how long the demonstrations would last, because calls to Chairman Zhou went unanswered, and DeeDee's staff refused to get involved. We did not even know who to contact in order to negotiate an end to the demonstrations, since the workers refused to disclose who had dispatched them and said their only instruction was to keep turning up every day at our office until further notice.

Meanwhile, Rebecca was inundated with daily nuisance calls from DeeDee's farmers and suppliers across various provinces. They all claimed Chairman Zhou owed them payments that were already overdue by at least a month. I was very surprised that Rebecca had taken this very well, answering each call as they came politely. "I've been well-trained by Susie to tune out the noise no matter how irate the caller is," she told me pragmatically. But by the thirtieth call, even her supreme patience was wearing thin.

On the third day of the riots, a state of emergency was declared at our office. We cancelled all meetings with external parties, barricaded the front doors, screened all mail and packages for signs of tampering, and did not step out of the office even for meals. Only Rebecca was allowed to leave the office to run errands and buy food for us.

Russell had dispatched Gary and Tom, All-Stellar's in-house lawyer, to Beijing. Gary's first move was to order me to call the local district police in for a meeting. He wanted to lodge a complaint about why they had still not disbanded the demonstrators downstairs. "They station two police officers here every day but they spend more time chatting up the workers instead of chasing them away," he fumed. "They are clearly taking the demonstrators' side and neglecting their duty."

The two officers arrived the next day. I was the translator as usual and addressed them with a Mandarin speech, before Tom or Gary could open their mouths. "Good morning, police officer Zeng and police officer Li. Thank you for taking your precious time to meet with us. You have seen the demonstrators downstairs. While the picketing had never once turned unruly, it nevertheless damages All-Stellar's image and causes us to lose face, even though we have always sought to abide by China's laws and respect its people. Most importantly, it is clearly a gross interference to the social harmony that President Hu Jintao has placed great importance on. Surely this is an issue that you are very concerned about?"

The officers smiled and started to speak, but were interrupted by Tom. "Why are you not doing anything about the demonstrators downstairs?" he demanded. "They have been here for almost a week! In the US, this is called unlawful assembly! Do you understand what I mean? Unlawful assembly is known as a group of people with the 'mutual intent of deliberate disturbance of the peace'."

I tugged gently at his sleeve, but he shook me off. "In the developed world, this law is under the criminal procedure code. The criminal procedure code, mind you," Tom intoned, as if he expected the two police officers to cringe at his intimidating legal lingo.

I had become quite skilled at managing difficult translations, but this one was trickier. How was I going to add a lighter and friendlier Chinese touch to the topic without offending the police officers?

I saw the more senior policeman slowly raise his eyebrow. He probably understood English and sensed where Tom was going with this. Visibly miffed at Tom's brusque remarks, he took off his metal-rimmed glasses, turned his chair towards me and said, "Unlawful assembly. What a ridiculous thing to say. Please tell your boss that this is not America. Our rules and regulations here in China are very clear and established. My men have already spoken to the person-in-charge downstairs, and ascertained that the workers have a legitimate claim against your company to return their unpaid wages. Chinese law does not give us a rightful basis to handle economic disputes like these. We urge you to resolve the matter directly with the workers quickly, as your failure to act is adversely affecting social harmony."

I translated this to Tom, and got an earful even before I could finish. "Are they out of their mind?" Tom hissed. "Toothless tigers! The police here can't even handle a riot that is obviously staged?"

The air in the room rippled with tension. The minutes ticked away as Tom and the police officers glared at each other, neither side willing to lower their gaze or back down.

Then suddenly, the confrontation ended just as abruptly as it had begun, when the clock struck 4:30p.m. It was the end of the work day for the two police officers. They smiled at me, stood up, and marched out.

Tom looked at me, dumbfounded. "I can't believe it! They just left like that? Can't they tell that this whole situation is a calculated, manipulative move to make false allegations against a foreign company that will destroy its reputation in China? Are they just going to shirk their duty like that by claiming this is an economic dispute?" he shouted, gesticulating so wildly that he almost knocked his bottle of Evian water off the table.

I sat there, piecing together how we had been cornered. Chairman Zhou knew that farmers and construction workers are viewed by the public and the authorities as economically disadvantaged groups. By stirring up a scene, he would be able to disgrace All-Stellar by portraying us as an irresponsible foreign company that owed hard-earned salary to these individuals.

On top of this, Chairman Zhou had taken advantage of the fact that the Beijing local police treated economic and workplace disputes as "civil cases" and would not interfere. The local police's hands-off approach in such civil disputes would be widely reported in American media a few years later in mid-2013, when Chip Starnes, an American businessman, was audaciously held hostage for six days by his own Chinese employees in a factory in suburban Beijing. The workers had detained him to demand more compensation after he announced plans to restructure his China business. The police did not intervene, and Mr. Starnes had to resolve it on his own through lawyers and local trade union officials.

Over the next three weeks, Chairman Zhou launched other attacks.

Alan—whom Chairman Zhou now treated as his number one enemy because the latter had led the invasion of DeeDee's headquarters—began to receive harassing phone calls and texts from unknown numbers originating from various provinces within China. His mobile phone would ring every few hours. Once he picked up, the line would automatically drop dead. Every evening after work, he spent hours scrapping off random paper notices stuck using obstinate Made-in-China adhesives on the windscreen of his brand new BMW X5 sedan and on his apartment door.

Meanwhile, negotiations with Chairman Zhou's old guards in DeeDee dragged on into the wee hours of the night every day. The interim new management, whom All-Stellar had legally appointed, ended up being forcefully locked up in DeeDee's office by staff loyal to Chairman Zhou. Several young men wearing black T-shirts and wielding wooden batons appeared one day and guarded the entrance of DeeDee's office, preventing DeeDee employees from going out for lunch or bathroom breaks. One of our advisors who came to Beijing to assist Tom in restructuring DeeDee was also roughed up by the men in black after trying to barge out of the room. We called the police for assistance and the poor civilian police officer who arrived to mediate the dispute got locked up as well. Both parties refused to budge. Using "anarchy" to describe the situation was not an overstatement.

The same China experts who had thought our takeover plan was fool-proof now admitted that Chairman Zhou's aggressive counter-measures had taken them by surprise.

Amid this mayhem, the advisors decided that Alan and I faced the biggest risk of being targeted for "aggressive and potentially destructive retaliation" since we had interacted the most with Chairman Zhou and his aides.

The advisors suggested appointing twenty-four-hour bodyguards for us in case our safety was compromised. I did not resist the idea, even though I knew Chairman Zhou would never hurt me. The next day, I found myself paired up with Zheng Ma, a Chinese version of Arnold Schwarzenegger who had biceps almost the size of my thighs. We became buddies as he followed me around throughout the day and slept outside my door at night.

"How many rounds are we jogging tonight?" Zheng Ma asked, slipping on his running shoes as I prepared to head out for a midnight jog around my neighborhood to de-stress.

"Four rounds? Possibly five?" I replied hesitantly, as I tried to ascertain how long I could possibly last, having not slept much for the past three nights.

"I think you should run a comprehensive check of your house to see if it is tapped," he suggested, as we completed our third round. He had already done a through security review of my apartment two days ago to assess the risks of enemy infiltration.

"How much would it cost my company?" I enquired curiously.

"About 1,000 yuan per square meter," Zheng Ma replied. That was a cool US$16,000 for my apartment. I already found out from the advisors that his dedicated services were costing us almost RMB1,500 (US$240) per day.

"So who exactly is after your life?" Zheng Ma continued.

"Some crazy Chinese businessman," I replied falteringly, before adding, "But I think he's not after me, he's after my boss."

Zheng Ma smiled, as we raced to finish our final round.

Every day brought a new emergency. Within days, we received a court order summoning us to turn up as defendants to a pending lawsuit that Chairman Zhou had filed against us. The hearing was scheduled to commence two months later at an intermediate people's court located in the south side of Beijing.

Next, we received letters from Chairman Zhou's lawyers purporting that certain members of a foreign fund had "illegally intruded into a Chinese enterprise's property."

The letter claimed that we had directly caused the IPO to be pulled. The letter also alleged that All-Stellar's management and employees were "despicable liars with no integrity," who had tricked Chairman Zhou and sent teams to illegally enter his company's premises and forcefully seize company property. They included several photos of the staged demonstrations at our office to claim that All-Stellar had been mistreating and exploiting Chinese workers. The letter concluded by alleging that Russell Wen and Alan Dong had "behaved improperly and should be discharged from official duties".

Emails, professionally crafted in English, were also circulated to our Limited Partners requesting them to step in to resolve the dispute. Russell nearly went mad. How Chairman Zhou managed to get the e-mail addresses of our Limited Partners was puzzling, and I knew a few suspicious looks were cast my way.

Still, what we were most concerned about was the possibility that Chairman Zhou would utilize the internet to spread photos of the staged demonstrations as well as unfounded allegations about us to incite public fury. So far, the Lao Qianbei had shrewdly refrained from doing so, implying that he was still prepared to let us "save face" if we would surrender.

Russell ordered us to prepare media responses. But even the Chinese public relations agency that specialized in crisis management to handle our case told me frankly that the damage control would still be a poor second best outcome, compared to working out a compromise with Chairman Zhou as soon as possible.

Time was not on our side. Bathroom breaks became a luxury and I found myself tempted to use the empty wine bottle on Fang Xing's table to relieve myself when I was stuck in unending conference calls, and could not dash to the bathroom. "Now, who was it who assured me that PE professionals would not need to pee secretly under their desks?" I asked myself sardonically.

What bugged me most was that I had not seen Alan for days. Did he get into some kind of trouble? Was he abducted by Chairman Zhou? I asked the team but they did not know.

Finally, I found out from Russell's secretary that Alan had applied for leave of absence and had already left China. He had gone into hiding—on doctor's orders, he said. Chairman Zhou's endless fusillade of threats—which allegedly included a threat to abduct Alan's children – was causing him "severe psychological and physical distress" that required him to take a complete break from work for an indefinite period.

I found it quite unbelievable that Chairman Zhou would actually make such a threat against Alan's kids. Despite his gruff exterior, he had shown many times to all of us how fond he was of children, and had made big donations every year to orphanages as well as causes to protect abused and abducted children.

But I had no time to dwell on this. With the key man down, the pressure on me mounted. I was the only one left in China to deal with the mess while my local boss ran to Singapore to hide.

Russell tried to drum up my morale with his battle cries: "We are not going to admit defeat so easily. As an established foreign fund operating in China, we are held in high regard by international investors. More importantly, we have the money to pay top-notch lawyers and advisors who have the best brains to formulate the right strategies to resolve the dispute. We are confident that we can wrestle back control over the company. Moreover, we have legal ownership over all the company shares. It's time for us to even the score."

Our lawyers told us that we could try evoking the China Public Gathering and Protest Law. So we filed a parallel lawsuit against

Chairman Zhou for disruption of social harmony. In the court filing, we claimed he instigated construction workers to illegally gather at our office complex to demonstrate. Russell encouraged us to come up with creative solutions.

Gary suggested we hire private investigators to probe into Chairman Zhou's private wealth, both onshore and offshore, and file court orders to freeze his personal accounts. One of our restructuring advisors suggested that we should find stress points to pressure him to budge through shaming him. Did Chairman Zhou have any mistresses, for instance? I refused to answer that question, claiming ignorance.

Yet another advisor suggested that we seek the cooperation from China's Public Security Bureau and the Internal Affairs Department, to allow us to cut off electricity and water supply at DeeDee's operations.

However, we never did carry out any of these ideas. Instead, we spent copious amounts of time debating the pros and cons of each option. Our efforts to maintain a democratic airing of views, and to secure a majority vote on the best course of action smothered our ability to act decisively.

In the meantime, Chairman Zhou, wielding his authoritarian style where everyone either obeyed his orders unquestioningly or got chopped, charged on. Mark Hensworth, who had expressed alarm to the Great Leader that things had gotten "completely out of hand" and tried to suggest a more conciliatory negotiation approach with All-Stellar, was told to leave.

"It is about time, I guess," he told me sheepishly. After the relationship between All-Stellar and DeeDee fell off the cliff when the IPO was pulled, Mark's role had slowly diminished.

"Do you know Chairman Zhou hasn't paid me my salary for the past three months?"

I had read in the news that it was quite a common practice among Chinese companies to owe salary to their staff. Still, when Mark described the details to me, I was taken aback.

Mark's salary at DeeDee consisted of two parts: the base salary or *jiben gongzi* 基本工资 and the performance salary or *jixiao gongzi* 绩效工资. The base salary, which was automatically credited to his bank account, was reported to the tax authorities for the computation of personal income tax. The substantially bigger chunk of the salary, termed "performance salary," was paid in the form of reimbursements. Every month, he had to find RMB20,000 worth of *fapiao*, ranging from meal and taxi receipts to electricity bills—expenses that he could use to claim for reimbursement. If he did not collect enough *fapiao* for the month, he would not be able to get his "performance salary" entitlement. This was a very common technique that Chinese companies used to reduce the tax burden for their staff, they claimed.

In DeeDee's case, Chairman Zhou told all the employees that because the IPO did not materialize, the company's cash flows had been severely impacted and he could not pay them their full salaries for a few months. He had withheld the performance salary from everyone, so Mark had been surviving on his base pay for the past three months. "I rarely get my full performance salary anyway. More than half of my *fapiao* are usually rejected by the finance department for being fake," Mark said ruefully.

"Well, maybe it's time to return to the US," he continued. "There are a lot more job opportunities since many American parents want to teach their kids Mandarin and Chinese culture. Hope you fare better here than I did, China Hand."

> *Yi Shou Zhe Tian* 一手遮天: **Shutting out the heavens with one hand, referring to someone with great power who can hide the truth and hoodwink the public.**

CHAPTER 21

Seizure

Tang Shou Shan Yu 烫手山芋

"ARE YOU IN, OR ARE you out?" Russell snarled at me. He had a short fuse that day. We had been up for four nights in a row strategizing how to snuff out Chairman Zhou's incessant advances.

On the whiteboard, the advisors had mapped out the plan, grandly termed "the bottoms-up approach".

"We will send new management teams down to the local provinces to take control at the subsidiary companies' level. The duck farms are the cash cows of the business, so if we were to succeed at acquiring control of these assets, it would deal a huge blow to Chairman Zhou. DeeDee would lose its key source of cash and lifeline," explained Tom.

By taking over the local operations in the rural areas first, we would be able to squeeze Chairman Zhou financially, and then seize control of the urban prize—the Beijing headquarters—when his base of power had weakened so much that most of his staff abandoned ship.

Everyone had voiced their support for the plan, except me. After a conflicted silence, I decided it was still better to speak up earlier than later. "This plan would involve fighting in unchartered territory and we would need a lot more time to prepare. Taking over all the farms would require at least four times more resources and effort, compared to just taking over the Beijing headquarters—which we barely succeeded in doing in the first place," I appealed to Russell directly, avoiding the icy glare of the legal advisors.

"And how are we going to change out the *faren* 法人 (legal representative) at the local subsidiaries, given that they are all loyal to Chairman Zhou?" I continued. In China, the legal representative had broad powers to act on behalf of the company, and held the company stamp as well as access to the company's bank account.

"We can sort out that nitty-gritty later. The key thing now is that Chairman Zhou had been playing dirty and rough with us, so we should fight back and retaliate before it is too late," barked Tom.

"Well, with all due respect, I would like to point out that we need to retaliate in a way that maximizes our chances of success and does not cost us another arm and leg," I said pointedly.

By now, we had already owed over US$1 million in fees to the advisors, and that figure was escalating by the minute. This new "bottoms-up" attack meant even more advisory fees out the door. From the best Chinese lawyers to restructuring specialists, private investigators, interim management and security guards, we had engaged a formidable local army. Their fees were so breathtaking that I suspected they must have been jacked up on the assumption that All-Stellar was foreign and therefore ignorant of local market conditions. Some of the service providers even demanded to be paid up front.

I soon got into a heated argument with one of the Chinese lawyers who kept chasing me for payment. "You and I both know that your company is already making a windfall from this assignment. We will eventually pay you, but we need to see results first!"

After that dispute, I was bothered enough to ask Russell, "Should we review the terms of engagement for these advisors? I think we should pay them on a success basis, and not by the hour. That way, they will have skin in the game and align their interests and incentives with us more closely."

Russell was also miffed enough by the exorbitant fees to promise to consider my suggestions carefully. But when our advisors turned up with their "bottoms-up" strategy, he was so sold on the plan that he had made no mention of the fees issue. And now, he was threatening to dock my salary for "being the only one who keeps opposing our plans".

"You are getting too friendly with the Chinese, don't get sucked in and side with them," Russell added. The very boss who had deployed me to China to be his eyes and ears on the ground was now getting suspicious of me. I realized that Russell had already started to lose faith in me a few weeks back when I had fallen ill. "He probably thought I was pulling off a trick like Chairman Zhou's medical holiday," I thought miserably.

The battle began. On August Fourth, we sent notices to each of the subsidiaries notifying them that their legal representatives and management had been replaced. In the provinces of Shandong, Henan and Guangxi—Chairman Zhou's traditional strongholds— we made legal arrangements to take over control of the local duck farm subsidiaries. Then we waited for Chairman Zhou to respond. For twenty-four hours, all was quiet.

Then, two days later, we received calls from phone numbers we did not recognize, requesting us to go over to the duck farms to take over operations.

In the southern province of Guangxi, a man identifying himself as DeeDee's local representative asked us to come down to the farm the next evening, so that he could hand over the company chop and business registration certificate to us. This, our advisors exulted, was ample proof that Chairman Zhou had finally surrendered. "Bottoms up," they cheered.

I was dispatched to handle this handover process, along with Mr. Lim, a Singaporean whom Russell had picked as the interim CFO, and Mr. Ding, the newly-appointed operations manager who was a Guangxi native. The only flight out of Beijing to Liuzhou in the afternoon was Air China flight 1875 arriving at 7:30p.m. The local representative insisted on meeting after dinner, so we agreed to meet him at 9:15p.m. at the duck farm.

The stench of duck manure and rotting carcasses filled the air as we walked past the entrance of the farm. I heard the sound of squawking ducks in the distance. Were the ducks having problems sleeping? I wondered, as we squelched through the mud. Fang Xing and I had visited the Liuzhou farm in early 2009 shortly after All-Stellar invested in DeeDee, and recollections of our friendly meeting with the well-organized local management were still fresh in my mind. This time, the farm was in disarray, with tools and sacks of duck feed scattered everywhere.

Suddenly, a pack of scowling farmers appeared and surrounded us. Without any greeting, they shoved us into a blood-streaked slaughtering house. Photos of dead ducks and red banners hung on the walls.

"We have ceased operations and have not fed the ducks for over two days. Do not leave here without resolving the farm problems," shouted the leader. I recognized him as the "local representative" who had called us the previous day.

It was also clear that he was acting on Chairman Zhou's orders. He had gathered over thirty duck farmers who lived within a ten-mile radius of the farm to meet us and stage a demonstration. These farmers were the outsourced vendors who formed a crucial part of DeeDee's supply chain. They reared the ducks in their backyards on behalf of DeeDee's local operations until the ducks were ready for slaughter. The local operations provided the baby ducklings, animal feed and technology to the farmers, and then bought the full-grown ducks back. Most duck producers in China operated under such a model nowadays, as it required less capital investment. Many of these farmers had worked for DeeDee's local operations for over a decade, and depended on the income from rearing ducks to raise their families.

"Chairman Zhou told us that you foreign thieves have forced him out and taken over his business! Who is the new legal representative you appointed? What proof do you have that he is legitimate?" the leader yelled over an old karaoke microphone. The microphone crackled so much that I could hardly make out his words. The farmers waved hammers, knives and other farm equipment, while their wives and children stood at the sides cheering for them.

"We are a reputable international investment fund and we have full legal rights to take over DeeDee's operations. We assure you that we will make every effort to keep the operations running smoothly and to protect your livelihoods, once we have completed the takeover," I said, trying to keep myself from stuttering in fear.

"Well then, why isn't your scoundrel legal representative here? He needs to prove that he can solve our problems!" yelled the crowd.

The leader pointed to the photos of dead ducks on the walls. "The supply of animal feed had been interrupted because of your takeover and the ducks had not been fed for days! Many are dying. You will suffer huge losses if you let this continue."

"Can you guys say something to them?" I pleaded with Mr. Lim and Mr. Ding, who were dumbly watching the crowd as they chanted, "Out with the foreigners!"

"Mr. Huang, I am new to the company and I do not know anything about this situation. What should I say?" whispered Mr. Lim.

Before I could reply, Mr. Ding said firmly, "I'm going to tell the local representative that I am just accompanying you to the farm but

I am not employed by DeeDee or All-Stellar. That way, they will let me go and I can contact your boss for you..."

"Don't you dare! You can't sell us out like that!" I hissed. "Just talk to the farmers and distract them while I send an e-mail to my bosses to get help as soon as possible."

"This is a quarrel between you and the farmers. I am just an innocent bystander," Mr. Ding said very loudly, so that the farmers would hear him.

The leader of the pack cut in impatiently. "Stop wasting time! When are you going to address our grievances? You still owe us over 120,000 yuan of overdue payment for the last batch of ducks we delivered. If we don't get the money, don't ever think of leaving Liuzhou!" shouted the leader. He looked at Mr. Ding, who backed further away into the shadows, showing by his body language that he had nothing to do with me.

Thankfully, Mr. Lim stepped forward. "I am extremely sorry about the problems caused by the takeover, but it is only temporary," he addressed the crowd. "Let me assure all of you that we will do everything we can to ensure that things return to normal soon."

As he distracted the farmers, I fished out my blackberry and furtively typed an e-mail to All-Stellar's headquarters:

Subject: Ransom payment

We are trapped in the Liuzhou city duck farm by thirty farmers. They will not let us go unless we pay them RMB120,000 for the previous batch of delivered ducks. SOS.

After over an hour, the commotion simmered down. One by one, the farmers sat on the floor, blocking the entrance to the slaughter house.

I checked my blackberry. To my horror, my e-mail did not get sent out—data network signals were almost non-existent on the farm.

It was already midnight and it was clear there was no way to leave before morning.

I sent a text message from my personal phone to Russell and Rebecca. A few minutes later, she responded, "Haha. Will try to get help. But be prepared to wait. As the Chinese saying goes, *yuanshui jiubuliao jinhuo* 远水救不了近火 (faraway water cannot save a nearby fire)."

I got permission from the representative to take a toilet break, and was marched out by two burly farmers to the nearby duck pond to pee. As I stood there pants down, I reflected over how crazy the situation had become, and let out a strangled scream of frustration.

It was not until late afternoon the next day that two policemen as well as a group of lawyers and mediators dispatched from Beijing appeared at the farm. Most of the farmers had already gone home by that time, but we were not allowed to leave the slaughtering house. Only the leader of the farmer pack, the farm manager and the plant manager were left at the scene. Negotiations continued until almost midnight before we were finally set free.

We signed a handwritten note stating that the legal right to the company chops and business registration certificate would remain with the local representative. We also surrendered almost all the cash the three of us carried in our wallets—about 15,000 yuan in total—as compensation for all the allegedly dead ducks. I had also given the local representative my watch in exchange for something to eat, as we had been starving for almost twenty-four hours. He had given me a bunch of sweet potatoes that the farmers had been roasting on a charcoal stove, but they were so hot that Mr. Lim and I scalded our fingers and tongues.

As we finally headed to the airport, I called Russell, who gave me an earful. "Where was the new operations manager, that Mr. Ding? What was he doing? Did you not register his status properly with the local authorities?"

"Mr. Ding came with us to do all the paperwork at the Administration of Industry and Commerce three days ago. We officially changed out Chairman Zhou's legal representative and replaced his name with Mr. Ding's," I assured him. "Problem is, Mr. Ding was so scared when he saw the demonstrators that he denied to the farmers that he was our guy and tried to distance himself from us."

"Fire him! He was supposed to help us on the ground to seize control, not sell us out!" roared Russell.

"Ok, whatever you say," I said weakly. "Are we still going ahead with the bottoms-up takeover of DeeDee's other farms?"

As it turned out, the very advisors who urged us to take over the local operations now switched gears and advised us against making any such further trips.

> ***Tang Shou Shan Yu*** 烫手山芋: **A delicious potato that one desires to eat but finds difficult to seize because it burns the fingers. Describes a very difficult problem that requires skill and risk-taking to address, but once resolved will bring about great benefits.**

CHAPTER 22

Fight

Da Da Chu Shou 大打出手

A WEEK OF UNEASY CEASEFIRE passed. We stopped our push to take over DeeDee's operations and change out the farm managers. Chairman Zhou kept the demonstrators loitering every day at our Beijing office lobby, but at least, they did not cause any disturbance and quietly played cards all day. They even stopped drinking beer.

Then, in late August, I suddenly received a text message: "How are you? Dear comrade, I have always treated you well and taken care of you. Why did you trick me into this? This is a matter that deeply hurts one's feelings. It is shameful!" It was from Chairman Zhou.

I wondered how to reply. Then, my phone beeped again: "You have known me for several years. I am a down-to-earth person. I really am not as bad as you think! Let's talk."

I called headquarters at once. "Russell, we need to talk. Chairman Zhou just reached out to me with two long text messages. I've forwarded them to you to take a look."

A few minutes of silence ensued as Russell struggled to make out the characters. To his credit, he had been ardently learning Mandarin so that he could "deal better with the Chinese, and cut out the interpreter and middleman". I waited eagerly, glad that he would be able to understand the friendly overtures in the Chinese text messages that an English translation could not quite convey.

Suddenly, Russell snorted. "Are you kidding me? This isn't some sick joke? Why would that old man reach out to you and even call you his friend and his *tongzhi* 同志(comrade), who has hurt his feelings deeply?"

"Russell, just because Chairman Zhou calls me his friend does not mean that I am secretly on his side or in cahoots with him. If you suspect me of betraying you, you can put all those fears to rest. I only work for All-Stellar and I am a loyal employee," I said firmly.

"No, Matt, what I mean is, why are you so sure this is from Chairman Zhou? In China, you need to be extra skeptical of everything, especially all the rubbish texts sent to your mobile."

I groaned inwardly. It was awesome that Russell was picking up on the Chinese social mentality of distrust so quickly, but we were wasting precious time in this case.

"So what are you suspicious about?" I asked.

"My Beijing driver has been teaching me street Mandarin, and he says that the modern meaning of *tongzhi* is 'gay'. So if the texts are really from Chairman Zhou, then he is calling you comrade because...?"

"No no no!" I protested. "Chairman Zhou is in his fifties and grew up in the Maoist era where everyone called each other comrade. Even now, he still has a habit of calling his wife *nvtongzhi* 女同志 (female comrade)!"

"The texts sound like a jilted lover's complaints to me," Russell went on, undeterred.

"Believe me, Russell, hurt feelings is a common phrase and it isn't as personal as you think! Officials often complain that the US has 'hurt the feelings of the Chinese people' whenever some bilateral diplomatic incident happens! I believe these two text messages are authentic and Chairman Zhou is indeed reaching out!"

"Chill out, man, just pulling your leg," roared Russell, letting loose a huge guffaw. "If he sends another text asking you to meet him at a hotel, I'll have my driver send you there immediately, okay?"

My phone beeped again. "Are you still in Beijing? You should leave immediately! If your bosses do not want to cooperate with us, the demonstrations will be just the start!"

This time, Russell was convinced. His advisors were triumphant—Chairman Zhou must be reaching out because he was suffering from battle exhaustion, or he was running out of money, they exulted.

I kept my mouth shut this time. I was not going to be the party-pooper reminding Russell that "in China, there is always more than meets the eye".

With communication channels reestablished, it was left to me once again to continue the dialogue with Chairman Zhou. I was anxious to reply quickly: both parties were losing precious time and resources. The only winners were the third-party advisors and lawyers who were still charging fees by the hour. But I still had to seethe for three and a half hours while the experts held a rigorous debate on how to craft "the most appropriate, measured and tactical response".

Finally, we sent it out on my phone: "Chairman Zhou, glad to hear you're well. We are happy to hear from you, but we are very upset about the demonstrations at our office building. Can you do something about it?"

Just 141 characters. And crafting it cost us US$12,300 in fees.

In less than three minutes, Chairman Zhou shot back a text. "I will ask my friend to speak to the leader of the group of men outside your office. We will see what can be done to help you restore order at your office. You know I am a man of integrity, and I will keep my promise. As for your company's investment, I will find a solution to repay you."

As our advisors exulted over how their cunningly crafted message had elicited what they interpreted as a white flag from the enemy, I wondered what Chairman Zhou had up his sleeve. I was a little nervous about his stated intention to repay us for our investment. Was he going to turn the tables on us by taking over our stake?

The next morning, all was peaceful and quiet at our office lobby. There were no sign of the protestors—not even their cigarette butts and melon seed kernels. Still, I waited with bated breath, not daring to believe that the ceasefire would last long. Perhaps Chairman Zhou was just buying time while he planned his next maneuver, and would send the rabble back to assault us again the very next day.

But after thirty-six hours of undisturbed serenity, even our office building management personnel started to celebrate. The roly-poly building manager bounced over to our office to congratulate us on our unexpected progress. "I was expecting it to last a few months," he marveled. "How did you make it go away so fast?"

I shrugged. The way I saw it, all it took to engineer this turnaround was a few short, cordial text messages, not dramatic lawsuits or invasions by SWOT teams. But I would have been lynched for saying that out loud in front of my team.

I did, however, send a quick personal text message to Chairman Zhou to express my gratitude—a move that I was made to regret ten minutes later. He responded again almost immediately, his conciliatory tone underlined by his characteristic barrage of exclamation marks: "I did not want all this to happen either! But you guys started this, so I had to retaliate! Especially when you mess around on my territory, do you understand? This is Beijing, my home! Thank you for your understanding! Look forward to cooperating with you!"

I showed the message to Russell, eager to show him that Chairman Zhou was willing to settle things in an amicable manner. But it unexpectedly fired up Russell's fighting spirit.

"The latest development proves just one point—the demonstrators were actually hired by him to harass us," he declared triumphantly. "Keep a record of those SMS exchanges. Do not delete them as we now have sufficient proof for the court case. I think we need to file another police report. Let's call that Chaoyang District policeman and surrender the new proof we have!"

We submitted a new police report, claiming that we had new evidence against Chairman Zhou—"a crook who had instigated acts of harassment that threatened the personal safety of foreigners living in Beijing". This description was crafted by our advisors, who recommended that the more we could depict Chairman Zhou as a devious character who deliberately disrupted social order, the higher the chances of convincing the authorities to side with us. At the same time, we, as foreigners, should always maintain a high level of professional conduct and show ourselves to be law-abiding when dealing with the government authorities as well as the police.

My work cell phone containing my dialogue with Chairman Zhou was also confiscated and submitted to the police as part of the new evidence.

Chairman Zhou discovered what had happened when a few friendly policemen from his district made a courtesy call to DeeDee's headquarters the following afternoon. He was incensed and had Manager Wang relay a message to me: "The only person left in All-Stellar that I thought I could still trust was you, and now you have betrayed me once again!"

Any hopes of resuming reconciliatory talks were shattered for good. Notices appeared on our office lobby walls every morning. One notice claimed that All-Stellar had "inflicted irreparable damage" to Chinese companies, while another listed the huge economic damages resulting from its "illegal intrusion into private property".

Letters from Chairman Zhou's suppliers were sent to our office. They were addressed to the new owner All-Stellar Asia Fund L.P., and revealed tens of millions of yuan owed by DeeDee for long-dated electricity bills, rental arrears and even duck feed invoices that went as far back as 2007. We were horrified. As more letters from new suppliers demanding payment poured in every day, I decided to drop Mark Hensworth a call just to vent. I caught him just in time before he boarded his flight to Hunan to tour the famous Zhangjiajie Mountains.

This time, Mark was much more candid when discussing DeeDee's affairs. He laughed at my story about the letters. "Are you sure Chairman Zhou isn't just taking you guys for a ride?" he asked. "He is extremely friendly with his suppliers, some of whom had actually participated in setting up DeeDee many years ago. He could have easily asked them to bombard you with debt letters to make you think the company is in horrible shape."

"But what makes you think he would do this?" I asked wearily.

"It's just a hunch. I'm not a business person, so I'm just relating what I've observed," he replied tentatively. "I've seen him do something similar before. Once, he asked me to pose as a foreign lawyer and write a letter to DeeDee's foreign supplier who wanted to raise prices. I was supposed to claim that DeeDee was going bankrupt and could not pay the supplier anymore. But thankfully, Chairman Zhou somehow managed to negotiate the prices down so I didn't have to send that letter. I've also seen him get a powerful contact to write letters to get out of another sticky situation with a local official, and I remember it worked miraculously."

"What sort of sticky situation?"

"Hmm…I think it had to do with an official to whom Chairman Zhou had given gifts earlier to help him get the bank loan and expedite the IPO process. The official wanted even more—a stake in DeeDee," said Mark.

I raised my eyebrows. "Wow, that official's greedy."

"Chairman Zhou tried all sorts of ways to get out of it, but he was nervous because he didn't want to get on the wrong side of this official. In the end, he got somebody from a company called Quanli to write a letter to the official and the demands immediately stopped."

I tried to Google the name "Quanli," but only hit blanks. "So what do you think Quanli is?"

"It could be a supplier, or maybe just another company that Zhou has close ties with," said Mark. "I don't know. But I noticed that Zhou's secretary was receiving a lot of calls from Quanli in the last two weeks before I got fired."

"Do you think Quanli is a shell company set up by Zhou and he is siphoning funds into it?" I speculated.

"Hmm, I don't think Zhou is a crook, as much as you may dislike him for using all these crazy tactics to thwart your attacks. Remember, it was Alan or Russell—or whoever the masterminds are in your fund—who started all this first," said Mark reflectively. "As for Quanli, I think it's probably just an influential company who has an important business relationship with Zhou. It must have a vested interest to help him get out of trouble," he added.

With this in mind, I started to dig into DeeDee's corporate relationships and discovered that many of the suppliers who sent us letters were companies set up by Chairman Zhou's relatives. But none of them bore the name Quanli.

In the end, we decided to simply ignore the creditor letters. And after a month, they stopped coming.

⟫◆⟪

It was around three o'clock in the afternoon when my phone rang. It was Russell. He was in Beijing for a series of follow-up meetings with the advisors and the police. "There is a Chinese guy blocking my path right now, and not letting me buy my lunch. I can't understand what he is saying. Would you translate for me?"

Surprised, I took over the phone. It was Manager Wang. I was relieved to hear Wang's voice at the other end of the line. I thought Russell had been accosted by some bloodthirsty Chinese gang member.

"Lao Wang, how are you?" I began.

"Hey Huang zong, we haven't spoken for a while!" Wang said cheerfully. "I bumped into Russell downstairs at your office and he is now with me. You know Chairman Zhou is extremely stressed lately. You guys have taken over operations, but the farmers are not getting the animal feed and veterinary medicine in time from the suppliers. The ducks are falling ill and some are dying from hunger. We cannot find Alan. Where is he now? We need to talk to him urgently."

He then passed the phone over to Russell. "Mr. Wang is just trying to find out from you where Alan is. And Wang says the ducks are falling ill and dying," I translated.

"Tell Mr. Wang in a friendly manner that our people have gone to the farms but the incumbent teams are not allowing us to get in," Russell said.

I relayed the message and added, "Lao Wang, what is the actual situation at the farms?"

"You know, since your guys took over the farms, operations have ceased. Your boss Alan is the mastermind, correct? Now he has disappeared and we can't find him. Can you please ask Russell when is Alan is coming back here to deal with the messy farm situation?"

So Chairman Zhou thought Alan was the "mastermind" behind our takeover plan! Russell did not refute this. Instead, he replied: "Tell Mr. Wang that Alan is away on a business trip and will not be back for a month. Meanwhile, for any issues, please ask him to come directly to you."

When I relayed the message across to Wang, he replied, "Okay, but please act fast. We don't want all the ducks to die of starvation. Do take care of yourself in the meantime." He passed the phone back to Russell.

Ten minutes later, Russell stormed into the office, and summoned me into the meeting room.

"This Wang guy accosted me and invaded my personal space! Why did you not call the police? You should have had the common sense to come over to rescue me immediately!" I wondered why Russell was giving me such a big dressing-down when the conversation with Wang seemed to have been so cordial.

"Russell, based on my knowledge of Wang, he would never touch anybody. He was pretty respectful to us over the phone!"

"You don't understand. You were not even there. He tried to raise his arms against me and blocked my path!" Russell yelled, his temples throbbing.

I blinked rapidly, thinking, "Come on, you think calling the police will resolve matters? Even if I had called the police, they would not have come to 'save' you because they would call it yet another civil dispute!"

Russell, even more incensed by my silence, yelled even louder: "You are showing complete disregard for authority here! You know I can fire you right away for blatantly disobeying orders? I can tell you are taking DeeDee's side and are strongly against what we are doing. You either voice out your objections up front, or you do what you are instructed to. Resign and get out, or stay and help the team get out of this mess!"

His accusations pierced my heart. I had never felt so wronged in my life. I was trying my best to avert further warfare by mediating between the two sides and presenting what I thought was the honest truth about Chairman Zhou and his people. Instead, I was being blasted for not kowtowing to Russell's perspective.

How I wished I had left together with Fang Xing earlier in the year! I was not mentally prepared to manage a culture clash of this scale and wondered what Fang Xing would have done if he were in my situation. But I could not find any way to connect with him again.

His mobile number appeared to have been cancelled, emails went unanswered and he was no longer active on his Weibo microblog or LinkedIn account.

We filed a police report again for the second time in three days. This time, we alleged that one of our senior foreign employees was forcefully detained against his will by a Chinese gangster employed by Chairman Zhou.

The next day, an unsigned letter appeared via the routine mail delivery to All-Stellar's office. It simply stated in Mandarin: "We know that All-Stellar has been involved in bribing a high-level official to expedite the IPO process. We will report this to the relevant authorities and ensure that you face serious consequences if you do not sell your stake in DeeDee to a third party within three months."

My efforts to trace the sender were futile. And I was already too swamped to do in-depth detective work on the origins of the letter. Russell originally dismissed this as yet another prank by Chairman Zhou. But I was genuinely alarmed, because the letter boosted my suspicions that Chairman Zhou might be working on a plan to boot us out of the company and force us to sell our stake. So I decided to share with him what Mark Hensworth had described earlier about the powerful business contact that DeeDee had. Would Quanli now be aiding Chairman Zhou into pressuring us into selling our stake as soon as possible?

"Quanli," Russell repeated thoughtfully. "Can you find out what the heck this is?"

I tried calling my contacts to see if anyone had heard of this name. I even tried to call Susie, who was amused that I was so desperate that I would reach out to her. "I'm on a yacht. I've never heard of Quanli so it must been set up quite recently after I left Beijing. I've been focusing on advising wealthy Chinese on offshore philanthropic projects and tax optimization, so I haven't had as much time to catch up on the latest on China's PE scene. Why don't you ask Fang Xing?"

After another two weeks of futile searching, Quanli Private Equity Co. came to find me.

A man who claimed to represent the investment fund came to our office. Only Rebecca was there at that time. "He's middle-aged, bespectacled, with a branded watch and a branded man-bag," she said. "You could be describing almost any Chinese male in this office building," I sighed.

He had left a message: "If Huang zong is interested to discuss All-Stellar's exit options from DeeDee Duck, he can meet with the managing director of the fund, Mr. Han, this evening at eight o'clock at the Ritz Carlton bar."

I rushed to report this to Russell, but he dismissed this as yet another scare tactic from Chairman Zhou. "You can meet this Han guy but make sure you don't reveal anything or promise anything. We don't want to give this Mr. Han or anyone in the PE world the impression that All-Stellar is going to admit failure and bail out from this investment."

That evening, I nervously made my way to the Ritz Carlton bar and sat there till 10:30p.m., but nobody approached me. It occurred to me that I had no way of identifying Mr. Han. But he obviously knew who I was. As I rose to go, a bartender brought me a jade paperweight, inscribed with the Chinese saying *renyishi fengpinglangjing, tuiyibu haikuotiankong* 忍一时风平浪静、退一步海阔天空. "This is from Mr. Han. He sends his apologies that he was not able to make it to the meeting."

I looked blankly at the inscription. If we endure and step back, the waves will diminish and we become as boundless as the sea and sky. What could that mean? I was getting more and more creeped out.

When I related the incident to Russell, he seemed indifferent. "That just proves that Chairman Zhou is just messing with us all over again," he said absent-mindedly. I knew he was busy with a potential deal in India, and he seemed to be losing interest and stamina to keep fighting Chairman Zhou. He was already exploring options for All-Stellar to exit from its involvement in DeeDee, after several members of the Investment Committee questioned the long-term viability of the investment.

That night, I pondered the meaning of the inscription again. It seemed that if we were only to take a step back to look at the bigger picture, we would find the solution. Our differences would no longer look so insurmountable, if we could go back to the first principle of preserving harmony.

The word he 和 (harmony) holds a special place in the hearts of many Chinese, who would rather bang their skulls against the wall in private than have an open, head-on confrontation with an adversary. What might seem hypocritical to westerners was simply a social norm for Chinese, who would coo words of endearment to the same person they were plotting to take down.

I pondered what that mysterious Mr. Han was trying to do by standing me up and then leaving this cryptic message. Was he just testing All-Stellar's reaction to see how willing we were to discuss our exit options? Perhaps he was hinting to us that it was in our broader interests to step away from our investment in DeeDee, before further warfare destroyed the value of the company—and our own investment—completely?

It was true that we had lost our best chance for reconciliation with the Lao Qianbei when we filed a police report, instead of responding graciously. Now, it seemed like there was no turning back.

But a small part of me still stubbornly chose to interpret the inscription in another way: when we are willing to take a step back, the sky could be the limit once again. If both sides were to back away from the tension, reaffirm our harmony of interests, and let time soothe over our differences, we still had a shot at rebuilding DeeDee.

It might take years. It would certainly take a ton of patience. And stepping back may seem like passive inaction. But in China, it could also be considered a solution.

> *Da Da Chu Shou* 大打出手: **Fists out for an all-out fight, referring to a violent attack.**

CHAPTER 23

Black Hand

Mu Hou Hei Shou 幕后黑手

I T WAS NOW SEPTEMBER, AND still no sign of a breakthrough.

DeeDee was hemorrhaging cash fast, and had lost more than half of its customers. We started receiving demands for payment again—this time from suppliers that I ascertained were genuine. The bills piled high on my table, and I was forced to report to Russell that if DeeDee were to continue in this state for another few months, its revenues would plummet and it may start making losses. I also heard rumors that Chairman Zhou was diverting the output of his local farms to another company he had set up, but there was no way for me to verify the information without personally going down to the farms—something that our advisors had instructed me not to do after the humiliating experience in Guangxi last month.

My efforts to track down Mr. Han still came to nought. But I heard talk among my PE contacts that Quanli's name was surfacing among the bidders in a number of high-profile deals, including some involving SOEs. In addition, Quanli was said to be close to acquiring some nightclub assets seized during the government's anti-corruption drive, and its stated aim was to turn them into luxurious private clubs for Chinese billionaires. It made me certain that Mr. Han must have high-powered connections: a mafia boss perhaps? An official?

But if Quanli was involved in such plum deals, why would it be interested in a relatively small, now-struggling company like DeeDee?

I suddenly recalled a stray comment made by Fang Xing once that one of DeeDee's farms on the outskirts of Beijing was located in a strategic area that could potentially be circled off for top-secret central government use. "What would the government want to do with a duck farm? It doesn't have oil or gold reserves and it's not near any airport or port, right?" I had asked incredulously at that time. "All we know is that the soil there is well-watered, fertile and not prone to disease or contamination."

He shrugged. "Park military tanks? Or grow more organic food for the top leaders?"

Intrigued, I had fished out the copy of the Ministry of Agriculture map that farm manager Lin had given to me during our first visit to the Beijing farm. We studied it together, but since neither of us knew much about geography and agriculture, the markings and symbols on it did not make sense.

After two minutes, Fang Xing exhaled and said lightly, "Anyway, whatever. Who cares about this old map and all these crazy rumors about Land Encirclement Programs? Maybe somebody made this up to hike up the land prices there."

I had laughed it off too and soon forgot about the incident.

But now, my interest was piqued. I rifled through the drawers in our office looking for the map, but could not find it anywhere. I asked Rebecca if she had seen it. She was busy painting her finger nails a bright red color "in honor of the upcoming October 1 National Day holiday" and could not help me to sort through the papers. "Your desk is so messy, it's no wonder that you can't find anything," she chided me. "What do you want with an old map anyway?"

"Strange. The last time I saw it was in end August. Did you let any strangers into our office for the past two months?"

"Oh come on, who wants to come here when there are no deals or money on the table? The last time anyone visited was that strange man from Quanli and I made sure he didn't step past my desk."

I tried to check the surveillance cameras in the office, but the security guards asked if I had already filed a police report for the missing map. That was the last thing I wanted to do, so I decided to drop the issue for the time being.

I did send a casual e-mail to Fang Xing's personal account, jokingly asking if he had heard anything new about the Land Encirclement Program. "Wish you were still here. I'm sure you have heard gossip about our issues with DeeDee. Maybe if you were around, we won't be trying so hard to get out now," I added.

The week-long National Day holiday passed uneventfully. Then, on Monday, an e-mail sent by Chairman Zhou's lawyers to the All-Stellar team sent my phone ringing off the hook again.

The letter stated that DeeDee's management was ready to start reconciliatory discussions, with the objective of paving All-Stellar's exit from its investment in the company.

The timing was uncanny: our Investment Committee had been pressurizing us to find a satisfactory exit from the investment as soon as possible.

Then, Manager Wang broke months of silence and called me, asking me out for tea. We had a long, friendly chat about everything under the sun except the conflict between DeeDee and All-Stellar. The next day, Chairman Zhou called me on my personal mobile phone, sounding effusively cordial. "Hi Xiaohuang, how's your golf game going? We should play some time after we finish negotiations for All-Stellar to sell its stake in DeeDee."

"Things have not been easy," I admitted. "But I still have utmost respect for you, Lao Qianbei. I am very grateful that you have made contact with me."

"I know you are a good lad so that's why I still talk to you. Frankly, if you leave All-Stellar, I would make sure that you guys lose every single dollar of your investment. I am just giving you face! Will you still be around in the company for the next few months?"

I assured him that I had no plans to leave and was eager to continue building the relationship with DeeDee. He seemed pleased.

This time, I decided that I would not report the conversation to Russell, since Chairman Zhou's words were bound to throw him into a fit. As soon as I put down the phone, Russell called me, eager to get this horrid mess off his hands once and for all. He told me to craft a formal, positive e-mail response to Chairman Zhou, asking for negotiations to be re-opened the following day.

Russell booked the next flight up to Beijing. I met him at his hotel and was surprised to see a burly body guard in the room. "He's my security detail to protect me from any more gangsters like the one that attacked me last time," said Russell.

I was taken aback. That incident had happened so long ago and yet Russell was sore over it. As I gazed at his towering athletic frame, I wondered again how Russell could have thought the skinny Wang was out to intimidate him, let alone physically cause him harm.

I mumbled, "I'm sure such an incident will never happen again..."

"Yeah you'd better make sure of it," snapped Russell, before pausing for a while. Suddenly, he seemed to think better of his outburst and continued in a more cordial tone: "Actually, I should thank you for helping me in that situation because I couldn't understand a word of what that Wang guy said even though my Mandarin had improved a lot. He had such a thick accent. We really need you to stay on the ground to keep the communications channel open with DeeDee, so we can get this divestment completed."

I assured him I would do my best.

"Since it is annual appraisal time back at headquarters, why don't we just take this time now to discuss your performance?" Russell continued. "We all know that your year has been a pretty tough one, and things have turned out much worse than we expected. So it's only reasonable that I cannot affirm that you have achieved any of the KPIs (Key Performance Indicators) we had set out for you, since we are likely to incur a net loss on this DeeDee investment."

My heart sank. "Russell, I have done my utmost and worked my hardest. I hope the company will at least reward me for my loyalty in staying with the company when others like Susie and Fang Xing have left..."

"Yes, we will acknowledge the fact that you continued to stay on with the company, and that you are playing a key role in helping to bring this mess to a closure," interrupted Russell. "We still need you to help us get through this final stretch. If we can pull this off well, your performance rating can still be very good."

As I left the meeting with Russell, I tried to look on the bright side: at least he had acknowledged my loyalty and my role in helping to set things right. And there was finally light at the end of the tunnel. Chairman Zhou was clearly eager to have foreign shareholders removed from his company to ensure his company's ultimate survival. As for All-Stellar, it had the go-ahead from our Investment Committee to initiate talks with potential buyers for our stake.

The next day, we arrived at our first meeting with Chairman Zhou, flanked by lawyers representing each side. Alan, All-Stellar's official Head of China in name, was still missing in action, despite the fact that we were trying to sell out of our first—and only—Chinese investment.

The Chinese side wanted us to divest our investment immediately at whatever market price we could get, while Russell wanted to drag out the process to find the best price possible. As the translator and mediator for the negotiations, I was caught in the worst possible position: I had to manage two men with bruised egos, who spoke different languages and had conflicting objectives.

This made the process unbearably painful. Putting Russell and Chairman Zhou together at the same table was like locking two famished lions in the same cage. They roared at each other at the slightest provocation, and negotiations were on the verge of breaking down on several occasions.

Finally, we agreed that All-Stellar would run a competitive bidding process. This involves multiple buyers submitting sealed bids detailing the price and terms of the offer, after which the seller would then select the bidder that offered the highest price or best terms.

Russell insisted that we find more bidders to take part, as competition theoretically meant we could drive the selling price higher. However, the auditor resignation and thwarted takeover plans made finding new interested parties very difficult.

All-Stellar tried to bring in a few potential bidders, but our discussions always hit a snag when the mystery of the auditor's resignation was inevitably raised. We still had no satisfactory explanation for that issue. Still, that was not the ultimate reason why the bidders backed out. The real stumbling block was Quanli.

The PE fund expressed its interest in buying over All-Stellar's entire stake in DeeDee a month after we opened the bidding process. My Singapore bosses were immediately suspicious of the company and berated me once again for not finding out more about Quanli. My feeble response that it was so secretive that it did not even have a website or a publicly available office phone number did not appease them.

Then, by bizarre coincidence, after Quanli made public its intention to bid, the other players started to fade out one by one. "We had a chat with Quanli's managing director recently and decided that this deal is not quite right for us," the managing director of one fund told me vaguely after I pressed him several times for a reason.

After one more month of searching for more bidders, further clashes with Chairman Zhou and ever-mounting advisor bills, Manager Wang came to us one day with an interesting proposition: Chairman Zhou had found two new bidders. "With three different bids, that should make the process competitive enough, right?" he asked.

Tom advised us to "settle for whatever you can get now, before the valuations get even lower". "It's clear that bidders view this divestment as a distressed sale so it is very difficult to even recover our investment cost," he told us.

I knew this already, but my heart still sank—Chairman Zhou was making us pay a hefty price for daring to challenge him on his home turf.

Exactly how huge a price was not evident until that nerve-wrecking day arrived, when Quanli and the other two funds submitted their bids.

Russell cursed. "The highest bid comes from Quanli."

"How much did they bid?" whispered Gary, almost too nervous to speak.

"Only US$73 million. That's US$5 million below our initial investment cost."

I gaped. We were going to lose several million dollars on our maiden investment. And the loss would be even greater when we took the massive advisor fees into account.

"Was this rigged? How can the bids be so low?" moaned Gary.

There was an oppressive silence in the room that nobody had the energy to break.

> *Mu Hou Hei Shou* 幕后黑手: **A mastermind manipulating a situation from behind the scenes.** 幕后 **means "behind the curtain,"** 黑手 **means "black hand".**

CHAPTER 24

Takeover

Gong Shou Er Qu 拱手而取

TWO MONTHS LATER, I STOOD in front of an imposing office building in Beijing's financial district waiting nervously for Russell to arrive. We were going to Quanli's office to sign the papers completing the sale of All-Stellar's stake. Our lawyers had already arrived and were waiting for us on the thirtieth floor.

I had not seen Russell nor spoken to him since that depressing day when Quanli won the bid for All-Stellar's stake. I heard he was up to his eyeballs in work, churning out reports for our Investment Committee. He also had a massive fall-out with Alan in Singapore the previous week when he told the latter that he would not be getting any bonus at all since his performance for the year was far below expectations. Alan would also be demoted if he did not produce exceptional results within three months. My enraged Chinese boss banged repeatedly on the table and started a ten-minute shouting match with Russell. Then he stormed out of the office and returned half an hour later with a scribbled resignation letter. While all this was supposed to be confidential information, Russell's secretary leaked the news, and within a few hours, Rebecca and I were gossiping about Alan's abrupt departure.

A week had passed, and I was still waiting for Russell to tell me my own performance ratings. He said he had his hands full with a few big deals in India and Indonesia, and he was travelling too much to get on a call with me. The longer he delayed, the deeper my dread as I anticipated bad news.

Sure enough, the night before Russell flew to Beijing, he sent me an e-mail informing me that my bonus would be cut by 45 percent. My performance was "far below expectations". He did not explain why.

Even though I had braced myself for the worst outcome, I was still shattered. I emailed Russell immediately, asking to discuss this in person. No response.

I knew my only chance to speak to him would be the precious few minutes before we entered Quanli's office. So I waited on the curb to make sure I did not miss him in his chauffeured black Audi. I was shivering and a little heady from inhaling the charcoal fumes wafting in the air by the time he arrived. Russell grimaced when he saw me rushing to open the car door. "It's so bloody gray and murky here," he growled without saying hello.

I wasted no time. "Russell, I need to speak to you about my appraisal…"

He swung around and blasted me. His words sliced me like Chinese sword play: "You refused to support the fund in our counter-attack… you put your boss in danger…it is clear to the Fund's shareholders that the inexperience and disloyalty of the China team undermined my best efforts to protect our interests in DeeDee."

It dawned on me that Russell had no intention of rewarding me for being the sole person in the China team to stay on in Beijing to see the deal through. Instead, to protect his own reputation when explaining the situation to the Investment Committee, Russell had pushed all the blame to Alan and me.

Somehow, I made it into Quanli's office. Just minutes earlier, I had still been full of curiosity about meeting Mr. Han: he must be around Chairman Zhou's age, I thought. Someone who had spent years perfecting his hand at this game.

But now I could only stare at those doughy yet dexterous fingers, and his USA-made Avanti cigar paired with an oriental jade ashtray, wondering at the mass of East-West transfusions that embodied this young China Hand. He was young, no doubt about it. Probably in his early 30s. And he had obviously been in China's private equity game long enough to exploit distressed companies and asset price inflation.

An image that had increasingly haunted me over the past two years appeared again: a bubble that swelled and sank and swelled and sank…and yet somehow managed to stay off the ground.

Then, Han—what the heck, Fang Xing—turned around in his gigantic armchair and waved at us.

He looked at me first, not Russell. And I knew why. I was the one he felt a slight twinge of unease about betraying. For the rest of All-Stellar, it was just their bad luck to have picked a battle against Quanli, the unofficial advisor to—and now majority-owner of Dominant Duck.

Fang Xing was even more charming and charismatic than the last time we had met. He had packed on the pounds, which simply made his gregariousness spill over even more.

"Huang zong, how are you? You're thinner," he said with exaggerated concern.

"Fang Xing, long time no see! *Ni fafule* 你发福了," I mumbled, using a common saying, "you're looking more prosperous," which hints that a person has put on weight.

He shook hands briefly with Russell, who was still too aghast to say anything. Then he gestured to the Chairman of Quanli. Unlike the suits around him, this elderly man sported a white golf shirt, blue tweed trousers and a cigarette that he sucked on greedily—a sharp contrast to Fang Xing's leisurely sip of his cigar. "This is Mr. Han," Fang Xing said, speaking in Mandarin. "I represent him – and I aspire to be like him." The older man, who seemed bored perhaps because he did not comprehend much English, suddenly looked up with a flicker of interest, and the corner of his mouth twitched upwards.

Han did not speak during the entire conversation, but looked up whenever we switched from English to Mandarin. Chairman Zhou was not present and Fang Xing did not explain why.

We were introduced to two other men in suits—the managing directors of the two funds who had submitted bids. Russell glared at them in fury: they had been unreachable for further negotiations shortly after putting in their bid. We had tried repeatedly to call them to ask them to reconsider their price, hoping to avoid selling our stake at a loss to Quanli. Now they sat quietly beside Fang Xing as part of the new investor consortium controlling DeeDee. I knew that we had been taken in for a ride, and I knew who Russell would blame.

Quanli's foreign lawyers walked in with copies of the printed contracts. "Are these the final versions?" Fang Xing asked in his crisp New York accent.

Russell looked murderous and gestured to our own lawyers to leave the room with him. I sat there helplessly while they argued in hushed tones for ten minutes. Fang Xing seemed to understand my paralysis, and chatted inaudibly with Han. Then he gestured to one of his lawyers to go out and speak to Russell.

"Mr. Han is someone you do not want to mess with," the lawyer proclaimed loudly. "He has connections you do not know about." I could see our Chinese lawyer's face turn a little pale as he turned around and studied Mr. Han's lined face more closely.

Finally, after more arguing—this time between our lawyers and Russell—the whole group strode back in the room. Russell, red-faced, picked up the pen and signed. He marched out, without waiting for me. I stayed put, too scared to be left alone with him.

Fang Xing picked up the contract and handed it to Mr. Han with two hands, bowing respectfully.

Then he slapped me on the back: "Are you going to stay in China?

As the Chinese saying goes, *lairifangchang* 来日方长. There are many more days ahead, and the road is long – hopefully we will meet again in better circumstances, and maybe we can cooperate on new deals."

I was too choked up to say anything. After shaking hands again, I went out and felt a desperate urge to jump off the ledge somewhere.

That decides it, I told myself. Free fall from 15,000 feet.

⬤━◆━⬤

The sky was overcast in Wanaka where I was scheduled to go sky-diving—my childhood dream. I had arrived by bus from Christchurch, New Zealand in the morning.

The storm clouds were gathering. Before long, it started drizzling. All skydiving activities were suspended for the day. My blackberry kept buzzing non-stop as we prepared the last pieces of documentation for Quanli before it would release its final tranche of payment. Finally, the money came through in the late afternoon. I also received an e-mail from Donovan promising me to repay me a portion of the money I had invested in the failed hospital project.

I heaved a sigh of relief mixed with resignation. Looking out of the window of my hostel room, I thanked God that I had survived this incredible China adventure, and fell into a deep sleep.

When I woke up, the rays of morning sun shone through the translucent floral curtain, leaving petals of colored light on my bed. As the early morning mist started to clear, I set off for the air field. Fears of exploding blood vessels and sudden seizures that had gripped my mind earlier in the week vanished. I was ready to test my limits once again.

I shouted at the top of my voice as I dropped out of the plane, strapped alongside the flying instructor. A photographer jumped after us, videotaping my 15,000 feet descent. The mountains and fields came at me at breakneck speed as the icy air pierced my skin. It must have been fifteen seconds later when I felt my exhilarating fall halt abruptly as my parachute opened. I drifted dreamily back to earth.

After falling so far, it was time to rebuild my life again in China. I needed to pick up the pieces after what I had melodramatically described to my alarmed parents as a "seismic clash between Eastern and Western cultures". Indeed, a brawl had almost broken out over this topic during a debriefing meeting in Singapore. We were trying to dissect how we could have done something so ridiculous as to sell All-Stellar's stake at an obscenely low price to a former employee's new shop. Gary and Tom had blamed Chinese crooks.

Alan, the sole Chinese person who dared to speak up, asserted that such ingenious plots could have been hatched anywhere in the world, not just in China, and started listing a slew of corporate fraud scandals in North America and Europe. Before long, the quarrel about whether westerners or Chinese were more unscrupulous disintegrated into shoving and bottle throwing. Alan, who had been hauled by Russell into the meeting for interrogations, was quickly dragged out again.

Nobody asked for my views. It was just as well, because my assessment of the situation would not have gone down well: we failed because we did not respect our Chinese partner enough and tried to control his company too much. We thought that by pouring huge amounts of money to hire expensive consultants to manage the crisis, we could emerge as winners. But as it turned out, our heavy-handed approach in dealing with Chairman Zhou only pushed him closer to Fang Xing and Quanli. That cost us dearly. Finally, we wasted precious time and resources fighting for power, only to be outwitted by a young China Hand, someone who was so familiar with us and who also knew China from the inside out.

> *Gong Shou Er Qu* 拱手而取: **Both hands held in front of one's chest in an easy position to receive or take over something.**

Epilogue

Three Years On...

WITH THE FINANCIAL BACKING OF Quanli, Chairman Zhou's company ballooned into one of the largest poultry players in China, big enough to garner the attention of hungry SOEs.

Fang Xing, leveraging on Mr. Han's connections with SOEs, angled for a big buyer to take over DeeDee at a substantial profit. It was an opportune time to woo these state giants: they were flush with cash and cheap loans from the state banks, and the central government was encouraging them to consolidate fragmented but strategic industries like agriculture. Many SOEs were paying top dollar to gobble up mid-sized companies, who had few other exit options since the Chinese securities regulator had slapped a moratorium on local IPOs. Quanli was not the only fund exiting an investment through a trade sale—Carlyle had sold their ownership in an industrial company to state-owned Sinochem International Corp in 2012 at over two times their 2008 investment. In another chemicals M&A deal, Carlyle made 400 percent profit, according to Chinese media.

In November 2013, an influential state-owned agri-food company took the bait and bought DeeDee. The deal was brokered within just three months and Quanli made a profit of 100 percent on its investment in DeeDee. Post-merger, DeeDee's duck farms would be run by the SOE's existing management team and fully integrated into the latter's extensive value chain, local media said.

I had left All-Stellar in 2013 to join a new Beijing-based firm and read about the merger in the news. I decided to send congratulatory text messages to Chairman Zhou and Manager Wang, who must now be rich beyond their dreams. The SOE had offered them two options: to continue working in the newly merged company as senior managers, or to leave with a handsome golden handshake. Both decided to take the cash.

Chairman Zhou chose to retire, while Manager Wang tried his hand at setting up organic poultry farms in his hometown province, where he had built a sprawling five-storey mansion for his elderly parents. He was now a father of two. Both he and his wife did not have siblings, so China's policies permitted them to have a second child.

"I was given a second chance at striking it rich—when the IPO failed, I thought I was doomed. We should celebrate my good fortune together at a karaoke session, what do you think?" Wang wrote in his text message reply to me.

I suggested tea at his favourite haunt the next time he visited Beijing instead. Two weeks later, he was in town, and I marvelled at how stylish he looked in his fitted Sartorio sports jacket.

"Wow, you look like a completely different person. And you even don't smoke anymore?" I asked, flabbergasted.

"No, I quit at Fang zong's advice. It was easier after Quanli bought the stake in DeeDee and I didn't have so much stress anymore. After I made my first million, I took up recreational cigar-tasting instead," he said.

"Fang Xing must have persuaded you to take that hobby up?" I asked.

"Yes, he says you don't actually smoke the tobacco, it's a whole ritual of preparing and appreciating the smell and finally taking a small puff…very much like tea appreciation. So I like it a lot. And Fang zong says it's the new fad among young Chinese elite," said Wang proudly.

"Fang Xing must be teaching you a lot about how to enjoy life, now that you are a rich man," I said teasingly.

Wang reddened. "Yes, I'm looking to buy my first sports car, and Fang zong let me test-drive his new Ferrari. He said I was the first person to ride in it. I'm very grateful to him for thinking so highly of me. He actually offered me a job last month when he left Quanli to set up his own private equity fund, saying that he values loyal employees. But I told him I'm just a simple farmer, not a financial guy."

"Wow, Fang Xing is striking out on his own: *cibang yingle* 翅膀硬了, his wings have hardened," I said, impressed.

"Yes, he is very successful in raising tens of millions from second-generation wealthy heirs," said Wang. He leaned forward and continued in a whisper: "But his personal life hasn't been as successful. I heard Fang zong's wife had an affair with another man after she found out that he had brought one of his mistresses to a Formula One race in Singapore instead of her. Fang zong was so angry that she had cheated on him that he divorced her immediately. They are fighting for custody of their son now."

My mind wandered to Rebecca, who had been dumped by Fang Xing just before she left All-Stellar in early 2011 for another job. We had lost all contact since then.

Wang broke my reverie: "I'm sure you have lots of questions about what has happened at DeeDee over the past three years. Ask me whatever you like. Now that I've left DeeDee and Chairman Zhou has retired, I can speak more freely."

I was delighted. "So how did Quanli turn things around so easily after we left? I thought the company's cash flows were turning negative and Chairman Zhou even gave us the impression that there was a real risk of bankruptcy because DeeDee had lost so many customers."

Wang laughed. "Well, the company was indeed hit hard when it was fighting with All-Stellar, but I think you may have been misled into believing it had lost all its business and was in big financial trouble. In 2010, it actually made about one billion yuan in revenues and kept its profit margins at 30 percent. And staff numbers actually rose to 600, from 500 in 2008."

I was flabbergasted. While the revenue number was less than our original target of about 1.2 billion yuan, the 20 percent growth rate in 2010 was still a very respectable performance given the adverse circumstances.

"Chairman Zhou has strong relationships with his customers whom he has served for decades," Wang continued. "So they all came back once he told them that the crisis was over. Fang zong also used Mr. Han's name to bring in some new customers."

"Who on earth is this Mr. Han?" I asked.

"I don't even think Han is his real surname. They say he comes from a top political family. He uses Fang zong to handle all his deals, and rarely appears in public."

"Then why did he show his face at the meeting when Russell signed the papers to sell All-Stellar's stake to Quanli?" I asked.

Wang shrugged. "Beats me."

I had a flashback of Fang Xing's lawyer telling Russell about Han during the meeting in Quanli's office. "Hmmm…perhaps Han was there to pull weight and get our Chinese lawyers scared so that we would back down," I wondered aloud. "Han knew Russell was going to put up a big fight once he realized it was Fang Xing who had undermined our competitive bidding process, by getting the two other funds to submit fake bids."

Wang looked impressed. "Russell is not an easy laowai to deal with. Mr. Han must be powerful to make him back down so quickly. Mr. Han was instrumental in getting the SOE to acquire DeeDee very quickly too."

He went on to describe how the SOE's investment bankers had described the operating quality of Chairman Zhou's duck farm assets as being "excellent".

"But didn't our auditors resign because of accounting irregularities? How were all those issues resolved so quickly?" I asked.

"Oh, you didn't know? A new big-name auditor took over shortly after All-Stellar exited, and they issued clean audited statements for DeeDee. No problem at all."

My mind was spinning. Suddenly, Wang suddenly snapped his fingers and said: "Oh yes, I've been meaning to ask you...do you still have that map of the Beijing farm that I had given to you during our first visit there together? What did you do with it?"

"That map?" I was surprised. "I haven't been able to find it since late 2010, even after cleaning out my desk."

"Oh...that's ok then. After Quanli took over, Fang zong had all copies of that map confiscated. Not sure what he did with them, but I still wonder till now what sort of important or confidential information was on that map...I heard a senior manager mention something about state assets, but I'm not smart enough to figure out this sort of thing."

I was intrigued. "I recall Fang Xing mentioning something like that too. A Land Encirclement Program for government use. Too bad I can't find the map anymore."

Wang looked excited. "Maybe someone broke into your office and stole it," he exclaimed. I shrugged. I had briefly considered this possibility myself in the past, even listing the people with easy access to our office: the cleaning lady, the building management, the security guard, Rebecca or a former All-Stellar employee.

But I decided that it was not something I wanted to investigate any more for now, especially if Mr. Han—be it the man himself or his former right-hand man Fang Xing—was somehow involved. I might revisit the mystery again in future if I ever decided to see a psychiatrist, or write a novel based on my adventures. But kiss-and-tell memoirs were obviously out of the question, I told myself pragmatically. I would get into too much trouble if I were to write an expose of the truth—even if it were my incomplete version of the elusive truth.

Meanwhile, my attention was arrested by another interesting development. I heard from industry insiders that B&C was under investigation by the local securities watchdog in the Asian market where DeeDee had planned to launch its IPO.

The regulator asked for evidence from B&C to prove that DeeDee had indeed conducted fraudulent accounting or other misconduct that would have warranted the auditor's resignation. However, B&C had refused to hand over working papers to assist investigations, pointing to China's state secrets law which banned auditors from taking papers out of the mainland. Now, B&C was being summoned to court by the regulator for refusing to comply with the regulator's request for working papers.

As I digested this news, I began to recall how vacuous the reasons B&C gave to justify their actions seemed. At that time, we were never really convinced by their explanations and had felt that their decision to quit had been too abrupt. I personally was not sure whether the audit team had considered just how serious the consequences of their resignation would have been. For us, it was millions of investment dollars gone down the drain. For Chairman Zhou, it shattered his IPO dream, hurt his company's reputation and led to the loss of jobs and livelihoods for many of the company's staff.

I also wondered why the auditors could not have been more forthcoming to a seemingly harmless procedural request for documents in relation to their resignation. If they had reason to suspect the company had indeed falsified accounts, why not let the evidence speak for itself?

It now seemed there was more than meets the eye than just the minor land dispute and falsified contract documents which they claimed to have discovered back in 2010. Did B&C stumble across some information that DeeDee had tried to withhold from them?

Why would this information make them so uncomfortable with the accounts? Why would the audit partner himself resign after the episode?

It might take years for a final verdict to be released and even then, the real reason behind the auditors' puzzling resignation may never be made public.

Perhaps one day, if I were able to reconnect with Fang Xing, he may be able to give me another key piece of the inside story. He was the ultimate beneficiary of the deal after all.

As I reflected on all this, I realized that Quanli's choice to do a strategic trade sale to a SOE made even more sense. Fang Xing had taken the shrewder approach to exit the investment in a way that avoided any possible scrutiny from public markets and even from the local securities watchdog.

I recalled how I had voiced concerns to him about whether the company's financial numbers would be in good enough shape to impress investors and to pass the audit. His flippant reply: "Investors will believe anything if you spin the story properly. And you just need to find the right kind of local auditor." Then after a pause, he had added pensively, "Or we could have simply avoided the IPO route and found a buyer in a trade sale. There's always money to be made as long as you know the right time to get in and out."

The court case made me wonder again what would have happened if All-Stellar had taken a more measured, subtler approach after the resignation of B&C. If we had resisted the temptation of staging a hostile takeover of Chairman Zhou's company after the failed IPO attempt, and clung on to our investment for another two to three years, would the outcome have been different? Or if we had rejected Quanli's rigged offer, swallowed our pride and found a way to cooperate with Chairman Zhou again to revive DeeDee, we might still have a shot at exiting the investment decently later on.

Or maybe, just maybe, we might have uncovered the secret hidden in that mysterious map. That might have given us a compelling reason to hold on to our stake, instead of exiting so hastily. I did not know if that secret had anything to do with B&C's resignation and refusal to hand over its working papers, or if it were simply the key to unlocking a hidden asset. In any case, it would have been useful information to consider when negotiating a deal with a new buyer.

I began to see more examples of the hugely profitable deals made by princeling-connected funds in Bloomberg, Reuters and other news agencies. What impressed me was how young some of the western-educated founders of these funds were, and how much capital they attracted from big-name foreign investors and sovereign wealth funds.

Through the grapevine, I also found out that a new PE fund had been set up and had revived some potential China deals previously rejected by All-Stellar. Its founder was none other than the young man whom Fang Xing had introduced as a potential candidate to take Susie's position before Alan was hired. Having absorbed enough experience from various international banks and PE funds, he was now raising money from the very employers he had worked for in the past.

All these developments made me revisit the hypothetical "what if's" that might have ensured All-Stellar's success in China. What if Russell had hired a well-connected young China Hand who was able to put us back into a position of power and help us handle the likes of Mr. Han? What if All-Stellar had been able to cooperate with well-connected Chinese PE funds in a legitimate and above-board way to invest in China? Or if it had attracted some heavyweight Chinese Limited Partners who could have helped us gain access to big deals?

Indeed, I had seen major PE funds forge key local connections and raise yuan-denominated funds over the past three years. Carlyle had formed a joint venture with a Beijing SOE in 2010 and raised its first yuan-denominated fund. Goldman Sachs, Blackstone Group and TPG Capital all launched their first yuan-denominated funds in 2011. Goldman partnered with the Beijing municipal government while Blackstone received commitments from Chinese government entities, SOEs and large Chinese corporations.

In contrast, All-Stellar failed to close a single deal in China, after the DeeDee drama. It eventually exited the market, as it deployed most of its US-dollar capital elsewhere in Asian markets like India and Southeast Asia. Russell cited myriad factors, from regulatory hurdles on foreign investment in China to a spate of accounting scandals at US-listed Chinese companies that made it more difficult to convince the Investment Committee of the credibility of potential Chinese deals.

But it was also clear that the failure of All-Stellar's maiden China venture had caused so much damage that it was almost impossible for a new China team to stage a recovery. Russell struggled for months to find a good replacement for Alan, as top-notch rainmakers who had heard about the DeeDee debacle shunned the fund while the mediocre ones failed to win Russell's respect and trust. He did, however, manage to hire two local associates. But the first jumped ship within months, while the other hardly showed up for work after barely a month of joining, citing medical reasons. I seemed to be the only China employee Russell could rely on.

After almost three months of probation following my humiliating appraisal, I was ready to leave All-Stellar. Despite working round the clock in a final attempt to redeem myself, I was still making no headway in getting approvals for any of the new deals I pitched.

Then, out of the blue, Russell called to reinstate my bonus and remove me from probation. "I can tell that you are trying very hard, and we value your loyalty," he said stiffly and hung up the phone, as if too embarrassed to wait for my response. Stunned, I wondered if my boss was slightly schizophrenic. Or perhaps he was simply driven to desperation to keep me because he was unable to find a new China head or retain the other local staff?

I was still tempted to throw a vengeful resignation letter at Russell's face—something I had visualized myself doing many times over the past few horrid months. But in the end, I chose not to quit…just yet.

Being an eternal optimist, I still hoped to help rebuild All-Stellar's business in China. I had seen how quickly things that went haywire could also move back in the right direction, if one just had the right skills, like building harmonious guanxi, identifying the right local partners who had skin in the game, finding solutions that are both local and lawful. Such traits took time and discipline to cultivate.

So I decided to stop grumbling that our Investment Committee's heightened caution about Chinese companies had made it much harder for me to close deals. From another perspective, it was a good way to keep me disciplined. It honed my skills in finding the right companies to invest in, instead of jumping at any juicy but risky opportunity that came along.

More importantly, staying on at All-Stellar would also allow me to broaden my contact base. While the DeeDee saga had hurt the fund's reputation, it ironically helped open doors for me since quite a few people were curious to meet me and hear the story from the only person in the China team who had seen the deal through from start to finish.

A few business contacts found my story so interesting that they even offered me jobs. Donald Wang, the billionaire hedge fund manager, was one of them. After it became clear that All-Stellar was going to exit the China market, I decided it was time for me to seek new adventures.

Donald had just set up a new company offering discreet advisory services to rising Chinese elite who needed more hand-holding as they deployed their wealth across global asset classes, high-end lifestyles and the like. He asked me to manage his international business development team. When I told him frankly that I did not know a lot about luxury lifestyles, he responded, "A lot of these Chinese rich families don't know much either. You just need to gain their trust first, and the rest will fall into place."

This conversation made me think of Chairman Zhou, whom I had not seen for three years. He was happily retired by now. I figured this was a good time to reconnect with him. Just to enjoy a good chat, like we did in the old times; not to dig up more of the past hurts. By now, I had grown accustomed to the idea that many of my questions about what really happened between All-Stellar and DeeDee might never be completely answered.

"Shall we have a round of golf together again some time?" I wrote in a text message to the Lao Qianbei.

In less than three minutes, Chairman Zhou shot back a reply: "Sure, what time?"

———⋗◆⋖———

It was a rare blue-sky day on the Guantang Golf Course, a stone's throw away from the Beijing Cascades Country Golf Club where the showdown between Russell and Chairman Zhou had taken place three years ago. Chairman Zhou had asked me to pick the venue for our meeting, and I was careful to pick a course that was luxurious enough to impress him, but would not inadvertently open old wounds.

The Lao Qianbei was looking good—he told me he had been enjoying retired life by gardening, working out at a gym and experimenting with new roasted duck recipes. "I'm keen to go to Sri Lanka, Japan and the US to play golf at all those luxury courses overseas you told me about too. Can you get me a big discount?"

I smiled. Chairman Zhou, despite being a multimillionaire now, was still as thrifty as ever. But he was not such a big dreamer anymore. When I described Donald Wang's lofty ambitions to list his new start-up—whose valuation he estimated to top US$500 million even without any revenues—on the New York Stock Exchange in five years, Zhou simply shook his head. "You mentioned an English saying to me once: don't count your ducks until they are hatched. Only now do I understand the need for sound business plans to achieve big goals."

Keeping with old times, we spent most of our golf session chatting randomly and admiring the two Mandarin ducks gliding on the man-made lake. The weather was perfect for golf. Huge gusts of wind had blown away the smog the previous night, allowing us to enjoy the sunshine for the first time in almost a week.

Finally, Chairman Zhou brought up the subject of All-Stellar. "How is Alan? Is he in Singapore?"

I grinned. "I've no idea actually. I've lost touch with him ever since he left the fund. But I did hear he just bought a Guantang club membership for over 600,000 yuan (US$96,000)."

Chairman Zhou snorted. "He did? That rascal was always more interested in his own property speculation and stocks than in managing companies like DeeDee."

"Alan had bought five or six memberships across different courses during the year before he was fired from All-Stellar. They must have brought him a tidy profit since he is still investing in new memberships," I recalled.

"Well, I never did believe that buying memberships at Chinese golf courses is a sound investment idea, it's too gray an area. Let's see what happens—I've heard rumours that the government may crack down on some of them[33]."

Chairman Zhou continued, "In China, projects can rise and fall

---

[33] Guantang was torn down abruptly by the local authorities in 2014, provoking an outcry by its wealthy members, some of whom are friends of this book's co-author. The members staged a demonstration outside the gates to demand their money back. Guantang's well-connected owner subsequently tried to rebuild it, but its final fate appears to be unclear, amid a nation-wide clampdown on illegal golf courses which started in early 2015. The National Development and Reform Commission stated on March 30, 2015 that sixty-six illegally constructed golf

unexpectedly. You can be on a high one day and then fall very fast the next. The only thing that can help you protect your interests in the long term is guanxi."

I nodded soberly. "Yes, I've realized that after All-Stellar's failed investment in DeeDee, building up the relationship is as important as—if not more important than—building the business. I'm…I'm… very sorry that I did not turn up that day at the golf course, Chairman Zhou."

The Lao Qianbei laid an arm on my shoulder. "You should just call me Lao Zhou, we're friends after all. I was indeed very angry when you tricked me into going to the golf course to meet Russell, but I understand your dilemma and I heard about the hard times you went through afterwards."

Somehow, I found myself unloading all the pent-up feelings of regret and self-blame to Lao Zhou: I did not pick up the warning signs about Fang Xing even though I was the closest one to him in the All-Stellar team. I did not know China well enough, even though I had prided myself on knowing it better than others because I was, well, Chinese. Now I knew it took more than my skin color or language ability to be China-savvy.

Lao Zhou sighed when he heard Fang Xing's name. "Xiaohuang, you are just not in his league. He is a gaoshou. An expert hand."

"So why is it that some western-trained Chinese like Fang Xing always get the upper hand in deal-making in China, while other haigui like Alan or Asians like Randy or myself are unable to match up?" I asked bitterly, talking more to myself than to Lao Zhou.

"You young people are all very smart and well-educated," replied the old man. "But Fang Xing is a gaoshou for a different reason—he grew up in China in a well-connected family, he has the *tiegemen* backing him up and he knows Mr. Han. It's very hard for a foreigner

_____

courses across the country had been shut down, and indicated that it will continue to investigate.

like you to match that. So you shouldn't beat yourself up too much because you became a pawn in his scheme."

I was not comforted by his words. "If one lacks the kind of special guanxi that he has, is it still possible to become a gaoshou in China?" I asked.

Lao Zhou shrugged. "It's hard to say. Even gaoshou like Horse Cloud have found the vital need to keep forging new and stronger guanxi. You know, he recently formed the Jiangnan Club[34] for people from his home province of Zhejiang?"

I shrugged. This club seemed to me yet another example of an inner circle that I could not join. Lao Zhou did not seem to notice. "For me, having lived so long and seen so much, I'm not sure I would aspire to be the kind of gaoshou Fang Xing is," he continued. "He is too cunning, and he also lacks the loyalty and perseverance that you have. You need those virtues to build not just guanxi, but trusting relationships which I still believe are more important in the long run."

I did a double take. Was the stern, exacting Chairman Zhou actually complimenting me?

"Well, there are things about China that I can never learn unless I jump into the mud and suffer some hard knocks," I said thoughtfully. "At least I'm still in China after these years."

"You appreciated the value of resilience and patience in a place like China," the old man smiled. "The story is not over yet, Xiaohuang. There will be a lot more highs and lows to come. But if you stick on long enough, maybe one day you can become a gaoshou in your own right."

---

[34] The Jiangnan Club's primary purpose is to build an exclusive network among a close group of business owners outside the trusted family circle, and the members met at a private property next to Hangzhou's famous West Lake.

THE END

Acknowledgements

Matt Huang

WRITING "YOUNG CHINA HAND" WAS a process of self-discovery. Trying to make sense of my tumultuous experiences in China gave me the impetus to pick up the pen, but it didn't take me long to discover I knew nothing about writing. Nor did I fathom how massive this task would be.

Nevertheless, the traits I learned from surviving these years in China—grit, determination, and perseverance—kept me going. As the late American writer and producer Sidney Sheldon puts it, "A blank piece of paper is God's way of telling us how hard it is to be God." From disjointed ideas and disparate experiences jotted on random sheets of paper, I slowly crystallized and pieced them together into a coherent storyline. What you have just read is the culmination of two years of research and synthesis.

I am forever indebted to my tireless and enormously resourceful co-author Grace Hsu. She spent countless nights re-writing and editing the manuscript, while tending to her hyperactive newborn. Her intellectual prowess and relentless questioning refined my thinking about China issues, and provided me with a highly structured way to reflect on my roller-coaster adventures. While it is my voice in the book, it was her hand that gave it expression–down to this very sentence.

To my mom and dad, thank you for over three decades of

unconditional love. You provided me with a nurturing environment to re-discover my Chinese roots, and equipped me with the skills to rise up to the China challenge.

I would like to express my heartfelt gratitude to my dear family and friends who have supported me throughout this process—Huimin Chong, James Hu, Joan Fong, Benjamin Cher, Liyen Tan, Geraldine Lam, Kok Kee Chong, Andy Heng, Kevin Woo, Michael Cronin, Brad Burgess, Terry Yan, Samuel Lipoff, and Katharina Lange. Your generous advice and insights were invaluable. Special thanks also go to Mr. Tim Clissold, whose first book *Mr. China* was a major source of inspiration for us when we brainstormed ideas for this novel.

As I write this, my understanding of China and its people continues to evolve. In particular, many of my young Chinese friends never cease to inspire me with their "supersize me" dreams, their formidable drive, and their relentless desire to succeed. This book is dedicated to them. I am privileged to be part of this dynamic generation shaping China's mind-boggling transformation.

Grace Hsu

China is a land where Mark Twain's quote, "Truth is stranger than fiction," became a reality for me. Here, the unthinkable can truly become possible. To all those who gave me the opportunity to experience, learn and write about the impossibilities that China does not limit itself to, my heartfelt thanks.

Printed in the United States
By Bookmasters